HEART OF ICE

GREGG OLSEN

PINNACLE BOOKS
KENSINGTON PUBLISHING CORP.

For Derek,
who loves to read

PINNACLE BOOKS are published by

Kensington Publishing Corp.
850 Third Avenue
New York, NY 10022

ISBN-13: 978-1-60751-762-7

Printed in the United States of America

Prologue

Miller's Marsh Pond, outside of Cherrystone, Washington

Hauling a dead body around isn't easy. *How could it be?* There's always the possibility that something can go wrong. An earnest young cop could flash his heart-racing blue lights, signal the figure behind the wheel to pull over, and step up to the driver's side window. He sees a hand dangling from the neatly bound package. In such a situation, a handgun on the passenger seat can be the perfect solution.

And then, one body might become two.

A couple of teenagers without a place to go or even the money for a motel might choose the wrong spot to have sex. They select a place for its very seclusion, the same reasoning a body dumper would employ when choosing his locale. They see the man with a corpse but it's too late to leave. Pulled from their steamed-up car, they scramble, crying and begging for their lives, to a gulley.

Pop. Pop. Skulls are pierced by the bullets from a practiced shot. *Sweet.*

And then, one body might become three.

The risk is always there, but at least one man knew, just

then, that it also had its benefits. It brought a rush. Such jeopardy produced a kind of euphoria that was as real as the high he felt when the life oozed from the woman's body. It was almost the same kind of charge that came when the light in the victim's terror-filled eyes went flat and dead like the buttons on an old overcoat.

He looked to the west toward the pond, sheathed in ice. It looked like sheet metal in the light of a cloud-shrouded sky. The wind nipped at his face. If he'd remembered how hard it was to lug a dead body, he'd have moved his vehicle closer to the water's edge. Dead weight had new meaning, for sure.

A car sped by on the highway. Even though it was a half mile away, he crouched slightly and watched as its beams gashed through wisps of fog. Ghost fog, he imagined, as he caught a glimpse of the swirling motion of heavy, cold air.

He'd packed up the woman's body in a blue down-filled sleeping bag. A nice one. The killing had been done in haste, which of course was never a good idea. That didn't bother him just then. He had more pragmatic concerns and they made him wince. He hated that he'd wasted a perfectly good sleeping bag when a ratty old blanket would have been just as serviceable. It had gotten to that point. The whole thing— the murder, the body dump, the return to where it had all played out. All to make sure that nothing, no clues—hair, blood, fibers—could tie him to what he'd done.

It was all about convenience.

It was as if he was that Starbucks barista he'd seen absent-mindedly pushing the buttons to make a latte for some woman who babbled incessantly about her busy life ("I'm not just a mom, I'm a lawyer, too") and how she needed "a boost" to make it through the day. He no longer had any doubts about what he'd done or why he'd done it.

"I'm addicted, you know," said the woman who reeked of coffee and baby wipes.

He smiled faintly, the cold air biting his handsome face.

Pushing buttons. Killing a woman. So easy. He was addicted, too.

He shook off the memory.

He widened his stance and braced himself; his feet slipped a little on the icy mud as he lifted her body from the back of his truck. As he heaved and flung her over his shoulder, he let out a soft groan. She'd seemed so much lighter in life. Wispy hair. Tiny hands with pretty pink nails with carefully applied white tips. Her ankles were so thin that he was sure they could wear the rings from a shower curtain.

A shower curtain would have been cheaper, he thought.

He moved toward the frozen water's edge. A fortress of weather-ravaged cattails guarded the flat plain of ice, with the exception of the point of entry that he'd selected for what he had to do.

She'd left him no choice. It was that simple.

He flopped the heavy bag onto the hard ground and spoke. He was quiet, but his words cut through the chill of the night.

"Jeesh, bitch, couldn't you have worked out some? Skipped the mochas? Called Jenny Craig?"

Considering her condition, she wasn't even *that* fat. She was just dead. She was doing nothing to help him and that made him angry. He tried to roll her; however, the leather cord from the bag snagged a log.

"Damn it! You make *nothing* easy, do you?"

He pulled the hunting knife from his hip and slammed its blade into the cord.

Snap.

Realizing he needed his insurance that she'd sink in the mud, he returned once more to the truck bed and procured a pair of heavy chains. A beat later, he was at her body, spinning the chains around her like a spider in a frigid night.

"Down you'll go," he said softly, a puff of vapor came with his breath. "Down, bitch, you'll go."

He steadied himself and pushed once more and the body rolled onto the ice. From the edge of the shore, he nudged it just far enough away so that he could crawl behind it, pushing it across, commando-style. He looked over his shoulder, back at the truck. *Nothing.* The wind blew over the ice and he figured he'd gone as far as he needed. He took the knife and started to pierce the ice. It was about a quarter-inch thick and it took some doing. Finally, a hole. He dragged the bag toward the opening and shoved it inside, the water making the bag heavier as it began to sink into the blackness below.

It was a perfect night. Snow was coming. Ice would form a frozen scab over the wound that had taken her body. The sleeping bag weighted with chains would sink into the ooze of the springtime thaw.

She'd never be found.

He'd be free.

He felt nothing for her. Just a little inconvenience that came with the territory of having to take her late at night when no one would see what he'd been doing. He felt the flush of exhilaration that came with a job well done. That mocha that he'd thought about sounded kind of good just then. He got into his vehicle and did what busy moms, dads, students, and killers do after a trying day.

He went for coffee.

It was five minutes to closing and both the young women in the coffee and pastry shop wished to God that no one else showed up so they could get out of there the second the big green clock hit the hour mark. The night had been as intermittent as the storm, customer-wise. A flurry of latte-sippers after eight, then nothing outside of a trio of high school kids who managed to stretch their coffee drinking into what seemed like a two-hour marathon. The women working the counter were authorized to give refills to customers at their discretion, but those teens weren't getting another sip. The workers wanted to go home. Snow had fallen and it looked like it would be a total bitch to drive.

Then he came inside, just before the lights would be dimmed.

The young blonde behind the stainless-steel counter had a concerned look on her face. She was petite, with lively blue eyes and a kind of knowing countenance that comes from either personal tragedy or too many years of retail experience. She smiled at the man in front of her, looking him over for a cue of recognition. Face. Eyes. Shirt. *Anything.* He wasn't a regular. He was handsome, trim, and had a killer smile, which seemed to be on autopilot as he entered the store. He wore a heavy navy blue coat, from one of those expensive outdoor recreation companies that specialized in outfitting men with outdoor dreams and office realities. His jeans were old-school 501s, stained wet and dark at the knees. He seemed vaguely familiar, as though they might have met somewhere, or had shopped at the same grocery store. But she knew she hadn't seen him at the coffee shop. She was required to know every customer by first name—if they came in more than twice. He must be passing through.

"You OK?" she asked. "You look hurt." Her gaze landed just above his brow.

For a second, he didn't quite track what she was saying. *Hurt? Like feelings hurt? Hurt, like an injury?*

"Huh? I'm OK," he said. "Tall mocha please. Extra hot."

She handed him a napkin. "You've got a cut on your head."

Oh, that hurt.

He took the napkin and dabbed at the small wound. Blood bloomed between the paper fibers. It was too high up—on his forehead—so he couldn't use the old "cut myself shaving" excuse.

Which he'd used at least once before.

"Must have scraped it on the darn tree," he said, adding a quick smile, and gesturing toward his pickup truck. "Those noble firs are spiky. Been out all evening getting the perfect tree."

That explained the dirty attire. Good one.

The girl was frothing the milk and the noise howled in the space of the coffee house. "And I thought *I* was rushing the season," she said. "They made us put up this Christmas stuff Thanksgiving night." She rolled her eyes and indicated a heap of faux gift boxes around a hot pink feather tree.

He shrugged. "Can I use your restroom?"

"Over there." She handed him a key with an oversized foam core cutout of a coffee cup with REAL MEN DRINK MO-CHAS emblazoned around the rim.

Once inside, he locked the door and turned on the faucet.

Stupid. Stupid. Stupid.

His own interior monologue mocked him as he scrubbed away the crusted-on blood from his temple. She had hurt him. She goddamn made him bleed. She paid for it, of course. Nevertheless, why did she have to go and do that? *What was the point, bitch?*

He looked at his face in the mirror. Normally, when he did so, it brought an appreciative gaze from his own eyes. This time, his heart pumped a little faster. Not as fast as it had earlier that evening by the frozen pond, of course. But faster, nevertheless. The blood he saw at his left temple brought worry and a touch of fear. He knew it meant something that he hoped would never surface. That she, literally, would never surface. It was possible that his DNA was lodged underneath one of her prettily painted fingernails. How come he hadn't thought of that? He could have chopped off her fingertips and fed them to the dog. He could have killed her faster to avoid that burst of adrenaline that gave her the upper hand for just one second.

Stupid. Stupid. Stupid.

Water ran down the drain as he scrubbed his hands and pulled himself together. Though he hadn't used it, he flushed the toilet. He'd been in there a long time.

Thinking. Cleaning. Worrying. But also reliving the triumph of what he'd accomplished in the flat, cold light of a snowy winter night in the middle of nowhere.

His drink was ready when he emerged from the restroom and slid the key at the girl. She was pretty. No denying that. Yet not his type. She had a tattoo on her wrist that appeared to be some kind of tropical flower, maybe a hibiscus. The tattoo artist who'd rendered the image was either a hack or a newbie. Either way, it was *permanently* a very bad tattoo. If her wrist was any indication, she likely had more of them wallpapering her young, lithe body. Probably some piercings, too.

The man liked his women a little more on the traditional side. More conservative. Pretty, like the coffee girl, but not so wild. Not so reckless with the beauty God had bestowed on them by virtue of His grace and their parents' genetics.

"Whip on this?" the girl asked.

"Oh, yes." He smiled, set down five dollars pulled from a gold monogrammed money clip, and winked. "I love whip. Keep the change."

The girl at the counter caught the eye of her coworker, a pudgy brunette who never flirted with customers. They watched as the man with the mocha got into his truck, turned the ignition, and drove away.

"Do you want some creepy with that mocha?" the brunette teased.

"No kidding. Make that a venti creepy."

"Extra hot, though."

The young women laughed. Both knew that the man, no matter how handsome or fit, was too old for them anyway. Besides, it was against company policy to even think about hooking up with a customer. The last one to do that got a week of corporate-sponsored ethics training and a new assignment repacking scones in a warehouse. Not worth it by a long shot.

As the truck backed out and pulled past the windows of the shop, the blonde walked to the door and turned the lock. Her coworker flipped the overhead lights and the store went dark. As they looked out at the moving truck, which was slightly shrouded with swirling snow, they noticed something that seemed a little strange. There was no Christmas tree in the truck bed.

It was empty.

"I thought he said he'd been out getting a tree," the brunette said

"Jesus. It figures. Everything is a pickup line these days."

The blonde rolled her eyes. "You got that right."

PART ONE
Mandy

Chapter One

Cherrystone, Washington

Emily Kenyon was proud of her deep blue suit and the polished silver star of the sheriff's office on her jacket, yet the idea of an A-line skirt in late November was more than her thin blood could take. *Why wasn't there a pants option?* She was the first female sheriff for Cherrystone, but surely someone had thought that through before. It was an annoyance on chilly November days and thankfully she only had to wear the suit for official occasions that had more to do with public relations than law enforcement. Moreover, she had the sneaking suspicion the getup made her look like a flight attendant as much as anything.

That afternoon she had lunch with the Rotary Club to kick off the annual "Teddy Bears for Tots" fund-raiser, a statewide drive in which officers collected plush teddy bears for the littlest victims of crimes, accidents, and fires. Emily spoke for five minutes, shook the hands of several Rotary officers, and thanked them for the "teamwork that makes us great."

The line felt hokey; even so the crowd applauded.

As she exited the restaurant banquet room, she knew that

she needed a warmer coat than her old trench if she wanted to keep from freezing. She ran through her mental list of things that had to be done. She needed to get her roots touched up at the salon. She also had to do something with the turkey carcass that occupied the top shelf in her refrigerator following Thanksgiving with Jenna, her twenty-two-year-old daughter, Chris Collier, her boyfriend—though she loathed the idea of a grown man being called a *boyfriend*—and her friend, Olga Cerrino.

Her cell rang. It was Jason Howard, her deputy.

"Kenyon here," she said.

"Hi, Sheriff. It's Jason."

That they even bothered to identify themselves was almost a joke between them. Only a dozen employees made up the Cherrystone Sheriff's Department. It wasn't the smallest law enforcement organization, but it certainly wasn't in Washington State's top ten. "We got a call from Jeanne Parkinson at the clerk's office. She's worried about an employee."

Emily knew Jeanne. She worried about everything.

"What's going on?" she asked.

"An employee didn't come to work today."

Emily wanted to laugh, yet somehow she held it. "Is this what we've been reduced to? The attendance monitors for the county?"

"That's what I thought, but this could be different. They're worried that something might have happened to Mandy on her way to work."

"Mandy Crawford?"

"Yeah. She's pregnant, you know."

"I know. She's due any day, isn't she?" Emily checked her teeth in the rearview mirror of her Kelly green county-issued Crown Vic. Spinach salad was never a good choice for a luncheon. Why didn't caterers understand that spinach leaves gripped teeth like Velcro?

"Mitch says when he left for work, she was already gone."

Mitch was Mitch Crawford, Mandy's husband.

"I'm not far from there," Emily said. "I'll stop by and follow her route to the office."

"Need the address?"

"I know where everyone in Cherrystone lives. That's how exciting my life is."

"Gotcha, Sheriff. We're in the same boat."

She almost said something about the *Titanic*, but thought better of it. Jason Howard was her subordinate and admitting to him that they were both in dead-end jobs was counterproductive. The fact was that adrenaline junkies would die a slow death in Cherrystone. Nothing earth-shattering happened in Cherrystone. No murder in five years. There had been three rapes, twenty-eight burglaries/robberies, eighty-three assaults, and a couple hundred drug busts, mostly for meth—the scourge of small towns and rural communities across the West.

No one had to tell Emily who Mandy's husband was. Mitch Crawford was a good eight to ten years younger than she, but the Crawford family was well known for having the region's car dealership. Cherrystone was certainly out of the way, with Spokane being its nearest major city. Mitch's father, Eddie, however, had shown a knack for marketing that turned the car lot into a destination. He'd fly people into Spokane from Seattle or Portland, pick them up in a limo, and make sure they returned home in one of his cars. He ran ads on TV and radio, and was inducted into the Marketing Hall of Fame in Reno, Nevada. When he died, Mitch took over.

The car lot wasn't looking so sprightly these days. Mitch Crawford, it seemed, was no Eddie Crawford.

Mitch and Mandy lived in a hopelessly hokey develop-

ment crafted for those who think showing off their money is
the better part of having any. Their address was in the ridiculously named Bristol Estates—ridiculous because Cherrystone was nowhere near England, and the only thing English
about the town was that most people spoke the language.

When Emily arrived, she showed her badge and a guard
opened the gate. Bristol Estates was a small development
with only fourteen homes on "equestrian lots" built with
garish architectural embellishments. Each home had a "car-
riage" house for their cars and a turret that presumably fed
fantasies for the would-be princes, Rapunzels, and Lance-
lots.

Emily parked the Crown Vic behind Mitch's German-
made sedan and wondered why Cherrystone's biggest car
dealer didn't drive a Ford like all his customers.

The leaded glass front door swung open.

"Emily," Mitch called out. "Sorry you've been dragged
into this."

He was better looking than she'd remembered. He had
broad shoulders, a strong, handsome jawline, and hair cut
short in the way that men sometimes do when it is thinning.
He was far too vain for a comb-over. He wore a Ralph Lauren sweater and slacks that looked a little too matchy-
matchy, as though he'd purchased them without the help of a
woman who knew what really looked good on a man. A gold
chain that hearkened back to his dealership origins was nestled in his manscaped chest hair. He'd tried to leapfrog from
his car dealership lineage, but the gold jewelry, the bad taste,
and a whiff of Calvin Klein's Obsession were clues that he'd
not made it as far as he'd liked. Despite the grand house. Or
maybe, because of it.

"Dragged? It's my job," she said.

"I know. Just seems silly. I'm sure Mandy just went out
shopping."

"How come you're home?"

"Oh, just had to zip home for some stuff I need at work."

"I see."

He cracked the door open a little more, but still didn't come outside or offer Emily to come in out of the cold air.

"She was supposed to be at work," she said.

"Oh, no. She'd taken the day off. She had some things to get for the baby."

Emily stepped a little closer, craning her neck to see what, if anything was behind him. "They were expecting her at the clerk's office."

Mitch looked unconcerned. "Signals crossed, I think. I'm not saying this to sound like a Neanderthal, but you know, she's pregnant. She's not exactly dotting all the i's and crossing the t's these days."

Emily let the remark fly by. He *was* being a Neanderthal, but something was drawing her attention more than his words—the overpowering odor of bleach.

"Can I come in?" she asked, a calming smile on her face. "Have a look around?"

He looked at her warily.

"Sure. I was doing a little cleaning. I'm done now."

"Smells like bleach," she said.

Mitch offered a kind of lifeless smile that seemed more for effect than for the conveyance of any warmth or charm. "Nothing works better for cleaning."

"I know," she said, thinking at the same time that nothing obliterates blood and other body fluids better than bleach, too.

Mitch led Emily into the kitchen. Atop the black granite counter, Emily noticed a plastic bucket with soapy water. A mop was catawampus on the floor. Mitch followed her gaze, and picked it up.

"Trying to clean up, you know, baby coming soon, and the help has the day off."

Emily surveyed the room, wondering if the help was his

missing wife or a maid service with an 800 number. "Sure," she said. She noticed a cappuccino machine that had to be commercial grade, a wine refrigerator, a walk-in Sub-Zero refrigerator, and a range with more burners than the nicest restaurant in Cherrystone.

"Nice kitchen," she said.

He pulled his sweater sleeves up to his elbows, bunching up the fabric in soft folds. *Cashmere.* "We like nice things. Mandy and I."

Mitch kept his body between Emily and the rest of the house. It was clear that he'd invited her in, but only so far.

"Can I see the bedroom? You know, to be safe. I might see something that you've missed."

Mitch put his hand out, a gesture that meant to push her back—though she was already at arm's length.

"I'd rather not," he said. "Mandy didn't make the bed and she'd die if you saw the way we lived. She thinks so much of you."

"She's a nice girl. But I don't mind."

"But I do. I mean, Mandy would."

With his dark brown, penetrating eyes, Mitch stared at Emily for a second, maybe two.

Dead air. Emily resisted the urge to fill the empty space. *Let him. Let him say something he'd regret.*

Finally Mitch spoke.

"I hate to do this, but I'm going to have to ask you to leave." He started for the front door, and Emily followed. Past the kitchen, through the living room, down the hallway with its art gallery vibe—mostly modern, though she spotted a Thomas Kinkade painting of an English cottage dipped in pink roses and candlelight.

"Mandy likes that kind of crap," he said. "Mall art. Jeesh."

This guy was too much. His wife didn't show up for work

and he was throwing her taste in art under the bus. Emily figured that Mitch Crawford was all about pretension, keeping up appearances. *Control.*

"What about your wife?" she asked. "Where is she?"

"What about her? I told you she was shopping in Spokane." His tone was impatient and he tried to reel it back in. "You know, for baby things."

"You hadn't told me *where*. Where in Spokane?"

He escorted Emily toward the door. "Riverside Mall, downtown. Better stores than the valley mall." He held open the door.

"All right," she said. "Tell Mandy to call the department when she gets in."

Before Emily finished her sentence, he'd already shut the door and turned the dead bolt.

Emily parked the cruiser in the SHERIFF spot in front of the terra-cotta facade of the City and County Safety Building, and walked to her office overlooking Main Street. Each time she passed the "Wall of Fame"—portraits of the sixteen men and the lone woman who'd served as sheriff—she felt a wince of pain. It had been two years since Brian Kiplinger succumbed to a heart attack, an event that not only broke the hearts of all who worked there, but put Emily in line for the job as the sheriff. She'd never wanted to be the damn sheriff; moreover, she never wanted to work for anyone but Kip. She was appointed interim sheriff and the following year she won the election by a whopping 88 percent majority. That she ran unopposed probably did more for her landslide victory than unbridled support from a hometown electorate. A woman sheriff was a bit of a novelty, to say the least.

"How was lunch?" The voice belonged to Gloria Bergstrom, the office dispatcher and, really, the glue that held the whole place together. She was in her midsixties, had steel-gray hair that she kept short and stylish, and never showed up for work without four-inch heels. There was good reason for that: in stocking feet, Gloria was only five feet tall.

"An inch shorter and I could have been a Munchkin in another life," she joked whenever anyone made mention of her stature.

Emily smiled at Gloria. "Lunch was fine. Lots of promises of support. You know, working together, making a difference. The word will get out that those teddy bears are important to the kids."

"Did you track down Mandy? The women from the clerk's office have called twice."

Emily shook her head and pulled off an earring that hurt like hell and picked up the phone. She pushed the speed-dial code for the clerk's office.

"Nope, her husband says she went shopping—" She cut herself off and turned her gaze from Gloria to focus on the phone call she was making. "Jeanne? Emily. I did a drive-by of the Crawford place and Mr. Personality said Mandy took the day off to go shopping for baby things in Spokane."

"She did no such thing," Jeanne said in her fluty voice. "She never would do that to us here. She is our best employee."

"Maybe she left a message with someone else that she was sick or something?"

"No. There's no way she would do that. You see, Emily, today we were having a baby shower for her. It wasn't exactly a surprise. She even picked out the cake."

"I see," Emily said, her mind flashing on the house she'd just toured. There wasn't a thing out of place. Not only was Mitch Crawford a social climber who'd rejected his middle-class roots for the accoutrements of a rich lifestyle, he was a self-absorbed ass. A lot of husbands were. She'd had one of those herself. "Was anything going on between Mandy and her husband? Was she angry at him?"

"No, not that I know of. She was focused on the baby. That's all she wanted."

Emily nodded. "All right. I'll check with Mitch this evening to make sure she came home."

"Emily, one more thing."

"What is it?" She held her breath as if Jeanne was about to reveal some critical clue about why Mandy Crawford might skip work. Maybe she was mad at someone. Maybe Mitch had been beating her up.

"Can you send someone over here to get some of this cake? No one here feels much like celebrating."

Emily let out a sigh. "Of course," she said. She hung up the phone and went down the hall to find her deputy. He was at his desk surfing a Web site for ski conditions in Idaho. He clicked his mouse to close the window.

"Jason? Can you find someone to go over to the clerk's office? Jeanne has something she wants to give us."

"Right on it, Sheriff."

Emily smiled as her deputy leaped to his feet and started for the door.

Jason Howard was always hoping that something would happen around Cherrystone. What no one knew just then was it already had.

It was half past six and already dark. The snow-threatening cloud cover was a snug lid over the town. Despite the elements, the Bryant-Thompsons were still out stringing lights to outline every architectural detail of their two-story Victorian across the street from Emily's charming but more modest home. The Bryant-Thompsons—Trevor and Mason—were one of those couples who insisted that it wasn't Christmassy if it wasn't over-the-top. *Way over the top.* No bush was left unadorned, no skeletal tree left without a coating of little white lights. This year, Emily thought as she waved at the two men on ladders, she wasn't going to give into her half-hearted attempt at trying to keep up with them. There was no point in it. She was doing a lighted wreath outside her front door and an artificial tree in the front window. *That's it.*

She let herself inside and reached for her phone. The house was quiet. Jenna, home from her job consulting for a sorority's national office, was in the shower.

Emily left her number with Mitch Crawford, but he hadn't called back. She pressed redial and it went to his voice mail a second time. She went toward the kitchen, dropping her shoes by the back door and her purse on the stainless-steel island. She dialed the Crawford dealership next. A young woman answered.

"Mr. Crawford went home an hour ago, Sheriff Kenyon," she said. "He didn't say if he was stopping anywhere. You should be able to reach him there. Is everything OK?"

"We're worried about his wife, that's all."

"Oh, nothing to worry about. She's fine. I'm pretty sure she called in here and he talked to her."

Emily felt a surge of relief. She thanked her, swung open the refrigerator, and looked at the foil-wrapped turkey.

Mandy Crawford is fine. I'm in trouble here. What do I do with this thing? I can't make soup for twenty!

She retrieved a large kettle from the rack over the island and started filling it with water. She wrestled with the turkey carcass, snapping the bones and cramming it into the pot. Two cups of mirepoix, a cup of rice, and some salt and pepper, and she was done.

It wasn't going to be the best turkey soup anyone ever made, but there would be a lot of it.

"Hi, honey," Emily said as Jenna came into view, a ratty

old robin's egg blue robe wrapped around her slender body. "Maybe Santa will bring you a new robe."

Jenna twisted her hair into a knot on her head and wrapped a thin, white towel around it.

"Only if I'm good." She smiled at her mother.

Emily held the image of her daughter in her mind's eye. She had a lithe figure that thankfully proved at twenty-two that she had her mother's good genes, and not her dad's. She had perfect teeth—without the utter sameness of a row of orthodontia-manufactured smiles. And she was smart.

"I thought you might have left for your father's," Emily said, stirring the kettle.

Jenna took a seat on a bar stool next to the island that held the Viking range Emily had splurged on when she remodeled the kitchen, a project as complicated as a murder investigation. "I'm going in the morning. How could I miss your famous turkey soup?"

Her change in plans had nothing to do with turkey soup, of course. Jenna, having been away at college and now traveling with the sorority job, had a new perspective about the most important relationship she'd ever had—the one with her mother. Certainly there had been the silly fights over boys, but that was long ago. The worries about who she was with and when she'd be home had abated. The talk about whether she should go to law school or find something that didn't keep her so close to the dregs of society had waned.

"Like me, Jenna," Emily once said as the two of them toured the Cascade campus when Jenna was eighteen. "Don't be like me. Some jobs come with a high price. I know."

Jenna watched her mother as she turned the peppermill over the bubbling soup pot. She wanted to burst forth with the words: "Mom, I love you. Mom, you've always been there for me."

Instead, Jenna teased her.

"The soup looks a little watery."

Emily made a face and reached for the yellow box of cornstarch. "I can fix that," she said.

"You can fix anything, Mom."

Neither mother nor daughter had a care in the world just then. Neither noticed that a pair of eyes had fastened onto them . . . onto their every move.

He had come for her.

His warm breath mixed with the cold air outside the big white Victorian. White puffs of vapor rose above him where he stood watching the scene through the backyard windows. He almost heard their laughter as the mother and daughter passed from one room to another, enjoying their lives.

Yes, they had lives.

He'd stalked her online. That was easy enough, of course. She'd left a trail all over the Internet—Web sites, blogs, e-mails. He knew so much about her—her shoe size, her best friend's flailing love life, her plans for life after Cascade University. Seeing her in the flesh was the necessary step. A precursor to the plans that were forming like a disease, for which he alone held the cure.

He aimed a penlight at the photo of the three young women, all blond, all pretty.

Yes, it was her.

The girls were posed in front of a Greek revival mansion that had been their home away from home. It was summertime. They wore shorts and strappy tank tops and flip-flops. No cares. Just bright, shiny futures. They were blue-eyed Barbies, with perfect plastic skin and figures that only a doll maker could conjure.

He focused on their smiles. Their obvious joy was like an ice pick to his gut.

"I'll wipe that smile off her face," he thought looking at the girl in the center. *"She's the reason. She's the leader."*

He told himself when he first got on the airplane in California that it was only to see her, to confront her. He wanted to tell her that her stupid decision had catastrophic results.

"Better be more careful next time," he'd planned to say. "Some one else might not be as reasonable as I am."

His interior monologue made him grin as he stood outside in the cold, watching. Waiting. Thinking of what she'd done. What they all had done.

He'd known the kind of pain that few endure. He was proud that he'd sequestered all of that. In the past, he'd done his share of handing out hurt like it was an appetizer to be enjoyed by the recipient. One little poisonous bite at a time was all he needed to find relief from his pain. One gulp. All of that had been a long time ago. But something was stirring inside and he knew that the girl in the center of the photo had become a kind of lightning rod for his anger.

He wrestled with it. Fought it hard. That night as he watched her from across the street, he knew that in the end, he'd have no choice. He'd argue it in his head over and over, and ultimately the dark part of him, the part hidden from all who thought they knew him, was about to become unleashed . . . again.

He looked down at the photo one more time and knew Jenna Kenyon would be the last to die.

Chapter Two

It was 8:05 A.M., the Tuesday after Thanksgiving, and the Cherrystone Sheriff's Department smelled of donuts and coffee. Gloria had brought in a dozen from the bakery across the street, as she did at least five times a month. The donuts were good—sugary, greasy, and lighter than air, of course—making them nearly impossible to resist. Only one person in the department seemed to care about the net result of too many donuts on a cop's waistline. Emily, of course. At least bagels were a somewhat healthy choice. *Why not bagels?* Emily knew that her own willpower to stay away from the donuts was a better solution than making a directive that Gloria stop bringing them in.

Although past forty, Emily Kenyon wasn't ready to "give up" and let the forces of nature and donuts take over her body.

She barely had time to acknowledge the donuts with her usual "Gloria, you shouldn't have!" before being accosted by Jeanne Parkinson, the county clerk.

"Emily," Jeanne said, her breath short and her hands fluttering. "Mandy's still not at work."

Emily glanced at the wall clock. "It's only ten past the hour." She peeled off her coat, gloves, and scarf. Her cheeks were bright pink from the walk from her cruiser to the back door. It was the coldest day of the year, just 18 degrees. The crusty berms of snow on the sidewalk had frozen solid. The sky had cleared.

"It doesn't make any difference," Jeanne said. "Mandy always came five minutes *early*. She missed her baby shower yesterday and she's still not here. I tell you, something's wrong. She's missing."

"Who's missing?" It was Jason Howard, donut in hand, sugar on his upper lip.

"We don't know who's missing," Emily said. "Or rather, if *anyone* is missing at all."

"She's missing," Jeanne said. "I know it. I couldn't sleep a wink last night."

"We're jumping to conclusions here. I talked to a girl from Mitch Crawford's dealership. Mitch had talked with Mandy a little while before I called."

Jeanne brightened a little. She had all the charm of a concrete block, but now and then allowed a trace of human emotion to wash over her face. It was clear that Jeanne the county clerk was very fond of Amanda Crawford.

"Where is she?" she asked. "What did he say?"

Emily felt a surge of embarrassment. "I guess I misspoke. I don't know what *she* said to him. I didn't talk to Mitch. I talked with his customer service manager."

She knew immediately that her response sounded lame. Yet at the time, it was good enough. She followed procedure. She only swung by the Crawfords' house as a courtesy to those who'd called in worried about Mandy not showing up for work. For all intents and purposes, Mandy was, in fact, off shopping in Spokane. That's what her husband said. He ought to know. She wasn't a missing person. There was nothing more to be done. Mandy Crawford hadn't hit the twenty-four-hour mark that would mobilize law enforcement from Cherrystone to Spokane.

Jeanne stepped a little closer, not threateningly so—just close enough to let Emily know she was very, very concerned. She was a tall woman with sea-green eyes under overplucked and overarched brows. Not pretty, but swathed in stylish earth-tone Jones New York clothes, she did the best she could with what she had. She'd won the county clerk job fifteen years prior and had no intention of ever giving it up. She had a particular type of toughness that belied the kind of sweetheart she could be. This morning she was almost in tears.

"Look, Emily, I know this girl. She's in big trouble." As she looked around the room, each person—Gloria the dispatcher, Jason the deputy, and Emily the sheriff—had a pretty good idea of what was coming next. None would be disappointed.

"She's dead, I'll bet. Her husband didn't want kids. Didn't want Mandy once she got pregnant. It was as if she ceased to exist from the moment she came back from the doctor with what she thought was great news. Joyful news. I'll bet the son of a bitch killed her."

"I didn't realize that he didn't want kids," Emily said. She turned to Jason. "You and I are going over there in five minutes."

She didn't have to say where.

Emily Kenyon parked and she and Jason went up the cobbled walkway ringed in pyramidal shrubbery to the front door of the house at 21 Larkspur. Emily hadn't noticed on her first visit there, but there were some scratches at the base of the door. *The Crawfords must have a dog*, she thought, as she rang the bell and looked around. The neighborhood was serene, devoid of any activity. In fact, the whole "gated community" seemed out of whack. Why would anyone want to live in a place with a guard posted out front? Especially in Cherrystone, of all places.

Nothing. No answer. No dog barking. No Mitch.

Jason offered to circle the house, and Emily nodded.

She rang once more. Again, nothing.

"All clear back there," Jason said coming around the south side of the house. "Nice digs. Big pool back there."

"The inside's not too shabby, either," she said. "Let's head over to the dealership."

It was after 9:00 A.M. when they arrived, and the sharks in the form of a crew of young men were already circling the car lot, looking for the first bite of the morning. Their pasted-on smiles fell when they noticed it was the sheriff getting out of her hopelessly uncool behemoth of a car. *No trade-in here. No getting a ninety-year-old into a car he doesn't need.* Christmas music piped over the car lot. It was José Feliciano signing "Feliz Navidad." A little peppy for the hour, and certainly wrong for the reason for the visit.

"Mitch around?" Emily asked, as she and Jason approached the dealership's snowflake-adorned glass front doors.

"Yup," said a young man in dark green parka over a suit jacket and tie. "He's in his office."

A young woman's voice went out over the loudspeaker. "Eggnog lattes for all customers on the lot right now. Come inside and shake off the chill. It's our treat!"

Jason followed Emily inside and they walked past three cars festooned with gigantic bows of silver and gold ribbon. One arrow pointed to the manager's office, another to the service department. A young woman in a Santa hat smiled from her desk.

"Hi, Mrs. Kenyon! I'm Darla! I went to high school with Jenna!"

Every sentence was punctuated with an overkill of enthusiasm. Emily remembered Darla had been a cheerleader.

"Oh, hi, Darla. Didn't recognize you with your hat." Emily smiled warmly. "Nice to see you." She indicated the door behind her horseshoe-shaped desk. "Is he in?"

"Sure is! How's Jenna doing?"

"She's fine. She's back from Tennessee for the holidays. She's at her father's in Seattle right now. Did you know she was working for her sorority?"

"Yeah. Cool. I heard that. I still want to go to college, but, you know, being a single mom hasn't made the timing for that so good right now." She pointed to a picture of a little boy on the credenza behind her.

Emily studied the little boy's photo, and suddenly felt sorry for Darla. The timing of the pregnancy, of course, was what had been out of whack. College first. Then a job. Married next. Baby last. That's what she told Jenna over and over, and so far, it seemed that the mantra had sunk in.

Mitch Crawford poked his head out of his office. He appeared irritated.

"Enough of the photo," he said. "I thought you'd never get here."

Darla looked hurt and embarrassed, and it was apparent that the man who took his father's job was absolutely nothing like the man who'd built the dealership on brains and undeniable charm. Mitch was devoid of any of that.

Emily turned toward Mitch. "Would have been nice if you'd called us, if you've been waiting for us to show up."

"I did call. Earlier." He let out an annoyed sigh and commanded Darla—without saying a word—to sit down and get back to work. She did.

It was a peculiar conversation, and Emily made note of its strangeness. None of Mitch Crawford's words were about his concern for Mandy, which was the reason they were there. He seemed more bothered by how he'd been inconvenienced by the sheriff and her deputy not being there earlier.

But they'd come because of Jeanne Parkinson's apprehension. Not because *he* called anyone.

"Look," he said, "the end of the month is a hectic time around here. We've got sales goals to hit."

"Of course. I have a goal, too," she said measuring her words. "It involves finding your wife."

Mitch toned down his conspicuous irritation. His eyes meandered from the sheriff to the deputy. "I understand. I'm busy. I'm sure she'll turn up."

Emily wanted to smack the guy and she was pretty sure, judging by the way Jason looked at him in contempt, he'd have told the review board that he'd seen nothing happen.

"I'll try to move this along. Can we sit down?" Emily asked, taking one of two visitor's chairs in an office that resembled more a trophy case of his father's achievements than anything Mitch Crawford had done. Number 1 Dealership in the Northwest, Grande Champion for Auto World's Contest of Excellence, and other over-the-top plaques that make no sense to anyone outside the auto-sales industry.

"I talked to one of your employees last night," Emily said, removing her coat. "She said you'd talked with Mandy."

Mitch's eyes were alternately fastened on Emily, then on Jason. It was like a Ping-Pong match.

"No, I didn't. Must be a misunderstanding. I told the crew I was worried about her. Wanted to see if her car ran into a patch of black ice or something. I drove the highway all the way to Spokane and nothing. Not a trace."

Jason glanced at her, but Emily ignored him. She made another mental note to tell him not to do that again. The best reaction when you want someone to keep talking is *no* reaction.

Darla, who was listening to every word, popped her head into the office.

"Mrs. Kenyon—I mean Sheriff Kenyon, I can clear up the phone call thingy. I told Tracee Connors, the night receptionist, that Mr. Crawford *wanted* to talk to his wife. She screwed up."

Mitch glared at Darla. "Not the first time around here, that's for sure."

Darla went back to her desk, her face red.

"Let's take a moment here," Emily said, turning back to Mitch. "We need to locate your wife. So let's calmly review what you've told us to see if we've missed anything."

Mitch slid into his leather office chair and swiveled toward the window. "Right. We need to find Mandy. She could be hurt. The baby could be in trouble."

"That's right. So, like I said, let's go over what you remember."

"That morning she told me she was going to take Toby out for a walk, then she was going to Spokane."

"OK, what was she driving?"

"Her car, a silver Camry, 2003."

It seemed odd to Emily that a car dealer had his wife driving an older car, not to mention one that was neither make nor model sold at his dealership. Jason wrote down the plate number.

"Why was she going to Spokane?"

"She said she was sure the baby was going to come early and she wanted one last chance to get some things she'd been wanting."

"OK, good. That's a detail we didn't have. But what about the baby shower at work?"

Mitch stared, blank-eyed. "Maybe she screwed up the date? That would be just like her."

The remark caught Emily by surprise. It seemed cold, harsh. He didn't know where his wife was, and Mitch Crawford was happy to disparage her. Either Mandy was a ditz or her husband didn't care much for her.

"Where did she shop for the baby?" Emily asked. "Do you know?"

"Baby Gap and Chelsea's."

Emily narrowed her brow. It was a name she hadn't heard of, and she figured it was because she hadn't been asked to a baby shower in three years. And, well, her own baby days were long behind her with Jenna out of college and on her own.

"It's an overpriced boutique on the first floor of the Riverside Square," Mitch said. "I don't know why she wanted to buy that crap. It's *just* a baby, for Christ's sake. A baby doesn't know what the hell it's wearing. But Mandy knows how to spend the dough. She's not the Walmart type."

Jason took notes while Emily focused on getting all the information she needed.

"OK. Now, about the morning walk with Toby." She stopped herself for a moment. She recalled the scratched door at the Crawford house and how silent the place had been when she'd come by the day before. "Where *is* Toby?"

"Good question. I haven't seen him since yesterday when I left for work."

"Doesn't that concern you?" Jason asked, for the first time inserting himself into the conversation.

Mitch looked at the young deputy. They weren't that far apart in age, but it was clear that Mitch regarded Jason Howard as someone well beneath his station in life.

"No, as a matter of fact, it doesn't. The dog gets out all the time and runs up and down the street. If I had a dollar for every time I had to go out and call for him in the middle of the night, I could close this dealership and retire. Trust me, Toby will be home tonight. He'll be hungry."

"So what happened next?" Emily asked. "Did Mandy take Toby for a walk?"

Mitch shrugged. "I don't know. I guess so. I wasn't there. One of us has to work, you know."

Emily wanted to say something about how Mandy *did* have a job. And about how if Mitch had been half as good a man as his father, his dealership wouldn't be hemorrhaging customers. Instead, she smiled.

Anything to keep him talking.

"Did Mandy phone you? Text you? Contact you in any way yesterday? After you—you saw her last?"

He shook his head. "No. We're not like those couples who have to check in with an 'I love you' every five minutes."

Duly noted.

"Look, I know you're here to find my wife, but I get the vibe from you that you don't like me. I don't care. You don't have to like me to find her, now do you?"

Jason piped up. "You're right. We don't have to like you."

Emily glanced at Jason. She let a slight smile break across her face. "But, yes, we will find her."

"Good. Now, if you need me to sign some paperwork for the missing persons report or whatever, let's do it. I made a list of her friends. Here."

He shoved a piece of paper at Emily. It held the names of friends and family members. Many of the names were familiar to her. Three were from the county clerk's office.

"If you turn up anything, call Darla. She knows how to find me."

As they walked past a sullen Darla, Emily turned to Jason and, in a very low voice, said what both of them were thinking.

"This guy's really broken up that his wife is missing, isn't he?"

"Yeah, crying a river."

Chapter Three

The drive from town to Spokane was monotonous under the best of circumstances. The two-lane highway was frosted with gray snow that resembled concrete in texture, color, and, if the night's freeze was deep enough, strength. An APB had been put out by Gloria, indicating a pregnant young woman was missing from Cherrystone. The local paper and a Spokane radio station with a pretty good police-beat reporter had already called.

Every day in Cherrystone was a slow news day.

Emily Kenyon told her deputy that she wanted to check out the stores that Mitch Crawford said his wife had frequented. She wanted to do something that felt like real police work again.

"I've been stuck behind a desk or at a banquet table for months," she said. "I'd like to play cop while I still remember how. You hold down the fort and start checking out where else she might have gone. Hit up her neighbors, too."

Jason wasn't disappointed in the least. He had a home-cooked dinner waiting after work and he figured that Mandy Crawford was ticked off at her husband and would turn up before the end of the day.

"Got it," he said. "The guy *is* an ass. If he treats his wife like he treats his dealership secretary, I'd have left him, too. Pregnant or not."

Emily started for the door. "We're in sync. I'll run up to Spokane and see if anyone saw her yesterday."

The saleswoman behind the counter at Chelsea's Natural Baby probably hadn't eaten a full meal in five years. Her gaunt visage was a sharp contrast to the lovely photographs of pink-cheeked babies and their madonna-esque mothers in designer clothes that ran along the back wall of the boutique. She had black hair that she wore swept back, held in place with an impossibly large tortoiseshell clip. Her skin was pale, almost the color of chalk. Her nails, blood red.

Emily approached her and she snapped her cell phone shut.

"I'm Caprice. Are you shopping for a grandbaby?"

Emily shook her head and wondered how bad she looked. *Not that bad.*

"I'm Emily Kenyon, Cherrystone Sheriff. I'm not a grandmother, thank you. I'm here on business."

Caprice had small birdlike eyes that she tried to make look larger by applying bold strokes of black eyeliner. She glanced at Emily and then away across the store at a teenage girl who entered from the main mall entrance.

She gathered her lips in a puckered frown. "Sorry. How can I help you, Sheriff Kenyon?"

Emily held out a photograph from the county's security badging office. In it, Mandy's hair was a little longer, and her face a little thinner than when she'd last been seen. She set it on the counter and waited.

Caprice looked down at the image. Recognition came quickly. "She's bigger now. Yes, she's a customer. A good one with negligible taste, but charge cards with plenty of room. Amanda Crawford is her name."

Caprice had insulted Mandy, but at least she had a good memory.

"Thank you. When did you see her last?"

"It's been awhile. Not for a couple of weeks. I can check our records, if you want to wait a moment. I'm the manager here."

Chimes sounded that indicated another shopper had entered and Caprice looked a little distracted as she kept her eyes on the teenager who started hovering by a hanging garden of baby dresses.

"Dior," she said, whispering. "I have to watch that girl. You wouldn't believe the number of shoplifters we get in here. Having a baby apparently means being a thief for some of these younger ones."

Emily nodded, not because she believed for one minute what Caprice was saying, but because Caprice was the type of woman who needed to deride every person that came into her shop.

"Maybe you can arrest her if she steals something," Caprice went on. "You know the type. Pregnant and stupid. Or stupid and pregnant." When the shop manager took a breath, Emily steered the conversation back to Mandy.

"About Mrs. Crawford. Are you sure it has been a couple of weeks? You didn't see her here yesterday?"

She let out a sigh. "I'm sure. Yesterday was slow. I could have used a new mom with a decent credit limit. I had a shipment of pink blankets from Paris that she would have liked—or that I could have sold her, anyway." She laughed, like she was trying to be facetious. Emily knew better.

"She was going to have a girl?" Emily asked.

"Pink and lavender, that's all she wanted to see."

Emily thanked her and went down the mall to the Baby Gap.

No one had seen Mandy there, either. It was likely Mitch

Crawford's wife had disappeared before she ever made it to Spokane.

As Emily departed the mall, she wondered why a dour hard-liner like Caprice felt a need to run a place in which she loathed her clientele. What happened to the women who worked in such shops and radiated the joy of motherhood? Mandy wasn't a missing woman to Caprice, but a missing *customer*.

Emily scoured the parking lot for her car. As she walked across the lot, she couldn't help but think of her time in places like Chelsea's when she was a young mother looking for the perfect little dress for the daughter who ultimately would always be the center of her life. She favored mint and lavender for her daughter, no pinks whatsoever. She wanted her to be the pretty little girl, Daddy's Girl, as she'd been, but strong, too. She carried a bittersweet image of those early years with David and Jenna. He'd been the young, handsome intern and their baby had been a delightful surprise. In the beginning, as she worked her schedule as a Seattle Police detective around a new baby and a husband who was always at the hospital, she'd held out hope that easier times would come. All young couples struggle in the beginning.

Emily sat in her car, taking in the flood of memories. She watched a woman and her three children climb into the gleaming silver of their brand-new SUV. The car was expensive. More than fifty thousand dollars, she thought. She wondered if the husband part of that family's equation was more welcoming of the children than David had been of Jenna.

David Kenyon could not take the spontaneity, the uncertainty that comes with a free-willed child. At the hospital, he was God; in control of the very lives of his patients. At home, he was a husband and a father. He couldn't make the tiny pieces of a real, dynamic life fit in his ordered, unyielding world of medical emergencies. He couldn't understand why Emily had wanted to catch the killer, put the baby rapist in prison, and stop the murder plot of an old man's greedy family.

But most of all, he could never understand why Jenna had to come first.

She'd loved David so much back then. *Deeply so.* She'd seen his need to keep things ordered and under control as central to who he was as a doctor. But she had needs, too. Her life was about being a mother, a wife, a cop. She saw no shame in those ambitions, in that order.

She turned the key in the car and pulled into light traffic.

Chapter Four

"Sheriff Kenyon," she said, holding the phone to her ear. Outside her office door, she could hear Gloria chatting with Jason about something—judging by their laughter, it had nothing to do with the case at hand. There was nothing to laugh about there. Just the uneasy feeling that Mandy Crawford's vanishing act might not have been her own doing.

The person on the other line gasped. A *crackle*. Then, silence.

"Are you there?" Emily asked.

Another crackle.

"Hello?"

"Sheriff Kenyon? This is Hillary Layton. Mandy's mother." There was anguish in every syllable.

Emily had been expecting the call. She both dreaded and longed for such calls. They were always enveloped in worry, regret, and heartache, but they were necessary to move any investigation forward. She'd left messages at Luke and Hillary Layton's Spokane home. The answering machine indicated that they'd be "in and out" but would be checking messages. Mitch Crawford had told Emily that Mandy's parents were vacationing in Mexico and he had no way of knowing how to reach them.

"Mrs. Layton," Emily said, "I'm so sorry."

It wasn't much, but it was heartfelt, and really, all she could say. Right then, they had not a scintilla of evidence pointing to Mandy's whereabouts. The rest of the conversation would be driven by the mother of a missing young woman.

"Any sign of my daughter?"

Emily could tell that the woman, so far from the snowy Northwest, was about to shatter into a million pieces. "Nothing. But we're working every lead we can. Where are you?"

"Puerto Vallarta. Mandy and Mitch sent us down here for a week—they have points in a timeshare. I didn't want to go, because she's so close to her due date. But she wanted us to go. She was so insistent. I can't believe that she's left him. She never told me anything." Mrs. Layton took a deep breath. "Just a minute."

Emily heard Mandy's mother put her hand over the mouthpiece of her phone and say something to someone standing nearby. The break in the conversation gave Emily a split second to collect her thoughts. She wondered why Hillary Layton would leave her daughter with her first grandchild due any day. It seemed peculiar.

"That was my husband," Hillary said, getting back on the line. "He wants me to tell you that he doesn't trust Mitch as far as he can throw him."

A man's voice could be heard in the background. It was the heavy growl of a big man. An angry man.

"The guy's a self-centered sack of crap!"

"Shhh! Luke. That's not helping!"

Emily tried to defuse the anger, with a calming tone. "Mrs. Layton—"

"*Hillary*, please."

"Hillary, then, where do you think Mandy might have gone? Are you close?"

"I don't know where she is. And yes, we are extremely

close. I saw her once a week and we talked on the phone almost every day. We're as close as a mother and daughter can be, yet still have our own lives. After I got your message, I called her girlfriends, Sammy, Dee, Caroline, and Sierra. No one knows anything."

One name caught Emily's attention. "Who's Sammy?"

"Samantha Phillips, her best friend. She lives on West Highland Drive. Married to a dentist."

Emily knew who Dr. Dan Phillips was. He'd taken over Dr. Cassidy's dental practice—the one that had seen half of Cherrystone through their first cavities in grade school to the trauma of impacted wisdom teeth in college. Cherrystone was more than a six-degrees-of-separation type of town, she thought. More like three degrees. Emily seized on Samantha's name because she never heard it mentioned before. When Mitch gave Deputy Howard a list of those with the tightest bonds to his missing wife, Sammy's name hadn't been among them.

Emily's eyes landed on the photo of Mandy that the women from the county clerk's office had brought in for a missing persons poster they'd made. She wondered when the photo had been taken.

"When are you coming back?" she asked.

"Tonight. We're leaving PV tonight. First flight we could get seats on. Alaska Airlines through LAX."

"All right. We're doing everything we can to find her. I want you and Mr. Layton to come to my office when you get back home."

Hillary Layton finally lost her fractured composure and started to cry. "Sheriff, do you think she sent us away because she wanted to leave Mitch? Or maybe . . . you know, something really bad happened to her."

Emily had worked missing persons cases in Seattle. She knew that the first hours were crucial, and in the absence of any reason for Amanda to flee, chances were that she was either abducted or injured somewhere. Or dead. Few people went missing longer than a day without one of those reasons accounting for their disappearance.

Yet to the mother on the phone, hope was essential just then.

"Hillary, please, *don't* think the worst. Right now, we have to turn every stone. We need to focus our energies on finding your daughter. That's what we're doing. We're rolling on this at one hundred miles an hour."

Hillary stopped crying. "Thank you, Sheriff. My husband and I will see you tomorrow."

Emily hung up and picked up the photo. She felt a small surge of hope. If Mitch Crawford was, in fact, involved with Mandy's disappearance, then he'd made his first mistake. He'd lied when he said he didn't know exactly where to reach his in-laws. Even if there was some reason that he didn't know which timeshare unit they'd been sent to, he surely could have tracked them with a call to the resort company's customer service center. After all, Mr. and Mrs. Layton were using his resort points for their stay.

It was a stupid lapse, all right, but it made Emily smile.

There was also the matter of Sammy Phillips, Mandy's closest friend, another oversight on Mitch's part. He'd never mentioned her.

The Phillips residence was everything Mitch Crawford's house could never be. It wasn't in a gated community, with the pretentious accoutrements of a wannabe estate. It was grand and authentic, a vintage home decked out in holiday finery that was subtle and respectful for the season. The two-story white colonial had an oversize gilded eucalyptus wreath on each of the double doors. Tiny faux candlelights were set in each of the fourteen windows on the street side of the house.

It was dusk when Emily arrived. She parked on the street, slick with melted snow. She'd never been inside the house; however, she knew its history. No matter how long the Phillipses would live there, Cherrystone old-timers would always call it the Justin House. It was named for Herbert Justin, a banker who'd had it built and lived there with his wife, Matilda, until he died at eighty-one and she was shuttled off to a rest home in Portland to be near her kids.

It was sold three weeks after the old lady was sent packing "for her own good."

Samantha Phillips was a stunning blonde with green eyes. She stood in the doorway as Emily made her way up the steps, wrapping her arms around her black-cashmere-clad torso and shuddered at the cool air.

"Come inside, it's getting a little more than brisk out here again," Samantha said, looking out across the sky, which was dark with the threat of rain or snow.

Emily followed her into the two-story entryway, across blue Persian rugs with a pile so deep that it nearly sucked the heels off her shoes. Samantha had a teapot on a tray with some of the delicate rolled cookies that Emily knew were krumkake, the same that her mother had made for the holidays. The room was dominated by a ten-foot-tall tree that, by fragrance alone, indicated that it was a real Balsam fir.

"I see you're Norwegian," she said, looking at the cookies.

A warm smile came over Samantha's face. "The krumkake. Have one, please. My great-grandmother's family was from Oslo, and these cookies are about the only Norwegian tradition that I have." Samantha motioned for Emily to sit. They faced each other in matching mohair love seats, obviously real and perfectly at home in the grand old house, stuffed with tasteful antiques and paintings.

"Your home is lovely," Emily said, taking it all in.

"Thank you, but I take no credit for it. My husband had

the guts to buy it when we really didn't have the money. We do now, of course," she said, catching herself in a flutter of weakness that she didn't like to share with strangers. "The practice is thriving, I mean."

There was a kind of awkwardness in the air. Emily knew that Samantha was chattering on to fill up as much time as possible, so as not to have to talk about what was really on her mind.

"I voted for you," Samantha said, as odd a non sequitur as Emily had ever heard.

Emily smiled graciously. "Thank you. I appreciate your vote. We need to talk about Mandy, Samantha. This is very important. Her mother tells me that you're her best friend. Is that right?"

Samantha poured tea, a cup for each of them. She motioned to the sugar. Emily declined.

"We knew each other in college," Samantha said, swirling sugar into the steaming amber liquid. "We were freshman roommates. We were that strange pairing of girls that actually clicked. Most of the girls who were paired off with high school friends ended up hating each other by Christmas. Not us."

"You're not from here, are you?" Emily asked, already knowing the answer. She knew everyone with deep roots in Cherrystone, because she had them herself.

She shook her head, and Emily noticed for the first time that the diamonds on Samantha Phillips's earlobes had to be at least two carats each.

"No, but I'm here because of Mandy. I was out here visiting her and Mitch, and I met Dan at a party."

"Did you know Mitch well?"

"Well enough to hate him, if that's what you want to know."

Emily set down her cup. "How come?"

"I don't know. Sometimes I hated him because Mandy

could have done so much better. She always dated decent guys in school. Mitch was such a jerk. He never let her do anything that went against whatever he thought best. It was like the second she married him, I had to make appointments to see her."

"So he's controlling," Emily said. "But what else? Was he abusive?"

"Not that I know of," she said. "I mean, he didn't hit her. I know she'd never put up with that and I know she would have told me."

Emily searched Samantha's worried eyes. "You're holding back on something."

"I know you're here for some big revelation, something that will give you a clue about what happened to her, where she might be. I just can't help you."

"Was she happy?"

"She hadn't been for a long time, but when she became pregnant, Mandy changed. She seemed to be her old self again. There was some joy in her voice. She'd wanted to have a baby for so long, but Mitch kept telling her the time wasn't right."

"So last year, the time was right?"

"I think so. I really don't know. One time when we were having coffee at her house—which, by the way, she hated the place—she told me that if she didn't start a family with Mitch she'd leave him. She said, 'I don't care about the things he cares about. I want to be a mom. I will be a mom.' "

"So, she must have convinced him it was time?"

"Or tricked him," Samantha said, looking like she'd spoken ill of the dead.

"Tricked him?" Emily prodded.

"I'm overstating, I think. You know what I mean, she just wanted a baby so much. She'd skip her pills and make things happen. She wouldn't have been the first woman to do that."

Emily could no longer resist the cookie. The buttery crunch reminded her instantly of her own childhood, of holidays with her family, and later with Jenna and David. There was a bittersweetness to the memory.

"Mitch was looking forward to the baby, too?"

"I think so. I think it took awhile. Dan and I went out to dinner with them in late October and they both seemed excited that they'd be parents by Christmas. Mitch was bragging about how he'd have a son to follow in his footsteps at the dealership."

"But it wasn't a son."

Samantha looked across the room then back at Emily. "I know. I almost dropped my fork. I nudged Dan to keep his mouth shut. I knew it was a girl, but it was clear that Mandy hadn't told Mitch. You could have knocked me over with a puff of air."

"I'll bet. Did you ask her about it?"

When Samantha started to answer, her cell phone rang. The ringtone was "Jingle Bells." She looked at the number and let it go to voice mail.

"My husband's late," she said. "And, to answer your question, I did ask her about it a week or so later."

Samantha Phillips had been out running errands. She made a trip to the bank, the cleaner's to drop off her husband's shirts, and she picked up two bags of Halloween candy because the old Justin House had been rumored to be haunted; every year, it got more trick-or-treaters than probably any other residence in Cherrystone. She knew that Saturdays were Mitch's biggest day at the dealership and that Mandy would be home. She parked behind a dark blue Lexus on the street in front of the house.

When she rang the bell, Mandy met her at the door.

"Oh, hi, Sam," she said.

"Hi, honey, I thought I'd stop by for coffee. I tried your cell, but it must be off."

Mandy lingered in the doorway, not really opening it for Samantha to come inside. "I guess I forgot to recharge it again."

There was a beat of uncharacteristic awkwardness.

"Can I come in?" Samantha asked.

Mandy stood still. Her hair was clipped back, as if she hadn't had time to brush it out. It looked like she was getting a late start on the day. "Not a good time."

A flicker of worry came over her. "Are you all right? Is the baby all right?"

"The baby's fine. I'm just trying to take it easy."

The excuse seemed so hollow, so completely unlike her friend.

"Are you sure?"

"Sure. Let's get together later. I'll call you."

"But I wanted to talk about last night. What you said about the baby . . . I thought Mitch knew it was a girl."

"I can't go there right now," she said, narrowing the opening of the doorway. "I'm sorry."

"Can I come in? We need to talk."

"Not now. Now isn't a good time."

Before Samantha could change the subject and offer to go to the store or run an errand to help out, the door snapped shut. It was as if she was selling magazine subscriptions door to door or maybe handing out pamphlets for a fundamentalist religious group.

She stood there and looked at the grand front door.

What just happened here? What's going on?

Two days later, Samantha got Mandy on the phone at her job at the county clerk's office.

At first, she thought that Mandy's cell phone had died and

that had been the reason why she hadn't called back, despite several messages.

"Are you mad at me?" Samantha asked.

"Not mad," Mandy said, keeping her voice office-low. "I'm going through some things."

"With Mitch?"

"I can't talk about it."

"Is he being an asshole again?"

"Listen," Mandy said, "I know you're worried about me." Her voice grew curt and now, very final. "I'm not going to talk about this. I need you to back off. OK?"

Then she hung up.

That was the last time they ever spoke about it.

Jenna Kenyon's cell phone vibrated somewhere in the depths of her purse. She'd been dispatched to the basement bedroom that her stepmother Dani had said was built with her in mind.

"You father wants you to feel you have a home here, too," Dani Kenyon said as she first revealed the unfinished bedroom, more than a year ago. "I want you to help pick out paint colors and fabrics. I'm thinking of chocolate with mango accents."

"That sounds yummy," Jenna said, knowing that Dani wouldn't get the irony of her pun, nor the literal distaste she had for orange and brown. The colors reminded her of the design scheme used by her junior high.

"Having you happy here is a big, big priority," Dani said.

The passage of time *proved* that. The room hadn't changed a bit, save for a few more items shoved inside the space. Jenna knew where she stood with Dani, and by extension, where she stood with her father.

She found her cell phone and let out an audible sigh.

It was Amber Manley.

She let it go to voice mail and turned on her laptop, waiting for it to whirl into life.

Amber Manley was a sister from the Beta Zeta House at Cascade University, Jenna's old chapter. Amber had stumbled onto a cache of food and clothes that had been squirreled away by Pepper Raynor. The problem was that while Pepper was a thief—stealing food from the kitchen and ripping off bits of every size two in the house—Amber had become the target of disciplinary action because she opened Pepper's closet.

Jenna started typing.

Dear Amber,

I know you've been trying to reach me. As much as I'd like to help you, I'm afraid I can't. The chapter rules are very specific. Despite the odor coming from Pepper's closet, you had no right to open it . . .

More than a thousand miles away, he stirred as she came online. His computer know-how came in part from the endless loneliness that draws a boy into the insidious depths of a computer screen, searching for connections to people, and for his own place in the world. He liked how the keyboard felt; cool at first, then hot as he pounded the keys to take him to places he thought he'd never go. His screensaver had been an image of the jade-colored waters around the sandy edges of Oahu, a place he thought he'd never see. But he had. He'd been all over the country, and to Europe. No place he visited, however, made him feel better about himself.

Nothing could.

And just when he thought it could be different, it was all snatched from him.

She was to blame, because she'd stolen from him all that mattered.

He'd e-mailed from a dummy e-mail account a seemingly innocuous message that he cleverly outfitted with a Trojan horse—spyware that allowed him to capture every word she typed on her laptop. If he was logged on to his computer at the same time, he'd actually see her words in real time. She wasn't a stupid girl, he knew. She wasn't weak. She handled those self-absorbed and dimwitted girls with an impressive toughness and logic. There were things about her he might have admired, had he not blamed her for the darkest tragedy of a life that had been marked by so many.

As he formed his plan, created his list, he learned to loathe her over the others. Of the three, she'd been the one in charge. She could have changed the course of her own destiny. She was responsible for everything that was coming to her. Jenna Kenyon could have kept her name off the list.

The first two had no choice. No voice. They would be the disposable practice dolls that he'd once tossed in a fire pit behind his foster family's house. They were trash. Not even human.

Jenna would be the prize. He'd save the most-deserving for last.

Chapter Five

The next morning, Emily caught a glimpse of Cherrystone's least favorite—albeit most successful—car dealer as he slowed his car in front of the copy center on Washington Avenue. She found a spot right behind him and parked the Crown Vic. Running into a "person of interest" is always a good thing.

"Hi, Mitch," she said, emerging from her vehicle. She could see him tense a little, but his slight smile stayed intact.

"Sheriff Kenyon," he said, pressing the key button to his automatic door lock. The horn beeped.

She took a breath. "I was going to call you. No need now."

"How lucky for you," he said, through taut, angry lips.

"I was thinking that we could get some more traction on Mandy's case if you stopped by the station."

Mitch Crawford's eyes flashed. "Oh, I see. After you've treated me like a freak and embarrassed me in front of my own staff, you want me to make nice? That's just goddamn beautiful. Thanks to you and your careless insinuations, my own mother-in-law asked me what I did with Mandy."

Emily shook her head. "I'm sorry. Sometimes people forget that you're a victim here, too."

Most people would have seen the emptiness of Emily's words, but there was no risk of that with Mitch Crawford. He only saw the things that fit his overly inflated self-image. Anything that stroked his ego, got him attention, or made him feel that he was the wronged one—it was a safe bet.

"Will you help us?" she asked, this time, her voice a little softer. She wasn't aiming for sexy, although there was no doubt that she was a beautiful woman with a stunning face and lovely figure. The days of charming a guy with an un-buttoned blouse were long gone, but she still could see the value in suggesting vulnerability.

Because that's exactly what catches a guy like Mitch Crawford off guard.

"I'm in the middle of some stuff here," he said, waving a manila envelope in Emily's direction.

"Oh, I can see that," she said. "Why don't you come by later this afternoon?"

"Do I come alone? Or do I get a lawyer?"

"You can always bring a lawyer, Mitch, but I think you're smart enough to see that we're only trying to help. I mean, really, why would you need one if you just want to help us find your wife?"

Mitch was probably a decent poker player. If he was wor-ried right then, he didn't let on.

"All right, Sheriff. If we clear the air, will you get Mandy's mother off my back? Tell her that I had nothing to do with any of this disappearance BS? She won't let up. It's distract-ing. It isn't exactly helping me move cars off the lot, you know."

"Look, Mitch," she said, trying to keep her cool, "she's worried about her daughter. She loves her daughter. She wants to know where she is. You know, most people in your position would feel the same way."

"You don't know how I feel," he said.

"Come in and tell me."

Mitch let out an exasperated sigh. "This is stupid. But I'll be there."

Back in her office, the smells of a burning coffeepot and popcorn emanated from the break room. Emily dialed the prosecutor's office and was patched through to Camille's desk.

"Hazelton," Camille said, her voice throaty from a cold that had declared war on her immune system.

"I ran into Mitch Crawford," Emily said. "He's agreed to come in for an interview. Thought you'd like to know. You'll never believe what he was concerned about."

"Try me."

"He's worried about his mother-in-law and car sales. He barely even mentions Mandy."

Camille let out a laugh, which started a series of coughs. "Sorry. Working on a cold. That's priceless. Remind me never to buy a car from that guy. I'd hate to boost him in a time of real need."

"Do you want to be there?"

"No. Too formal. Just chat with him. Press him gently—and I know that will be hard because I'd like to shove him against a barbed-wire fence until he screams."

"You must be sick," Emily said. "You're holding back now, Camille."

"Just a little. You know what I mean."

Emily did. The two women talked a moment longer. Emily told the prosecutor that she intended to videotape the interview with Mandy's husband.

"I'm not sure he'll go for it," she said.

"If he likes what he's wearing today," Camille said, "I'll bet he says yes."

* * *

An eleven-year-old snowboarder noticed the gleam of silver under a pile of snow on the back end of a Walmart parking lot near Spokane. Casey Broder's mother wouldn't let him go to the slopes with his older brother and friends, so the kid took to the heap of snow plowed into a minimountain behind the store. It wasn't much of a slope and he cursed his mother for not letting him do what he wanted to do.

All of that changed, when the sun hit the minimountain just right and a small mirror blinked right at him.

Casey thought it was a girl's compact at first. He bent down to pick it up, but it was frozen into the minimountain. Using his board, he started to chip away at the crust of snow. A couple of whacks and he discovered that the mirror was attached to a car.

A silver Camry.

Casey told the Walmart greeter what he'd found and the man called the police. Within an hour, the police arrived and determined that the car belonged to a missing woman from Cherrystone.

"They found Mandy's car behind a Deer Lake Walmart," Jason said, catching Emily in her office. "The store's snowplow operator has lousy peripheral vision and buried the car by mistake. It sat there because no one complained their car was missing."

She could read her deputy like a book. There was neither sadness or hope in his words, just the rote recitation of the facts.

"She wasn't in the car, was she?"

He shook his head. "Nope. State police will process for trace."

Emily had a sinking feeling. "Thanks, Jason. I'll tell Mitch. I'll bet you a beer that the vehicle's clean."

"You're on."

If there had been any hope that Mandy had left on her

own, it evaporated with the discovery of her Camry. She might have had plenty of reasons to escape her husband—last trimester or not—although it seemed unlikely that she'd vanish from a Walmart parking lot.

"She's not the Walmart type," he'd said.

Chapter Six

Mitch Crawford's eyes were bottomless. Flinty. Cold. Sheriff Emily Kenyon felt the sparse hairs on the back of her neck rise. She'd been close to evil too many times to discount the feelings that niggled at her. It was as if somewhere inside there was a malevolent barometer telling her to be just a little more wary.

But not so wary that you let fear stymie you.

On the credenza behind her, the face of her daughter, Jenna, beamed in her graduation photo. Nearby, a little pink purse decorated with an eyeless flamingo and filled with pennies served as a paperweight.

And as a touchstone to terrible things in the past. Things that made Emily and Jenna closer than ever.

"I'm surprised at you," she said, as they faced each other from across her desk. "You seem . . ." She paused to irritate him.

"What's the word I'm looking for? *Indifferent.* That's what I'm feeling from you here."

It was a lie, and a strategic one.

Mitch, however, didn't blink.

"Are you expecting me to cry?" Mitch asked.

"Some emotion would be nice, Mitch."

He gripped the stack of fliers that he'd had made at the copy center. They were facedown, but through the cheap goldenrod-colored paper the photo of a woman was visible. The headline in squat block letters was also bold enough that it could be read backward through the paper: MISSING.

Mitch kept his arms folded tightly across his chest. The muscles that enveloped his sturdy frame like cables spun around a rigid spool tensed beneath a powder blue Hilfiger lamb's wool sweater. He didn't smile.

"Look," Emily said, still sizing him up, "I don't want anything from you but the truth."

Mitch clutched his papers and stood up. "Jesus, Sheriff, you *know* me. You know my family. You *know* that I didn't do anything to her."

She asked if he'd mind if they spoke in the conference room.

"I'd like to record our conversation," she said, waiting for him to decline.

But he didn't.

"I have nothing to hide. You wouldn't know it by the way you are treating me."

She wondered if it spoke of arrogance or innocence, his willingness to be filmed.

With the stationary video camera recording, Emily sat across from Mitch so that she could meet his gaze head-on. She noticed how he hadn't yet said Mandy's name. She stayed quiet, hoping that her silence would invite the man with the ever-so-slowly-receding hairline and beefy biceps to reveal something of use in the investigation. *To spill more.* It was a technique that had served her well as a Seattle cop, then as a sheriff's deputy, and finally as the sheriff.

"You need to be forthcoming," she said. "We understand that things weren't that—and I don't mean to be unkind here— great between you," she said, stopping herself and playing his game of not mentioning his wife's name. "And your wife. You know your marriage was in trouble."

The veins in his neck started to plump. "We had problems, but not any more than anyone else around Cherrystone or anywhere in this country!"

"Yes, but she was going to leave you."

Mitch's face had gone completely red. "I'm sick and tired of all the innuendo coming out of your office. I loved my wife."

Loved, past tense.

Emily opened the folder and handed it to him like a menu. Inside was a photograph of a pretty blonde in a periwinkle sweater over a blouse with a Peter Pan collar. Emily noted that Mandy was apparently a very traditional pregnant lady, in that she had chosen the same look her own mother's generation had sported—pregnant woman as child. Big bows. Babyish prints. None of the trendy hipster black pregnancy duds for her—no bump-clinging spandex tops revealing a thin slice of tummy.

"I know what my wife looks like," he said.

"Say her name."

Mitch shoved the folder back. "Damn you, Emily. Mandy! *Mandy* is her name! Is this some kind of a test here?"

"Calm down, Mitch," Emily said, her voice steady and commanding. "I want to find Mandy, too. I need some help here. Are you sure you've told us everything?"

Mitch turned away from her and headed for the door. "There isn't any more to tell," he said over his shoulder. "You've been to my place. You've interviewed everyone that I've ever known."

"OK, then a few questions for you. I'm wondering why it is that you didn't know where your in-laws were."

"Because I didn't."

"You sent them there, Mitch. Essentially paid for it."

"Look, I didn't. Mandy did. Mandy decided to give them a free ride on our dime. I wasn't lying. I didn't know they'd gone to Mexico until after they got there. I was so pissed off at Mandy, I didn't want the details of Luke and Hillary sipping margaritas. That trip was for Mandy and me."

"I see. Seems like you don't like anyone much, Mitch."

"What's the big deal? So what if I don't get along with them? I'm not the first husband to have a lousy relationship with his in-laws."

"Fair enough," she said, not doubting that the Laytons didn't care much for Mitch, but still unsure if he was being honest. Mitch Crawford was that kind of guy, overselling his story like he was trying to upgrade her into a car she couldn't afford. "I need to know more about Mandy. Did she ever leave like this before?"

"No. She was very reliable."

"Why did she leave, Mitch?"

"I have no idea. This interview is over. I'll look for her myself. Thanks for nothing."

From the hallway, Emily watched Mitch Crawford's retreating figure. It was more than a hunch. She knew it in her bones. Mitch was holding back. Crime statistics indicated that Mandy was dead and that her husband had killed her. But there was no evidence. No blood.

"There's a reason for that," she told Jason.

"Yeah, he didn't kill her."

"But you saw the plastic bleach bottle in the trash."

"Yeah, but if you went to my house you'd find two bottles in our trash. Bleach kills germs. I've got two germy nephews."

Emily smiled. "I don't know. Something's with this guy."

"Yeah, he's full of himself, for one. I'll bet his home gym is the biggest room in the house."

"Wouldn't be hard to guess his priorities," she said.

"Anyway, Sheriff, just because the dude is a self-absorbed ass, that doesn't make him a killer."

Emily wasn't so sure. "That remains to be seen."

Across town, in the floodlit darkness of a snow-clad backyard of weed-free grass and four thousand daffodils yet to bloom, a man's voice called out.

"Toby! Here, boy! Toby! Come!"

Mitch Crawford's voice was nearly raw from calling. He'd turned on the pool lights and the patio lights, even the up-lights that forced a cheery, warm glow up the trunks of artfully grouped aspen and birch.

He banged a metal food dish against the flagstone patio that ran from a pair of ten-foot-tall French doors to the edge of a lapis-tiled pool. It being winter, the pool was entombed in a covering of blue plastic bubble wrap. A crust of ice formed in patches where it had splashed on the patio.

"Toby!" A wisp of white vapor rose from the edges where the warm water seeped against the pool's lapis tile work. "Where are you?"

Something seemed odd, and Mitch moved closer to the pool. A piece of the bubble-insulated sheeting had curled along its edge. The covering was custom-made for a perfect fit and he wondered if he should ask for his money back. He bent down and started to adjust it, when a shadowy figure caught his eye.

A cat wandered across the white-dusted lawn. Balls of snow clung to its furry belly.

"I guess you haven't seen Toby, have you?"

The cat barely regarded the man and continued on its path over the grass, onto the flagstone, and then off under the dark green of a precision-trimmed yew hedge.

"Toby!" he called once more. "Where are you, boy? Come here. Come home!"

Mitch pulled the covering taut and pulled himself to his feet.

As Mitch turned to go inside his oversize empty house, an indistinguishable dark shadow at the bottom of the pool near the cascading Jacuzzi caught his eye. *What the?* At first he thought it was a pile of leaves that had somehow become sucked under the plastic overlay. He ran to the electrical panel next to the cabana and turned on the overheads. *Flash!* The yard lit up like a high school football game. He bent down and lifted the plastic.

"Oh God! No!" he cried out. "Please!"

Chapter Seven

Emily looked out the window of her office and a smile came to her face. It had snowed for two hours and Cherrystone that December looked as if it had been dipped in white glitter. Main Street had been decorated by city crews the day after Thanksgiving, but the decorations—faux fir boughs with big plastic ribbons that had been a fixture on the streets since the 1960s—had long passed from kitschy to charming. They looked even better with a touch of frosting.

The rest of the world—the more sophisticated cities in which she'd lived or visited—could keep their fancy holiday accoutrements. Emily still saw what she'd seen as a child—the sparkle of a fake fir bough and the whimsy of an oversize red plastic bow.

And yet, this year brought with it a touch of the melancholy, too. Jenna was a grown woman with a real job. Certainly, she'd be coming home for Christmas. But that wouldn't always be the case. At some time, in a flash like all of life had been, she'd be waiting for Jenna, a husband, children—maybe even a dog—to come visit.

At forty-four, Emily knew she was far too young to give up on herself and live through her daughter. But she'd screwed things up with Chris Collier and probably had missed her chance at a happily ever after. It had been her fault, and she knew her inability to move their relationship forward had been a crushing blow to Chris. Over Thanksgiving, she suspected that he was going to ask her to marry him, and she was right. She loved him, no doubt, but she said she wasn't sure about getting married again.

"We need to move this forward," he said, without any anger, but with the calmness of a man who knew what he wanted. "Or end it and get on with our lives."

Why didn't I just say yes? she asked herself. Why can't I be ready?

Cars slowly passed by through the sparkle of the snowfall when the phone rang, snapping Emily away from her thoughts. It was Jenna, calling from Memphis, her first stop on a three-college tour to promote the Beta Zeta Sorority.

"Hi, honey," she said.

"Hi, Mom," Jenna said, her voice buoyant. "Just thought I'd check in with you."

Emily loved that she and Jenna talked nearly every day; the only exception was on the occasion when the day had gotten away from them and it was late at night. In that case, they'd text *I love you* and *Good night*.

"How's it going with the Crawford case?" Jenna asked, knowing that her mother lived and breathed an investigation on a 24–7 basis.

"We'll sort it out, but until we find her, we're a little stuck right now."

"You know that jerk killed her."

Emily could hear her own voice coming from Memphis and it brought a wry smile. Jenna didn't cut a suspected killer any slack. She'd make a good prosecutor someday.

"What we know and what we can prove, as you know, are completely different."

Jenna murmured something that Emily couldn't quite make out.

"Sorry, Mom, I'm between recruitment planning meetings and the chapter president here said I could get some privacy in the TV lounge, but these girls keep barging in with their complaints and criticisms about what they did last year and how they are sure that I don't know what I'm talking about because I'm from up north and I have a regional bias. They won't give me a minute."

"What happened to the good manners of the South?" Emily asked.

"Gone like everywhere else. This is the most self-centered bunch yet. Seriously, Mom. All they care about is drinking and looking like they're Paris Hilton."

"Sounds like your sisters at Cascade University."

"These girls are over-the-top in everything they do. We were never so bad as these girls. I'm not kidding you."

"That's not what I remember," Emily, said, a slight edge to her tone, meant to remind Jenna of life's lessons learned the previous year as the chapter president of her BZ sorority. She remembered the time Jenna had to kick a girl out of the house for stealing money from the cook's rainy-day fund. Or the time one sister came home so drunk that she was found on the couch the next morning with her thong on backward. And nothing else. There were other incidents that made Emily wonder if sending her daughter to CU had been the right thing to do—scholarship or not. She held David responsible. He'd promised to send Jenna to a top-tier school out of state, but Dani, his new wife, balked. They were going through a major house remodel and she was sure there wouldn't be enough cash for Jenna's education.

"She can get a job," Dani had told David. "I had to."

Emily played that back in her mind, and almost lost the feeling of joy she had at hearing her daughter's voice.

"P.S., Mom, these girls are driving me crazy. They really are the worst. Ever!"

"How so?"

"Mostly the same old, same old. Disorganized. Selfish. Boyfriend troubles. One told me she thinks *two* of her old boyfriends have joined forces to stalk her. I mean really, Mom, how self-absorbed do you have to be to think that one stalker isn't enough?"

Her daughter's comment amused Emily. "I didn't know stalking could be a group activity."

Jenna laughed. "That's what I thought. There's also this girl who spends all day crying that her brother gets all the attention, and her dad, some meatpacking bigwig out of Oklahoma, doesn't do anything but send her money."

"I wish someone would send me money," Emily said, teasing Jenna.

"Gotta go. I have a P.S. for you."

"What's that?"

"P.S., I had an airport layover in Chicago and got you your Christmas present."

"A snow globe or a Graceland T-shirt? I know," she said drawing out her words as she pretended to ponder it, "a Graceland snow globe. Will I love it?"

"Did you raise me right?" Before Emily could answer, Jenna cut in. "Love you, Mom. Back to the bitchfest in the dining room."

"Talk to you tomorrow."

"Good luck with the case, Mom. You'll figure it out. You always do."

Luck would be good, Emily thought, snapping her phone shut. *A pregnant woman doesn't just evaporate into thin air.* Amanda Crawford had to be somewhere.

By the end of the day, Mitch Crawford had found himself on all three Spokane TV affiliates with news feeds across the Northwest. Emily, Jason, Camille, Gloria, and all the others working the case let their jaws fall to the floor when he uttered a line that surely had to qualify for a place in the annals of crime reporting.

"I'm a successful businessman, a *very* successful businessman," he said, dead-eyed to the camera. "Guys like me don't kill our wives. We trade 'em in and get a new one."

"He thinks she's a used car," Emily said, staring at the TV. "Unbelievable."

Chapter Eight

The number on the minuscule screen of her cell phone had long been committed to memory.

She answered it immediately. Before she spoke, she heard his voice.

"Your Crawford case is making noise all the way over here in Seattle."

It was Chris, of course.

"No kidding," she said. "Gloria's been fielding calls from the Seattle media like nobody's business," she said, almost feeling a little awkward. She was unsure if he'd called to talk shop—or to ask her to reconsider his proposal. She felt her face grow a little warm and looked around her office to make sure she was really alone just in case the conversation veered toward the personal.

"I hope some of the media attention does us some good out here."

"Reporters are like maggots on a corpse," he said. "They have a job to do."

Emily let out a laugh. Chris always had a kind of cut-to-the-chase perspective when it came to everything. She watched as a pair of reserve officers walked by her office window. She waved at them. The sight of the young men snapped her out of the place that she was revisiting in her mind.

"Em?"

"I'm here. Just thinking. Sorry. Chris . . ." She let her words trail off to a whisper. "I miss you."

"I know. Me, too. I'm coming to Cherrystone this weekend. I thought maybe this would be a good time to see where we stand."

"In the middle of a possible murder investigation?"

"You were always best when you were on the hunt for a killer," he said.

She laughed. "I think you might have something there. I know that I'm always happiest when I'm going after the bad guy."

"Yup. And the guy you have in Cherrystone is as rotten as they come."

"Mitch Crawford is really something, isn't he?" she said. "What did you think of his TV performance? Made me sick to my stomach."

"We only got a snip of it on the Seattle news, but yeah, made me sick, too. He seems preoccupied with how clever he is, how much dough he has in the bank, and absolutely everything in the world except for one thing."

Emily nodded as he spoke, before interjecting, "Mandy."

"He's your guy, all right."

"I can take care of this on my own, you know."

"Of course you can. But you know how much fun we'll have going after him," he said. "And, Emily, don't worry about my fee. Dinner with you will be satisfactory."

"Let me think about that," she said, kidding him to within in an inch of his life. "OK. Sounds good. When can you get here?"

"In my car now."

Emily heard a car honk and she spun around and looked in front of the sheriff's office.

Chris Collier, his lightly graying hair framing a handsome face that still retained the chiseled good looks of his youth, smiled and offered a quick wave through an open window.

Gotcha! He was already here.

While she was glad and surprised to see him, Emily felt a weird flutter of annoyance come over her. *Had Chris come because he thinks I can't work the case without him? Did he think I was too proud to ask for help on my own, when I determined I could use some?*

His smile disarmed her and she glanced at her schedule to make sure nothing was pressing. *Good. Quit overthinking, Emily*, she thought.

On the way over to Cherrystone, a simple phrase reverberated during the drive. *There was no other life without Emily. No other life he wanted.* Chris Collier felt twinges of that from the day they'd reconnected after all those years of being apart—years of being married to the wrong people. Emily had David, the doctor. He had Jessica, the librarian. Neither spouse was the right match. And neither could be.

From his own failed marriage, Chris knew both the joy and the heartache of trying to make two people into an unbreakable unit. The love he had for his ex-wife had been lost long before Emily came back into Chris's life. At first, he figured he could chalk up his mistakes to the fact that the life of a cop held little room for anything that resembled a real life. He'd been called away on a murder investigation in the middle of his oldest son's Little League game—the game in which the boy had pitched a near perfect game. For the rest of his son's life, there would always be the idea that "your job always came first." Jessica Collier would not have a problem concurring when her son said those things. She, too, had felt the chilly glow of a cop's blue light.

"I can't compete with a dead girl. No woman can," she told case-obsessed Chris the morning she packed her bags, took the kids, and returned to Idaho where she had family.

Chris said he understood, but at the time he was so wrapped up in a murder investigation that he really didn't process his own personal loss—or the truth behind his wife's analysis of the state of their marriage.

With Emily, there was the promise of a do-over. They were no longer kids, no longer bound to make the same mistakes. Their children were grown. Their lives were pitched toward a time when the focus was aimed more at themselves, their needs. They'd had their breakups. They had their passionate, endless nights. The time for being together was now. *That moment.* Chris Collier was certain.

He practiced the words in his head.

"Emily, we've had our ups and downs. We've been through things so dark and dangerous that we almost have no right to be here anymore. But we are. And I know now, more than ever, that life with you is the only life I want to have."

Chris smiled at the idea that he needed to rehearse. *Why was it so hard to be vulnerable to the ones who love us most?*

But that evening, after dinner, talk about the case, Jenna, Chris's condo, the subject of their future just didn't wind its way into the conversation—rehearsals or not. It just didn't seem to fit.

"The temp is dropping," Emily said, pulling another comforter from the bench at the foot of her bed and spreading it across the mint green and white quilt that her mother had made.

Chris bent down to help her with the covers, and he placed his hand on the small of her back. She turned around and they kissed. She had missed the warmth of his touch, how he tasted. *The way that he pulled her close.* He undressed her in the pale light of the bedroom lamp, letting her blouse and dark wool skirt fall in a heap by her feet. He unhooked her bra. Emily returned the favor by unbuttoning his shirt. His body was lean, muscular, but not through some ridiculous workout regimen. Chris Collier played racquetball, ate right, and was blessed with genetics that kept him off the treadmill like so many men his age chasing after the body that they never really had, even in their twenties. The scar from the gunshot five years before had lightened somewhat; the hair on his chest encircled it with a light brown fringe.

Emily touched her fingertip to the scar. It was smooth, harder than his skin.

"I could have lost you forever," she said.

"I'm here now."

"I know," she said, as they fell onto the bed. As they kissed, he embraced her with the right mix of tenderness and passion. Emily felt like she was falling into a warm pool, being carried away. She knew she'd always loved Chris. His touch, his taste, his body were everything she missed and everything she needed. She kicked the top quilt to the floor.

"We won't need that extra blanket," she said.

Chris kissed her again, deeply. "No, babe, we won't." He reached over her and turned off the light.

Sweat pooled under Mitch Crawford's arms, and his lips were chapped from a nervous habit that had him constantly moistening them with his tongue. He'd had bad days before, but nothing like the ones that were pulling him downward right then. It was one of the late nights at the dealership, with two salesmen on the floor and Darla Montague at her desk answering phones and keeping the glass coffeepots from burning to black bottoms.

Mitch stared out the window at the lot.

"You all right?" Darla asked, entering the room with the

week's sales reports, commissions, and payrolls. She set the file on his desk, but Mitch kept his gaze toward the window.

"I don't know," he said.

"Do you need anything?"

He turned to look at her. His eyes had flooded. "I'm sorry, Darla."

"Sorry?"

"Sorry for everything I did to you. I'm a lousy person, I know that. I guess everyone does."

Darla didn't want to argue. She knew what kind of man Mitch Crawford was. He was older. He was her boss. He'd taken advantage of her. She probably could sue for something. She recognized all of that on some level. But she didn't want to do anything but forget her own foolishness.

"It's OK," she said. "We were both at fault."

"I've really screwed up," he said. "I've really made a mess of things." He opened the file folder and glanced at the reports. "Maybe next month will be better." He fanned out the payroll checks and started to sign each one. The last one was a check made out to himself. He looked at Darla as he tore it up.

"Maybe next month," he said. "Can't really afford to pay myself right now."

Darla stayed mute. The owner of the dealership hadn't drawn a salary for two months. If he had, she was sure that a couple of the car cleaners would have to be let go. He kept telling her that "those guys have kids" and "Mandy and I will get by. We have savings."

But then Mandy was gone.

Darla wondered if financial problems had driven Mandy away, away and into the arms of another man. Sure, Mitch was a jerk and a cad, but there were times when it almost seemed as if he'd had a heart beating somewhere inside.

It looked like Mitch was about to cry.

"Mr. Crawford, what can I do?"

"Nothing," he said. "I found Toby."

"He came home?"

"No, the damn dog must have fallen into the pool and got caught under the plastic cover. He's dead, Darla. I thought Mandy took him. But she didn't. Toby's dead."

Darla looked like she was going to cry. She knew what that dog meant to her boss. "You need to tell the sheriff. This is important."

Mitch lined up three pens in a faultless row and looked out his office window to toward the showroom.

"Why bother? They think I killed her. They'll probably think I killed the dog, too."

She wasn't the jumping type, but Emily almost jumped for joy when Camille Hazelton finally secured a warrant to search Mitch Crawford's home on Larkspur. It had taken some doing. Certainly there was probable cause within hours of the first report of Mandy missing, but the Crawford name still had a residual currency among the county judges. Camille kept saying she needed more. Finally, there had been enough. The car, the fact that none of Mandy's credit cards had been used, and that her dependable nature at work had been compromised by her sudden absence all played a role. Techs came from Spokane to comb through the house, spray luminal, and procure the Crawfords' laptop. Emily and Jason oversaw the small army of CSIs as they poked and prodded the contents of the massive home. No blood was found anywhere. In fact, there was no trace that Mandy had even been there—outside of clothes in her closet in the master suite. Even her hairbrush was devoid of any hairs.

The strobe of a camera flash swept over every space.

"Jesus, Sheriff," Jason said as they stood in the kitchen

and watched the swarm of techies wave their ultraviolet lights over every surface, "you'd think Mr. Clean lived here."

Emily shuddered as a cold breeze blew in from the open front door.

"Even Mr. Clean can make a mistake," she said. "Just takes one."

Chapter Nine

As a waitress swooped around the bar, carrying beers and mounds of nachos with enough cheese to choke even a young person's arteries, Cherrystone County Prosecutor Camille Hazelton zeroed in on Emily as she sipped a glass of hot spiced wine. Camille had asked—actually *commanded*, was more like it—to meet after work. With Chris waiting for her at the house, Emily agreed a little reluctantly.

"He did it," Camille said. "You know it. I know it."

The words came at Emily like the authoritative pounding of the keys of an old manual Underwood typewriter, the kind her mother used for writing letters to the editor each week until her death.

"He did it. You know it. I know it."

Camille Hazelton never minced words. She probably didn't even know how. She was, without question, the single most powerful woman in the county-city building. At fifty-five, she was lean-faced and not at all unattractive—at least when she smiled, which detractors insisted wasn't nearly often enough.

Camille and Emily had been friends since arriving in Cherrystone about the same time—Emily coming from Seattle to start over and Camille to pick up where her father

had left off. Dan Hazelton had been the prosecutor for an as-
tonishing twenty-seven years.

When he died, his lawyer daughter moved back home
from a successful law practice in Chicago and did what only
the prodigal daughter could do. She ran against three men
and was elected. Like Emily, Camille had deep roots in
Cherrystone, but she'd also lived outside the insular community. She'd learned that there were dress shops with more to
offer than Delano's on Main Street. She knew what really
good ahi was and the difference between Dom Pérignon
champagne and André. And yet, like Emily, she found that
nothing resonated deeper in a caring person's heart than the
place called home.

Emily sat across from the prosecutor with hot spiced
wines in the cozy confines of TJ's, a downtown bar that was
frequented by law enforcement—pool tables on one side, a
long battered bar that had a century of scuff marks and dents
from cowboy boots, and later, steel-toed boots. It wasn't
fancy. But neither was Cherrystone.

Emily looked down at her wine, a curl of steam still rising
from below the rim.

"Of course we know Crawford did it. Homicide stats. His
unconcerned affect. Both point to him."

Camille motioned to the cocktail waitress that she wanted
another.

"You know it. *I* know it. All of Cherrystone suspects it.
But suspicion, as you know, is not enough. We need evidence."

The waitress deposited a basket of peanuts, and Camille
lowered her voice. "I don't know any other way to say this."
She stopped, clearly pained at the prospect of what she was
about to say. "Look, I have to ask. Do you think we need
more help on this?"

Emily didn't pounce, though if it had been anyone other
than Camille asking, she might have. Instead, she took a

breath. Emily thought of telling Camille that Chris was in town and that she was going to run some things by him, informally. She didn't volunteer it because she felt somewhat awkward about it. Chris was a seasoned pro, but he was also the man she loved. She could separate the two aspects of their relationship just fine, but she doubted everyone else could. Jason, for one, had made subtle remarks about sometimes feeling like an outsider in the sheriff's office. Besides, he'd offered to help. She didn't see her acceptance as a sign of weakness. *Why should she?*

"It isn't that, Camille," she said. "We've done everything. We don't need to contract this out to Spokane PD. We're just a little stuck."

Camille let the warmth melt from her face. She set down her drink. "You need to get unstuck. My office is being crucified. You can't believe the calls we're getting. If the election were held today, I doubt I'd get enough votes to stay on the job."

Emily, having had her own run-ins as a publicly elected official, understood. Working as a public servant felt meaningful most of the time, but there were occasions in which the public pushed hard. Too hard.

"I'm sorry," she said. "We're doing our best."

"Let's *do* better."

Emily wished she'd asked for a second drink. Just then, she could use one. She held her tongue, partly out of friendship, but also because there was no arguing Camille's point. Mandy Crawford had to be dead. Everyone figured her husband had done it, but nothing concrete had turned up.

"If you can't get me something in the next week, I'll have no choice but to call in a special investigator from Olympia."

"Fair enough," Emily finally said.

But it wasn't, not really. She put on her coat, told Camille good-bye, and hurried home to Chris, who was spending the night before heading back to Seattle to meet with real estate agents about selling his condo—it was do-or-die time for their relationship. Marry or move on. She'd planned a quiet evening alone with him, but Camille's obvious challenge put an end to a much-desired romantic interlude.

Murder always had a way of messing things up.

Chris met Emily at the door with a bear hug that would have snapped a frail woman in two. He kissed her, feeling the chill of her skin from the winter air. Judging by the wonderful smells emanating from the kitchen, she knew that his promise of a delicious meal had been genuine.

"Hope you're hungry," he said, taking her coat and leading her to the kitchen—replete with the savory smells of roast pork with the woodsy hint of rosemary.

"Why do you keep saying you don't cook?" she asked.

"I don't. But, I can. There's a difference." He poured her a sauvignon blanc that had been chilling in the refrigerator, instead of the cabernet he'd purchased at a wine shop in Seattle. "Seems like this will be just perfect with the dish."

She took a glass and sipped. "Perfection."

"Tell me about your day," he said, filling his own glass.

"Look, don't get me wrong," she said, watching Chris slice off a medallion of pork. "I adore Camille. But, honestly, she can be a bit aggressive."

"Like you can't handle *aggressive,* Em."

She swirled her wine in the glass. "I didn't say I *couldn't* handle it. Cammie is pushing because she thinks, she's *sure,* that Mandy's dead and Mitch is her killer. She doesn't have a body, and as confident and forceful as she can be, she's not about to prosecute without one."

Chris shrugged. "I don't blame her. It's a tough call."

Aware that she'd just dove into shop talk, Emily changed the subject. "How was *your* day?"

Chris put his hands upward and shook. A wry smile on his face. "Thanks for asking. I've been cooking and cleaning all day."

She kissed him and whispered in his ear, "Oh you have, have you?"

"Cooking a little, but no cleaning," he said. "Not my forte. Besides, I had a lot of reading to catch up on. A good day for Cherrystone."

"The place where nothing happens," they both said together.

Emily was thankful that she and Camille hadn't succumbed to the charms of the mountain o' nachos. Everything Chris prepared was perfection for a late evening winter meal. The roast was the star of its platter. But the green beans, pan-braised in brown butter, and the Yukon gold potatoes looked fabulous, too.

"I got the photos back from the techs," she said, indicating a cream-colored envelope she'd brought inside and placed next to her purse. "Want to look at them after dinner?"

Chris brought the steaming platter to the dinning table and grinned.

"That's why I'm here, babe. If spending time with you means going over case notes and photos, count me in. Now, eat. OK?"

"It isn't as if you're forcing me. This looks wonderful." She pierced the meat with her fork and tasted.

Handsome, and he can cook, too.

Jenna Kenyon fixed her attention to the rolling LCD departure screen at the airport. Her flight was delayed because of severe weather in the Midwest. She didn't mind the delay, however. As much as Jenna loved a good roller-coaster, she preferred such a ride with its tracks bolted to the ground, not in the confines of an airplane at 30,000 feet. She tried to get comfortable while she went wireless on her laptop, checking her e-mail, seeing if any new comments had been made on her BZ blog. *Nothing.* As a diversion, she went to the stat counter tool that tracked who'd been landing on her blog.

As was typical, there were a number of hits from young women at the chapters she'd just visited, with even more coming from those who were on the schedule. With or without the "detective's gene" from her mother, it was easy to see who'd been coming to check on her. She saw the ISP of a girl who'd asked her lawyer father to defend her in a grievance over her having sex with a frat boy under the grand piano at her chapter. Her dad's law offices were also logged. Another who left an electronic bread crumb was Tristan Wyler, her last serious boyfriend. She liked Tristan, but with law school next year, she didn't really want to get deeply involved.

He, apparently, was still interested.

An anomaly got her attention, too. She noticed a flurry of hits coming from Southern California. The ISP for one was coming from Garden Grove; the provider was a local phone company. The other came from a company called Human Solutions, Inc., in nearby Anaheim.

Interesting, she thought, powering down as her flight was called. *One of my chapter sisters must be living down there.*

After dinner, Chris and Emily cleared the dishes from the old dining table and scooted aside the candles that were all about ambience, but offered no real illumination. At least not of the kind needed to review the photos she'd brought home from the office. She turned the dimmer switch on the chandelier to full power.

"Good shots," Chris said, "if you're making a brochure

for your house. Maybe I should use your photography for my condo brochure."

"Smart ass," she said, fanning the images over the glossy tabletop. "Take a look."

Emily could almost smell the bleach as she looked over the photos of the pristine environs of the Crawford home. Chris was right, of course. Everything *was* in perfect order. At once, the place with its twin oversize couches studded with artfully, but casually arranged throw pillows, reminded her, too, of one of those "staged" homes on TV real estate shows. Those were the shows in which the host intoned that sellers couldn't live as they really did when trying to unload a house. Everything had to be ridiculously perfect.

"The Crawfords, apparently, lived every day like they were expecting company," she said.

"Or maybe after Mitch killed Mandy he did a cleanup that would have made the cover of *Better Housekeeping*," Chris said.

"*Good Housekeeping* or *Better Homes and Garden*, but you're right. *If he killed her. If he killed her there.*"

No appliances littered the kitchen's gleaming, expansive stone countertops. The towels in the master bath were rolled into cream and sage pinwheels of terry cloth, casually arranged in an antique breadbasket.

She flipped the photos to a scene that depicted the master bedroom. *Gleaming. Immaculate.* A duvet billowed without a wrinkle over top sheets that appeared to have been pressed by a steam iron: crisp and white. Everything was perfect. Not a thing out of place. On the highboy. On the dresser. All perfect.

The photograph of the largest of the other four bedrooms, a guest room, she figured, was in stark contrast. The bed was made, but hastily so. The nightstand had an empty dish that might have held a midnight snack. The dresser's top had barely a patch of mahogany visible through all the clutter—an uncoiled belt, a paperback novel, a jewelry box.

Mitch had told Emily that he and Mandy had not had any guests. There'd been no one to their home in the past month—a cue that the only fingerprints the techs might find would be theirs and theirs alone.

Emily thought of the bleach once more. She remembered how incredibly ordered things had been in Mitch Crawford's office at the dealership. Not a slip of paper was askew. Even the paperclips had been lined up in order—reds next to reds, blacks next to blacks. No jumble of unsorted paperclips for Mitch Crawford.

"He's a neat freak," Darla Montague had said. "That's just the way it is around here."

And, at home, too.

"So if Mitch was such a neat freak at home, how was it that the guest bedroom was such a lived-in mess?" Chris asked.

Emily mulled it over as she worked the tight muscles in her neck by rolling her head backward, then side to side. Then it came to her. She looked over at Chris.

"The guest in the guest bedroom had to be Mandy," she said.

Chris swallowed the last of his wine. "Maybe she'd banished herself to the guest room because she wanted to get away from him?"

She looked at the photo again. "That's right. She left the master bedroom on her own. Most women would send their husband to the sofa and keep the bedroom for themselves. I know I did that to David a time or two."

She was sorry that she mentioned David's name. But Chris didn't seem to mind.

"Angry at him? Annoyed by him? Sickened by his touch?" he asked. "Seems strange."

"I don't know," Emily said. "It is curious, I'll give you that. Why would a woman leave her husband's bed, and camp out in the bedroom down the hall? Why didn't she just leave him? Go to her mother's in Spokane, for example?"

"You know women better than I do," Chris said.

"She was waiting for something. She didn't think she had to leave. And learning more about Mitch Crawford, I can bet he didn't want her to leave. He didn't want to look like a loser."

"Waiting for what?" Chris asked.

Emily tilted her head slightly as she thought it through. She stared deeply into the photograph, like some miniscule text would give her the answer. "I don't know. But I intend to find out."

It was late and there was only one thing more that had to be addressed, and it wasn't the saga of the missing mother to be.

Chris got up and put his arm on her shoulders and held her. He'd practiced what he'd say, his final plea, on the way over to Cherrystone. He'd make the dinner, help her with her case, then ask her.

He pulled a small black box from his pocket.

"Oh, Chris," she said. "I don't know."

"I haven't even asked you. But seeing you're a detective you've figured me out. I love you, Emily. I always have."

Emily could feel tears threaten to spill from her eyes. "I love you, too."

He opened the box. It was a platinum band with a row of emeralds, Emily's favorite stone.

"Will you be my wife?" He took the ring from the box and held it out to her.

She pushed back a little. She was surprised that she hadn't seen it coming. Not then. Not that night. "I think so, but not now. Let's wait until this case is over."

Chris looked a little hurt. He'd given it his best shot. She didn't give the answer he imagined, but she hadn't said no yet, either.

"All right," he said, "but I can't wait forever."

There were times when Emily suspected that she was the biggest fool in Cherrystone, maybe even on the planet. She studied her reflection in the mirror as she undressed for bed. It was as if by looking into her own eyes she could have some kind of a silent conversation with herself. She loved Chris.

Why can't I just give in to what I know is right? She thought.

Her answer came as she brushed out her thick, wavy hair. She and Jenna had been alone for years, forging a life together in the town where she'd grown up. She'd dated a few locals. She'd wanted—*desired*—the kind of solid relationship that her own parents had enjoyed. David had been the man of her dreams when she was young. She foolishly thought that they were a team, destined for great things together.

But all he'd wanted was a pretty woman on his arm—a woman he could control.

Chris was nothing like that. He loved her for *who* she was. He sought a life with her because he knew that the two of them together was some kind of magic, which it was. He'd also been good with Jenna, though he had his own children and knew that he was no replacement for a Seattle doctor who'd carelessly discarded the best things he'd ever had.

Emily studied her face in the mirror. She wondered if she was looking at a woman who had built a wall around herself under the guise of protecting her child. The excuse that she didn't want to disrupt Jenna's life was an empty one. Jenna was grown. A college graduate. Preparing for law school. She was no longer a little girl who needed protection from the world.

Emily could not have known how wrong she was as she slipped into the bed next to her lover. Her sense of safety was a vapor. She had no idea that a malevolent force of evil had come to Cherrystone already . . . and that it would return.

Chapter Ten

The Cannery was Cherrystone's stab at being hip. The restaurant occupied the entire floor of the old Fruitland Packing Company's first processing plant, two blocks west of the Courthouse. The building had been gutted by the new owners, leaving exposed brick walls, a ceiling lattice of ductwork, and a salad bar converted out of the steel juicing unit that, in Cherrystone's glory days, had provided apple and pear juice to moms and kids in a seven-state region. The food was mostly vegetarian and the presentation was more New York than Spokane. Everything was pretty. And pretty expensive.

At least for Cherrystone.

Camille Hazelton and Emily Kenyon met there at least once a month to visit, discuss county and city government, and any cases that were on the docket that warranted a once-over before trial or pleading. This time, however, Mandy was on the menu.

While Camille ordered a tomato basil soup with pancetta confetti, Emily went to the salad bar. She put a layer of a chiffanade of romaine on a pale yellow plate and moved her tongs toward a marinated heart of palm.

That looks interesting, she thought, with a wry smile. *I'd rather be sitting under a palm tree than eating one.*

"Cary, great to see you," a voice called from the other side of the salad bar.

Her smile faded. Emily's heart sank to the floor. There was only one Cary in town. It took an extra breath to regain her composure, although she did so without so much as flutter of an eyelash. Few names and few people brought that kind of reaction. The ones who usually did were already in prison or, in the best of all worlds, six feet under in a grave dug in the Potter's Field section of a cemetery. But not this one.

She looked over and there he was. His eyes caught hers and locked.

"This is old home week," Cary McConnell said, with his perfect smile in place. "Hi, Emily Kenyon, lady sheriff."

She swallowed. "Hello, Cary."

He was a handsome figure, in a nearly black suit cut to fit a lean, athletic frame. His dark hair showed no signs of receding. He combed it back in a tousled look that Emily was sure he considered very sexy. His blue eyes were lasers. His eyes were whiter than the dish of peeled quail eggs that were next to the heart of palm.

"Been awhile. I guess that we'll be seeing each other more now," he said.

Emily looked puzzled and moved on to the feta. "How so?"

He looked over in Camille's direction. "I'm surprised your pal over there didn't tell you."

"Tell me what?" The feta clumped too much, so she moved on to the Kalamata olives.

"I'm going to be representing Mitch Crawford."

Emily started to leave. "Oh that," she said.

"Hey Emily," Cary said. "Aren't you going to get some sweet peppers? I remember how much you liked hot things."

Emily didn't turn around. She didn't want him to see her red face, her embarrassed and angry reaction to his comments. He'd said the "hot things" in such a salacious way that she was sure he meant it to be sexual.

"Why didn't you tell me?" she said, taking her seat.

"Emily, I know you have some history there," Camille said, pulling back to get a better view of the man who'd just accosted her lunch companion. "But you're going to have to deal." The prosecutor's eyes lingered on Cary and he flashed a smile in their direction.

Camille looked at Emily. "I am as surprised as you are that Cary would be handling this case."

"Seems a little out of his league," said Emily, who clearly wasn't enjoying lunch anymore.

Her remark was a dig, and none too subtle. Cary had been her divorce lawyer, and he'd been a good one at that. He'd made sure that the split with David was fair, that the custody arrangements for Jenna favored Emily's interests. Things took an unfortunate turn, when out of loneliness or just the need to be romanced, she'd dated Cary briefly. After a few dates, Cary became too attentive. *Too interested.* He'd fixated on her in the way that seemed unhealthy, almost scary. He'd even followed her to Seattle when she was working a big case. If he'd pushed her one iota harder to keep things going, she'd have arrested him herself for stalking. Their relationship had been consensual, of course, but Emily knew that she'd made a mistake nearly from the first time they'd been intimate.

God, I had more sense in my twenties than I do in my thirties, she'd thought at the time.

She'd forgiven herself, but she'd never forgotten how stupid it had all been. Whenever she heard his name, saw him in Cherrystone at the market, she was reminded that age didn't always bring wisdom.

"So when did Mitch hire Cary?" Emily asked.

Camille swirled some fake sweetener into her iced tea. "Yesterday, I guess."

"How come I'm only finding about this now?"

"Look, Emily, probably no one wanted to be the one to tell you that the rumor mill was churning with news of Cary getting involved in the Crawford case."

Emily looked down at her salad and stabbed at an olive. She'd just lost her appetite.

"There is no problem here," she said. It was a bit of a white lie. She couldn't stand the man. The only saving grace was that she would never have to talk to him. Camille would provide discovery if an arrest of his client was ever made. The only thing that would drag Emily into a face-to-face conversation with Cary would be when and if Emily took the witness stand.

That was a big *if*. No one knew for sure where Mandy was, and if she was even dead. It didn't look good for Mitch Crawford's wife, but Camille never silenced her mantra: *We need evidence. Get evidence, Emily.*

That, and the combination of a man she loathed and his client, a probable killer, fueled Emily's desire to get at the truth all the more.

Back in her office, the sheriff glanced out the window as a city snowplow ambled back to the garage next to her office. The snow was so scant that the machine almost looked defeated. Like Emily. The news that Cary McConnell was back in her life had tied her stomach like a Nantucket knot. It was visceral. *Sudden.* And it bothered her. She didn't like holding on to any negative feelings about Cary. Lurking in her consciousness was slow-burning worry that Cary and their past relationship could find its way into her investigation, knocking her off her game.

He was everything she thought she'd wanted when her

marriage to David unraveled. Cary was smart, charismatic, and even kind. There had been things about him that were so appealing. For a while, she imagined that his controlling nature—about everything from the cut of his suit coat to his confident manner on a case—cloaked a kind of insecurity that came with the need to always be right, to always win.

To be the best.

She understood how people wore masks of certainty and even false arrogance to make their case, to get what they wanted. One incident gave her a little glimmer that, perhaps, there was something deeper inside that perfectly groomed man with the nice car, expensive clothes, and top-of-his-law-class pedigree. There was a heart beating there, too. After she hired him to take care of her divorce, she sat in his office and admired a silver plate that hung on the wall.

"That's lovely," she said.

"Some friends gave it to me."

His words had seemed so final, that she didn't press the point. Later she learned that Cary had made seven trips to a village in Mexico to help build homes for children who'd taken up residence in a city dump outside of Tijuana. The plate was a gift from Hands Across the Border, a nonprofit group recognizing Americans who do more to help others than merely writing a check. Cary's brashness and bravado were counterpoints to the real man, the one she'd wanted to know.

Of course, she'd been wrong.

As another light dusting of snow fell on the streets of Cherrystone, Emily looked at the clock with the stuttering second hand that had been hung on the wall by Sheriff Kiplinger. The clock had been given to him by the Cherrystone Jaycees and Emily thought that it would stay put until the thing died. It was inscribed with: "There's Always Time for Justice in Cherrystone." It was so corny—and so true—that Emily had grown to love it as much as her beloved boss.

It was five minutes before the news. Emily turned on her old office TV and called over to Jason Howard, who had just come in from his routine run-through with the next shift of officers who'd be taking over the mundane traffic and minor theft cases until the graveyard shift. "Let's see what Crawford's lawyer has to say," she said. "He's on the news." She purposely did not use Cary's name.

"Should I bring some popcorn from the break room?" Jason said. His smile was a little sheepish. He already knew the answer.

Emily made a face. "Only if you want me to barf it up all over my desk."

"No, thanks." Jason parked himself on the corner of the desk. "We can definitely do without that."

As the picture came on, Emily was glad it was only the Spokane affiliate. She knew Cary well enough to know that he'd gunned for the national media, or the Seattle TV stations at the very least, when he was looking to capture the attention of news producers. It must have been a blow to his oversized ego that all he could lure to his office for an interview was the lowest-rated affiliate from Spokane. When the news anchor led with a house fire in rural Spokane County, Emily caught herself smiling.

"Good, he didn't even make the top story," she said.

As the anchor breathlessly recounted the turn of events that involved a dog knocking over a candle to ignite a Spokane Valley mobile home, the crawl on the bottom of the screen teased the interview: NEXT, CHERRYSTONE LAWYER SAYS HIS CLIENT IS UNFAIR TARGET OF INVESTIGATION.

A commercial for an apartment complex offering a "move-in" bonus and a "holiday ham" was next. Another was from a florist.

Finally, the anchor, a sunny brunette who couldn't have been more than twenty-five, was back on the air announcing the story.

"And now, an exclusive interview by Anne Yakamoto with the lawyer representing the Cherrystone car dealer now under suspicion in his wife's disappearance."

An Asian woman with blond hair gripped the microphone like she was about to warble on a TV singing show, her fingertips doing all the work. She stood in front of Crawford's dealership and did the news reporter bobblehead nod as she was introduced. Her hands must have been frozen, Emily thought, but apparently Anne Yakamoto wanted to show off her slender fingers and perfect nails—admittedly, her best feature.

"I'm standing here in front of the world-famous Crawford's car dealership in downtown Cherrystone. . . ."

Emily winced at the first sentence. *World-famous?* She wondered if Mitch Crawford had been the copywriter for the opener. It would be like him to insist upon that kind of a promo line to secure the interview. She rolled her eyes at Jason and he returned the gesture.

". . . and as Christmas comes, this whole town is wondering where one of their own has vanished. Mandy Crawford has been missing since just after Thanksgiving. Police have investigated, but have come up empty-handed. No one wonders where Mandy has gone more than her husband, the owner of this hugely successful dealership. He's been putting up posters and working the phone lines of the volunteers who are searching for his missing wife. I sat down with Mitch Crawford's defense lawyer this afternoon."

The video cut to a shot of Cary on the telephone. He looked serious as he made some notes on a legal pad.

Emily doubted Cary had made notes on anything or even that he talked to clients on the phone. He always said he had "associates" to do the jobs he didn't like. The only thing he liked to do, apparently, was grandstand in the courtroom.

Or, apparently on subzero-rated TV.

Next, Anne Yakamoto faced the camera. "Mr. Mc-

Connell, you're pretty upset about what's been happening to your client."

Cary, in a crisp white shirt, charcoal jacket, and a Tiffany blue silk tie, unfolded his arms. "You bet I am, Anne. Mitch Crawford has suffered an unbelievable tragedy here."

"*Unbelievable* is right," Jason said, his eyes fixed to the TV.

". . . His wife, the mother of his child-to-be, just flat-out disappeared. Immediately the sheriff put the focus on Mitch, when she should have been looking for Mandy. We don't even know what happened to her, but we do know that Mitch didn't have a thing to do with her disappearance."

The camera went back to the reporter. "Why do you think the sheriff focused on your client?"

"Lazy. Inexperience. I don't know. It probably was convenience."

Emily felt her blood boil, but she said nothing.

". . . There isn't one shred of evidence that ties my client to anything here. He was looking forward to the holidays with his wife and the birth of their first child. Turning him into a suspect is outrageously cruel. Leave him alone. Find Mandy. Do your job, for crying out loud."

There was a quick cut-over to an image of Mitch Crawford, shoveling the snowy sidewalk in front of his fabulous house. Emily doubted he'd ever done that before. He struck her as the type who'd made sure that he kept plenty of "the little people" around to do that sort of thing. Bossing people around made him happy.

Anne Yakamoto turned her head slightly when the news anchor asked if she'd talked with Mitch Crawford. "Mitch talked to me briefly off-camera. He's still wrapping Christmas presents for his wife and expected new baby. He says he just wants them to come home safely."

Jason looked over at Emily. She sat stone-faced. Even the

reporter had bought into his charm; she'd referred to him by his first name.

A photograph of Mandy went up on the screen. It was fairly recent. She smiled broadly, holding up a baby quilt. There was no mistaking the joy the young woman had for her impending motherhood. If the photo was meant to tug at the heart, it succeeded.

"If you see this woman, please contact Mr. McConnell at his law offices in Cherrystone."

Another news story came on and Emily turned off the TV.

"That was probably the most insulting bit of news reporting, if you can call it that, I've ever witnessed—and, believe me, I've seen more than my share," Emily said.

"Yeah, looks like the reporter was on the wrong side of that story from the get-go."

"I guess that's Cary's strategy. He's going to be the mouthpiece for his client now. Letting us know how hard this has been on Mitch, how rough we've been on him."

"I'd like to be rough on him," Jason said. "The guy's a prick."

"That, he is. But we'll get him. His arrogance and his lawyer's arrogance will be their undoing. In a way, I'm relieved."

"I'm out of here. See you in the a.m."

"Night, Jason."

As her young deputy departed, Emily winced at the thought of the blue tie that Cary McConnell had been wearing. It had been held in place by an antique tie tack with his initials. She wondered if it was a coincidence or a maybe even a kind of snarky sartorial wink directed at her. She'd purchased the tie and the tack—the only gifts she'd given to him.

She wished now that she'd asked for them back.

Chapter Eleven

Emily Kenyon pulled the Crown Vic to the side of the road. The Cherrystone Sheriff's Department hadn't yet ordered the hands-free phones that were a state safety requirement at the beginning of the New Year. She answered her ringing phone. The young woman on the line was one of those who masked her nervousness with inappropriate laughter. The end of every sentence was punctuated with a giggle or quick laugh. Throughout her years as a detective, Emily Kenyon had interviewed so many of her ilk. Also, the criers, the derailed train-of-thoughters, and the story-changers. The story-changers were always the worst. As long as people kept the basics of their information consistent, they'd probably make it through the trial process.

A crier was better than a laugher, though. Laughers frequently turned off members of the jury. *What's so funny about homicide?* A crier could win a case for either side.

"My friend says I should call because we saw something that might help your case," the woman said, laughing.

"What is your name? What case?" Emily felt a little annoyed, but Gloria had taken the call and said that the girl "might have what we're looking for—a real lead."

"Steffi Johansson," she said. Again, the laugh. "I think

Mitch Crawford was in our shop just after Thanksgiving. He was a total freak, too." Another laugh.

"I see," Emily said. "How about I come out to see you. Are you at your shop?"

"Yes, I am. It's Café Patisserie on the north end of Griffin Avenue, just off the highway."

Emily knew the place. "I'll be there in a twenty minutes. Tell your boss you'll need a break."

"I *am* the boss," Steffi said, letting out a short laugh. "At least, for this shift."

Steffi Johansson was waiting just inside the front door of the café when Emily arrived. "I made you a mocha, double-shot, no whip."

"You didn't have to do that," Emily said, taking the paper cup and moving to a table by the front window, away from another patron reading *USA Today* and sipping a chai latte.

Steffi smiled. "I nailed your drink, didn't I?"

Emily hated mochas. "That you did," she said.

The young blonde laughed. "I have a real knack for that. Don't ask me why. I just know what people want."

"Well then, you know what I want," Emily said, not caring that her segue was silly and obvious. Finesse wasn't needed with Steffi Johansson. The girl was annoying as hell.

"Right. OK." She sat down. "It was late one night, just before closing. Cherie and I were working and wanted to get out of here on account of the snow. We were kind of ticked that he came in."

"Cherie?"

"Cherie Parks, she was here that night, too."

"All right. And you think it was Mitch Crawford that you saw?"

Steffi sipped her own concoction, a frozen ice cream drink that had about a million calories and zero nutritional value.

"Pretty sure," she said. "I saw him on TV. Actually, Cherie *saw* him on one of those TVs at Seattle's airport and called me. She doesn't work here anymore," she said, with a laugh. "She's in Hawaii, lucky bitch. She got fired for coming in late too many times. The owners are really strict."

Emily knew the type. She was pretty strict herself. "Yes, so Cherie made the connection between the TV and the customer in your shop. How is it that *you* remember him? It's been awhile."

Steffi swirled her plastic straw in the cup. "He was a total freak. One of those customers who thinks he's so hot and hits on you. Not only that, he had a cut on his head or somewhere. Yeah, I remember that."

"A cut?" The revelation interested Emily.

"Yeah, he went into the bathroom while I made him his drink. He seemed a little put off that I even mentioned the blood."

"So he was bloody?"

Steffi pointed to a spot on her forehead. "Around here. Said he hurt himself cutting a Christmas tree out in the woods. That—besides the fact that he was a creepy letch—is the reason I remembered him at all."

"Because he had been cutting down a Christmas tree?"

"Because he said that's what he'd been doing."

Emily tilted her head and lifted her shoulders slightly. "I don't follow."

"He didn't have a tree in the back of his pickup. We thought it was odd. Like, why would he say he'd been out getting a Christmas tree and was on his way home, when he didn't have a tree?"

Emily liked what she was hearing. The timing made sense. Steffi's details could be believed. The right details— the cut, the lack of a tree, the man's attitude—seemed to be in sync with Mitch Crawford and the disappearance of his wife.

"The prosecutor will probably want to do a lineup tomorrow," Emily said. "Would you be able to come in or should I send a deputy to pick you up?"

Steffi looked around nervously. "Oh, I'll be there, I guess. Just tell me when. If the guy who came in here that night is there, I'll remember. I never forget a customer's face. Or a name, if they tell me. Actually, we're rated on how many customer names we know. They want us to make everyone feel like we give a crap about them when really all we want to do is serve them a latte and get them out of here."

Emily didn't doubt that, and she waited a beat while Steffi did her little laugh. She looked around. The whole place was set up to be cozy, but not too comfortable. Turnover was everything to a place like Café Patisserie.

"Can you describe the truck he was driving? Anything about it? Plate? Decals? Color?"

Steffi shook her head, her blond hair bouncing against her shoulders. "I'm not good at that. Maybe blue. Or black. Newish, I think. I'm not sure."

Emily got up to leave. She smiled at the young woman. She wasn't much, but she was all she had just then. "All right. Thanks, Steffi, I'll call you in the morning."

"Want a biscotti? On the house."

"No thanks, I'm good. Thanks for the mocha, though. It was divine."

She walked out to the cruiser, and dropped the half-full cup into the trash. It was without a doubt the worst thing she'd ever sipped.

Sweeter than a box of sugar cubes.

Lineups were rare in Cherrystone. Most everyone knew everyone in town, so identifying a perpetrator was as easy as recalling what year he or she graduated high school. In the odd instances in which a lineup was called for, the prosecution and sheriff's staff emptied a conference room in the jail that had been outfitted with a two-way mirror. The table was pushed to one side, the chairs to the other. It was rinky-dink in every way, a far cry from the setup Emily Kenyon had been used to in Seattle.

Emily and Prosecutor Camille Hazelton, smartly dressed in a dark blue suit that looked much more CEO than Emily's sheriff's uniform, waited in the hallway with a nervous—and laughing—Steffi Johansson as five men were ushered inside the room.

"Is she going to be all right?" Camille asked Emily, just out of Steffi's earshot.

Emily nodded. "She's a laugher. Sorry. We get them the way they come to us."

"The jury will hate her. If we ever get that far."

"Tell me about it."

Camille approached Steffi with a warm, welcoming smile. "I'm Camille Hazelton, I'm the Cherrystone County prosecutor. I'm very grateful that you've come in this morning. I'm also grateful that you called the sheriff's department. Steffi, you'll see five men. I want you to look carefully at each one and let me know if any one of them is the man that came to your coffee place just after Thanksgiving."

"OK. Can I ask them anything?"

The question surprised Camille. Most potential witnesses just want to look and leave, kind of hit-and-run identification. "No, no questions, but I'm curious," she said. "What would you ask them?"

"Well, I'd guess I'd ask them what they'd order for a coffee drink. I never forget what a person orders."

Camille looked over at Emily. "We can't ID someone based on a coffee drink. The things that you told Sheriff Kenyon are crucial because of what you said you saw. The man's injury, for example."

Steffi took a deep breath. "Got it. OK. I'm ready." She

dropped another laugh, this time softer, and Emily and Camille detected the fear emanating from the pretty blonde. It was clear that she wanted to be helpful, but she was also scared.

"Where is defense counsel?" Emily asked, not wanting to say Cary's name.

Camille looked at her watch. "Can't make it, something about a personal emergency at home. He's sending an associate." She looked down the hallway. "And right on time, here comes Donna Rayburn now."

Emily knew Ms. Rayburn, of course. She was an attractive brunette with a law degree and implants that she made no bones about ("They're not D's," she'd been heard to say at a law office party, "but lowercase C's."). She was nice enough, but she was one of those people who'd come to Cherrystone with the idea that it was a stepping-stone to a better job elsewhere—and ended up staying. The newspaper had three reporters and an editor who'd done that; the hospital had four doctors. And of course, she knew that Jason Howard had once planned to leave.

Donna walked purposefully toward the three women. She wore a charcoal suit, four-inch heels, and carried a large Kate Spade bag that swung back and forth like a wrecking ball. As always, Donna was in a big hurry.

"Let's get going on this," she said, still ten yards away. "I have to catch a flight. I'm speaking at a conference in Chicago."

"Well, Donna," Camille said, sarcasm apparent to all, "by all means we wouldn't want to hold you up."

Clearly annoyed, Donna Rayburn made a face. "Look, I can't help it if I'm busy. Really, dragging me over here for a latte-stand clerk's ID is beyond the pale. I can't see how it is of any relevance whatsoever. Mitch Crawford is a very, very busy man. And I'm a busy woman."

It took everything she had for Emily not to pull the Kate Spade from Donna's hand and bop her upside her head with it.

A jailer popped his head from inside the doorway to the conference room. "Lineup's ready."

"Steffi, remember," Camille said, ushering her toward the glass.

"It isn't a latte stand," Steffi said, turning to Donna. "We're a full-service restaurant and patisserie."

Donna nodded, her affect smug. "So I hear."

The lights went up inside, and the miniblinds that covered the window/mirror rose.

Five men stood in a row. Three were jail inmates; two were DUIs, and the third was a burglary II. One was an assistant jailer who often pulled duty for a lineup. He had the kind of bland face and average build and height that made him good filler for lineups. Mitch Crawford was also in the mix. He, like the others, was clad in jeans and a button-down shirt.

Steffi inched forward and studied each one.

"Take your time," Camille said. "This isn't about being fast. We're looking for truth here."

"All right," Steffi said, this time without a laugh.

"I'm going to have each one move forward and turn to the right and left," Camille said.

One by one, each man followed the command.

"Number five looks familiar," Steffi said.

"Take your time," Camille said, her heart sinking a little.

Donna impatiently shifted her weight and pulled her handbag close. "I think she's doing fine."

Steffi looked at the defense lawyer, then back to the five men. She was so far from laughing by then, that Emily wondered if Steffi Johansson was about to cry. Frustration on her face was unmistakable. Her lips were tight and her eyes seemed glossy with tears.

"I'm sorry," she finally said. "Number five seems so familiar, but I can't be sure."

Donna Rayburn turned to leave. "This identification is over. Thanks, ladies. I'm off to Chicago."

No one said good-bye to Donna. She slipped away and headed toward the jail office.

"I'm sorry," Steffi said, a tear rolling down her check.

"You did your best, Steffi, that's all we can ask."

As the three women started to leave they saw Donna walking down the hallway. She wasn't alone. She was chatting with man number five.

It was Mitch Crawford.

Chapter Twelve

The next day, Emily Kenyon's morning started as it always did: She pulled into the line at Java the Hut, and ran through a mental checklist of what she'd be doing that day. She wrote a quick "luv u, jenna. see u soon!" to her daughter, using the instant-note feature that allowed her to scroll down and select a prewritten message without having to write each letter. It was cheating, in a way. But at 7 A.M., what in the world was a mother with a murder investigation supposed to do?

She ordered a quad latte instead of the usual triple and tipped the girl a dollar instead of the remaining change. It was the holiday season, of course.

Her list for the day:

Call Chris about condo listing.
Thank Mandy's supporters.
Talk with Mandy's parents.
Review Crawford financial documents.
Check cell phone records.
Check Internet activity and e-mail.
Review ATM and credit card transactions.
Pray for a miracle.

Christmas music was playing softly in the background of the Landon Avenue Methodist Church meeting room, where three women worked in unison to find Mandy Crawford. With the color-coordinated finesse of the champion scrapbookers that they were, they'd set up a Mandy Central that rightly would be the envy of many larger organizations. Even professional ones.

When Emily stopped in on her way to the office and did a quick once-over, she half-expected missing child advocate John Walsh to pop out of the men's room down the hall. They'd made two trips to the copy center for fliers and had made two dozen outreach calls to community leaders who might be able to spread the word. Not a bad amount of work already done, considering that it was barely half past eight in the morning. The three women all had jobs, but had taken the early part of the morning off so they could get a start on their efforts to bring Mandy Crawford back home.

Emily was troubled by something she'd heard on the Spokane newscast she'd watched with Jason the day before. She entered with a smile, said hello, and then got right down to business.

"Has Mitch Crawford been over here to help with the search?"

Erica Benoit, who'd been friends with Mandy through a scrapbooking group, let out a laugh.

"I saw that SOB on TV last night, too. He's only been over here one time. I asked him to bring one of Mandy's photos—a recent one—so we could put it on the flier and on the Web. The way he put us off, you'd think we were going to swab his mouth for DNA or something."

The other women laughed.

"My daughter, Michelle, is making a MySpace page for Mandy," Alana Gutierrez said, looking up from her laptop.

"Good idea. So did Mitch get you the photo?" Emily asked.

Alana looked disgusted as she snapped her laptop shut. "Begrudgingly, I'd say. He made sure we cropped him out of the photo."

"Like we wanted to include him," Erica said, rolling her eyes.

"The guy's ego is so big," said Tammy Sells, another scrapbooker. Tammy was older than the other two, a heavyset redhead with a penchant for gauzy tunics even in the dead of winter. "I've never liked him. I've never, I'm glad to say, *never* bought a car from him, either. Gives me the creeps. I'd rather pay twice the amount to some other car dealer than to line the pockets of that abrasive piece of scum."

"You seem to be holding back," Emily said with a smile. "Tell us how you really feel about Mitch Crawford."

Erica and Alana laughed a little, but Tammy didn't crack a smile. "I guess you know how I feel. Good God, we're trying to help bring home his wife and he's too busy to come down here."

"So," Emily said, "he hasn't been down here making calls, pouring coffee, preparing fliers?"

"Are you kidding? It seems like he's the last one on the list when it comes to people in Cherrystone who care about Mandy."

"I know what you're getting at and I'd say that his lawyer is as big a liar as his client," Erica said.

Emily didn't argue with that, in fact, Tammy's remark made her feel pretty good just then.

"Coffee, Sheriff?" Alana asked. "We'd love to find out what's going on with the case."

Emily shook her head and did what she hated more than anything. She lied. "I'm sorry that I can't tell you anything right now. But as soon as I can, you'll hear it from me before it's on the news, OK?"

It was a lie because there really wasn't much to report—

and when there was, they'd be among the last to know. That fact pained her.

"Fair enough," Tammy said.

Emily thanked them for what they were doing, told them how they exemplified the best of the community. The words might have seemed canned, like those given to the Chamber of Commerce or the Rotary. They surely weren't meant that way.

"I promise to keep you up to date. You do the same," she said, referring to the big whiteboard with the color-coded notations of calls that had come in with tips, who'd made the call, how the calls had been handled. None had panned out, but it was the continuing effort that really mattered.

As Emily turned to leave, Alana stopped her by standing up.

"Sheriff Kenyon," she said, her voice brimming with emotion, "you don't think that Mandy's dead, do you?"

The other two women looked at her with sympathy. It was clear that they had already made up their minds about what happened to Mandy.

And who was to blame.

"We're doing our best to bring her home," Emily said, looking through the open doorway toward the church sanctuary down the hall. "But you're in the right place here, I'm afraid. Right now, we need a bit of a miracle."

It wasn't that she could feel the warm breath of another person, but Emily could *feel* the presence of someone right behind her. Emily turned on her heels in the parking lot of the sheriff's department.

"What are you doing here?" she asked.

Cary McConnell stood in front of her next to her car. It obviously wasn't a court day for Cherrystone's brashest and most self-absorbed lawyer. He wore indigo-dyed jeans, a tan jacket over an olive-colored button-down shirt. The cut of everything he wore was athletic—tight enough to show the world what he had, but not so to reveal an extra pound if he'd eaten too much for lunch. The cold breeze mussed up his hair, and for once, he didn't seem to care. She thought the clothes he was wearing were too thin for the winter weather, but she loathed him so much, she considered him nearly reptilian anyway.

Cary folded his arms. "That's not a very nice greeting for an old friend."

Emily reached for her car keys and pulled them from her purse. "Is that what you're calling me these days?"

He stepped a little closer. "Very funny. Seriously, Emily, this whole Crawford thing is pitting us against each other. I don't like the guy any more than you do. He's a client."

"I'd love to quote you on that," she said.

Cary smiled. It was a grin as dazzling as ever. It didn't melt Emily's heart like it once did, but it was, without a doubt, completely disarming. "Look," he said, "I feel really bad about my behavior back when we were seeing each other, and even more recently."

"You should feel bad, Cary. You were a Class A jerk."

"All right, guilty as charged. I'm here because Cherrystone is too small of a town for us to be bitter about the past. I want you to forgive me. OK?"

Emily pushed the button for the Crown Vic's automatic locks and they popped up like soldiers at attention. She reached for the door handle. "We're OK."

"No, really, I wanted to talk about Mitch. Do you have a minute?"

Emily waved her hand at him, pushing him back from her personal space. "We can't talk about that. I mean, you don't want to talk to me about it. Do you?"

"Some things are bothering me. You know, I care about the truth. That's why I went to law school."

Emily seriously doubted the revisionist rationale for the profession he chose. She figured that Cary McConnell had gone to law school to make big bucks.

"What is it?" she asked.

Cary looked around, his dark eyes finally landing back on hers. "I don't want to talk about it here. Trust me. I'm very concerned."

Trust him? Emily felt a flutter of anxiousness. Camille would pitch a fit if Cary had some kind of information that he'd offered up on a silver platter and she turned a deaf ear to it. Even so, the conversation should be between the prosecutor and the defense lawyer—not the sheriff and the man with whom she'd had an affair.

"You really ought to tell Camille."

"I don't know her like I know you."

The comment made Emily's skin crawl. She wondered if he was referring to the fact they'd had sex, and not the bond of a long-term friendship.

"What do you want to tell me?"

"Follow my truck, OK?"

"I didn't know you were driving a *pickup*. What happened to the Mercedes?"

The question was meant to sting a little because all that Cary used to talk about was how expensive his car was and how it was "the most kick-ass car in Cherrystone."

Cary ignored the intent of her remark. He was good at that, she thought.

"I like hauling stuff around on the weekends," he said.

"I'll pass on following you, Cary. Thanks," she said. Cary was a jerk, maybe as much as his client Mitch Crawford, but he was also an astute judge of people. She remembered how when they were dating he pegged a local mail carrier as

Cherrystone's panty thief—a man who broke into women's bedrooms to steal their underwear. Cary's reasoning was a little disturbing at the time, when she thought back on it. All he said was: "I know the type."

But he had been right. If there was something that was troubling him about the Crawford case, which she assumed he was intimating, then she ought to hear it.

"What's with you and Chris Collier?" he asked.

The question was out of bounds, inappropriate, pushy. *Very Cary.*

"None of your business," Emily said, turning her attention to her Crown Vic and getting inside.

"Sounds like you still care," he called out.

Emily didn't bother opening her driver's window, something she would have done to give a homeless person a five-dollar bill despite the icy weather. She merely mouthed the words she hoped he could read: "The only thing I care about is forgetting that you ever laid a hand on me."

Chapter Thirteen

Cascade University, south of Spokane

He'd been watching her all night. She never paid him a single glance. Her sole focus seemed to be on herself. She'd made several trips with her carbon-copy sisters to the Kappa Chi upstairs bathroom, her purse slung over her shoulder like she was headed into battle. In a way, she was. The frat bathrooms were notoriously filthy. No TP. Just squat, do your business, and flush with a well-placed foot. *If not too drunk, of course.* When she and the pack returned to the party they were giddier than ever, with lips lacquered and hair fluffed up to look messily styled.

Bet she loves the bedhead look, he thought. *Bet she's not as hot as she wants everyone to believe.*

Tiffany Jacobs brushed right by him as she made her way to the basement. She could feel the heat of a hundred bodies rise in the dank passageway. She caught the peculiar blend of odors—vomit, beer, pot.

Guys are so gross, she thought.

The frat boys were playing boat races with some of the other drunken sorority girls down there. Upturned plastic drinking cups floated on a slimy beer surface on a sheet of plywood suspended between a pair of sawhorses procured for the game. Drink. Slide the cup. Push it to the edge. Drink. With each heat, a cheer erupted with the kind of enthusiasm that might have greeted the winner of the America's Cup.

But this was the big blue plastic beer cup.

The room was crowded and the walls were so hot, they practically wept condensation. Tiffany's rubber flip-flops stuck to the concrete floor from the coating of spilled beer that shined like shellac.

"I'm going to get some air," she told her crew, all teetering woozily on a chilly night of beers. One of her Beta Zeta sisters, an unfortunate girl with brown hair and teeth that had never seen the benefits of orthodontia, started to follow. She was one of the four Lindseys who had pledged that year. Tiffany knew she was a mistake, but they needed another girl to make their quota. Lindsey S. wasn't really BZM— Beta Zeta Material—but she had a high grade-point average.

"No, Lindsey S. I'll be back. I'm going to call my mom. You stay here."

Lindsey S., drunk and bored, complied and returned to the boat races.

Tiffany shimmied through the tightly woven human mass on her way to the door. Her mom had called earlier in evening—*twice*.

He was right behind her, just close enough to keep her in his sightline, but not enough to make her feel uncomfortable.

The cool night air blasted her face and sent a welcome chill down her body.

If Satan threw a party, he'd have it at Kappa Chi, Tiffany thought, as she walked up the concrete steps from the basement to the yard. Bits of broken glass shimmered.

She could hear the sound of a couple making out by a massive oak tree that sheltered much of the yard. She went the other direction, toward the pool, reached for her cell phone, and dialed the speed number for her mother.

"Hi, honey," her Mom said. "I wondered if you'd call me back tonight."

"I'm sorry, Mom," Tiffany said, sitting next to a leaf-filled pool. "I've been studying my butt off tonight."

"That's why you're there, honey."

"I know." Tiffany rolled her eyes.

"I called earlier because I wanted to let you know I can come a day early for Mom's Weekend."

"How early, Mom?" Tiffany was annoyed and had no problem letting her mother know. "You know I have a lot of responsibilities."

"I know you do, Tiff."

"Just a minute," she said cutting off her mother. She took her phone from her ear.

"Do I know you?"

Mrs. Jacobs tried to speak to her daughter again, but Tiffany was arguing with someone. She couldn't make out anything that was being said. The tone of it, however, seemed angry and confrontational.

"Tiff? What's going on? Tiffany?"

No answer.

"Tiff?"

Then the phone went dead.

Emily Kenyon's phone vibrated and she looked down at the small LCD screen. An electronic envelope rotated in the window. A new text message had arrived. She snapped open the phone. It was from Jenna. She knew it even before she opened it. No one else sent her a text message.

"Tiffany Jacobs is missing. I'll call u in a few. Something's not right."

Jenna was working at the Beta Zeta chapter at the university in Knoxville and wasn't expected home for a couple of weeks. She told her mother in a memorable text message that the chapter was one of the better ones in her region.

"No trouble, these girls. Only one drunk and one bulimic. Might be new low record."

About an hour later, Emily answered the phone. It was Jenna.

"Mom, can you believe it about Tiffany?"

"Hi, honey," Emily said, flipping through a notepad on which she'd logged a few details. "I really don't know much. I checked the police logs for Cascade and they indicated Tiffany disappeared from a frat party two days ago. They don't even know that she's really missing."

"She is. I know she is, Mom. I *know* Tiffany."

Emily met Tiffany only once when visiting Jenna at Cascade. Both Tiffany and Jenna were involved in BZ recruitment the year before. Tiffany, as Emily recalled, was a smarter girl than her fluffy-headed name suggested. She was a stunning girl with piercing blue eyes and a pretty, slightly turned-up nose. She was studying to be a pharmacist; a job that she teased "would let me know what's wrong with my friends and neighbors without even having to ask."

"What makes you think she didn't run off somewhere?" Emily asked.

"Two things, Mom. One, she'd never leave without a bunch of clothes. The girls at the BZ house there say she didn't pack anything."

"OK. Maybe spur of the moment."

"No, Mom, that's not it. The other thing is that the police found her phone outside of the Kappa Chi house. That pink razor was like her other brain. Tiff wouldn't be caught dead without her phone."

Jenna's own words stopped her cold. The expression had slipped from her lips merely to prove a point, not to make a prediction.

"Jenna?"

"Yeah, Mom," her voice now deflated.

"I called down to the university police. I offered to help, of course. I told them pretty much what you've said. Tiffany was a good girl. This could be very, very serious."

"Thanks, Mom."

Garden Grove, California

The concerns about where he would kill his prize came at him like a drumming rain on a tin roof. Her mother was a cop. Her mother's *boyfriend* was a cop. Those two elements upped the ante considerably. It would be harder to capture her, slit her throat, and rip out her insides when Mom and the boyfriend lurked around Cherrystone, Washington. He was anxious to get things going. It was, after all, a very busy time of year.

He smiled. *Hard to fit in Christmas shopping and another sorority bitch.*

"You look happy," his wife said, handing him a platter of tamales her mother had made.

His smile stayed frozen, but it was tolerably real-looking. "You know how I feel about mama's tamales. I think they're the best in the world."

She smiled back. "Me, too."

He took the platter, wondering why the woman who knew him better than anyone knew nothing about him at all.

He decided he'd take Lily Ann Denton next. She was but a day trip away. So convenient; a drive-through window kind of a killing. Jenna Kenyon would be the finale. And as much as he'd love her mother to find her blood-drained body on Christmas Day, he knew that killing her in Cherrystone was too great a risk.

Chapter Fourteen

Cherrystone

That Mitch Crawford seemed solely motivated by money raised the very dark possibility that the car dealer might have placed a value on having a dead wife. The specter of an insurance payout could not be ignored.

"So you still think he did this for the money?" Jason asked Emily as they went over the timeline of Mandy's disappearance for the umpteenth time. They had several sheets of computer printouts and note cards that outlined what they knew so far. It was old-school police work, but the new system was still in transition. New technology usually came to Cherrystone when it wasn't quite so new.

Jason had duplicates of the printouts as they faced each other across Emily's desk, but he left the highlighting up to his boss.

Emily conceded that money did run Mitch's world, but she was unsure if they could really fix the motive in that direction.

"First of all, he has assets far beyond what most people around here have. Let's see, three houses, a yacht, a fleet of classic cars, and more gold around his neck than a hip-hop star."

"No kidding. I didn't notice the gold chains."

She rolled her eyes. "Men don't pick up on it, I guess. Nothing turns off a woman more than ropes of gold nestled in a thick patch of chest hair."

"I'll keep that in mind," Jason said, touching his shirt's top button, and then laughing.

"Sorry," she said, smiling back. "No offense meant. Back to Mitch. If his balance sheet showed some irregularities, I'd be more concerned about the possibility of money being the motive here. So far, we know that the dealership is doing just fine and that he's not leveraged to the hilt on his other assets."

"It makes me hate him even more," Jason said.

"Tell me about it. I'd like to get a new car, but I really shouldn't. Anyway, I'd say money is too obvious a motive."

But what was the reason? Jason didn't quite get it. He had a wife. He had kids. He couldn't imagine another man snuffing out all that was so dear to him personally.

"If not money, what?" he asked.

Emily selected the pink highlighter. It was dry, so she took the cap off the yellow one. "I'm getting the distinct feeling that Mitch Crawford has other agendas when it comes to his wife," Emily said.

"An affair, maybe?"

Emily ticked off bullet points on the printout.

"Maybe he was tired of her?" she asked. "Maybe he just didn't want to be bothered being a dad."

"Like Tony Ryan?"

Emily put down her pen. "Yes, exactly. Like Ryan." It was, she thought, a pretty good example.

Tony Ryan was a Seattle beer truck driver who made local, and then national, news after his wife went missing two years ago. Carly Ryan was pregnant with the couple's first baby. Friends said that Tony didn't want to be a father; that he preferred spending his time away from work playing Xbox and hanging with his buddies. He repeatedly made remarks that indicated that he felt having a son or daughter made him "old" and moved him up to adulthood in an irrevocable way that he just didn't want. One of the key lines from the trial came from Carly's sister, Miranda. She told the court that Tony "told me that having a baby made his needs irrelevant. He was pissed off that he might not get all of Carly's attention. He actually told me that 'if she thinks for one minute that I'm not gonna have sex when I want it because of some brat wanting her attention, she's dead wrong.' "

Dead Wrong, of course, was the phrase used by headline writers the next day.

The jury found Ryan guilty of murdering Carly and their baby. That sad story would have been nothing more than a repugnant footnote in the annals of crime, if not for the theory of the case. The prosecution and the media ratcheted up the stakes by casting the killer as the bone-chilling representative of young men who assumed that the world revolved around them, as it had in sports, high school, and at the gym.

Mitch Crawford didn't really fit that profile. Not very neatly, anyway. Sure, he was self-absorbed and filled his three-car garage and off-site garage with the spoils of a lavish lifestyle. He ran his office as more a king than a manager, demanding employees do things that had nothing to do with their jobs. Emily learned how workers were told to detail his personal cars once a week, pick up his dry cleaning, even shine his shoes.

And while he seemed spoiled and entitled to all that he could see, he did actually have a work ethic. If his father had created the dealership from nothing, then Mitch Crawford wanted to make sure everyone in the region knew that he'd taken it much further.

"My dad had a vision, but my eyesight's a lot sharper," he used to tell people when they came in for a test drive.

As far as the Crawford case was concerned, Emily felt, insurance didn't appear to be the motive.

Cherrystone used the American Insurance Control Bureau as its primary tool in determining when and if crimes could be linked to an insurance motive or fraud. AICB was little more than an end run around a subpoena. Carriers liked it because it helped connect the dots when a person involved in a potential crime procured multiple policies. In the old days, law enforcement agencies had to issue a subpoena for each insurance company—and the defendant was not obligated to say even which company he or she might have procured a policy. It was shooting in the dark. With AICB, an alert would be sent out to all members—most of the insurance industry—and they'd be able to chime in with a yes or no.

In Mandy's case, there were no other policies outside of the one she held from her job at the county. Her life was worth $75,000. Her baby held no value. A baby isn't worth anything because it isn't drawing an income and it doesn't have a dependent.

"So what did AICB really turn up?" Jason asked.

"Nothing. I highly doubt that a man like Mitch Crawford would break a sweat, let alone kill his wife, for seventy-five grand."

Jason agreed. "Maybe ten times that."

Emily nodded. "I've never thought this was about money, but now I'm certain that it isn't. This man was all about convenience."

Later that afternoon, the office phone rang. To Emily's utter surprise, it was Mitch Crawford. He was huffing and puffing mad, but she was glad for the call.

The more you talk, the more you'll hang yourself, she thought.

"How can I help you, Mitch?" she said.

"Help me? You have to be kidding. You could stop harassing me, for one."

Emily swiveled her chair and looked out the window. Cars passed by. "You'll need to be more specific. No one here is intending to harass you."

"My insurance guy just called me saying that you put out a goddamn alert on me. Like you think I killed Mandy for insurance money. What a laugh!"

"I'm sorry you think this is so funny."

"You know what I mean. I know that you sent out a bulletin to everyone in the country asking if I had policies on Mandy's life. Why didn't you just ask me?"

"You haven't exactly been cooperative, Mitch."

"I've done what you wanted me to do. Nothing more. I think you're wasting my time. You're wasting Mandy's time, too."

"You don't happen to know where she is?"

"You know I don't."

She thought he'd hung up, but he was only gulping a breath of air to fuel his rage.

"I'm so sick of you and your office. If you had asked me, I would have told you that she only had one stupid policy from that cheap-ass county. There would be no windfall in Mandy's death."

"I don't know. Seventy-five thousand dollars is a lot of money."

"To you maybe, but not to me. I haven't done anything wrong and you've been treating me like trash. What's with you? I know you're single. Man-hater? I've heard some things about you."

From Cary, no doubt.

Emily hated losing her cool. It took some doing, but she held it.

"This isn't about me, Mitch. This is about you and your missing wife. Let's remember that. All right?"

The phone went dead with the sound of a thunderclap.

Imagine that, Mitch Crawford, mad enough to slam down his phone. Nice.

Chapter Fifteen

Garden Grove

They were a beautiful young couple, by any measure. Michael Barton, almost thirty, had an athletic build with penetrating brown eyes and dimples that never looked childlike or silly. *Only disarmingly handsome.* He was more reserved than shy, though he could come into his own when the situation demanded it. The only problem with Michael was that he was only able to reflect the moods of others. He seldom seemed comfortable enough to make the first move when it came to displays of warmth or charm.

Olivia Barton was a stunning Latina with smoky brown eyes that never needed shadow or mascara, and full lips that she enhanced—when she had time—with a pretty plum-colored gloss.

When Michael and Olivia bought their house in Garden Grove, they knew the first bit of remodeling would be the basement that the previous owner had outfitted with a cheesy, knotty-pine bar and air hockey table. Olivia saw the bulk of the dingy downstairs real estate as a potential playroom for the kids. Michael knew that he needed a home office.

Yet they had a son, Danny, and shortly thereafter, a daughter, Carla.

So of course, he and Olivia compromised. The bar was ripped out; the space that housed the air hockey table was replaced by a playhouse and the other side of the room was set up with a desk, PC, fax, printer, and telephone. Two slits of glass let in the sunlight of the outside world. Whenever Michael worked, he did so with the chirpy noise of the children and their friends. He didn't mind. In fact, their little voices, their *happy* little voices, seemed to make his day.

Laughter like that was completely unknown after he and his sister had been abandoned by their mother. Certainly, he had been miserable in Portland. As his own kids played, little Lego-like pieces of his past would snap into place and he'd remember a few of the things that led to his desertion by his mother.

With the perspective that comes with time, Michael began to see that his mother, Adriana Barton, had probably done the best that she could. He didn't even call her "Mom" in his mind when he thought of her anymore. It was always just Adriana. It was like she was some mythic, albeit vile creature. She was colored in his memory as the darkest shade of evil, a woman worse than Snow White's wicked stepmother, or any of the Disney bitches.

Die, Adriana, die. I hate you.

When he was being abused by the adult who'd preyed on him when he was only a child, he wondered where Adriana had been. She should have been there. With him. With his sister. Had she left him and Sarah to endure this kind of an existence?

An existence like her own? Had she left them so she could be free?

Sometimes tears came when he thought about Portland and how Adriana had been beaten by Sarah's father so badly that everyone thought she'd die. He remembered the time she came to see him at school and the teacher told her she had to leave.

"You're scaring the other children," the teacher had said.

Adriana had black-and-blue eyes that day. She'd tried to cover them with makeup, but she was never really good at such subterfuge. Her flinty eyes were incapable of lying. In fact, the only time she was ever successful in making up a story was the one about the ride to Disneyland.

"We are going to have the best time there," she said. "I haven't been there in a long time, but I've wanted to go on Space Mountain."

"The Haunted Mansion and the pirate ride, too," Michael said.

"All of that. Just us three."

Later, when he revisited the trip from Portland to L.A., he remembered how they hadn't brought any luggage. He remembered how Adriana had only thought to bring a carton of cigarettes for herself, and nothing for him or for Sarah. She cracked the window an inch as they drove over the snow-coated Siskiyou Mountains. The icy air reached inside the car.

"Mom, we're cold," he told her.

She just stared straight ahead.

"Mom!"

She pulled the cigarette from her lips and jabbed it at him. He pulled back, whimpering.

Adriana turned on a Dolly Parton tape and the little girlish voice of the country singer kept them company the rest of the way there.

He looked at the small circular scar on the back of his wrist. Adriana had left him with more than memories. She had left him with her mark. It was faint, but it never tanned, so it never really went away.

Down in his basement office so many years later, the PC

whirled as it booted up. The screen rolled and a desktop messy with Word files, jpegs of the kids, came into view. Michael pulled down the Favorites tab and hit the bookmark named: *Jenna's BZ Blog.*

An icon of a little yellow face with a frown advertised her mood. Her latest entry had been made earlier in the day.

Michael's anger swelled; his brown eyes were pools of incontrovertible anger. He knew that he'd screwed up badly, but somewhere along the way he thought that just maybe the news reports were wrong. That he'd truly done what he'd set out to do.

Danny came from around the partition.

"I need new batteries," the boy said, holding up a laser gun.

Michael opened a drawer. Paper clips, staples, even masking tape. No batteries.

"Sorry, pal. Better tell your mama. I'm all out."

The little boy shuffled up the stairs and Michael returned his gaze to the computer screen. The mask that he fashioned for his son's benefit melted from his face. It was like a shade that he could pull up and put down. He knew there was falseness to half of what he did. It was mimicry. Sometimes, he'd look over at parents with their children, knowing that the connections they felt were different than his.

It hurt. And the hurt gave him hope.

Just maybe I'm not the monster I think I am.

Olivia Barton carried a laundry basket heaped with dirty clothes down to the basement, past Michael's office and over a carpeted floor littered with red, green, and blue cardboard bricks that were the obvious remnant of a hastily built and destroyed fort. *Danny and Carla!* Holding the basket against her hip, she opened the laundry room door and went inside the dark little room. A lightbulb illuminated by a pull of a chain swung as she turned it on.

With Michael at work, she went about her Tuesday routine, sorting the whites from the darks. Each item of the kids' clothing was like a memo of what their day had been. The food they ate. The grass stains. The pet hair. Whatever had been the activity was there waiting for a spray of prewash and the hope of a mother that the stain would get clean.

It irritated her that Michael never seemed to get the hang of making sure his clothes were right side out before he unceremoniously dumped them into the laundry basket on the floor of their bedroom closet.

The least he could do . . . Olivia's thoughts trailed off and she noticed a dark, reddish smear against the white of one of Michael's usually pristine T-shirts. The T-shirt had been nestled inside a blue pullover shirt. She pulled the shirts apart and looked at the smear. *He wore that Tuesday . . . what did we have for dinner? Spaghetti? Tacos?*

She looked closer. The stain wasn't hot sauce. She remembered they'd had a shrimp salad that night. No red sauce.

She ran her fingertips over the stain, about the size of a half dollar. It was smooth, penetrating the fabric like a dye stain of color. No lumps. No bumps. She wondered if it was blood. If it was, she didn't recall him saying that he'd injured himself.

"Honey," she asked later that night as they prepared for bed, "did you get cut or something?"

Michael seemed unconcerned. "Not lately. Why?"

"Oh," she said, "I thought I found some blood or something on a dirty shirt of yours."

"Nope. I'm fine." His reply was brisk. *Curt.* It was almost as if he thought his short denial was all he needed to say to stop her brain from ruminating on whatever it was that spun over and over.

Leave me alone. Leave me be. You can't know everything about me. I won't let you.

He went into the bathroom and looked at himself in the mirror.

Why is she pushing me? Why is she ruining what we have?

Olivia stood outside the bathroom door. No water was running. No sound of him urinating into the bowl. Silence.

What is wrong with my husband? They lay side by side, drifting off to an uneasy sleep.

Olivia woke as the moonlight poured though the slats of the miniblinds and fell on Michael's bare upper torso. He'd gone to bed with a T-shirt on, but in the heat of the night, he'd shucked it from his damp skin. The retrofitted central air-conditioning of their bungalow was just that . . . *central.* It was barely a puff by the time it reached the master bedroom in the back of the house. Olivia shifted her weight and lifted her head from the pillow. *Gently. Slowly.* It hadn't been a dream that stirred her from her restless sleep, but the worry that sometimes crept up in the dark of night.

You really don't know him. No one really knows him.

Michael was on his back; blades of light played over his muscled chest. She rubbed the sleep from her eyes and shifted a bit closer.

The injury was the color of rust, jagged and positioned just below his collar bone.

Michael's brown eyes snapped open and Olivia let out a gasp. "What are you looking at?"

"You scared me! I just couldn't sleep," she said, recoiling into the sheets.

Michael stared hard at her before turning his back and facing the window. "Oh. Me, too. Hot in here. All I can do is rest my eyes."

Olivia pulled the blankets up around her neck. Suddenly, she felt a chill in the air.

The two of them lay side by side, the digital clock rolling over to morning.

Chapter Sixteen

Cherrystone

The silvery fringes of his thick, wavy hair askew from the winter wind, Chris Collier stood at Emily Kenyon's front door, a smile on his face and an overnight bag in hand. With barely a hello, Emily planted a deep kiss on his lips and led him inside. He smelled of the cologne she'd given him for his birthday. She was happy to see him for a thousand reasons, not all of them business, of course.

But business was on her mind.

"You feel like a movie?" Emily asked, pouring a glass of garnet-colored merlot from Stone Ridge, a local vintner that had once won a gold medal at a competition in Napa. It was the first winery in Cherrystone to be so honored. After a bacterial blight killed the largest of six remaining cherry orchards in the 1980s, some farmers jumped on the grape bandwagon. Signs were encouraging. Cherrystone might soon be better known for something other than cherries.

A glass for her. A glass for him.

Chris grinned. "I know what movie you're talking about," he said. "And I thought you were going to try to get me drunk."

Emily retrieved a DVD from her purse and slipped the disk into the player. "I don't need to get you drunk for *that*." Their eyes met and she smiled back. "But I thought I might have to in order to get you to look at this Crawford interview with me."

The blue screen of the flat-screen TV—which had been her sole splurge the previous year—turned black, then the image of Mitch Crawford came into view. She picked up the remote control and pressed the button that froze the image.

"You already know that I think he's your guy," Chris said, settling on the couch, facing the TV. The Christmas tree twinkled from across the room.

"We *all* think so," she said.

Emily pressed PLAY. The video display showed a small conference room with acoustic-tiled walls and an oversize clock. A voice—Emily's—could be heard, but it was slightly out of range. It seemed she was giving instructions on where Mitch Crawford was to sit.

"Nice interrogation room," Chris said. It was a gentle jab, meant to make Emily smile.

It did. "Thanks. We try out here in Podunkville."

Mitch took a seat facing the table-mounted camera.

"He looks like he's ready to go out to dinner or something," Chris said, noting the man's deep gray suit, red silk tie, and silk pocket square. "Who wears a pocket square, anyway?"

"Except to a wedding."

"Or maybe a funeral."

From the couch, the pair sipped their wine from large balloon goblets and watched as Mitch Crawford alternately kept and lost his cool as Emily, off camera, asked him about Mandy's disappearance.

"He's a peach all right," Chris said. "The last bit was interesting to me." He reached for the remote and backtracked on the DVD.

It was Emily's voice asking the question. "I need to know more about Mandy. Did she ever leave like this before?"

"No. She was very reliable."

"Why did she leave, Mitch?" Again, Emily.

Mitch's eyes darted to something off screen. There appeared to be a slight wetness on his upper lip.

"I have no idea." He hesitated. "This interview is over. I'll look for her myself. Thanks for nothing."

Chris got up and poured himself some more wine, and then returned to the couch. Mitch Crawford's face was frozen on the flat screen. "All right. He's everything you've said he was, including a world-class liar. He's holding it together pretty well, but you can see he's starting to sweat. That's probably the reason he ended the interview—not that you weren't pushing him hard, because you were."

"I tried. I think I did push too hard," Emily said. "His holier-than-thou attitude brings out the worst in me."

Chris shrugged. "No worries, Em. I find it interesting that he never mentions the baby."

"Me, too. It's as if the baby doesn't figure into his worries whatsoever."

"I also noticed how he says Mandy is so reliable, yet says he has no idea where she'd go, and that she'd never done that before."

Emily agreed. "Reliable people don't run off."

"Not without a reason, they don't."

She locked her eyes on Chris. "You don't think she left him, do you?"

"Not at all. But I wouldn't have blamed her if she had."

"The more I get to know him, the more I wonder *why* she stayed with him at all."

"You know the answer, don't you?" He looked over at Jenna's portraits taken with Santa Claus from babyhood to high school. They were set in a row on the mantel among sprigs of holly Emily had plucked from the backyard before she'd given up on fighting the couple across the street for best decorated house on Orchard Avenue.

Emily followed his eyes to the pictures.

"Of course," she said. "She wanted a baby. She'd waited for the SOB probably to tell her when the right time would be for her to have one. Not the right time for her. But—"

He cut off Emily. "Right. The time that suited *him*."

"Maybe there was no right time."

"Exactly."

"Most pregnant women who are murdered are victims of the men who fathered their babies."

Chris finished his wine. "He didn't want that baby, did he?"

Emily set her glass down, too. "He probably never wanted the competition a baby would bring."

Emily Kenyon adored Chris Collier. She loved being with him, loving him. That part of their relationship had always been fulfilling, exciting, and something that fueled all of her fantasies when she was alone and longing for his touch. He was her dream. He was a broad-shouldered six-footer, with lively eyes and wavy dark hair that had begun to silver at the temples.

"I like it this way," he once told her, "kind of reminds me of my dad. He was gray by fifty-two."

Chris had often told Emily that after he retired, he wanted to sell his downtown condo and buy a farm in the rural part of the state.

"Maybe I could find a place out near you?"

"Are you a stalker or just looking for cheap real estate?"

He winked at her. "Oh, a stalker, for sure."

Emily knew that she'd once used Jenna as an excuse to forestall talk that she and Chris should be something more than lovers. There had been very good reasons for the delay of her own personal happiness. Jenna was sixteen when she'd been traumatized by the bizarre events that led her into the web of a serial killer. That crime had brought Chris and Emily back together after having been partners on the Seattle police force earlier in their careers. She loved Chris, there was no doubt about that. Loving him, however, meant carrying that old burden.

But Emily also knew that Jenna was right, that Chris was good for her, and she for him. Listening to a twenty-two-year-old never seemed like a good idea, but Emily knew her daughter never failed when it came to wanting Emily to find the joy in her life that had eluded her since she and David divorced.

Why don't I allow myself happiness? Love?

Chapter Seventeen

At twenty-two, Cherrystone Reserve Deputy Ricardo Gomez was a techno-geek who knew his way around computers like Emily Kenyon knew her way around motherhood and blood spatter evidence. In a very real way, his high-tech prowess was a curse. Whenever anyone had problems with their home PCs, it was Ricky who'd get the desperate call for troubleshooting.

Sometimes he'd even be asked to come over to make a house call. Doctors didn't make house calls, but a guy who knew the difference between byte and bite me did. He often wondered if anyone had heard of a help-desk phone number, but he never said no. He'd graduated from Cascade University with Emily's daughter, Jenna, and went looking for a job before going back to school for a master's degree in knowledge management and criminal justice. He'd been hired on a one-year contract to work with the software company to move the Cherrystone Sheriff's office from paper to paperless.

Ricky looked like anything but a nerd. He worked out three days a week, kept his longish black hair styled, and wore dark jeans and a sport coat every day. He was handsome, with brown eyes and teeth so white they almost glowed.

Since Ricky was trained and had been deputized, he fit within the standard protocol for chain-of-evidence rules. That was good. Cherrystone couldn't afford an outside lab to go over the Crawfords' laptop computer. After all, they'd barely had enough dough for a year-end holiday celebration. Emily had Ricky in mind when she needed someone to take a look at the computer that Mandy Crawford used before she vanished.

"You won't find anything on it," Mitch Crawford had said as he watched Emily and Jason Howard carry it off on the Friday after his wife disappeared. "We're pretty good about wiping out most of the websites we visit, no cookies saved either. We're not going to be victimized by some crook try-ing to steal our information by spying on us. We use Compu-Clean every Sunday on an automated cycle."

Emily felt like saying something along the lines of "how convenient," but she held her tongue.

Nevertheless he must have read her mind.

"Well," Ricky said when Emily handed off the laptop, "it's not exactly the latest and greatest."

Emily knew he was right. The laptop was at least seven years old, which made it nearly a relic as such things go. It was the size of a small attaché case, not one of the slim little notebooks that students and executives have made the day's status quo. She told Ricky how Mitch used a program to lessen the risk of spyware.

"Or so he told me," she said, her tone sardonic at best.

"I can poke around. Give me an hour or so and I'll pick the low-hanging fruit. If I think there's more there, and I can't get to it, I'll let you know. I'm not going to try to play superstar info finder here. Let's leave that to someone with real experience. OK?"

"Fair enough," she said. She watched as he booted up the machine and started clicking through the icons on the desktop. "I'll leave you to your work. Come and get me if you find something."

"Sheriff Kenyon?" Ricky Gomez stood in the doorway of her office, with the look of a man who'd won a drawing for a new car or maybe a trip to Hawaii—excited and satisfied.

Emily looked up from her paperwork. "What is it?"

"I think you'll want to see," Ricky said, barely able to contain his excitement.

"You're not a good poker player, are you, Ricky?"

He laughed. "No one thinks so."

Emily set aside her papers and followed Ricky to his office at the end of the hall. It wasn't much of an office. Before he moved inside with a telephone and cables that ran from four computers, it had been an employee smoke break room. It still smelled of it, years after the ban on smoking in the workplace. His mom brought in a faux Oriental rug to cozy up the gray and white speckled linoleum floor.

It was a thoughtful attempt, but the big sink behind Ricky's desk let it be known that this office wasn't an office in its former life.

Emily peered over Ricky's shoulder as he navigated the Crawfords' desktop.

"Check this out," he said, clacking at the keyboard and looking up at the sheriff at the same time.

"Here are her favorites, not really erased by the file cleaner," he said.

Amanda's favorites on her Internet navigation tab were an odd mix of household management websites and scrapbooking resource pages that she hit routinely as she downloaded stencils and design ideas. Emily could see that Amanda hadn't finished the template for the Christmas scrapbook that she'd ordered online.

"Looks like she hadn't done anything since Halloween," Emily said.

"That's right," Ricky said, pointing out that the cache, the location in computers where information is stored for faster downloading, was empty.

"I expected that," he said. "That's one of the chief benefits of CompuClean—the software company calls it their Cache-Out tool."

He clicked over to the e-mail folders, showing Emily that the inbox was empty. So was the sent box. He checked her trash can. All were a big zero.

"Ricky," Emily said, "I thought you found something."

"Hang on. I need to give you the background. Learned that in class last year. You need to see the process."

Emily liked Ricky all the more just then. He was doing things by the book, not trying to tease her with a buildup for crucial information that might never come.

He clicked his cursor onto Mandy's personal folders. Most of them, he pointed out, dealt with her scrapbooking hobby. He went through each file, text, and images. Most of the images were pictures of another woman—a sister, maybe, and her children. She had recently populated a template called "Before You Were Born" with images of herself, Mitch, and their house at 21 Larkspur.

"She was getting ready for something good to happen," Emily said.

"I guess. But here's what you've been waiting for. He found a text file that easily could have been missed. It was labeled: *Next Phase*. He clicked on it, and his eyes met Emily's as she began to read, simultaneously, reaching for her phone and dialing Camille's number.

If anyone is reading this message, I am probably dead. My name is Amanda Crawford. My husband is

Mitch Crawford. Whoever you are, you alone will know my fate. You and my husband. Mitch said he'd kill me if I left him. He's said it so many, many times. I've wanted to leave for a long time. I've wanted to find my way out of this mess.

Having a baby was not done to placate him, to make him love me, or feel sorry for me when he beat me. But for a little while, I thought that maybe he would change. He seemed to. When I found out that I was carrying a daughter, I told him that it was a boy. I did this to save myself and my baby. He only wanted a son. Anyway, if you've read this, then you know I didn't find a way out. Mitch will be very careful when he kills me. But he will make a mistake.

Please don't forget about me. You are my—and my baby's—only hope. Please tell my parents that I wish I could have told them what was happening, but after the first time, he said if I told anyone what he'd done to me, he'd kill them, too. He has a boat. If he finds me and kills me, I'm all but certain that he'll dump me in the water. Mitch doesn't like to get his hands dirty.

Amanda Lynn Crawford

"Can we authenticate this?"

Camille Hazelton looked up from the single laser print that Emily had brought from her offices in the sheriff's department.

The prosecutor had been in the middle of an employee-recognition event that included a chocolate cake and certificates of achievement for "going the extra mile" when Emily called with the news of Mandy's note. Emily caught her eye through the window of the conference room where the Cherrystone government support staff had gathered in their grim little celebration. When Camille's eyes met Emily's, she gladly bolted—cake in hand—for her private office.

"I love my people, but I hate those events," she said as she shut the door. "I can tell by your face that this is good, isn't it?"

"Better than good," Emily said, with a satisfied grin she didn't even try to hide.

The letter was only three paragraphs, but it said everything Mandy Crawford had needed to say.

It pointed an accusing finger squarely at her husband.

"Of course, we can't say for sure if she wrote it," Emily said, sliding into a seat next to the heavy oak desk that had been the county prosecutor's since 1910 when it made the front page of the paper under the headline: PROSECUTOR GUILTY OF EXTRAVAGANCE. A framed copy hung on the wall.

Camille slipped her chic Vera Wang reading glasses down the bridge of her long nose. "But we know that it was on Mandy's computer. We know that for certain."

"Yes."

"What else was on the computer? Is there more?"

"No." Emily shook her head. "Nothing relevant. A few scrapbooks in progress."

"Zilch?" Camille said.

"That's right. Mitch says he and Mandy cleaned the PC on the Sunday before she disappeared."

"And he left this there? Seems a little sloppy, don't you think?"

Camille was right, of course. But Emily had known plenty of criminals who'd thought they were so smart that their arrogance, their unbending belief in their own invincibility, were the keys to their eventual downfall. It was as if always being told they are smart, handsome, pretty, funny, and brilliant left no room for introspection. *To doubt themselves.* A lack of tendency toward doubt meant a tendency for errors.

"They all make mistakes," she said.

"Can your tech guy say when the message was written?"

Emily had already considered that. She knew that time-dating any computer file was an issue. "That's a problem. Just like we can't say if Mandy wrote the letter for sure—you know, anyone could have—we can't say *when* for sure. Microsoft Word automatically dates this kind of a doc, so a good defense lawyer can question all of that."

"This is good, Emily. But good isn't enough for an indictment. We need more."

"Don't I know that," she said.

Emily left Camille's office and went past the conference room where the employee party had been. The room was empty, but the big chocolate cake, half gone, called to her. She looked around and ducked inside. She cut a piece, and put it on a floppy paper plate.

Ricky loves chocolate, she thought. *Good work deserves a little something sweet.*

Even though a surge of adrenaline that came with the discovery of the note from Mandy lifted Emily, she still couldn't get past the grief she felt when she thought of Mandy and her baby. Certainly, an arrest, a trial, and hopefully a conviction would do nothing to bring her back. Justice in a murder case was not only about punishing the killer. It was for the family, the friends, and the community in which the victim lived. But unlike, say a rape case, or a violent assault, there was no payback coming from the victim.

The victim in a homicide had been silenced permanently.

Emily's job, she knew, was to speak for Mandy. She and Camille were the only ones who could.

"I hear you now, Mandy," she said to herself. "I only wish that I'd heard you before it turned out to be too late."

Chapter Eighteen

San Diego

"What a bitch!"

Lily Ann Denton cursed under her breath, but resisted the urge to press her palm against the horn. She let out a gasp of exaggerated anger. Some woman in a Dodge minivan stole a parking spot in front of the Circle K just as she was about to pull in.

Did she have to do that?

Lily Ann did another loop around the tiny, packed lot and found a space. She waited a moment for the Maroon 5 song that she'd fallen in love with to finish before she turned off the ignition on her sunny yellow Cabriolet. She was a grad student on a mission. At twenty-one, gone were the days when she relied on a pretty good fake ID and eye-catching breasts that acted as a winning backup plan—if the clerk was a male.

A horny male.

After a quick lip-gloss and hair check, she got out of the Cabriolet and hurried inside the store, eyeing the clerk— *good, a young guy*—as she made a beeline for the cold beer case in the back of the store. She rolled her pretty blue eyes at the woman who'd snatched her prime parking spot. She had three kids with her, all clamoring for candy bars and sodas.

"One or the other, Mattie, Diet Coke or Snickers. Not both."

Mattie, a chubby ten-year-old, started wailing and Mom gave in within a second. Lily Ann caught the little girl's eye and saw something in it. The little girl offered up what seemed to be a little too much of a grin, a-look-what-I'm-getting countenance that said everything about who she was and where she was headed.

Nice, a little manipulator. Probably Beta Zeta material, she thought.

Lily Ann leaned closer to the clerk, waving her driver's license like a dog dangling a bone. The young man barely glanced at the laminated card.

"Party up at campus?" he asked. He was referring to the fashion design college just east of downtown San Diego.

"Party everywhere I go," she said.

"Hot."

"That's right." She pulled a twenty from her purse and paid for the beer—she didn't have to show her breasts or her ID, really, which made the day a pretty good one so far.

"Have a good one," he called out.

"Always do," she said.

The mother with the three kids observed the exchange and figured that one day whatever attributes the young woman had she'd lose them to marriage and gravity.

But she wasn't the only one watching Lily Ann.

As she ferried her beer to her car, she didn't notice the man standing across the street watching her. He followed her movements like she was some kind of performer, a figure to be studied. He took in her long blond hair, and watched how it bounced up and down as she stepped toward the Cabriolet.

She was lovely. Maybe the prettiest of the bunch.

He could feel his rage swell as she started to back out of her parking spot.

Off to a party. Have fun. It'll be your last. Girls like you don't care about anyone but yourselves.

He got back into his own car to follow her; her yellow car was like a beacon in traffic. Lily Ann couldn't lose anyone tailing her if she'd wanted to. *Girls like her*, he thought, *always had cars that screamed "Look at me!"*

If she had known that she was being followed or that she was in danger, she might have pulled into the fire station she zipped past or the church. There were a half-dozen opportunities when she might have escaped her fate. A stop. A quick turn. A cop was writing a ticket on the side of the road, and she tapped her brakes.

She punched in a phone number on her cell phone.

"Kara, God, I almost got a ticket. Was going fifteen over on Lander and passed a cop. I swear we had eye contact."

"Close call."

"I'm lucky. Hey, I got the beer."

"Awesome," Kara said, "I just finished my psych reading and I'm ready to party."

"You're always ready to party."

"Look who's talking."

"See you in a few."

Lily Ann looked in her rearview mirror. She didn't notice the man following her. In fact, she didn't even look at the traffic. Instead, she checked her makeup one more time. A couple of cute guys were coming to their little pre-func get-together before the party at the frat house later that evening.

The man behind her slowed, too. He pulled out a cigarette and lit it, sending a curl of smoke out of the cracked-down window. He flicked on the radio and smiled when he heard a Maroon 5 song come on the radio. He'd known through her Facebook account that Lily Ann loved the pop band.

He wondered if she was listening to them now. She was

so predictable. So easy. He parked and waited and smoked, flicking out the ashes as they grew to quarter-inch points of gray. He liked to keep things neat. He even hated that he smoked in the car, but Jesus, smoking was the hardest habit to break.

Maybe even harder than killing a girl.

Lily Ann Denton was nothing to him. In fact, the more he read her online profile, the more he hated her. She posed for picture after picture, beer in hand, laughing and pointing at the camera like she was some goddamn superstar. Like she had no cares whatsoever.

He drew on the cigarette, sucking the smoke deeply into his lungs and nodding as if he was having a conversation with someone.

But the conversation was in his head.

"I hate her stupid little mouth. So tight and tiny."

"Yeah, she thinks she's so pretty. So special. She's nothing. Says she wants to be a doctor or a lawyer on her Web bio."

"She'd be lucky to need either when I get finished with her."

"Yeah. She'll need an autopsy, if anything."

"If they can find her."

"Right. That's right. They didn't find the other, did they?"

"They don't have a clue. Stupid. Stupid. Stupid."

He could feel his own lips moving as he had the conversation with himself, but he knew he wasn't really uttering any of the words. He wasn't crazy like that. They were only playing in his head. Over and over. The conversation sustained him, *fueled* him, as he waited for Lily Ann to drink a few beers and move on to the party. To move on to her final destiny. The one he'd scripted all on his own. Talking to himself, even silently, took the ennui out of the business of murder.

"Yeah, the truth is that killing is hours of boredom with ten seconds of ecstasy."

A couple of girls, both long and lean, with dark hair that curled past their necklines, walked past. One carried a coat, the other wore one. They were in a hurry. He watched as they headed up the steps to the house where Lily Ann was holding court. He checked his watch. They were punctual. The time for the pre-party drinking was half past the hour.

They'd drink for an hour.

And he'd kill Lily Ann Denton, put her in the trunk, and go to Arby's.

God, he was hungry.

Chapter Nineteen

Cherrystone

The greasy smell of french fries and buffalo chicken wings hung in the overheated air. It was 1:15, just after the lunch rush, when Jason Howard stomped snow off his feet in a puddle inside the door and hurried into Cherrystone High School's cafeteria/auditorium. The lights were dim, but he could see Emily sitting in a metal folding chair on the stage at the far end of the cavernous room. Seated next to her were the principal, Sal Randazzo, and a teacher he didn't recognize. And also a girl he expected was the student the office staff had said they were gathered to honor.

Dr. Randazzo stood up and took the microphone.

"Nothing is more important than the safety of our students," he said, as a slide show of young faces played out on a giant pull-down screen behind him. "We've gathered here today to honor Naomi Frye for her heroic actions that saved the lives of two of our students. . . ."

Very quietly, Jason went up the steps to the stage and cupped his hands around his mouth.

"Sheriff Kenyon," he whispered.

Emily didn't appear to hear him.

Dr. Randazzo put his hand on Naomi's shoulder.

". . . This young woman stopped at the scene of a terrible car accident and administered CPR."

Jason leaned in just little farther, trying his best to avoid being seen by the student-body audience who'd gathered, however begrudgingly, to honor one of their own. He called once more. This time he caught Emily's attention.

"E Mer Gen Cee," he mouthed at her.

As gracefully as she could, Emily said something to Randazzo and took Naomi's hand to congratulate her. She walked calmly across the stage, trying not to disrupt the occasion for which she'd been asked to speak.

"What is it?" She was clearly concerned. It made no sense for Jason to show up in the middle of a school event. For goodness sake, he could have waited an hour and she'd have been back in the office. She wondered if it was Jenna. "Has there been an accident?" Her heartbeat quickened. It was far from routine having Jason interrupt a public event.

"No. It's pretty bad. We might have found Mandy."

Emily knew by his dire tone that he didn't mean Mandy Crawford had been found alive. "Her body?"

"Yeah. Dumped off the highway by the old Highline."

An icy wind that felt like raptor claws on the back of a neck blew down the ravine behind the Highline Tavern, ten miles out of town on the Cherrystone-Spokane Highway. The tavern was nothing more than a biker bar, a place with six pool tables and a bathroom that had seen a flood of vomit and misaimed streams of urine. The dive had been closed for two years, having failed to hang on to the Goldwingers and Harley wannabes that came from Spokane on the weekends in their Citizens jeans and Ralph Lauren leather jackets.

Two cars from the Washington State Patrol were parked

out front. Shane Packer and Ron Oliver, both well known to Emily, had kept the area clear from the inevitable stream of lookie-loos hovering nearby. Such gatherings were always part of any major crime scene in small-town America, where police scanners still sell and where middle-aged men still live out the dream they'd be smarter than Columbo or Jessica Fletcher.

"Sheriff," said Shane, a tall black man with strikingly handsome features and cannonball biceps that made most women feel a little flap of flirtatious energy whenever he was around.

"Officer," Emily said. Her expression was grim. There were no real smiles for old friends at a time like this. "What do you have?"

He motioned over in the direction of the patrol car, lights flashing. "Ron's got the witness in his vehicle taking a statement now."

She looked over and saw Ron Oliver, a sandy-haired cop who'd become nothing more than Shane's sidekick. He was busy making notes on his state-issue pad while a young man, not more than eighteen, talked animatedly about what he'd found.

Emily turned back toward Shane. "What have we got?"

He motioned for Emily and Jason to follow. "Kid was looking for bottles for recycling and found her. Follow me." They walked from the parking lot, through some garbage left by the previous owner. Emily couldn't help but notice that a baby crib had been trashed and left in the blackberry brambles. It seemed odd to her that there'd ever be a need for a baby crib in a biker bar.

What's this world coming to?

The three of them stood on the edge of the ravine.

"Down there." He pointed to the figure of a young woman, her body wrapped in what appeared to be a sheet. But on closer examination, it seemed more likely that it was a painter's drop cloth. Her hand protruded from the covering, almost as if to call out to the world, *Come here. Find me.*

"Techs are coming from Spokane," Shane said. "Called you, Emily, because of your missing woman."

Shane's words were meant to affirm what all of them knew. Cherrystone had no standing there. The body was found in Spokane County. Outside of Mandy Crawford, Cherrystone had no reports of anyone else missing—man or woman.

With Jason just behind her, Emily looked down the ravine. She estimated it was about a seventy-foot drop, maybe eighty. The incline was layered with dollops of snow and a tangle of thistles and blackberries. A deer trail to the bottom cut a zigzag path from where they stood.

Emily steadied herself as she made her way down toward the body, with the sick feeling that came with the sad realization that someone's daughter had been murdered and dumped like garbage. The cold weather had been in their favor. There was no stench, no flies buzzing around the corpse.

She knelt next to the body. It took only a second and the abruptness of her own words surprised even herself.

"This isn't Mandy Crawford," she said.

"How can you tell? You can't even see her face," Jason said from two steps behind her.

Emily looked up at her deputy, and then locked her eyes on the arm sticking from its frozen wrapping.

"Mandy doesn't have a tattoo around her wrist."

Jason's mouth was a straight line as he looked at what was so sadly, but concretely, evident. A chain of blue violets spun around the dead girl's wrist. They were faded, having lost the crispness of a new inking.

"Yeah," he said. "This isn't Mandy."

Emily and Jason knew that Amanda did, in fact, have a tattoo. But it was a pink rose on her lower back.

The pair climbed back up to the edge of the ravine. Shane

Packer was smoking a cigarette and stubbed it out into the half-frozen ground.

"Still trying to quit," he said.

Emily nodded. "She's not ours. Someone's heart will be broken tonight. But she's not Cherrystone's missing mother-to-be, that's for sure."

The three of them talked a bit more. Jason said he was so glad that he'd never started smoking, though it seemed to go with a law enforcement job.

"No groups smoke more than cops and doctors," he said.

"You got that right," Emily said, without offering up that she and her ex, a doctor, had been heavy smokers back in the day. Both had stopped smoking before they had Jenna.

On the drive back to Cherrystone, snow skittered over the now-dry and bare highway. Emily was heartbroken with the realization that a dead girl's mother would be getting the worst-possible phone call once identification had been made. How that would hurt. Emily would probably never know the end of that story. She couldn't follow every case. She had her own, of course.

"You know Mandy's dead, right?" Jason asked.

Emily let out sigh. "We *think* she's dead. The absence of her body makes this difficult, of course."

"Not impossible. I mean, why can't Hazelton just indict that SOB of a husband of hers?"

Emily shook her head. "Because she's up for reelection next year and she wants to win. She doesn't want an opponent wagging a finger at her come election time saying that we rushed to judgment and arrested the wrong guy."

"A lot of other prosecutors would indict him now just to make him squirm a little, you know, see what he does once he makes bail—because you know he would."

"I'm sure. Camille isn't going to let us down. Once we

find Mandy, or have some physical evidence of foul play, she'll indict."

Jason looked squarely at Emily. She faced the darkening roadway, one hand on the steering wheel and the other fishing for a lemon drop from the tin she kept in the cruiser.

"You thought that was her at first, didn't you?"

She let her eyes light on him for a second. "I did. I hoped it was and I hoped it wasn't. I don't think she's alive, but, I guess, I'm praying something like this will come to an end."

"Yeah. Some news is always better than no news."

Emily didn't agree. She hated not knowing where Mandy Crawford was, of course. But she loathed more than anything the duty that fell on her shoulders when the worst outcome in a missing person's case came into play.

"Try telling yourself that when you have to make a death notification to a dead girl's mother and father."

Jason knew just what she was talking about. "Where in the world are you?" he asked, looking out at the dormant vineyards and their spiderweb rows of grapevines as they whizzed by in the speeding cruiser, the rows fading in the early evening. "Where did he put you, Mandy?"

Chapter Twenty

Gloria brought in three tins of assorted Christmas cookies—some she made and others she conceded were "filler"—as her countdown to the holiday kicked into high gear. She kept the Spokane radio station that played "holiday favorites" on low.

"Less than a week of shopping," she said, with a good-natured smile. "Still time to get me something I can't live without."

"Someone here to see you, Sheriff," she said, as Emily breezed in with latte in hand.

Emily looked down the hall, and mouthed, "Who?"

Gloria lip-synched back, "Wouldn't say."

The woman waiting outside of Emily's office was a wisp; a good wind and she'd blow away. She couldn't have been more than five feet tall, barely a hundred pounds after a full meal. She had strawberry blond hair that she wore cropped at the shoulder; bangs framed her blue eyes. It looked as if she'd been crying. Her mouth was taut, frozen in a kind of grimace that appeared to indicate that her reason for being there was a painful one.

"I'm Sheriff Kenyon," Emily said. "Gloria says you're

here to see me." She waited for the woman to say something, before adding, "But she didn't say why."

The woman stood up. She wore boot-cut jeans with heels, a stylish sweater and blouse. The sweater was jade-colored and expensive. In her arms she held a gray coat that probably weighed more than she did.

"Sheriff, I'm not a gossip," she said.

"Good. We don't have much use for gossip, around here. Gossip works better for the newspaper, anyway."

It was a lighthearted comment that was meant to relax, but it fell flat. Emily noticed for the first time that the small woman in front of her was shaking. Her hand holding her car key trembled noticeably.

"Are you all right?" She waved her inside. "Come in. Sit down."

The woman took a seat across from Emily's desk.

"I'm fine, and thank you."

"Who are you?"

"Tricia Wilson." She paused and looked nervously around the room.

She was afraid of something. Or someone.

"I used to be Patty Crawford."

Emily's eyes widened a little. While the last name rang alarm bells, the first meant absolutely nothing.

"I'm sorry. Are you a relative of Mandy's?"

Her visitor shook her head and set down her black leather satchel. Emily noticed a large envelope protruding from the silver jaws of its clasp.

"Not exactly. More like a kindred spirit, I'd say. I know what it's like to be married to Mitch Crawford. And I know now that I'm a lot luckier girl than Mandy is. I got away from that bastard alive."

Emily tried to keep her face from betraying her feelings. She could have kicked herself right then. How stupid they'd been not to know that Mitch had been married before.

"We didn't know how to reach you," she said. She felt foolish for lying, but she hated not knowing something that she should have known.

Tricia stayed expressionless. "I'm sure. If you even knew I'd existed, you'd have had a hard time finding me. I've changed my name, my hair, my address. I never wanted to be found by anyone from my old life as Mitch's wife. It was a complete and utter nightmare."

Again, Emily waited. Waiting always brought better results than peppering a person for the details. Tricia Wilson had come to Cherrystone with a reason. She was the ex-wife. Emily knew she might be there to settle the score, to get some payback for a bad marriage. Maybe she'd been dumped by Mitch. Emily didn't know. She wanted Tricia to do the talking.

They'd fill in the gaps later.

"I married Mitch when I was eighteen. He was ten years older. He was handsome. *Fun*. We had a lot of money. We had his parents' place on the Oregon coast any weekend we wanted. He was the dream. Hell, we were living the dream." She looked wistful as she remembered the good times.

Without taking her eyes off Tricia, Emily unbuttoned her coat and slid out of the arms.

"What happened? It sounds like things were good."

"Things are always good in the beginning."

Emily nodded, thinking of David and the early days of their marriage. Things had been good once between them.

"I feel stupid for even being here," she said, making a movement that suggested she might get up and leave.

Emily put her hand on her desk, a gesture indicating to stay.

"But what happened? You're here because you want to tell me something. Did you know Mandy?"

"No. But I know Mitch."

"I'm sure you do. Tell me. Have you talked to him about Mandy?"

"Not at all. I haven't spoken to him since the day we divorced."

Tricia stopped herself again.

"Go on."

"Sheriff Kenyon, I was afraid he'd kill me. I really was."

Emily felt a rush of sympathy. She's worked terrible abuse cases in Seattle. She'd seen women who shuddered with fear even when the man in question was safely behind bars.

"Did he hurt you?" she asked.

Tricia started to cry and reached for her purse. Emily looked around for a tissue, and she'd assumed that Tricia was doing the same. Instead, she produced a large gray envelope and scooted it on top of Emily's desk.

"Open it. I want you to see. I've never let anyone see this before."

Emily undid the little brass clasp and reached inside. She found three Polaroid photographs.

The first showed a very young Patty Crawford facing the camera. She had a black eye that a prizefighter might have bragged about. Her cheeks were streaked with tears; her hair pulled back over one shoulder. She looked fearful that at any second there could be another attack.

"Oh, my," she said, looking up. "Mitch did this to you?"

Tricia dabbed at her eyes with a tissue she'd retrieved from the bottom of her purse.

"Yes," she said.

The next image was similar to the first, but not nearly as brutal. Emily hated that she'd even made a judgment about the severity of the injury. No injury was acceptable. It was clear that this was a different incident than the first photograph. Tricia's hair was longer, and styled differently. Her gaze was less fearful, almost resigned.

Emily glanced up for a second, then picked up the next photograph. She found herself suppressing a gasp.

The final image was the most brutal. Tricia was naked from the waist up. It looked as if there was a large gash on her forehead. She had two softball-sized bruises across her rib cage. The framing of the photo was askew, as it had been in the other two, indicating more than likely that Tricia had taken the photos of herself.

"Dear God," Emily said, "what did the police say?"

Tricia avoided Emily's eyes. She kept her sightline fixed on the floor. Or the tissue in her hand.

"I didn't tell. I couldn't."

"But the photos? You must have taken them to prove what had happened?"

"This is very difficult. I know now that none of this makes sense. But at the time I only took them so that in case he killed me, someone would know it wasn't my fault. That he'd done this to me."

She was sobbing now, and Emily got up and shut the door. She took the seat next to Tricia and put her hand on her shoulder.

"I'm so sorry. You didn't deserve this, Tricia."

"That's not why I'm crying. I'm so damned embarrassed and ashamed that I didn't do anything. But I was so afraid of him. He told me over and over that if I told anyone what he'd done that he'd kill me and go have a big fat breakfast to celebrate. He told me that people would stop asking about me fifteen minutes after I'd been gone."

"Tell me about the photos."

"If I'd have been smart, there would have been more of them. He used me like a punching bag—and I'm not kidding—from the wedding night on. He said when I danced with a friend from high school that I looked like a whore. I should have known he was a control freak. Everyone else did."

Emily knew that something within Tricia's past had led her to choose a man like Mitch Crawford. Maybe her father had knocked around her mother. Maybe she'd been abused by a family member. It no longer took a psychologist to ferret out the reasons why some women made the poorest choices in a mate.

Sometimes a deadly choice.

Emily tapped a finger on the worst of the images.

"I've seen photos like this and I've talked to the women who've lived through the worst kind of abuse, and I know that you're like so many of them. You're a survivor. You did the right thing by coming here today."

Tricia twisted her Kleenex and balled up the sodden tissue.

"I got away from the bastard. All I can wonder is, you know, if I had said something, maybe Mandy wouldn't, you know . . ."

"Wouldn't what?"

"Be gone. Be dead."

"What makes you think Mandy Crawford is dead?"

"OK. I don't know that she's dead, but I'll never forget what Mitch told me after our divorce." She stopped and eyed Emily. Her look was pleading and sad.

"What did he say to you?"

"He said, 'I never make the same mistake twice.'"

"And you take that to mean?"

"At first, I thought it meant that he'd never get married. Now, I think he meant that if he ever found himself with a wife that didn't bow to his every whim, he'd kill her. The man was not complicated, in the way that a pit bull isn't complicated. They might look cute when they are puppies, but they grow up to rip the face off a ten-year-old. He's like that. Everyone thought he was a charismatic do-gooder. He ran his dad's lot in Portland like he was running for office."

"But he wasn't like that at home," Emily said, more of a statement than a question.

"Oh, to be fair—and that's how sick I think I still am, giving him the benefit of the doubt at all—but in the beginning we were happy. I thought that when he questioned what I was wearing, how friendly I was, or whatever, that he was just jealous. You know, that he cared about me."

"Does anyone know about the photos?"

"You mean, does Mitch?"

"That's right, that's what I mean."

"Of course he does. He gave me fifty thousand dollars to get out of his life and give him the photos and the negatives."

"But you have copies."

"That's right. I was an abused wife. I wasn't completely stupid."

"Of course not," Emily said. "You know that this will come out, now."

"Yes. But I'm glad about it. Even if it means that he'll sue me for the hush money. That's what I think of it—hush money. I really don't care. I don't want to leave feeling like I sold myself for fifty thousand dollars. You see, Sheriff," her emotions once more causing her words to fracture, "I have a daughter now. I don't want what happened to me, to my mother, to happen to Abby. I'm over it, but I don't know what residual damage might linger."

Emily knew that the cycle was learned and often generational. Predators like Mitch Crawford went after women who fit a certain type. She had never thought of Mandy Crawford, on the rare occasions when she saw her, as a passive woman. She seemed so outgoing. So confident.

It had been a mask.

It occurred to Emily just then that both the Crawfords wore masks of a sort. He pretended to be the consummate charmer; she was the adoring wife.

But neither was true.

"Tricia, you know what you'll have to do. If Mitch killed his wife, we might need you to testify."

Emily's words seemed to embolden Tricia. She leaned forward across the desk. She tapped a painted nail on the stack of photographs.

"I've been waiting for this for years. I'd like to pay back the SOB for all he's done to me. I only hope," she said, her demeanor softening, "that I'm not too late—that Mandy is still alive."

Emily studied Tricia, now fully composed.

"Is there anything else?" she asked.

"Yeah. He was screwing the help at his office here in Cherrystone. I heard he got the girl pregnant. He's such a pig."

"Who told you that?"

Tricia looked down at the photos, letting her eyes linger on the gruesome images. "A friend," she said. "I still have a few, you know."

After Tricia left, Emily fanned out the photos on Jason's desk. She told him about her story of being battered by Mitch and how she'd heard that he was up to his old tricks, sleeping around with the help.

"Holy crap!" he said. "Mitch Crawford did that? He's going down."

"I like it when you're direct, Jason. But let's see. I'm going to check on her story about Darla. Let's see if she had Mitch's baby."

A phone call to the dealership confirmed it was Darla Montague's day off and Emily drove over to the Cortina Apartments on Sycamore. She found Darla's apartment right away—the car with the omnipresent car seat and a decal of

breaching Orcas were obvious beacons. Darla had a SAVE
THE WHALES poster, coffee mug, and pencil holder at her
desk.

Darla looked crestfallen when she opened the door and
saw the sheriff. No reassuring words or warm smile could
placate her.

"Please don't tell my baby's daddy," Darla said as Emily
confronted her with what Patty Crawford, a.k.a. Tricia Wilson,
had indicated earlier that day in her office. The twenty-two-
year-old with the baby in her arms started to cry. "I don't
want my parents to know, either."

Emily felt for the young woman. She saw her as the type
who probably meant well, but through her own gullibility
was constantly a victim of circumstance. She was working
as a receptionist at the car dealership, she had a baby, and
she was worried about what her parents would think of the
fact that she'd slept with the boss.

"Is the baby Mitch's?" Emily asked as she took a seat on
a sofa half-covered in folded diapers and baby blankets.

Darla, in a rocker, held her son tighter. "Oh, no. I didn't
do anything with Mitch until *after* the baby was born. I
swear it."

"I see," Emily said, more of an acknowledgment than an
acceptance of Darla's story. "Tell me what happened."

"You mean about how we did it?"

"No. No, Darla. Not *how* you did it, if you're referring to
the sex act itself. What I'd like to know is what was the ex-
tent of the relationship? How involved were you, really?"

Darla became quiet. She turned around with her back toward Emily, her baby boy facing the sheriff. She looked out
the window.

"This is really embarrassing," she said. "We only did it
one or two times."

"Was it one or two?"

"OK, two times."

"All right. Now when did this happen?"

"This summer. After my son was born. I'd come back to work, from my extended leave. And you know, I was feeling bad about myself. I felt fat. My boyfriend called me a cow. Can you believe that? I just had his son and he called me a cow?"

Emily felt strongly about a two-parent family, but this baby daddy of Darla's was a piece of garbage.

She shifted the subject back to the concern at hand. "I'm sorry, but what happened with Mitch?"

"Well, Mr. Crawford, err, Mitch, said that my boyfriend was a jerk to call me names. He said that he thought I was pretty. He said that I had potential. *Real potential.* And then, you, know, one thing led to another."

Emily felt sorry for Darla. *Potential? Honestly, what didn't work when it came to getting a lonely girl into bed?*

"No," she said, "I don't know. Tell me."

"OK, it was after closing and he told me to come into his office. My son was at my mom's so I didn't have to rush out. It was a Friday night. I was going to go out to party. Anyway, he told me he was lonely. He said Mandy was cold to him. Then, well, then he kissed me and we had sex."

"In his office?"

Darla turned around, tears streaming down her face. "Yeah, and I'm not proud about it."

"Did he say he was in love with you?"

"No, he didn't."

"But he wanted to see you again, didn't he?"

"I guess I'm not explaining myself very well. He said that I was pretty and we had sex two times. I don't think he ever said he wanted a relationship with me. He just told me that his wife was cold to him and I was fun."

"Did you know Mandy?"

By then, Darla's tears were uncontrollable and her baby

started to cry, too. "I'd seen her come into the dealership a few times. She was nice enough. I mean, she pretty much acted like she was put out having to come into the dealership. She never stayed long and she didn't seem to appreciate how hard her husband worked."

It passed through Emily's mind that Darla Montague was probably the most naive person she'd ever met. Youth alone wasn't the reason she'd gotten involved with a charismatic man. She had also felt sorry for him. Maybe, she thought, Darla had hoped that he'd fall in love with her.

Yet he only wanted her for one thing.

"I have to leave now. My mom invited us to dinner." She balanced the baby against her shoulder and looked for her purse and car keys.

"All right," Emily said, starting toward the door. "We can talk more later."

Darla dug her keys out of the space between cushions on the sofa. She looked nervously at Emily. "OK. Please don't tell my mom. Please don't tell anyone."

"I won't say anything to your mother. But I do have to tell the prosecutor. If we get to the point where there is a need for you to testify, you best tell your mom, OK?"

Darla wanted to buy some time. "But that will be a long way off, right?"

"I hope not. But, yes, you have some time."

Right then, Emily wanted to give Jenna's former class-mate some motherly advice. But she resisted telling her that she'd be all right, that this would pass, that they'd all laugh about it someday. Because she knew she wouldn't. Darla Montague had been stupid beyond stupid. It was best for her to live with that and let it sink in.

Emily left Darla's apartment and its baby smells with more questions than answers. Chief among them was whether Darla's relationship with Mitch had anything whatsoever to do with the fact that Mandy was missing. She seemed to be a truthful young woman, one more worried about what her mother might think about her affair with her boss than being involved in a potential criminal matter. One question that gnawed at her was the source of the tip that led her to Darla. Who inside the dealership had it in for Mitchell Crawford? Judging by his reputation, she imagined that the line of people with a score to settle might a long one.

A very long one.

Emily looked out the window. The streets of Cherrystone glittered with ice.

"Jenna, where are you?" she said aloud.

She looked at her watch. It was half past the hour. Jenna's plane had landed long ago and she was due on the Inland Empire Airport Shuttle an hour ago. Emily chatted on the phone with Chris a while—he was doing things around the condo that he hoped to sell in a slowing Seattle real estate market.

"I'm worried. Something could have happened to her."

"I'm sure she's fine," he said. "Jeesh, Em, you act like you're going to put out an APB on your daughter because she's a half hour late."

"Don't think I wouldn't. And she's forty-five minutes late."

Chris laughed and asked Emily if she needed him to bring anything from Seattle when he came for Christmas.

"Chestnuts," she said.

"Really?"

"Yes, fresh ones."

He promised he would, though he didn't have any clue as to where he'd find them.

"Pike Place Market," she said. Just as she was about to tell him which stall to zero in on at the venerable farmers' market in downtown Seattle, a pair of headlights pierced the darkness in front of her house.

The van had arrived.

"She's here," Emily said.

"OK. Tell her I'm looking forward to chilling with her tomorrow."

"Chilling?"

"Hanging. Whatever. Love you, Em."

"I love you, too."

She snapped her phone shut and spun around in time to swing open the door for Jenna.

"Merry Christmas, Mom!"

Forgetting the nightmare of the Mandy Crawford investigation as she drank in her daughter with a hug that meant to convey all of her love *and* shake off the cold night air, Emily knew it would be a great Christmas.

Jenna was home.

Chapter Twenty-one

The white Victorian was full of memories, which was one of the reasons Emily could never let go of it. Her brother hadn't felt that way, so there was no problem in buying him out after their parents died. She wondered why it was that he hadn't felt the connection to the old place.

Maybe it was a girl thing?

The house was as decorated as Emily could manage, given the time she'd spent chasing down phantom leads on the Mandy Crawford case. Chris came over from Seattle on Christmas Eve and the two of them cut some pine boughs from the backyard and put them on the mantel. The woodsy fragrance filled the living room.

Chris put his feet up on the ottoman and leaned back, as if he'd been out working as a lumberjack in the woods of the northwest.

"A lot of work," he said, "but I guess it's worth it."

Jenna poked her head into the room. She brought with her an armload of presents.

"Work," she said, "is all this wrapping I've been doing. Wrapping packages so someone can shred it in two seconds. Some traditions are stupid. Give me a gift card any day."

Emily made a face. "You'd be the first to complain if all you got were gift cards and you know it."

Jenna eased her packages under the tree, while her mother stood back and regarded her handiwork. She'd done a nice job with the tree, putting up the ornaments that Jenna had made as a child alongside those she'd made for her own mother and father. Her favorite was a raggedy angel with a Styrofoam ball for a head, silver pipe cleaners for a halo, and wings made of cut pieces of a paper plate. It was tacky, all right. But sometimes, tacky can be quite charming.

"Oh, Mom," Jenna said, spotting the paper plate angel, "can't we put that in the back where it won't show?"

"Not on your life."

"Ugh. It's embarrassing."

"Only to *you*. When you have kids of your own some-day—not anytime soon, I hope—you'll do the same thing."

"I doubt it."

"Believe me, when it's your own child, you'll love almost everything they do."

Chris looked a little wistful—his own children were grown, then gone, evaporated into their own lives by a bitter divorce.

Emily caught the look and changed the subject.

"Let's see about dinner," she said.

Christmas Eve always meant the biggest turkey that could be found by the cook—first her grandmother, then her mother, then Emily. Emily made a duck sausage stuffing with the fresh chestnuts that Chris bought at Pike Place Market. Roasting the nuts on the stove was his sole contribution to the meal.

In her years as a daughter, wife, and mother, Emily had fixed a turkey every which way—in a paper bag, deep-fried, roasted under a tent of aluminum foil. Jenna had helped with some of the side dishes, of course, and though Emily was far from the point of handing over the turkey duty to her daughter, she enjoyed how much she'd grown into wanting to take over.

"Mom, you and Chris should relax. Maybe there's something on TV that'll keep you occupied?"

Emily smiled at Jenna. She was so glad to have her home for Christmas. She would have kept her disappointment to herself if Jenna had elected to have gone west of the mountains to be with her father and baby half sister, instead of staying put in Cherrystone.

"How about we do this together?" she asked, brandishing a whisk.

"Sounds good, Mom. You seem like you're letting go. That's good."

Emily thought of zinging Jenna back, just as she always did. But not that day. For most of the morning, mother and her daughter ruled the kitchen while Chris Collier staked his claim to a football game preview show.

No one said grace aloud when it came time to eat, but inside each of the three gathered around the table knew how blessed they were. After dinner, they opened their gifts. Chris gave Emily an emerald bracelet and a German gun polish that everyone in law enforcement coveted. She gave him a navy cashmere sweater and a tin of Virginia peanuts that she knew were the very best—and his favorite. Jenna was sure her mom had broken the bank with the lovely cream wool peacoat with gold-toned buttons with pink plaid lining from Juicy. She got a pair of black Ugg boots and a Tiffany heart necklace from her father.

"Nice necklace," Emily said as she fastened it around her daughter's neck.

Jenna touched the heart as it swung in place. "I circled it on a catalog when I was over there. I knew he didn't have an imagination, so why not pick something expensive?"

Chris nodded. "Good girl."

The best gift came from Jenna to her mother.

Emily could have cried when she opened the red box from Talbot's. Inside, was a pair of fully lined pants made in the same worsted wool fabric as her dreaded A-line skirt that paired with her Sheriff's uniform jacket.

"Where did you find these?" Emily said, clearly touched.

Jenna beamed. "Chicago, mom. The world's a lot bigger than Cherrystone and Spokane, you know."

"Thank you, honey." Emily hugged her. It was the most thoughtful gift she could have imagined. She could tell the county council members who complain when they see her around town, the truth. She didn't buy the pants as an FU to their archaic dress code.

"I'm a mother first," she'd say. "This was a gift from my daughter. I intend to wear them."

And stay warm.

Mandy Crawford's disappearance had dominated the week, even the *month*, as Emily Kenyon tried to put together a puzzle for which there were very few pieces. The photos of Tricia. The affair with Darla. The message on the laptop. Things, she was sure, pointed to Mitch as the purveyor of some kind of evil. But on the other hand, there was still no body. No direct evidence pointing to foul play. Just a bunch of innuendo swirling around a man who seemed to deserve all the bad press and rumormongering that he'd garnered. The pressure was mounting, but the investigation was going nowhere.

Chris stayed over through the weekend, in part to spend time with Jenna, who was back in her girlhood bedroom between consulting assignments at various Beta Zeta sorority chapters in the southern region. When there was a single knock on the door followed by the immediate turn of the knob, everyone directed their attention to the young woman who'd been expected for dinner.

And she wouldn't have it any other way.

Shali Patterson never went anywhere without making an impression. Subtlety in her dress, hair, and manner seemed utterly foreign to her. She worked at a Nordstrom store in Seattle after graduating from Cascade University but knew that she'd find something better someday. She just didn't know what it would be. Shali and Jenna had been best friends for years, sorority sisters at Cascade, and were destined to be maids of honor at each other's weddings.

If either found a steady guy that the other approved of, of course. A good guy was as elusive as a pair of sensible shoes.

Both knew that with true, undeniable adulthood holding them prisoner after graduation, the week between Christmas and New Year's was likely to be the only chance they'd have to really catch up and hang out together until summer.

Chris Collier hadn't seen Shali in a while, so when she flopped down on the couch next to Jenna and across from where he sat with Emily, all he could do was grin.

"I think doing hair would have been more fun than med school," she announced.

"I like the pink highlights," Emily said, from her place next to Chris on the sofa by the Christmas tree.

"Thanks, Mrs. Kenyon. Magenta is what I'm going for. I did it myself because, well, I just got tired of looking like everyone else."

"You've never looked like anyone else, Shali," Jenna said, peering up from her laptop, a wide smile on her face. "Not for one minute."

Shali beamed. "It takes some effort to be me, that's for sure." She looked over at Emily and Chris. "Look so cozy, you two."

"We're good," Chris said, resting his hand on Emily's shoulder. "Doing our best."

"That's what my mom says. Do your best!" Shali saw her mother's words as a rallying cry for mediocrity. She would never consider taking up the cause for "doing one's best" if that meant life in Cherrystone and nothing more.

"How is your mother? I haven't seen her for quite some time," Emily said.

Shali looked at Jenna. Obviously, she hadn't let the cat out of the bag.

"I thought Jenna might have told you."

"You asked me not to," Jenna said.

"I would have told, you know."

"I know. But this friendship of ours would never survive if it was between two people just like you. One of us needs to keep a confidence."

"I get that and I'm working on it," Shali said. She looked over at Emily and Chris, enthralled by the Ping-Pong match that was the two young women's disclosure. "Mom met a guy online. Texas, I think. She's sure he's the one."

Emily looked at Jenna, but returned her gaze back to Shali. "I hadn't heard."

"Well," Shali said, shifting her frame on the chair, "Mom never met a man who couldn't charm the pants off her."

"Shali, that's not nice."

"Not nice, maybe. But true." She nudged Jenna to change the subject. "So what's up with you? How's it being the sorority nazi?"

"Let's see," Jenna said, pretending to look at an imaginary list. "I've just entered battle number two with the Beta Zetas at the University of Kentucky."

"You get all the good schools, don't you? Seriously, what's going on with them?"

"Just a bunch of nasty and anonymous e-mails from the girls down there. They're mad at me because they were caught holed up in the lounge smoking pot, drinking rum shots, and watching *America's Next Top Model*—a marathon."

"I love that show," Shali said. "That's what I should have been, instead of doing hair or being a doctor."

Emily leaned closer to her daughter. Jenna looked at Shali, with a stern *shut up now* glance. "What's going on, honey?"

Chris seemed more interested than alarmed. He knew that Jenna could handle just about any situation. She'd proven that long ago. But whether she holds a badge or not, a mom is a mom.

"Just a big mess, Mom. I'm getting e-mails that trash the president, a nice girl named Sarah Lee."

Shali brightened. "Like the frozen cheesecake?"

"Yeah, like that," Jenna said.

"Mrs. Kenyon, do you have anything sweet around here?"

"You know where the freezer is, honey."

Shali got up for the kitchen and Emily, concerned about her daughter, moved into Shali's spot on the couch. Chris, Emily, and Jenna's eyes followed Shali out of the room.

"What are the e-mails about? And what's the national office doing to help?"

Jenna laughed, but it was a laugh choked with sarcasm. "First of all, Nationals does nothing. They talk like they're so concerned about the girls, their welfare. But all they care about is a smoke-free environment and diversity as long as you're white." She clicked on her laptop and read from her e-mails.

"Just so you know, the president here was drunk in her room earlier this week. Three sisters saw her. I'd give you their names, but I don't want to be dragged into this mess."

"It came from the same IP address as this one," Jenna said, scrolling down.

"My father's a lawyer and he says that he can make a

case against the BZs for the way they've treated some of the girls here. Sarah Lee is a big liar and a whore. She's not the kind of girl we want representing any of us here. She's also bulimic."

"Sounds pretty petty, Jenna," Chris put in.

"Tell me about it. I wish I never took this job. Dumb idea."

Shali came back in the room with a frozen Three Musketeers candy bar. She was so excited she looked like she'd won the lottery. "Mrs. Kenyon, you still freeze these. I love you!"

Jenna smiled at her friend, but resisted the opportunity to say something snarky about frozen candy bars. "I was telling them about those stupid girls back in Kentucky," she said. "I'm dealing with a bunch of whiners who feel like the whole world is against them when they all drive BMWs and have spray-on tans."

Shali took a spot on the floor next to the fire. "Tell them about your meeting last week. That sounded so fun."

"This is good, I guess," Jenna said, kind of enjoying the attention of her mother and her detective boyfriend. *Or whatever he was.* "I thought it would die down. You know, Thanksgiving, Christmas, the holiday season. No such luck. One of the girls called Nationals saying that someone peed on her pillow and cut the straps on all of her tank tops and bras."

"Sounds very mature," Chris said. "Aren't these girls adults?"

"Age has nothing to do with maturity," Emily said, doing everything she could not to land her eyes on Shali's pink hair.

Jenna was on a roll. "So they had this big meeting. Everything is supposed to be secret, of course. No girl who is being admonished by the chapter or Nationals is supposed to speak of it to anyone. But Sarah Lee did. I got to the meeting place—a banquet room in the back of a pizza restaurant off campus—and I had to walk past at least two dozen BZs. They glared at me and said that I was being unreasonable."

"Sounds like a Lifetime movie. You know the part, where the girl has to walk past all of her classmates that know that she was really raped by the quarterback with the shaved pecs and sexy stubble on his face."

"Tiffany Amber in *No One Heard Her Scream*."

"Yes. That's how it felt. A very Tiffany Amber moment."

Chris looked at Emily and Jenna. They clearly understood Shali's reference to a TV movie. He didn't have a clue, but said nothing. Admitting he didn't know who or what Tiffany Amber was, would only serve to make him older than his fifty years.

And he wasn't doing that.

"So, anyway," Jenna went on, "enough of that tangent. The bottom line here is that Sarah Lee's dad, the lawyer, threatened to take the BZs for everything they had if they didn't fix the problem. He used words that made the national office shudder with fear."

Chris, once more, looked puzzled.

Emily touched his shoulder. "This is a shot in the dark, but is it the *you're fostering a hostile learning environment*?"

"Yup," Jenna said, "the gold standard."

"So what happened?" Chris asked.

"Nothing. Same as usual. The nice girls get bullied by the ones who have the loudest parents with the most money."

"Sounds like a Little League baseball game," Emily said.

"That's about right, Mom. The only thing that I hate worse than the drama of a dispute that's escalated to the national level is making a road trip to help some failing house build up its pledge base."

"That doesn't sound so bad," Chris said. "I mean, it's all about marketing, right?"

"Honestly, Chris, sometimes it feels like it's all about babysitting. I know it isn't much longer and I'll be off to law school by this time next year, but I really do hate what I'm doing."

Emily wanted to kick her ex-husband and his greedy wife Dani to the curb just then. If they had helped out a little more, Jenna might have taken another route to finance more of her education. Emily wondered if she had miscalculated and should have pushed for more college loans. She just couldn't, having experienced the burden firsthand with her own student loans and David's from medical school.

"Who's hungry?" Shali asked. "Because I am."

"You always are," Jenna said, ending the conversation about money, her dad, and bratty sorority girls.

"Your mom can cook. My mom never met a can opener she didn't like. What's that I smelled when I came in here?"

Emily stood and looked toward the kitchen. "Nothing fancy. Just the best meal you'll ever have. Come on. Let's eat."

"Just a sec," Jenna said turning her attention back to her laptop screen. "I have to finish this blog post."

"What are you doing, blogging? That's so five minutes ago."

"I know. The headquarters women think it is so 'cutting-edge' to blog. But that's how we share the information that builds stronger sisterhood or something like that."

She finished typing the entry:

Hi Girls,

I'm looking so forward to seeing all of you in Dixon. I might be late, so dinner might not work out. Could someone save me a late plate, just in case? We'll have so much fun talking about recruitment and how we can maximize our efforts

to ensure that we have the very best new pledges.
Go BeeZees!

Love, Jenna Kenyon, your Southern District
Consultant

She posted a happy-face icon and powered down.
Dinner smelled so good.

A thousand miles away, a man logged on to Jenna's blog. Her picture filled him with an unbridled rage that he was sure would be transparent to anyone who saw his face, even days later. She was pretty, sure. He tried hard to read more into what she was saying on her blog. How it spoke of her frivolous nature. How it indicated that she was a callous bitch who cared only about herself.

And now she was about to get what she deserved. She was on his list.

Chapter Twenty-two

Tricia Wilson's photographs were haunting. Emily had seen horrific images similar to them before, of course. As a Seattle cop working homicide or special victims, she knew firsthand what the brutal hand of an enraged man could do to the small bones of a child or a woman without the strength to fight back. She knew that when people indicated someone had been beaten "black and blue" that it was really a shorthand for a range of colors from indigo to red to blue to yellow, even green. Human skin could change hues nearly as fast as gasping fish on a riverbank. *Just like that.* From pink or brown to splash of hideous color that told the world the color of pain.

But Tricia's photos weren't like that. Emily looked deeper into the Polaroids. The colors were crisp, rather than muddy. Distinct, rather than blurry.

Something's awry here, she thought. It passed through her thoughts that Tricia had said that she kept copies and returned the negatives. She figured that the woman, caught up in memories of the past, had made a mistake. Polaroid cameras didn't use negatives.

Jenna caught her mom by the coffeepot, waiting to steal a

cup before it finished brewing the next morning. It was clear that she was lost in thought, distracted by something.

"What's bothering you, mom?"

"Honey, it's the photos. Something isn't right."

"Mom, don't get caught up in this one. Not like last time."

In a way, the comment was sweet. Emily took it as such. Jenna was looking out for her mother. She knew how involved she could get when it came to abuse cases. The previous summer, thirty-one-year-old Maria Hernandez was beaten so badly by her husband that it took more than a hundred stitches and a metal plate to mend her injuries. Emily didn't sleep for weeks when she worked that case, hoping against hope that by the time Maria was released she would agree to testify against her husband, Carlos.

But it never got that far.

Carlos was there to pick her up the day of her discharge. The family's van was packed and headed south, out of town.

Family members in Cherrystone haven't heard from either since.

Emily couldn't get the photos out of her mind.

"I know. I know. But these are so graphic."

"Just keep doing your best, Mom. You'll get him."

They talked awhile longer, Jenna saying that things at the sorority house were a disaster. The girls wanted to host a party—as another sorority had done the week before—but they were dangerously close to being put on probation.

"Stick to your guns, Jenna."

"I will. Just like you."

Emily poured some more coffee and searched for another container of creamer. She knew what it was that bothered her. It was the fact that Tricia's injuries were so very visible. She hadn't been beaten until her kidneys failed. She hadn't been punched in the stomach. These were Nicole Brown Simpson–type injuries—visible and overt.

For a man who cares about what everyone thinks about him, she thought, *you'd think he'd have punched her where it didn't show. He wasn't only a wife beater, he was a stupid one.*

As they had since before they wore bras or even had a concept that they'd really like boys enough to touch them, Jenna and Shali retreated into her bedroom—a room that had once been her mother's and might one day be the guest room for a little girl of her own. Jenna half-smiled as the thought came over her. If she found a decent guy, got a job, worked awhile, well then maybe.

Maybe not in that exact order.

In some ways, the room was a museum to her past. The old Mac computer that she'd used growing up was on the desk, a collector's item, her mother mused when Jenna wanted to trash it. It had long since been replaced by a sleek new laptop. Next to a collection of dried corsages—from weddings, mostly—a framed poster of the cover of *People* magazine hung over the bed. The celebrity on the cover was Mariah Carey, but Jenna wasn't really a Mariah fan. She never had been. Just below Mariah's photo was a tagline that referenced when Jenna was held captive by Nick Martin, Cherrystone's crazed kid. Jenna had initially thought she was helping the boy, but in the end, he taught her the greatest lesson of all: Not everyone wants to be rescued.

Date in a Dungeon—Girl Held Captive Tells Her Story

Shali looked at the magazine cover as she flopped on the bed. "Why do you keep that shitty magazine, Jen?"

Jenna sprawled out next to her friend, tilting her head way back to take in Mariah's photo. "I don't know. I guess to remind me how close I came to losing everything. Mom said that it was better to 'own' your past then run from it."

"Your mom is a nut."

Jenna laughed. "She is, but I love her. She's my mom."

"Better by far than mine."

"No argument, there."

Shali picked at a small blemish on her chin. "So tell me about this so-called consultant job. Is it as bad as we thought it would be?"

"Worse." Jenna stopped herself. There were parts of the job she liked—meeting people and problem solving, to name two. But there was an overdose of self-pity and self-absorption that seemed to come with the chapter insignia.

"These girls have everything," she said, "but they think they have nothing at all."

Shali stopped picking at her pimple. "They sound like us, don't they?"

Jenna shook her head, and the bed rocked a little. "Look, I was mixed up with a junior serial killer and I have a father that would rather align himself with his new wife and re-placement kid than be a father to me. That's me. Let's talk about you, now."

"Let's not." Shali sighed.

Jenna got up and retrieved a brush from the bedside table.

"I like your hair that way. Looks prettier than that goth shit."

For a girl with pink hair, that was saying a lot and Jenna smiled. She'd dyed her hair black the summer before college, thinking that she needed a change. It also fit her mood at the time. She just didn't want to look like the girl who'd been held captive. Eventually she let it return to her light brown. That fall, for the very first time, she colored it blond.

"Being a blonde isn't edgy, but I think it suits me. It kind of makes me feel, I don't know, a little invincible, when I go after what I want."

Shali brightened. "A little blonde ambition is a good thing."

"I guess." Jenna set down the brush, pulling some long golden strands from the bristles and dropping them in the trash can. She thought about Shali's "blonde ambition" comment for a second. It was a very good line. She'd use it in her next Beta Zeta blog post.

Jenna had no idea that a thousand miles away, a man in his basement office was eagerly waiting for her next blog post. He was counting on Jenna to be as thorough as ever—detailing where she was going to be, who she was going to see.

It was all about timing.

Chapter Twenty-three

Miller's Marsh Pond, outside of Cherrystone

The thought of a decomposing body is enough to make the skin crawl on the living. But decomp is always the natural outcome of a death. A stealthy decomp is the killer's hope for lifelong freedom. Maybe even *life* itself.

A grave, not the proverbial shallow one, is always the best course of action. Bury the corpse deep enough in a remote location, scatter debris over the surface in a haphazard manner, and hope that no one stumbles upon it. That's been a successful path for all of the murderers no one has ever heard about.

Dismemberment works well, too. Chop up the corpse in the bathtub, disperse the bits and pieces as convenience allows, and keep fingers crossed.

The killer of the woman in the water had done a mental pros-and-cons chart and decided that while enhancing the convenience of disposal, dismemberment was too messy a course of action. Blood spatter from a power saw almost always goes in a place that escapes detection by the killer with a scrub brush. Luminol with its eerie blue glow is a chemical finger that points right at the killer.

When a human body is surreptitiously dumped in the water, it becomes food for fish, turtles, and the other scavengers of the dead. If the body doesn't get consumed, gases swell in the tissues and fill the cavities, distending the organs. Enough time in the water turns a dead person into a balloon, bringing it to the surface for discovery by a boater or in the nets of an unlucky fisherman.

Dead bodies and water don't mix.

In Florida, a body can be consumed by alligators in a sunny afternoon. In the open sea of the Pacific, sharks dine on the fleshy morsels of what had once been a human being with the kind of glee that brings to mind the phrase *feeding frenzy*. In particularly pure and deep waters like Washington State's Lake Crescent, bodies have been found preserved decades after they'd been hidden there.

That wasn't going to happen with the body that he'd dumped that flat, moonless night. That body wasn't going to be eaten, weighed down, or preserved at the depths.

The weather warmed and for a short time, the snow turned to rain. Mandy was about to make her return.

Chapter Twenty-four

Jack Fletcher had left his youngest son's tackle box in the trunk. All bundled in heavy coats, hats, and gloves, Jack and his kids had made it halfway down the path toward Miller's Marsh Pond. There, ice fishing was the order of the afternoon in the days after Christmas. *Damn, the weather had likely ruined this year's outing.* A seesawing patch of weather had brought a thaw and then another hard freeze—it was an unusual occurrence that the big-city weatherman liked to call "Pineapple Express" to indicate that the genesis of the storm had come from Hawaii. It meant a lot of rain on the western part of the state and snow on the eastern region, including Cherrystone. This season, the Pineapple Express blew through with a hot breath that drove temps up to 55 degrees for forty-eight hours.

And now it was back down below freezing. New snow was coming that evening and winter was headed back with a vengeance.

"Watch the boys, Stacy," Jack told his daughter, a fittingly sullen girl of fourteen. "I'm going back to the car to get Brandon's tackle."

"You always leave the boys with me," she said. "You ought to pay me, Dad. I'm the live-in sitter around here."

Jack pretended not to hear her rant about watching her younger brothers, Brandon and Kevin. He'd thought of asking Stacy to get the tackle back at the car, but he knew she'd complain about that, too.

"You use me like a slave, Dad!"

The Fletchers had packed up early that morning for their annual post-Christmas fishing trip, just to the west of Cherrystone. It was Dad's time with the kids. His ex-wife, Sherry, had a new beau and between the holidays the pair headed off for a vacation in Hawaii. Jack was Mr. Mom just then and he didn't mind it one bit. He knew that cold weather would come back in a flash and that day might be the very last one before rain, snow, and bundle-up weather. Jack had black curly hair he fluffed up to camouflage a receding hairline. He had a stocking cap, leaving his curls as fringe.

He made his way down the path toward the car. Only one other car was parked in the lot, indicating to him that the place would pretty much be all theirs that day. He smiled. Jack Fletcher's silver Prius gleamed in the winter sun, screaming out loud to the world that he loved the earth.

He pressed the trunk key into the lock, and it popped open. He stared into the blackness below and his heart sank.

"What the?"

He moved a blanket, just in case. But it was obvious. The box was gone. He'd left it at home on the kitchen counter.

"This is the kind of day I'm having," he said, closing the lid. "Stacy's going to blame me for this."

As he slammed down the trunk, he heard a scream.

"Dad!"

It was Stacy's voice. He turned around and looked for his daughter.

"Dad! Come here quick!"

Jack squinted into the sun, the light blinding him with the shimmer of gold off the icy surface of the water.

Something was wrong.

"Stacy! Kevin! Brandon!" He called out. "I'm coming." He started running to the spot where he left his children, but they weren't there. Instead, about fifty yards away, he saw them huddled at the edge. The sun wrapped them in a halo of light.

Were all three there?

"What is it? Brandon? Kevin?"

"We're fine, Dad," Stacy said, her voice breaking, as she turned around to face her father. "Oh, Dad!" She lunged for him, and he gladly held her. At that instant Stacy was no longer a flippant teenager. In the time it took for her father to go to the car, she was once more a little girl. A scared little girl.

"What is it, honey?" he asked.

She started to cry and pointed to a spot about ten yards from shore.

Partially cemented in the cracking ice among the degraded greenery of a winter-dead patch of aquatic plants was the swollen figure of a child, a teenager. It appeared she'd been wrapped in a dark blue blanket, maybe a sleeping bag. She was facedown in the water, her hair swirling like a halo on the re-frozen surface. Her ice-sheathed skin looked waxy and white. He didn't like what he was seeing, but Jack craned his neck to get a closer view.

No, it wasn't a child, but a woman. He could see a wristwatch and wedding band.

The boys just stood there, their eyes fastened on the corpse.

"Want me to poke her with a stick?" It was Kevin, the eight-year-old, whose mother once caught him eating canned dog food off the broken end of a hula hoop—with his older brother, Brandon, urging him on.

"I'll get a stick for you," Brandon said.

Pinpricks of sweat beaded on Jack's brow. He gently pulled his kids away.

"No stick. Let's go back to the car," he said. "I need to call the sheriff."

It was almost dark when Emily Kenyon and Jason Howard, along with two patrol officers, arrived at Miller's Marsh Pond.

His kids in a warm cruiser with a patrol officer, Jack Fletcher led the sheriff and her deputy to the body, half frozen, facedown in a sheath of ice and snow.

"How are your children?" Emily asked. "It must have been quite a fright for them."

"It was, but they'll be OK. I think my oldest—the girl, Stacy—is the most shook up over this. The boys wanted to prod the body with a stick to see if it was a doll or something."

"Not a doll, that's for sure," Emily said, as she bent closer to the still-frozen edge. She saw the watch and the ring on the hand that was curled slightly upward. She could see that the woman was likely clad in jeans or a different, softer fabric. Through the layer of ice that covered the torso like a shield, she could make out a bra and the fragments of a torn blouse.

It had to be her.

"Mr. Fletcher," she said, "we'll need to get a statement from you. But we don't need it tonight. Take your kids home and come down to the station tomorrow, first thing. Can you work that out?"

"Thank you. I appreciate that. We came here for a memorable day, you know, a tradition with Dad. A day that we'd remember."

Emily knew where he was going and her heart went out to the children. "They'll never forget what they saw and I'm sorry for that. They'll always remember how their dad kept his cool and called the police, just like he should."

He smiled. "Hope so."

Emily turned her gaze toward her earnest deputy.

"Let's cordon off the area, Jason. Spokane crime scene techs are on their way, but this dead girl's not going anywhere. We're going to have to chip her out and that'll take time and daylight."

Emily didn't say so to Jason and he didn't say it to her. But as they stood there watching Jack Fletcher and his family drive away, both had a pretty good idea whose body they just found. Even without the face, the long swirls of reddish blond hair were a big indicator, but there was something else that both of them had seen. The waistband on the trousers was elastic.

The dead body was wearing maternity pants.

It had to be Mandy Crawford.

The two Spokane crime techs set up a string grid that ran from the path by the shoreline to about four yards past the dead body in the ice. It was painstaking work and the wind nipped hard at their unprotected faces. They ran infrared lights over the soil, looking for anything out of the ordinary. The snow had come and gone, so it wasn't likely that any trace could be found, but the two women who'd come down to process the scene for Cherrystone left not one single inch undisturbed.

Chapter Twenty-five

Spokane

Casper Wilhelm had been Spokane County medical examiner for decades. So long that Emily Kenyon was sure he had to have been the ME when she was in high school, and she didn't want to do the math on that one. Dr. Wilhelm was white haired, foul mouthed, and as brilliant as could be. His reputation outside of the region was so stellar that many thought there had to be something wrong with him because he'd never left for a bigger city.

"Hell," he said, quite plainly at a conference in Chicago, "dead is dead. Doesn't matter much where you live when you die. A body's a damn body. I like Spokane. What's more, my wife does."

The ME's assistant, a pretty young woman named Denise in a spotless white lab coat, offered coffee and Emily thanked her. She sipped it from a disposable cup and waited on the blue couch just outside Dr. Wilhelm's door.

It was 8:45 A.M. When she called after Mandy's body had been found, Dr. Wilhelm told her to be there at 8:30.

"Not a second later. We'll start sharply."

He'd said it with a short laugh. "You know, all autopsies start with something sharp—a scalpel."

Emily resisted the eye roll at the time. "Yes, of course."

"My grandson thinks it's funny," he said.

In reality, she didn't think there was much to laugh at. A dead pregnant woman had been cracked out of the ice at Miller's Marsh Pond. It was clear that she'd been murdered. No one ends up in a frozen lake in a sleeping bag in the middle of winter by accident.

All the while on the drive up, Emily considered every bit of the terror that Mandy had likely endured. She could see the young woman in her mind's eye, battling the evil of a man who cared nothing for her life or the precious baby she carried. She could hear her voice as she screamed or begged.

I hear you, Mandy, she thought. *We all do.*

Dr. Wilhelm told her to be there sharply, but it seemed he was running late. She sat outside his office door, sipping on coffee Denise provided from a thermos carafe next to a counter crammed with medical supplies. She could hear his belly laugh as he talked with someone on the phone. Clearly, Dr. Wilhelm was a man who loved his work.

"Donut?" he said as he emerged from his office. "Denise! Get Sheriff Kenyon a goddamn donut to go with that lousy coffee of yours! I want one, too!"

He patted his protruding belly. "Like I need one more, you know."

Emily took a donut, because to say she didn't want one was akin to telling Santa to screw off.

"Delicious," she said.

"Let's get down to it. She's prepped and on the table. Water's running. Did you see Mr. Crawford?"

Emily looked puzzled. "When? I mean, not for a few days."

The ME shrugged. "Half hour ago. Just before you arrived. He came in and did the ID." The ME reached for a second—maybe a third—donut. Sugar rained on the floor and he pulverized it with his heel. "We tried to notify him that we might have found Mandy, but he wasn't home."

"But this hasn't been on the news. Did you leave a message or something?"

Dr. Wilhelm swallowed his last bite. The man ate like a snapping turtle.

"Negative. He said he heard it on the scanner that a body had been found. He was sure it was Mandy. He drove up first thing. Denise almost decked him to get him to wait his turn. Wanted him to take a chill pill. Didn't you, honey?"

Denise, a woman who a moment ago was a donut server, was a tough chick when she had to be.

"You got that right," she said. "The prick went right around me and found her in two seconds flat. He didn't want to follow procedure. Anyway, I don't care. He ID'd her. Cried like a baby."

The news surprised Emily.

"Really?"

"Yeah, you know the type. Big explosive sobs, followed by hacking and then the whole apology for being so 'emotional.' Jesus, the woman was his wife, pregnant with his baby. He had a right to fall apart."

Emily hated Mitch Crawford, but she almost felt sorry for him just then. The way Denise described it, the fellow was distraught—as he ought to be.

"Did he say anything?"

"Yeah, you'll love this. He says, 'Why, Mandy? Why did you do this to me? I don't know if I can ever forgive you.' "

Emily watched from the corner of her eye as Denise removed the pale gray drape that covered Mandy's body. Although the baby had been removed, her abdomen was still distended.

"Do what?" she asked, suppressing the horror of what she was seeing. Somehow it helped to focus on anger at Mitch

Crawford for something callous that he'd said, rather than the evil he'd done.

"I dunno. Die? But it bugged me that he seemed to blame her for doing something to him when she was laying there like a thawing turkey the day before Thanksgiving."

"I know the guy. Enough said," Emily said.

Chapter Twenty-six

Cherrystone

"You all right?"

Jason Howard stood in the doorway of Emily's office, his head cocked in concern.

Emily smiled tentatively. "I'm fine. I'm going to dig into the case again. Camille's out of town visiting her mother and I'm trying to button things down on Crawford before she gets back."

"Can I help?"

Emily knew that her deputy only wanted to be useful, but his offer only annoyed her. It wasn't that he wasn't up to the task, it was more about the fact that she couldn't piece together what was troubling her.

"No, I'm good," she said, a little too dismissively. She saw the hurt in his eyes. "You grab some lunch."

"Bring you back something? Going to the grill."

Emily declined the offer. "No, I actually brown-bagged it today. Such a glamorous life I have as the Cherrystone sheriff."

Jason tried to brush off the rebuke with one of his good-natured smiles. He buttoned up his heavy blue coat and left.

Emily knew that he'd bring back one of those big pink frosted cookies that she once remarked she liked, but could really barely eat half of one. One more bite ensured a sugar overload and an afternoon of the crash-and-burn.

Pink icing can be a real killer.

Everything she had was in front of her. Emily looked at the sheaf of reports that she, her deputy, and the CSIs from Spokane had compiled on the Mandy Crawford missing persons case. There was nothing there. She wondered how an inch of paper could contain so little information. Mandy was at work one day. Gone the next. She'd been seen walking the dog by a woman who also misidentified the breed of the Crawfords' canine. So that was no good. She hadn't been observed by any of the clerks in Spokane at the mall. Her credit cards hadn't been used.

She was gone. *Poof.* Mandy had vanished.

Every day put the young mother-to-be in greater and greater danger. Emily didn't tell the media or the local women who'd come to help search for Mandy Crawford about the dire statistics behind the disappearance of any pregnant woman. Most were dead at the hands of their husbands, control freaks who refused to have the focus shift from their personal and sexual needs to a child who'd suck up every last bit of their wives' attention. They viewed those babies growing inside the distended abdomens as parasites stealing the attractiveness of a body whose sole purpose had been to pleasure them.

Such murders were about rage fueled by envy.

She looked down at the paper with the stats from the coroner.

Name: Amanda Lynn Crawford
Height: 5'2"
Weight: 100 lbs
Age: 29

Hair: Blond

Eyes: Brown

Marks/Tattoos: A pink rose on lower back.

External evidence of injury: Postmortem ligature on wrists and ankles. Markings correspond with chains recovered from the scene.

Cause of Death: Asphyxiation.

Special note: The victim carried a full-term fetus, a female.

Emily had seen the body at the coroner's in Spokane, so she held the horrific visual whenever she went anywhere. Not just Mandy's case. But the others, too. Emily sometimes saw blood spatter in pizza sauce. The sound of a chopping knife against a wooden cutting board often conjured up images of extreme brutality. One time, when she had the misfortune of running over an opossum, she felt the wheels crunch and she thought of a little boy that had been run over by his older brother.

"You have that look on your face," her daughter Jenna had said one time when they were making stir-fry.

"What look?"

"Mom, the *look*. You know. The *look* that means you're thinking about those celery sticks as something disgusting. Something dead. Bones or something."

Emily tried to shake it off, protesting to Jenna that she couldn't be further from the truth.

"Honey, I did have my mind on work, but not that. Something boring. No bones."

But it was a lie.

In time, Emily improved upon masking the look. There was only one thing that troubled her more than the pictures and the thoughts of what sick men do to the weak and frightened. She loathed how a vital young woman like Mandy—after being brutally murdered—could face the further indignity of being nothing more than a few words on a report.

Name, height, weight, age, hair, eyes . . . cause of death.

She studied the pristine pages of the report. In time, they'd be covered with the oily spots of someone's lunch, they'd be folded, maybe torn, as the days and the weeks of the investigation passed. Cherrystone was going to a computerized system in the new year, and no doubt Mandy Crawford's murder would be the last of the old-school folders in the archive of a county that had seen only twenty-one murders in its entire history.

Emily looked at the photo of the body. There was a black swipe against Mandy's wrists, ligature marks had been determined by the coroner to be postmortem. The killer had tied her to some chains in order to sink the corpse into the icy water.

Hoping, of course, that she'd stay put.

But Mandy didn't. She literally rose from the dead.

Chapter Twenty-seven

Lewiston, Idaho

Nothing much ever happened in that remote patch of Idaho. But that day was to be different.

Every morning for the past decade or so, Leroy Evans pulled a cowboy hat over a stocking cap and saddled up his old bay mare, named Screamin' Demon, to survey the security of the fence that ran the boundary of his eighty-two-acre ranch just east of Lewiston, Idaho. Neighbors four miles away had crossed their German shepherds with wolves for some goddamn stupid reason. Ever since then, a pack ran free in the fields looking to wreak havoc and make a meal out of someone's livestock.

Leroy had raised sheep and cattle to great success, and had even dabbled in ostriches and emus. The mammoth birds were a complete bust—their low-fat meat and supple leather never really caught on with butchers or mass-market shoe manufacturers. He had kept only about fifty of the birds, and gathered their eggs for a fellow who etched them with tribal designs that didn't mean a darn thing but were hot sellers at craft shows.

It was cold that morning. Icy. Most mornings that time of year were. Leroy went east first, so he could catch the slight warmth of the rising sun on his face as it tripped over the Sawtooth Range. About ten minutes into his ride, at the point where his property hit the main highway, he stopped Screamin' Demon.

Strange place for an O egg, he thought, as he dismounted, then bent down to pick it up. Something wasn't quite right. He pushed back some bunched-up dead ryegrass with the toe of his range-scarred boots.

"Hey!" he said, loud enough to echo.

It wasn't an ostrich egg. At least, none that he'd ever seen had long strands of dark hair attached.

"Come on, SD," he said as he jumped back on her. "We got a call to make."

Leroy Evans didn't know it, but he'd found the skull of Tiffany Anne Jacobs.

The Idaho state crime lab in Boise made a quick study of the teeth and the dental work of two missing persons from that region. Tiffany Jacobs had lost a back molar when she cracked a tooth on a corn nut when she was fourteen. She had a dental implant to replace the tooth. The silver post gleamed under the lights of the lab.

Crime scene tape flapped in the wind as the sun went down on the day of the discovery of Tiffany Jacobs's skull, two ribs and a femur. Cops and crime scene investigators from Lewiston PD and the Idaho State Police canvassed the area, hoping to find more.

"Body must have been dragged around by coyotes or a pack of those ornery wolf-dog hybrids," one of the investigators said as he returned to his car. "She might have been dumped out here. Or she could have been dumped a mile from here and dragged. Damn coyotes are pretty strong."

From a vantage point on the highway, a TV camera focused its lens on the ongoing investigation. News reports had already leaked the discovery of the missing young woman.

A sorority sister still at Cascade called Jenna with the news. It hit her like a hard swung sap to the stomach. The truth of what happened to Tiffany had finally come; it was ugly and final. She was still processing the information when her mother came home.

"Did you hear the news?" Jenna said, not waiting a split second for Emily to shed her heavy woolen coat and set her purse down on the foyer table.

Emily wondered if Mitch Crawford had made another plea for the cops to back off. "What news?"

Jenna started to cry. "Oh, Mom! They found Tiff's body in Lewiston. Mom, she's dead."

Emily knew about Tiffany's disappearance, of course. But she'd almost half believed that she'd run off with someone. It was the story given by an old boyfriend, one usually not believed. Emily knew that Jenna and Tiffany were not particularly close. Even so, the information was devastating.

"I'm so sorry, honey. I hadn't heard," she said, wrapping her daughter in her arms. "That's forty miles from the university."

Jenna gulped a breath. "I know. She'd been there all the while."

Emily could feel Jenna relax a little, comforted by her touch, as always. "I'm so sorry, honey."

"Mom, I sort of hoped . . . You know, I *hoped* that she'd just come back. That she'd played a trick on us or maybe was just being a flake."

Emily, still holding Jenna, stepped back and looked in her daughter's eyes. "Is there anything I can do for you? I don't really know Mrs. Jacobs, but I could call her."

"No, that's OK, Mom. I'll do that. I'll find out when the

funeral is. Can you keep an eye on the investigation? I don't want to be the last to know if the killer is one of the boys we know from the frats."

"I'll phone the Lewiston PD now," Emily said.

This was a friend of her daughter's, and while they were not close, it was a tragic outcome. She piled her coat on the sofa and started for the bedroom. There were few secrets between mother and daughter, but such a call warranted some privacy. She dialed Lewiston PD, explained who she was and that her daughter knew the girl. A young woman working in investigations said she'd let her know if anything broke with the case.

"We're still figuring out jurisdiction issues. Not sure if we're the crime scene or the police on the other side of the river in Washington should handle."

"Thanks."

"Sheriff Kenyon, I will tell you that it'll probably take one of those TV forensic docs to give us the cause of death on this one. I'm told not much was left of her. Lots of animal activity."

Emily hung up, feeling the discouragement of the young woman's words take over. Cause of death was crucial to determining the *who* of a murder case. If she'd been shot, it might have been random, a stranger. If she'd been stabbed, it more than likely could have been someone she knew. Same with strangulation. Murders of the close kind were almost always personal.

Done by someone who knew the victim or selected them for a purpose.

A bag of bones would tell few tales.

More than a thousand miles away, a man logged on to his computer and typed into a search engine the words TIFFANY

+ JACOBS. The quest was a nightly ritual, one he'd under-taken since he dumped her body in a ditch in Idaho.

For the past weeks, there had been nothing new. Just the forty-some news accounts about the missing sorority sister from Cascade University. There were some photos showing the beautiful young woman, some of her parents, some shots of the campus. Until that particular night, the man wondered if she'd ever be found.

And I didn't even try very hard to hide the bitch, he thought.

On that particular evening, there was some news. The number of articles about Tiffany Jacobs had suddenly dou-bled.

Missing Coed's Body Found

A Lewiston rancher found the remains of what police have confirmed as the body of Tiffany Anne Jacobs, 21, in a field near his home yesterday morning, Idaho State Po-lice reported.

Exact cause of death has yet to be deter-mined, although the manner of death has been classified as a homicide.

"I'm sorry to be the one to bring bad news to the young girl's family. I wish I hadn't found her," said rancher Leroy Evans, 66. "I sure hope they catch the guy who did this."

The Idaho State Police crime lab in Boise has processed the evidence. Identi-fication was made with dental records.

A person of interest—a 25-year-old man from Washington State—had been questioned, and then released. CSIs at his apartment produced five plastic bags of evidence.

"We still need the public to help us,"
said a spokesperson for the ISP. "If you
have any information on Tiffany's case,
please give us a call."

A woman's voice called from another part of the house.
"Dinner's ready! Everybody wash up and come to the table."

The man at the computer shut down the computer and
grinned. He had information on Tiffany's murder, all right,
but he wasn't going to give any of it to the police. He hoped
that the twenty-five-year-old nameless man would be named
soon—as a suspect. It was always nice when the police
found someone to blame. They'd done it before and, he
hoped, they'd do it again.

"Coming, honey!" he called out. *A nice dinner sounded
so good.*

Chapter Twenty-eight

Cherrystone

Hillary Layton plopped herself down in the visitor's chair facing Emily Kenyon's desk.

"I left my husband in the car," she said.

The last time the mother of the murder victim and her baby and the sheriff who had vowed to catch the killer had met was at the church vigil more than a month before. Mrs. Layton wore charcoal pants and a heavy red wool coat. Peeking out from the triangle of fabric by her neck was a silver sweater with flecks of metallic yarn. It had probably been a Christmas sweater meant for an occasion far different than the one she was observing at that moment. She brought with her a small Monarch Vodka box, its top cut off on three sides and flapping at its hinge as she took a seat.

"Tell him to get in here," Emily said. "It's so cold outside."

Hillary brushed off the suggestion as she unzipped her coat. Sparkly drops of water fell to the floor. The snow on her coat had melted. "He'll lose it if he comes in here."

"Lose it?"

"You know, he loses his temper. He's got a pretty mean one."

Emily tried not to let her worry betray her. Nothing hurt more than attacks from a victim's family. She tried to keep a reassuring countenance on her face, but she could feel the knife being inserted.

The knife cut.

"I see," was all she could say.

Hillary Layton was a kind woman. Everything about her said so. She'd taught school. She'd volunteered for the state Democratic Party when they pushed for health care for children who weren't covered. She had six cats and a bird.

But she no longer had her only child. Mandy was gone.

"Look," Hillary said. "I know you are doing your best. But tomorrow we bury Amanda and Chrissy."

Emily hadn't heard that a name had been picked out by either Mitch or Mandy. She wondered if Hillary had taken it upon herself to name the dead baby. She said nothing, though. She let the woman talk.

"I know Mitch killed them. I know that you know he did. What I don't get," she said, her voice cracking, despite her attempts to hold it together, "is why you aren't doing more to nail the bastard."

"Mrs. Layton," Emily said, using as calm a voice as she could, "You certainly know better than that."

Hillary fidgeted with the box. "I know you've tried. But that smug ass is running around acting as though he doesn't have a care in the world. By the looks of it, I'd say he's right." Her gaze narrowed on Emily.

The knife was cutting.

"I know you want details, but we're not there. I know you are frustrated. I get that. We all do."

"You know something, Sheriff Kenyon?"

"What?"

"I really expected more than this from you. I remember reading about your daughter's disappearance and how you went after the killer with everything you had. You got him, didn't you?"

"Yes, I did."

"I'm asking for the same here. I . . . I . . . I know we can't bring Mandy or Chrissy back from the dead. I know that with every fiber of my being. But I still hear my daughter's voice when I pick up the phone."

"I'm so sorry," Emily said.

"When I hear a baby cry, I wonder what Chrissy's cry might sound like. Would it be like her mother's? Mandy had a wail that could crack plates when she was a baby."

The tears rolled down, but Mrs. Layton ignored them.

Emily handed her a tissue, but she refused it.

"I want your officers, your staff, here to see my tears. I want people to know that my heart is broken."

"We all know it. We all are devastated by your loss."

"Can I say something to you, mother to mother?" Mandy's mother asked.

"Of course."

"Did you let it pass through your mind even once when your daughter was missing that she might be dead?"

Emily's response was immediate. "Yes, I did."

"Did you ever imagine that you might never see her again?"

"It was my darkest thought, yes."

"Hold on to that. Take that deep inside, Sheriff. That's how I feel right now. I know that there is no end to it. Luke and I will never, ever hold our daughter again. We will never know what kind of joy a little girl like Chrissy might have brought to our lives. To the lives of others."

"We will not rest until justice has been brought in your daughter's case," Emily said, wishing she could reel back the

words. The phrase sounded so cold and impersonal. "I will
not rest," she said as if the echo of her own sentiments would
resonate with the grieving mother.

"My husband thinks that you will do your best. He also
thinks that Mitch is probably smarter than you. I don't know
about any of that. All I know is that I need you to fully understand that I will be a thorn in your side for the rest of your
life." Hillary looked down at the contents of the box, then
looked back at Emily.

Emily locked her eyes on Mandy's mother. "Mrs. Layton,
I am good at my job. I will do my best."

"I know. I know. We had to make an appointment to come
to the house to pick up some photos and things for the funeral tomorrow. We wanted to set up a memorial board and
table at the front of the church so people could pass by and
see the little pieces of our daughter's life. Small stuff. But
the fragments of her life cut short."

Emily wanted to do more than just offer words to comfort
the grieving woman sitting across from her, peering into a
box of all she had left of her daughter. But protocol, laws,
and common sense made it clear that boundaries were more
important that being human. She hated that part of her job.
Words were the only salve.

"That must have been so very hard," she said. "I'm
sorry."

"He—I hate saying his name—put what he thought we
wanted to collect in this box and set it outside the front
door." She reached inside the liquor box and pulled out a few
photos of her daughter. "She was seven in this photo," she
said, pointing to a vacation shot taken on a gray, windswept
beach. "You can tell we're in Washington because she's
wearing a coat with her bathing suit," she said. A faint smile
crossed her lips, and then faded.

Next she pulled out a Beanie Baby, a red bull. The smile
returned, this time more pronounced.

"This is Tabasco. She got him after she was injured so badly in a car wreck when she was twenty. My husband bought it from the hospital gift shop. Told her not to put up with anyone's BS about her injuries."

Emily took the red plush toy from her hand.

"She had four cracked ribs and a shattered pelvis. They said she might never have kids, but she proved them . . . *almost* proved them wrong, didn't she?"

"She did. She really did."

The unspoken part of the conversation was the fact that the baby that she'd so wanted had been killed, too.

"He abused her in life. He abused her in death. You know what he did, don't you?"

The cremation was troubling. Emily knew that the family had been extremely upset by what Mitch Crawford had authorized when the ME released the bodies.

"She would never want to be cremated. She was raised in Catholic schools, for goodness sake. I mean, we weren't Catholic, but a lot of that rubbed off on her anyway," Hillary Layton told Emily as they talked in her office, the morning of the ceremony at the Methodist Church.

"I know it feels wrong to you, but he is her husband. He has the power."

"I know. But it has to stop, Sheriff. You have to make him pay."

More than four hundred people showed up in the church that held so many memories. Mandy's wedding, her vigil, and now her funeral service. Mitch Crawford followed her family to the front row, but there might as well have been a force field between them. They didn't speak. They didn't sit close. No one knew that the pale pink casket was empty. People who filed up spoke to Mandy and her baby.

"God is watching over you both now," said Samantha

Phillips, Mandy's closest friend, her big green eyes raining tears. "I love you, Mandy. I love your sweet baby, your sweet Chrissy."

The Laytons went next. Mr. Layton rested his big hands on the casket and began to caress it.

"I had two dreams in my life, Mandy. Both of them involved you and your mother. No man, no father, could have ever asked for more. You're alive in my heart as you were the day we brought you home from the hospital." He had a million more things to say, but no more words came from his lips. Mrs. Layton took her husband by the hand and led him back to his chair.

As the Laytons huddled together in the front pew, a mass of grief and unfulfilled dreams, the entire congregation watched as Mitch Crawford walked up to the casket. His gait had lost its swagger and he dissolved into tears as he placed two white roses on the blue casket. He said only three words that anyone could hear.

"I'm sorry, baby."

The only real piece of evidence—outside of Mandy's body and the chains that had failed to weight her body into the mud of the Miller's Marsh Pond—was the down-filled sleeping bag that had encased her remains like a big, blue pupa. Jason visited all the local sporting goods stores in Cherrystone, and based on the photos Mountain Mania was identified as the manufacturer. The model—a down-filled, mummy-bag style—had been discontinued for at least ten years.

"It had leather ties," a clerk at the Big Five Sports Center said, while tapping on the photocopy that Jason slid onto the clerk's counter. "Now the ties are nylon. Vegans, I'm told, like to camp, too."

Later that afternoon, Jason arrived at the sheriff's office

with tired feet and little to show for his long day of digging for something to tie Crawford to the murder of his wife. He found Emily in her office finishing up a phone call.

"How'd the bag ID go?" she asked, placing the phone in its cradle. The brightness in her face faded as she read her deputy's transparent expression of defeat.

"About what we expected. Old bag," he said. "No one's sold one around here—around *anywhere* probably—for more than a decade." Jason slumped in a chair facing Emily's desk. He took a peppermint from her covered dish and popped it inside his mouth.

"State crime lab says that fibers on the bag are consistent with an array of GMC and Ford interiors—in reality just about every car company uses the same carpet suppliers, it seems," Emily said, taking a mint for herself. "Who knew that global outsourcing would trickle down to be a problem for forensics?"

"We're basically screwed on that, aren't we?" he asked.

Emily didn't want to say so aloud, but inside she agreed. "Nope," she said, "we'll find out where this bag came from and then we'll find our killer."

A search warrant served the day Mandy Crawford's body was found had turned up nothing to connect the sleeping bag with the Crawford residence.

"Mitch Crawford isn't the camping type," Emily said.

"Yeah, he's a condo time share or, better yet, a summer-place-on-the-lake kind of fellow."

She nodded. "That sounds about right."

The only other remotely remarkable identifier of the bag was a five-inch, nearly square hole at the top of the bag, near the ties. The lab team was unable to conclude when the tear had been made and if it had any relevance to the homicide.

The chains were so mundane, so heartbreakingly average, they could have been from anywhere in the country. There was nothing on them—no paint chips, no oil, no patterned markings—that could trace them to any life they might have had before they were wrapped around Mandy's corpse. It was as if Mandy's killer had been extremely careful, cunning, and deliberate.

Or, Emily thought, *very, very lucky.*

PART TWO

The Other Pretty Girls

Chapter Twenty-nine

San Diego

Two members of a litter crew from a San Diego youth detention home found Lily Ann Denton's body, the day after it was dumped in a gully behind the restroom of a rest stop. At first the boys who found her thought she was a blow-up doll that had been coated in ketchup.

"Dude, check this out. Some sick shit over here. One of those plastic chicks guys bone when they can't get a real chick."

The older boy, a Mexican gangbanger with an ironic name—*Angel*—bent down to take a look.

"Shit, that's no doll, dude. That's a dead ho."

"I'm not baggin' that. Let's get the boss over here."

"Bitch must have really pissed off her pimp."

"Yeah, stupid ho."

The young men went back to the van. Within twenty minutes, the rest stop was bathed in the blue light of ten squad cars and the red light of an ambulance—as unneeded as it was. An hour later, a coroner's van from the city of Rialto showed up.

"A mile west, and the dead girl would have been in San

Diego County," one cop said to another as they watched Rialto's finest bag the body for transport. "Getting murdered is bad enough, but Jesus, to end up in penny-pinching Rialto's system. That's just insult to injury."

Someone's daughter had been brought in the night before, unceremoniously dumped in the chiller until that morning. Dr. Kenneth Jensen looked at the body on the autopsy table, water running from a rubber hose around the figure like a bloody moat. Every now and then, water pressure would ebb and the bloody moat would drain completely to reveal the gleam of the stainless-steel construction. The table was a thing of beauty. Brand-new. Never been used.

Because of his age—fifty-nine—Dr. Jensen saw every young woman as a "girl" when she was splayed out and presented for the last conversation she'd ever have with another human being.

That it was a one-way conversation was irrelevant. Even though she couldn't say a word, her body told him so much. It was almost funny that way. But as he looked over the body, he could almost hear the voice of the girl telling him in breathless detail who she was and what had been done to her.

What had led her to his table for that last conversation?

She was white. Thin, but well-nourished. Her hair was shaved in strips, hastily so. She had the remnants of blond hair that had been bleached at a salon—a good mix of colors, not the cheap from the bottle look. She had perfect teeth, undoubtedly aided by expensive orthodontia. He noticed the front teeth had been fronted by porcelain veneers, again a sign of a person with means and with the desire for perfection. Her jeans, Sevens for All Mankind, were unbuttoned and dropped far below her waist. Her thong underwear had been torn at the crotch, so its waistband rode up high like a bloody and tattered ribbon around her waist.

Who was this pretty girl? he wondered.

Dr. Jensen spoke into his microcassette recorder, which rested on the dissecting tray that swiveled over her lifeless body. He gave his sad and final description of what he saw, the details as cold and clinical as they had to be. Earlier in his career, he'd made the mistake of showing emotion and his transcriber asked him about it. Emotion, he learned, had nothing to with medicine for the dead or the living.

He shut off the recorder.

"Now, my dear, tell me, what happened to your hair?"

It was a good question, of course. Her head had been crudely shaved. By her? By her killer? And why? He thought of the pop star who in some fit of lunacy had pulled into a California hair salon and grabbed the clipper and shaved her head. In two minutes, she'd turned from a beautiful young woman to a sad-looking alien being. She had gigantic eyes and a dome head that was the sickly whitish grey of a body drained of life, of blood. Pundits said that the pop star had been crying for help or had sought to cleanse her mixed-up life by shearing her locks and starting over. Renewal. New beginnings.

Balderdash, Dr. Jensen thought.

In this case, he doubted that the woman had cut her own hair. She was a girl, it appeared, who was very concerned about her looks. The killer must have done the hasty clip job. Track marks where the clipper hadn't done its job left a few thin bands of long hair. Those hairs, more so than the stubble, indicated that she had been a blonde in life. But the killer had taken all of that away. It was as if killing her hadn't been enough.

The killer.

Yes, it was obvious it was a homicide. The cause of death was staring him right in the face and it was incontrovertible. Even though it wasn't his job—that was the bailiwick of the detectives—he wanted more than merely the *cause*. Dr. Jensen was all about the *why*.

Fixing her weight at 110 was easy; a scale was built into the table. Height was easy, too. She was 5 feet 3 inches. There was a centimeter option, too. But he ignored it.

This is America, for God's sake! he thought.

Working from her feet to her waist, the medical examiner used heavy shears to snip through the fabric of her dark-dyed jeans. The shear's tips were bull-nosed so as not to snag her flesh. The poor girl had been through so much already. No need to add insult to injury.

A song came on the radio he piped into the autopsy suite and he pinpointed the artist and the date: Gilbert O'Sullivan's "Alone Again (Naturally)," 1972. He smiled. He had a grim job, and with no money in the budget for an assistant, the radio kept him company.

"You weren't even born when this was a hit," he said to the dead girl.

She was completely nude now. Jeans cut off. The tattered thong was snipped away and placed into a stainless-steel tub along with the jeans. She had been topless when she was found. No jewelry. Nothing else on her body.

He probed her mouth, vagina, and anus with three clean swabs. It was hard to tell if this girl had been raped. There were no injuries to those orifices, but the lab guys would be able to determine if there was any semen, any killer's DNA.

Gilbert O'Sullivan's depressing little ditty had ended and the radio offered up news about the weather. It wasn't what the ME wanted to hear. *Shit, more rain*, he thought. What happened to "It never rains in Southern California"?

Albert Hammond. He was unsure if the year was '71 or '73.

He made a mental note to remind himself to cancel Saturday's tee-time at the links. He hated playing golf in the rain and he didn't care who thought he was a pussy.

So there she was, this baldheaded girl on a stainless-steel table. Her eyes stared into the space of the autopsy suite. He turned the overhead light toward her exposed breasts and the hideously large gash in her chest.

He lifted a flap of skin, and water and blood squirted at him.

"Damn it," he said, taking a step backward, before resuming his exam.

The wound was enormous. It had been cut crudely, not in the fashion that had been suggested by the cops who'd found the body.

He cut a wider incision and reached for the rib spreader.

"Wonder if someone harvested her kidney or something. You know," the cop who helped transfer the body to the ME's office had said, "one of those black market deals."

The ME didn't think so. If someone had sought the girl's kidneys, they didn't do a good job. Both kidneys were in place.

More fluid oozed. It wasn't blood. It appeared to be bloody water, a kind of watered down Bloody Mary that came from a sprinkler system that had rained on her since she died.

Mary, he thought, *I'll call her Mary. Until we find her folks.*

The music playing was a Mariah Carey song, one of those in which the singer contorted her voice to such a degree that to Dr. Jensen's old-school way of thinking, he could no longer make out the tune. He didn't play his date-the-song game when Mariah came on the radio.

The rib spreader moved easily. Too easily. Normally, it took some force to pull apart the bones so that the ME could have access to the vital organs. They all waited there, in their protective cage to be plucked out, examined, weighed and photographed like an organic and hideous still life.

Something was wrong. The ribs on the right side of the body had been snapped. Car wreck? Beaten in the chest with a baseball bat?

No bruising to indicate that at all.

Dr. Jensen went inside. Something was missing. Yes, the kidneys were there. He aimed a light toward the right of the dark red cavity that was the girl's chest. It was empty. Dark. A void.

"I'll be," he said out loud, "the cop might be right, after all."

The girl's heart was gone.

Chapter Thirty

Dixon, Tennessee

Even though she lived in the inland region of Washington, Jenna Kenyon knew she was a kind of a geographic snob when it came to her idea of natural beauty. After her parents tried to make a last stand in their marriage by leaving Seattle for her mom's childhood home in Cherrystone, she reluctantly allowed herself to see some beauty in the arid part of a state split in two by the jagged edge of the Cascade Mountains.

Before she started traveling and actually seeing the "middle" parts of the country, she figured there was no compelling reason to go there. *If there wasn't a coastline, what was there to look at?* When she took the job with Beta Zeta national offices, she had her eye on the West Coast. She imagined herself touring campuses in California, Oregon, Arizona, and even Washington. She thought of foggy days in San Francisco, surfing in Malibu, hiking in the Sierras. Shopping in Portland, where there was no sales tax, was also very, very appealing to a young woman on a squeaky-tight budget.

It just didn't work out that way.

"Congratulations, Jenna, we want you to be our newest national consultant," the call from some woman in the personnel offices of the headquarters. "We have a very special assignment for you, my dear."

Jenna, who was at home when the call came through, motioned to her mother and mouthed the words "I got the job."

Emily put her arms in the air and mouthed back "wonderful."

Jenna's face fell as the woman on the phone detailed the specifics.

"You'll be the consultant for the Southern region, including Mississippi, Alabama, Florida, Tennessee, and Kentucky."

"But I applied for the West Coast," Jenna said, barely concealing her disappointment.

"I know, dear. But we're trying to lead the way in geographic diversity. Diversity of all kinds is important to being the best we can be."

At first it almost seemed an offer she could refuse. *Alabama? Mississippi?* Neither were places she'd ever imagined visiting if she lived to be a hundred. She'd have considered giving New Orleans a shot, but Katrina and the fact that there were no BZ houses on any campus there kept her from at least a little bit of Southern glamour.

Six months into the job, Jenna knew how foolish she'd been. She'd come to appreciate the warmth of the people of the South, a region in which it seemed there were no strangers. She loved the food, too. If eating real-crispy-buttermilk-soaked fried chicken and corn cakes meant an extra lap at the track that was fine with her.

With her mother immersed in the Mandy Crawford case, Shali drove Jenna to the Spokane airport for the flight to Nashville. It was a Friday morning and the next day had a full slate of things that needed her attention.

"I'd like to tell those old ladies in the BZ office that these girls have no interest in being the best sorority in America."

"When we were at Cascade, we didn't care either," Shali said, digging a candy bar from her purse with both hands—while she drove.

"Right. I know."

"You don't have to do this much longer." Shali pulled over at the passenger drop-off zone. A taxi honked and she resisted the urge to raise her middle finger.

Jenna smiled at her best friend. "I know. See you in a couple of weeks. Hey, maybe we'll have a wedding to plan for the spring."

Shali looked very interested. "Your mom's going to finally say yes to Chris?"

"I think so. I *hope* so."

"If she doesn't I might. He's old, but he's kind of hot, don't you think?"

Jenna rolled her eyes. "Shali, what am I going to do with you?"

Shali grinned and checked her makeup in the mirror. "Same thing as always. Keep an eye on me."

Jenna hugged her best friend and disappeared into the airport with a smile on her face and the feeling that despite her faults, her inappropriateness, her over-the-top behavior, Shali Patterson was a pretty good friend.

Jenna Kenyon had checked out the Dixon campus online and surfed a little on the Web about the region. Of course, all the images were of summer festivals, baskets of flowers, green lawns, and rose-covered fences. Even in the dead of winter, she could see that the rolling hillsides and massive oaks were the bones of a scenic region. Dixon, a town of 30,000, was halfway between Nashville and Knoxville on Interstate 40.

Jenna was more indie rock than Carrie Underwood, but she let the radio feed her the local flavor as she drove east. It wasn't a hard job that she had to do, and it wasn't the end of all of her career aspirations.

The flight from Spokane to Seattle to Nashville took forever and by the time she'd picked up her car from the Alamo lot and drove to the campus, she was beat. Although it was dark, a fresh layer of snow brightened the somewhat familiar drive. Last time she'd been to the house there, it had been summertime. It was actually easier to make out where she was with the canopy of leafy trees that were now dormant. Giant red oak trees defiantly clung to their shriveled, leathery leaves. She turned off the highway and drove toward campus.

She saw a couple of girls in short skirts walking without coats up toward the library, cell phones pressed to their ears and puffs of warm air coming from their mouths.

Don't they know it's cold outside? she thought, which made her feel like she was her mother. It was funny how much sense her mother made now when she observed the behavior of the kids younger than her.

Parking was always a disaster on campus, and she was glad when she got the message that she'd have a spot in the lot next to the steps to the front door.

With its half-timbered gables, narrow windows, and mix of light and dark masonry, Beta Zeta House was one of those faux Tudors that were inexplicably fashionable in 1930s America—even in a place like the South where they had no connection to anything. It had such a steeply pitched roof that workers who cleaned the gutters lashed themselves to the massive chimney because slipping on a slate roof almost guaranteed death or lifetime in a wheelchair. Unlike some of the other houses along the fringes of Greek Row, the BZ house had been built specifically for its purpose as a sorority. That meant on the main level it had a large living/meeting room, a cafeteria/dining room, and a lounge (originally it had been used for music, but playing piano and violin had been supplanted by watching *Oprah* and reality shows that would have made the sisters of the past cringe).

The basement level was outfitted with three dozen study carrels, and three refrigerators with diet soda in the front and a not-so-secret cache of beer in the very back.

The upper level was dominated by a sleeping porch which was nothing more than a darkened formation of bunk beds, like some kind of hospital ward with Hello Kitty sheets.

Two large dormitory-style bathrooms commanded the end of each hallway with a stash of pink and blue flip-flops in rambling rows stationed just inside each doorway. One pair was high-heeled because its owner said her feet hurt "even in the shower" if she was not in heels.

"It's what I'm used to!" she said as if high heels were a mark of fortitude and not fashion.

Adjacent to the sweeping staircase were four bedrooms, two to the right and two to the left. The largest belonged to the housemother; the other two were small and used by the highest-ranking women of the house caste system—the president, Sheraton Wilkes, and the social director, Midori Cassidy, who was the only Asian in the house. The fourth was the guest room, reserved for visiting moms, sorority alumnae, and representatives from the regional or national offices.

Midori, who never missed the opportunity for a social event, put up a sign shaped like a big pink heart on the front door.

WELCOME BIG SIS, JENNA!
"LET'S GET BEEZEE!"

She parked and noticed that she had a message on her phone.

It was her mom, of course.

"Hope you had a good flight. Call me when you get in. Chris got on a website called 'flight tracker' and says your plane was on time. Call me. Love you."

There wasn't time to call her mother back just then. She closed the phone, grabbed her bags, pulled her coat tightly around her, and started up the steps. The sign on the door made her smile as she turned the brass knob and breathed in the smells of a meal about to be served.

She didn't see the man in the lot, four cars down from where she'd parked.

Of all the BZ cooks, Glenna Tyler was probably the worst. It wasn't that there was a whole lot of competition, either. Most of the women who served as cooks for the sorority houses did so to make ends meet. They had children of their own to feed, but the job serving the more privileged set was a means to an end. If the housemothers or directors actually cared about their charges—and most did—the cooks just wanted to heat and serve.

Glenna was fixing her infamous "Tot Bar" meal that night. Tot Bar was five large bags of frozen tater tots paired with a variety of condiments—ketchup, cheese, chili, and sour cream.

That was it.

"The least she could do is deep-fry them," said the token plus-size sister, Jasmine Rhoades, a recent pledge who hadn't yet tired of the meal.

In time she would, for sure.

"Wait until you try her minipizzas," said Sheraton Wilkes, a pretty blonde with flawless skin and the kind of long legs that looked good even in capris—even in winter. Sheraton introduced herself as she found a seat next to Jenna.

"Glenna toasts English muffins and we top them with, you know, basically the same stuff we have here."

The familiar content of the conversation made Jenna smile. She'd been there. Done that. She smiled at a probable anorexic named Julie Lynn and took a seat.

"Hi," she said. "I'm Jenna Kenyon. I'm here from Nationals. I'm going to help out with the community involvement plans for the chapter."

"Won't be much to do," Julie Lynn said, moving a tater tot from one side of her plate to the other, like it was a hockey puck. She picked it up with her fingers and dabbed it into the ketchup. It never found its way into her mouth. Just back and forth, in and out.

"Why's that?" Jenna sat down.

"We do Relay for Life and Black History Month."

Jenna wondered why it was these young women, these supposed "future leaders," didn't have a bit more imagination. In fact, any imagination whatsoever.

"Those are great causes," she said, choosing her words carefully, "but Nationals would like us—all of us sisters—to try to do a little more."

"You mean more than Date Dash and Love Cruise on the river?"

Jenna nodded. "Yes, more than that."

Sheraton looked around the dining room and waited for everyone to stop their chatter and focus their attention up front, on her. Even a girl who had been measuring the number of tator tots that she could fit into a small plastic cup stopped.

"Sisters, our special guest has arrived from Nationals! Everyone, I want you all to welcome Jenna Kenyon."

There was a round of polite applause and Jenna stood up.

"Thank you," she said. "I'm glad to be here. I look forward to working with you tomorrow when we look at solutions to make our pledge drive more effective next year. You are an amazing group of young women. We can make this house even better if we work together."

Jenna hated the speech. But the women at Nationals wanted her to improve the quality of the sisters there, or the place would be shut down. It was that simple.

"We'll be meeting at eight a.m. sharp. I expect you all to be there."

Chapter Thirty-one

Saturday at the Beta Zeta House was filled with breakout sessions and pep talks. The forty girls that made up the current membership of the Dixon chapter were at their breaking points. Four were supine on the twin sofas; three more were curled up in a heap next to the turned-off big screen. Motivation and education were hard work. They'd worked on "Building Stronger Bonds with Your Sisters" and "Blonde on Blonde: How Recruiting Sisters of Your Own Hair Color Works Best."

Jenna hated that one. She presented the material exactly as written—which she was required to do—but with obvious disdain for the message. It clearly smacked of racism. She caught Midori's eyes and they felt like ice picks boring into her own.

"All right, sisters," she said, "we're done for the day. We've accomplished a lot, but we have more to do. Tomorrow, each of you will bring down your top three outfits for next week's recruitment. I want to see an outfit in our colors—taffy and mango—and an outfit in black accessorized with gold."

"What about the third one? You said three outfits," said a girl from the back of the room.

Jenna could finally see some lights come on in the brains of the women clad in an array of Juicy velour tracksuits. "Someone's paying attention. Thank you! The third outfit is your choice. It can be anything you want it to be as long as it is a skirt and sweater. We want you to show your individuality. That's what makes all of us special."

Again, it was a line that Jenna loathed, but she did what she was asked and followed the program.

As the girls filed out for the evening, Jenna went upstairs to her room and dialed home.

"It's me."

"Hi, baby," Emily said. "How's it going in the Deep South?"

"How's it going in the deep freeze?"

Emily laughed. "Things are OK here. Moving forward with the Crawford investigation. We're at a snail's pace, but we are making headway."

"How's Chris?"

Emily waited a second. "He's here," she whispered.

"Mom, that's so cool. Why don't you tell him 'yes'? Don't mess this up, OK?"

"Since when did you turn into the mother, here? That's my job."

"Since you started acting like a big baby. Kidding."

But she wasn't of course. Jenna felt that her mother's decision to not make a commitment to the man she loved was nothing short of stupid. It was about pride. About being hurt again. About all sorts of things that discarded the part of the equation that could end with a "happily ever after."

"OK," Emily said. "What's going on there?"

"Same old, same old. These girls got themselves into a bad situation and now they have to rebuild. We've been working on what needs to be done all day and I think I'm getting through to them with what's really important."

"You mean, purses and shoes to match?"

Jenna knew when her mom was pulling her chain. "No, I was thinking more about when to wear an up-do and when to wear a half-ponytail." She let out a laugh. "The girls are great, but this job completely sucks."

"Hang in there. Summer will be here soon and we'll figure out something else before you head off to law school."

"I have to pass the LSATs in March first."

"That's no problem. You're a smart girl. I love you."

"Love you more, Mom. Bye."

Jenna snapped her phone shut and looked around the room. Everything was in order. Her laptop was cable-locked to the sink. She had the complete data file of every living BZ member in the United States, which made it a security concern. She touched up her makeup and ran her fingers through her hair, giving it a little volume.

I'm in the South, and no matter what they say, hair is bigger down here, she thought, a mist of hairspray falling to hold everything in place.

There was a knock at the door. Sheraton and Midori were there to take her out to dinner at the Boarding House, a restaurant downtown that was popular with college students yet nice enough to take your mother. A little expensive, but the chapter had an account. The meal was on the BZs.

"Hi-hi!" Midori said, seemingly over the hurt of the presentation. "Ready to go out?"

Sheraton pushed the door open. "I'm soooo hungry! Let's get going! I saw your rental car." She paused and made a sad face. "We'll take my Lexus."

Jenna knew she was in for a night of mind-numbing conversation, but she was getting paid for it. What's more, she knew the food would be good. She'd Googled the restaurant before she left Cherrystone.

* * *

Just as they were about to leave the house, a voice called out. The three young women stopped.

"Aren't y'all little dolls?"

Shelby Barker's sweet voice was dipped in cornmeal, as Southern as could be.

"I'm Shelby Barker, but y'all can call me Ma Barker." She waited a second. "I know, I know. But everybody else does!"

Ma Barker had been the house director for almost twenty years. She was a warm woman, rather large, with spun-sugar hair and a penchant for housedresses that had to be from an old Rodgers and Hammerstein musical. They were shiny and full. Jenna had talked to Ma Barker on the phone the week before Christmas, letting her know she'd be coming.

"Don't call me the house director, either. I'm a house-mother, and that's good enough for me."

Jenna gave her a warm hug. She couldn't help herself. Ma Barker was like a kind sponge for good feelings.

"You are a good hugger," Ma Barker said, smiling and taking it all in. "You have the kind of spirit this place needs."

Jenna returned the smile. "I hope so."

Ma Barker cocked her head and looked over at the TV lounge, a half dozen girls staring blankly at a reality show about Hugh Hefner's Playboy mansion. "Ya'll gonna kick some ass? 'Cause these girls need it. I've been here longer than any of them have been alive and I've never seen a lazier bunch of girls. No wonder this place is going to hell in a handbasket."

Sheraton and Midori stood mute and Ma Barker didn't seem to care one whit about them and how they might regard her assessment of the house.

Jenna liked Ma Barker and the "eyes and ears" part of her job would have called for her to let Nationals know that Ma had spoken of her girls in a "less than flattering manner." But she wouldn't do that. The lady was probably one hundred percent correct. She lived with the girls every day. The women back at Nationals were living in a fantasy world of white gloves, teas, and closed-mouth kissing.

"That's why I'm here." Jenna said.

The old lady proceeded to tell Jenna about the house, the fact that it was built of the "finest materials of its time, but, well, things have gotten better since then." She indicated that Jenna would be staying in the only room with a private bathroom.

"The hot water heater has been givin' me fits, but I think we've got it fixed now."

"I hate a cold shower," Jenna said.

Ma Barker indicated she understood. "That's not the problem. The dang thing had been making a racket when it heated up. Hot water's no problem. But sleeping next to that contraption has been a nightmare for the last few moms who've stayed in there. We got it fixed, I think. I hope. I really do."

"I'm sure I'll be fine."

"I know you will be. Now, go ahead and head out to dinner. All y'all could use some meat on your bones."

"Thanks, Ma Barker," Jenna said, trying very hard not to laugh at the name.

"You're welcome. Now get. OK? Get some food!"

Chapter Thirty-two

Jenna set her alarm clock for 5 A.M., jumped from the bed, turned on her laptop, and headed for the private bathroom of the Beta Zeta guest suite. Despite the thumping of the stairs a few times during the night, she was remarkably refreshed and ready to tackle the issues that awaited her. She was there to get the house back on track. The chapter was in trouble or she wouldn't be there. Occasionally, once popular sororities found themselves in a state of decline. One of the women in the national office told Jenna during her training that the decline experienced by a formerly top-tier house was sometimes due to the trivial.

"Fashion, dear. Dark-dyed jeans work today, but acid-washed or lighter colored jeans make those of us who know better want to scream," said the woman, an attractive redhead with obvious extensions and green-tinted contacts. "We have a couple of, shall I say, *problem* houses. We started on that path and should have nipped it in the bud right away. But we didn't and now we pay for it. The girls were nice enough, but they didn't attract the correct kind of pledges and the spiral started."

"I think I know what you mean," Jenna said. "At Cascade,

we have a house that no one calls by its proper name because a couple of the girls two years ago were on the chunky side."

The woman talking from behind her mahogany desk nodded. "That's right. That would be Ate-a-Pie, right?"

Jenna smiled a little nervously. It seemed peculiar that this fifty-something-year-old would know something like that. "Yes, Beta Pi."

"We have to keep our chapters up to par, *beyond* par, really. As a national consultant, your job will be to be our eyes and ears. You'll be the keeper of our ideals and expectations. You're the one we've hired to stop the spiral and keep the quality of our southern region as it should be. No detail is too small. The way the girls dress. The GPA. The kinds of cars in the parking lot. All of it adds up to our Beta Zeta image."

Jenna understood, though she felt the "keeper of our ideals" comment was not only stupid, impossible to do. She didn't say so, but she knew the real reason was to keep the chapter dues flowing. A dying house is a cash drain. For all the talk about sisterhood, the Beta Zeta was a big business, too.

Remember, she told herself, *this job is only temporary. Maybe when I'm a lawyer I can help some "chunky" girl sue a sorority.*

Jenna looked around the guest suite and went into the bathroom. It was clear that the bathroom needed updating. It still had the orange-and-green daisy appliqués of almost forty years ago. It also had an accent wall covered by a mod print by a designer named Vera.

It sure wasn't Vera Wang. Just *Vera.*

As she let the water run over her, she picked at one of the edges of a daisy decal.

This could come off pretty easily, she thought, resisting the urge to remove it. God knew these girls needed help, but she was not there to help with their décor. She was there to save them from probation and the revocation of their status as a BZ sorority.

As she laid out her clothes for the next day—a "snappy professional" look consisting of a fitted pink blouse and black wool skirt, J.Crew—she replayed the conversation she had with Sheraton Wilkes before she went to bed.

"Of course," Jenna had said, "you know that what we said is between us."

"Yes, sister to sister."

"That's right. But not sister to sisters, if you get what I'm saying."

"I can't tell Midori?"

Jenna shook her head slowly and deliberately. "No. That's the way it's done. Nationals sent me to save you from being drop-kicked out of the system. It would be absolutely de-moralizing if your girls knew that."

"But wouldn't they work harder if, well, they knew we were bottom-tier?"

"We've been doing this a long time. You aren't the first to need a nudge in the right direction. If your girls knew, some—and maybe even the strongest girls—would leave. And we can't have that."

Sheraton seemed confused. "But they've taken the pledge. They can't leave."

"I like your attitude," Jenna said, unsure if the girl standing in front of her was naive or a dream come true.

Sheraton smiled. "Thank you," she said.

Must be naive.

Jenna ended the conversation reminding Sheraton that she'd have to be ready at 7:30.

"The day will be long," she said, "but I think we can do it. Yes, we can!"

She rolled her eyes at the thought of her own inane words. She knew that she was doing the sorority gig to make money for law school, but it seemed pretty tasteless. If the BZ organization was in trouble, it wasn't necessarily because its girls were not up to par. The whole organization needed to be Vera Wanged.

Jenna answered a knock on the door. It was Sheraton, dressed to the nines, holding a cup of coffee.

"Mocha, extra hot, extra shot," she said, with a voice that Jenna could only describe as a grating chirp. "Just like you like it."

Jenna looked surprised. "Thank you. How did you know?"

The girl beamed. "I Facebooked you!"

Jenna smiled at her. "Oh, I'll have to add you as a friend."

"Invite already sent," Sheraton said, beaming. "Just log on and we'll be able to stay in touch all the time."

"Oh-my-God," Jenna said, letting her vernacular drift not to Southern-fried, but to the kind of Valley-speak that still seemed to be the dialect favored by the young, blond, and educationally disinterested. "That's awesome."

She motioned Sheraton to sit on the daybed while they went over the PowerPoint presentation that the national office had provided. The first slide with its smiley-face art trumpeted the purpose of the meeting

IN IT TO WIN IT: RECRUITMENT MADE EASY.

"This looks amazing," Sheraton said. "Very high-tech. Do you want me to make it go to the next slide? I'm a communication major."

"I thought you said fashion merchandising yesterday."

Sheraton made a face. "I *did*. But I'm not sure. I might go to medical school. I just want to help people."

Jenna wondered for a fleeting moment how fashion merchandising fit into the category of "helping" people.

"Wonderful," she said.

Jenna refocused on the images of the pretty and perfect— and a few of the less so for diversity's sake—as they floated into view. The bullet points accompanying the images stressed sisterhood, the importance of a first impression, and how to ensure success when it comes to making sure the top girls pledge their sorority.

"I have to be honest with you," she said turning to look directly at Sheraton. "This recruitment effort is crucial. We have to fill up every bed in this house. We have to ensure that we never have another incident like what happened last fall."

Sheraton made a face.

Sad? Sorry? Regretful? Annoyed? It was hard to say.

"Oh, that. I guess that was pretty bad."

That was, without room for argument, the understatement of the century.

Jenna knew the story well. Everyone did. It was the reason this particular BZ house was nominated by the university newspaper as the sorority as the "Girls Most Likely to . . . Do Anything!"

The previous September, the Beta Zeta girls hosted a cruise on the Little Tobacco River that ran lazily through town and into the corn and tobacco fields that made up most of the area's agricultural economy. Such cruises were part of the BZ program—invite some potential sisters for fall recruitment, some cute frat boys, and maybe even a former valedictorian or two. Midori and the BZ social team ordered T-shirts silk-screened with the BZ logo, and the words "Cruisin' for Love."

The next day, the event was renamed "Boozin' for Love."

The sisters and their guests took a bus from Greek Row for the hour-long drive out to the launch for the cruise. Midori and Sheraton sensed trouble nearly from the outset. Two of the frat guys—handsome and hopped-up—brought a stash of vodka.

"No one can smell it. No one can tell we've been pre-func-ing," one of the guys told some girls in the back of the bus.

That might have been good advice, if the girls hadn't started so early and been so eager to have fun.

Misty or Missy Johnson—no one really knew her, or her name—was the first to start throwing up. The bus pulled off the highway in Bakersville and the rest of the girls who were drinking fell in line. A wave of vomit roiled through the back of the vehicle. In less then two minutes, the sympathy pukers started in.

The bus driver, a big barrel-chested fellow with an accent as deep as an oil well, ignored the entire scene. He had a job to do and if he didn't get the busload to the river in time, he didn't get paid. He cracked a window and kept driving. By the time he arrived, things had calmed down a bit and he could later feign no knowledge of the chaos of the drive.

But it got worse.

Once everyone got on board the boat, the booze continued to flow. The Diet Coke bottles—liter-sized—were spiked with rum. One of the potential recruits brought enough marijuana that she could have made one of those airplane travel pillows out of her stash.

Both Sheraton and Midori did their best to try to stop the debacle.

"Hey, you guys," Sheraton said, in near-tears, "we need to get control of this situation."

She was met by blank stares.

Midori steadied herself with her hands on her hips. "She means it!"

Again, no response.

The captain's voice over the loudspeaker did, however, get the point across. "I'll have no hanky-panky or drinking on my vessel. My crew will be watching your every move. You signed a waiver to come aboard and I'll hold you to it. No drinking. No smoking—or you're kicked off. Thank you."

The thank-you was a bit odd, but the man made his point. For a time, it seemed that order was restored. The boat went down the river. The DJ played eighties music stalwarts like Bananarama and Tears for Fears, and the girls who weren't drunk had a good enough time.

One had too good of a time.

Dressed in a quasi-sailor suit and tennis shoes, the woman in charge of the tortilla chips and salsa went back into the boat's storage locker off the galley. Despite the rumble of the motor, she heard the kind of noises that belonged more in a motel room than on a boat.

"What's going on here?" she asked once inside.

One of the BZs was on her knees, her bleached blond head down, in position while a frat boy with his brown eyes rolled back into his head moaned at her, "Don't stop! Keep going! You're doing good!"

"Enough!" the woman yelled at the two of them. The BZ snapped to, wiping her mouth. But the young man looked right at her.

"You next?" he asked.

"I'm going to tell the captain and you're going to swim back to the dock."

"Sure? In your dreams."

Of course, there was no walking the plank. The kid zipped up his pants and thought he'd be able to disappear into the crowd. But he couldn't. The lady in the sailor suit never forgot a face. The incident was written up and made its way into the annals of disastrous sorority social events.

The only saving grace for Sheraton and Midori was that they hadn't been drinking and that they'd done their best to thwart disaster. The women at the national office gave them copies of a popular self-help book that came with a promise in its title: *No One Will Ever Push Me Around . . . Again!*

* * *

Although a communication major, Sheraton Wilkes was technologically challenged when it came to helping out with the presentation part of the chapter meeting. She had an excruciatingly difficult time advancing the PowerPoint slides. Jenna took over the remote clicker midway through the presentation.

"No worries, Sheraton. I'm a bit of a control freak anyway," she said. The girls all laughed. Jenna, however, was disappointed. Part of the strategy from Nationals was to get the president involved in the presentation.

"If she clicks it, she'll stick with it," was the advice of the fifty-five-year-old sorority sister in the deep red suit and triple strand of pears. Real pearls, at that.

On the last slide, Jenna looked around the dining room at the girls who were about to be drafted into an army of representatives for a faltering chapter.

"Each of you holds a great power here," she said. "We want you to succeed. We want you to be all that you can be."

The girls stood and applauded. Jenna smiled, but she felt silly. She said the text as it was written, but it always felt a little over the top. Almost like it was an ad for the Army.

"Thank you," she said. "I know you guys can do it. I know you guys are ready to make sure that next year is unforgettable." She stopped and self-edited. "But not as unforgettable as last year, that's for sure."

The girls laughed. They got it.

Chapter Thirty-three

It was worse than a couple of angry midgets wrestling in the closet. A pillow over the head did nothing.

Thump. Whap. Thump!

The intermittent banging of the pipes reverberated from the bathroom with its Vera wallpaper and cheerfully outdated daisy appliqués. It was 2:00 A.M. and Jenna Kenyon knew she couldn't sleep in that room. She grabbed the pillow and a blanket, and started for the TV lounge, where she figured she could grab a spot on the couch. The TV was still on, and all of the couches were occupied with young women glued to a dating-show marathon that featured four pretty women in an RV vying for the affections of a smooth-chested hunk with a unibrow.

The BZ girls were sucking it in with a big fat straw.

"You'd think he'd wax his brow if he's gonna wax his chest," said one of the girls, a redhead in yellow pajamas with lips and fingers stained orange from Cheetos.

"No kidding," a brunette agreed.

"I still think he's so hot."

"Oh, yeah. Superhot."

Jenna lingered for a moment, but none of the girls saw her. And she decided that there was no way she was going to kick them out of their cozy cocoon and away from their inane conversation so she could crash there. She doubted they'd offer, and if they did, they'd do so begrudgingly. It was too late to impose anyway. It didn't matter that the TV show they were riveted to was nothing short of complete garbage.

Tired and beginning to feel stressed, Jenna decided to go upstairs to the sleeping porch. She hated the sleeping porch at her BZ house at Cascade University, and knew this was no better. Dozens of beds. Lights always out. A snorer or two in utter denial. It was a sleepy girl's nightmare. She tiptoed inside, and searched for a bed as far from the open window as possible. Fire codes mandated that the window next to the fire escape remain open. Jenna knew sleeping next to the open window only invited the inevitable—a drunken frat boy proving his prowess by slipping into his girlfriend's sorority bed late at night. It happened almost every night, on every campus, across the country.

As Jenna drifted off to sleep, she couldn't help but think that no parent would ever allow a son or daughter to join a frat or sorority if they knew everything there was about them.

If I ever have a daughter of my own, she's going someplace without the Greek system, she thought.

At first, the cry was unintelligible. Just a guttural scream that started loud and went even louder. It was coming from the second floor, up the stairway to the sleeping porch.

The girl in the bed next to Jenna jumped to her feet. "What's going on now?"

Jenna sat up and felt for the gooseneck lamp hooked to her bedframe and turned it on. The bulb was no more than twenty-five watts and it barely illuminated the faces of the girls who'd crawled out of bed.

"Megan must have forgotten the front-door combination," another said.

But the scream wasn't about being locked out.

"Oh, my God!" came the words this time. *The scream. The words. Something was very, very wrong.*

Jenna pushed past the girls in the hall and headed down the stairs. At the second-floor landing, she found Midori hunched over, sobbing uncontrollably. She reached down and put her hand on her shoulder.

"Midori, what is it?"

Midori was crying so hard now, she couldn't speak. She looked up, her face frozen in utter terror.

Jenna got on her knees and held her; in doing so, she felt a wetness on Midori's nightgown. She looked closer.

It was blood.

"Midori! What happened? How did you get hurt?"

By then, the entire hall was filled with girls—less the ones that were going to take the walk of shame home after spending the night with their boyfriends—and the air was thick with panic.

"It. It. It isn't me." She sputtered out her words and turned to indicate the guest bedroom. Midori started to shake. "It's Sheraton. Something's happened to her."

Jenna motioned for another girl to attend to Midori. She commanded a girl who had taken pictures with her cell phone to dial 911.

"I mean, right now."

Ma Barker scurried up the stairs, swathed in her inch-thick turquoise terry bathrobe. Her head covered with a nylon sleeping cap.

"Good, Lord! What's going on up here?"

"I don't know. Sheraton's hurt." Midori looked up. "She's in there!"

Jenna nearly lost her footing as she entered the bedroom. Looking down, she saw the smear of blood. But that wasn't the worst of it. The wall next to the daybed was splattered with a triple arc of blood that looked like the devil's rainbow. Three dripping arcs of blood oozed from the wall to the floor behind the bed. Her cream-colored wool coat borrowed by Sheraton in the chill of the night was striped with red.

And there she was. The body of a young woman face-down, the light from the bathroom reflecting off the dark wetness of her head.

"Sheraton?" Jenna said, almost in a whisper. "Are you OK?"

There was no answer, just perfect stillness.

Thump. Whap. Thump!

Startled, Jenna screamed. The noise of the water heater nearly jolted her to the ceiling.

"Ya'll pull yourself together. Campus police are coming!" Ma Barker called out.

A siren wailed louder and louder. The girls in the hallway started to cry. Ma Barker tried to gather them together to get out of the house.

"We don't know who did this," she said, "And I don't want any of my girls here to meet him, if he's still in the house."

Ma Barker was thinking of the slaughter of five girls by a serial killer ten years before. He'd crept into the sleeping house of a Chi Epsilon chapter near St. Louis and cut the throats of five girls. All but one bled to death. The deaths were painful, slow, and beyond anything anyone could have imagined. The lone survivor recovered and eventually testi-fied against Paul Walton, the boyfriend of one of the victims. He'd been angry that she'd broken up with him and was sure the other sisters were behind it. Today, he was in prison on death row.

As the girls followed Ma Barker down the stairs to the front door, Jenna hurried back up to the sleeping porch and turned on the overhead lights. Her heart pounded and fear gripped her so tightly she could barely breathe.

"Is everyone out of here?"

She ran over to a bed on the north side of the room. The girl curled up under the covers wasn't moving.

"Oh God, not another!"

Jenna pulled the blanket from the bed and prepared herself for the worst. But it was only a decoy, two pillows arranged by a girl who decided her reputation was something worth saving. Or at least worth lying about.

Jenna was acquainted with police procedure as well as anyone. She knew what was to come. The sad task of notifying the dead girl's parents. The questions. The follow-up. *All of it.* Not only had she been raised on *Law & Order* in all of its incarnations, she had a realistic view of police work through her mother's experiences as a cop. Few meals or evenings were left without some comment about some investigation in the news, or even closer to home.

Jenna wanted to cry, but knew that tears did nothing.

A man stood in a coffee line at the Nashville airport. His right hand was sore and he'd bandaged a small cut with tape he purchased from a drugstore. Despite the pain, he was nearly euphoric. He'd had a great business trip. *One of the best ever.* He could hear Wolf Blitzer's voice coming from the bank of TVs bolted overhead in at the gate. Wolf was talking about a breaking news story coming out of the college town of Dixon. Without turning his head toward the screens, he fixed his auditory senses on Wolf's words.

". . . The body of a college student was found earlier today at the Beta Zeta House on the campus of Dixon University."

No name was given. The audio had some quotes from some young people who were devastated by the grisly discovery. It was boilerplate reporting, and the only thing that made it interesting was the fact that the victim was young, pretty, and a college student. She was, as the story implied, too young to die. Too full of promise.

". . . a person of interest is being questioned."

That line made him smile.

"Tall latté, no foam," he told the girl behind the counter, still listening to the news report.

The real person of interest put Equal in his latté.

This is too good to be true, he thought.

He was right about that. It was.

Emily Kenyon was overcome with concern. Jenna was on the phone telling her about the horrific discovery of Sheraton Wilkes's blood-drenched body at the BZ house at Dixon University. Jenna called earlier in the morning, but Chris was staying over and she just let the phone ring. She felt like a bad mother just then. *A really bad mother.* Most women who attempted to build new relationships felt the twinge of regret any time they put a new love over their children, no matter if they were toddlers or grown.

"You must be terrified," she said. "The poor girl."

"Jesus, Mom, I've seen a lot in the past few years, but nothing like this. I'm talking like something out of a slasher movie. Spatter all over the wall."

She wanted Jenna to get on a plane right that very minute. Certainly, she knew Jenna's strengths. She was tough, because she'd had to be. They'd made it through a nightmare five years earlier with the three horrific murders that shook Cherrystone and the ensuing events that nearly cost them their lives. But that was past them. It was water under the bridge. It had to be. To let violence consume either mother or daughter would be letting go of the love they had for each other. The bond they had was unbreakable.

"I'm OK, Mom," Jenna said.

"Honey, I'm sure you are. But why don't you come home?"

"A grief counselor is coming in from Nationals, and they want me to stay until he gets here. I said I could do it. I mean, Mom, this girl was slashed to death and the sisters here saw it."

"Saw the murder?"

"No, no. The aftermath. What I mean is, most of them saw Sheraton's body and after the police came through with the crime kits, the room has been visited by everyone who lives in the house. One girl sent photos from her cell phone to her dad's paper in Knoxville and they put them up on their website."

"Nice. What's wrong with people?"

"That's what I thought. Mrs. Barker, the housemother, says that she'll clean up the mess. I feel a little bad that I didn't offer to help her."

"Are you sure you're OK?"

"I'm a little shaken, but I'm doing all right," Jenna said, tearing up a little.

Emily knew that Jenna was on the verge of falling apart, but to mention it would be to push her to the edge. She was a thousand miles away and there was no way to wrap her arms around her. "All right," she said. "Is there anything I can do for you?"

"No. I'm just going to stay until the counselor comes. Then I'm going to come home. Nationals wants me to take a couple of weeks off and skip Gainesville."

"Good idea. So when will you be home?"

"Monday night at the earliest."

"I'll meet you at the airport."

"Don't worry about me, Mom. I'm fine. I'm going to help these girls the best that I can, but really, I know that's not my expertise. So far two of the girls said they're going home, but I've seen their grades and I think they would have dropped out anyway."

"Do they have a suspect?"

"They won't say. At least not the police. The girls think Sheraton's boyfriend was mad at her. But mom, I had dinner with Sheraton last night and she said how much she loved the guy. There were no problems. Not on her part. She wasn't smart, Mom, but she was a nice girl. I liked her." Jenna almost said "really liked her" but she knew that was the kind of editing of feelings done after a tragedy. Sheraton was a nice enough girl, and she didn't deserve what happened to her, but she was hardly anyone with whom Jenna would ever stay in touch.

Now that was impossible anyway.

"Have the police picked up the boyfriend?" Emily asked.

Jenna didn't answer.

"Jenna?" Emily looked at her phone and the signal was strong. "Jenna?"

"Sorry, Mom. I have to go. They want me to come to the station to make a statement, so, of course, I have to do that."

"Call me when you get back. I love you."

"Love you more. Say hi to Chris."

Emily was overcome with worry. She'd done her best to keep up a calm front, but the idea that her daughter had been so close to a killer was more than unnerving. Sorority houses had been drenched in blood before, certainly. Whenever pretty young girls were sequestered in places like sororities, nursing dorms, or Girl Scout camps, men with evil in their hearts had a way of tiptoeing inside. *One deadly step in the darkness toward their prey.*

The women of Emily's generation knew of one case that brought an instant and deep shudder of fear.

In mid-January 1978, serial killer and jail escapee Ted Bundy entered the Chi Omega sorority house on the Tallahassee campus of Florida State University. He slipped inside around 3 A.M. No one heard him. No one had a clue that he was even in Florida, let alone on the hunt once more for young, female victims. In a bloody frenzy that lasted no more than a half hour, Lisa Levy and Margaret Bowman were bludgeoned and strangled to death; Karen Chandler and Kathy Kleiner were severely injured.

After that terrible incident, mothers and fathers across the country made hurried trips to see that their daughters lived in houses with security systems that could preclude a killer from gaining entry.

What the parents didn't know—and what surely would have given them even greater pause—was that most houses had alarms. But girls frequently gave out the alarm codes so tardy sisters could get home late at night.

Later, when David Kenyon got the news of Sheraton Wilkes's slaying and learned that Jenna had been there when it happened, he called Emily. By then, she was in her office reading Jason's latest report on what Mitch Crawford's neighbors thought of him.

"We need to get our daughter out of there," David said, without bothering to say hello.

Emily sent down the report and put her ex-husband on the speakerphone. She pushed her chair back and glanced at Jenna's high school graduation portrait.

"Nice to hear from you, David."

"There's a crazed killer out there and she needs to come home."

Emily let out an exasperated sigh. "She has a job. She's fine. She's safe."

"Emily, I think we have different ideas about what's safe and what isn't." The subtext of his remark was meant to hurt, to conjure images of the past when Jenna was, in fact, in grave danger.

Emily could hear a baby crying in the background, which meant that David was likely calling from home. *Dani had probably left to go shopping. She'd rather spend money than time with him,* she thought. *For once, I don't blame her.*

"Look, David. We don't need to have conversations like this anymore. We're done. She's over twenty-one. And, in case you've forgotten, she's working the Beta Zeta gig because you reneged on your offer to send her to law school. Stupid me. I should have had that written into the divorce decree, but I was dumb enough to still trust you. I didn't know you and Dani were already so involved."

"Does it always have to go there? Do you always have to bang the drum about Dani? Get over it."

Emily felt her face grow hot. *I'm not letting him do this to me. I'm not having my buttons pushed!*

"I am over it. And I'm over you. Consider this conversation over, too. Our daughter's grown. Don't ever, I mean, *ever,* call me again pretending that you care about her."

The baby's cries grew louder.

"David, give the baby a bottle. Try being a dad to her. You might like it."

She hit the speakerphone Off button. It felt so good being a bitch to a man who treated their daughter like an afterthought—like something on a list that had to be checked off.

Buy groceries
Fill up the car
Pick up dry-cleaning
Care about your daughter

A thousand miles away in the basement office of his Garden Grove home, Michael Barton read Jenna Kenyon's latest entry, posted around 3 P.M. that same day.

I'm still at DU. I'm sure most of our sisters have read or heard the sad news about one of our own. Sheraton Wilkes was savagely killed. Her parents

are going to hold a memorial service in her
hometown and I'll post all the details here later
in the week. Nationals is putting together a
tribute for Sheraton. I didn't know her well, but
she was a very nice girl. We're heartbroken in
Dixon.

In light of what happened, I'm canceling my
recruitment training for the BZ house in
Gainesville this week. I'm going home to
Cherrystone. You can call me on my cell, leave
comments here, or use my e-mail addy.
Thanks for understanding,

Jenna Kenyon, Southern BZ Consultant

Everything the young woman wrote made him angry. The
way he saw it, Jenna Kenyon pretended to be so concerned
about her sisters, the dead girl, and the BZ organization.
What a phony piece of garbage!
He glanced at the calendar and opened his e-mail account, selecting his boss's name from the address book. He
started typing:

Clay, I got a couple of leads I need to work in
goddamn Spokane. Leaving on Monday, back
Wednesday night. Tell the gang to feel sorry for
me. At least Nashville has Jack Daniels. Not sure
what, if anything, Spokane has. LOL

—Michael

He liked the LOL—laughing out loud—to close the e-mail.
It made him feel more fun. Sure, he could be fun.

Chapter Thirty-four

Cherrystone

Casper Wilhelm's voice was unmistakable. Every word he uttered hit like a punch to the face. The Spokane County medical examiner seemed impatient and a little irritated, which pretty much was the way he always was.

"I don't like being kept on hold, Sheriff." Dr. Wilhelm's smoky, deep baritone echoed in the concrete cavern of the parking garage where Emily imagined he'd gone to make the call so he could light up a Lucky Strike.

A car honked.

Yes, he was smoking in the garage.

"Sorry about that, Doctor." Emily knew him well enough to acquiesce whenever he chided anyone. Arguing only ensured a long and painful outcome—with the good doctor always right.

"I'm sure you are. But forget it. I'm about to make your day. I think. It's about the Crawford case. You know, the dead pregnant woman?"

As if she'd forgotten. He must have had Cherrystone mixed up with Detroit or someplace where murders could be confused. In Cherrystone they were an exceedingly rare oc-

currence. Emily walked to her door, and pushed it shut with
her hip.

"What's up? Tox screen back?"

"Not *that*. She was clean as a mother-to-be." He took a
drag. "The DNA swabs came back."

Emily could feel the doctor play with her a little, or
maybe just dragging it out so he could finish his cigarette.

"Well?"

"Well. If Amanda Crawford was alive, she'd have some
explaining to do. Turns out that Mitch Crawford wasn't her
baby's father."

Emily could feel the air squeezed from her lungs. "You're
postive?"

"We swabbed Mitch when he came up to do his 'cry me a
river' routine, and you know the rest. The other part of the
picture was on an autopsy table in my lab. Procedure. We ask
and if they give it, we call it a bonus. Saves everyone the
trouble later. Never paid off like this before."

"I'll bet it hasn't," Emily said, a mixture of excitement
and uneasiness taking over. They chatted a bit more and,
then, apparently done with his smoke break, the coroner
ended the conversation as abruptly as it had stared.

"I'll have the reports on your desk tomorrow," he said.

Click.

"Thank you, Dr. Wilhelm," Emily said, knowing he'd already gone. *Thank you for making my case harder than it
had been before.*

Jason Howard walked by as Emily was about to call prosecutor Camille Hazelton. She waved him inside her office
and indicated to shut the door.

"Don't go anywhere. You're going to want to hear this,
too."

Jason slumped into a chair as Emily got Camille on the line.

"You're on speaker," she said. "Jason's here, too. I just got off the phone with Dr. Wilhelm."

"How was Spokane County's favorite old cuss? Wilhelm. Not Jason, of course."

Everyone laughed.

Emily's eyes met Jason's. "He's fine. He had a bit of news. Turns out that Mandy's baby wasn't Mitch's."

Jason mouthed, "Whoa."

There was a beat of silence before Camille spoke. "Oh, really? That does make things even more fascinating."

Emily glanced at Jason, then back at the speakerphone. "I know. I was thinking of springing it on Mitch this afternoon."

"Let me think on that for a second," Camille said. The wheels were turning. "Do we use it to shake him loose? Or do we spring it on him later, when we have no other options? It's pretty hot, so I'm sure we don't have the luxury of time. You know McConnell is a bear when it comes to discovery."

"I'm sure." Emily hated the reminder that Cary McConnell was involved.

"OK. Thought about it. Spring it on him. Also, go back to the scrapbooking girls and anyone else who was close to them. If we tell them what we know, maybe they'll feel free to share something."

"People hate sharing the secrets of the dead."

"True. But they hate letting a murderer go free even more so."

Emily set down her phone and looked at Jason, who'd done an expert job of pulling in both sides of the conversation.

"Let me guess. I get the scrapbook girls."

Emily nodded. "I'll take Samantha Phillips."

"Who gets Mitch?"

Emily managed a smile, the first one of the day. "We'll make a party of it. Let's do it together."

"Thanks, Sheriff. I'll do my best. I won't let you down."

"You never have, Jason."

Emily had one more call to make. She knew that the information about the baby's paternity would leak from the ME's office. She dialed the number for Amanda's parents. Hillary Layton answered.

"Mrs. Layton, I mean Hillary, I have some news."

"You arrested Mitch for Mandy's murder?"

"No. This is upsetting news, but not that. I'm afraid that the baby that your daughter was carrying wasn't Mitch's baby."

Hillary Layton started to cry very loudly into the phone.

"I'm sorry. I'm so sorry. I know that this is hard to hear."

"It isn't that at all," Hillary said, calming herself. "I'm so happy that Mandy had found someone to love other than Mitch Crawford. I only wish I knew who it was."

Emily didn't say so, but she was thinking the very same thing.

Samantha Phillips was filling boxes with clothing and household utensils in the garage when Emily arrived later that afternoon.

"I don't suppose you're here to help," she asked, looking up from the pile of odds and ends that she was sorting.

"You're not moving, are you?"

"Oh no. I could never leave here. Bad memories will fade soon, and I'll focus on the good times with my family. And Mandy. This stuff is going to the Goodwill. The kids get so much crap at Christmas if I don't clear things out of here, I'll be featured on TV as one of those crazy hoarders."

"Not likely," Emily said, looking around. "You might be

the most organized person I've seen, Martha Stewart notwithstanding."

The garage was an organizer's fantasy. Almost a vision of organizer's porn with hooks here, labeled bins there, bikes hanging on racks like a row of Sunday suits, tools in perfect order above a workbench.

"I'm here about Mandy," she said.

"I figured. I saw Mitch in the paper the other day. He was quoted that he was innocent and that the case has been a witch hunt from the start. Said people are jealous of him or don't like him for this or that. No kidding."

"I saw that article, too. I'm here about Mandy and her baby."

Samantha set down her bundle of clothes. "What is it, Sheriff?"

"This isn't easy to say. I know how close you and Mandy were."

"Thank you. But *what*?"

There was no gentle way of saying it, so Emily was direct. "The baby Mandy was carrying wasn't Mitch's."

Samantha shot Emily the kind of look meant to sink a person to the lowest depths of their being. "Why would you say something like that? I thought you were on our side?"

"I am, Samantha," she said gently. "But it is the truth."

"It smacks of something Mitch's defense lawyer would say to smear her. How could you?"

Emily knew Samantha was right. But the evidence could work the other way, too—as a motive for murder. She didn't say any of that to Samantha. No argument was needed. The shock of the news had to sink in.

"The DNA results came back," Emily said. "I was as surprised as you are."

Samantha turned away and walked toward the workbench. "You think you really know someone. I guess the joke's on me. I told her everything about my marriage. How

I hated the idea that my husband had his hands in people's mouths all day long. It disgusted me. I told her how I thought my oldest wasn't very smart and I wanted to kill myself for thinking that."

"We all have silly thoughts. Every mother does." Emily said, as the woman crumpled in front of her.

"The point here," Samantha said, "is that I told her everything. If that baby isn't Mitch's, I wouldn't have the first clue as to whose it could have been. It makes me wonder if I ever really did know her at all."

"Nothing to suggest maybe she might have had an affair?"

Samantha shook her head. "Tell me something, Sheriff Kenyon."

"What?"

"How do you grieve for a best friend you really didn't know?"

Emily didn't have a good answer, but she offered one anyway. "There are things we don't know about each other, but our love is just the same."

Samantha looked around her perfectly organized garage. Order amid the chaos. "She was like a sister to me."

"I know. She still is."

"But I didn't really know her."

"Maybe she didn't want to disappoint you."

On the other side of Cherrystone, Jason Howard made the rounds of the scrapbooking group. Neither Erica Benoit nor Alana Gutierrez had an inkling about who might be the father. He caught up with Tammy Sells as she trudged out on the crunching snow to get her mail.

"If Mitch knew about it, it's the reason he killed her," she said, stuffing her mail into her coat pocket and bracing herself against the chilly air. "In a way, though, I'm kind of happy for Mandy. Maybe for the last few months, she really did have a little happiness after all."

"Thanks for your time," Jason said. "I'm sorry about your friend."

She looked at the young man and smiled. "Be good to your wife, deputy. She's depending on you."

"Thanks, ma'am. Will do."

Darla Montague, Mitch Crawford's assistant, was cleaning the "guest" tables from a day of free hot dogs. The dealership smelled more like a fast food place than a place that sold cars. Her spirit seemed to brighten when she saw Emily and Jason enter the showroom. She always expected good things would come her way, simply because she was good. *Or tried to be.*

"Hi, Mrs. Sheriff Kenyon," she said, letting out a little laugh.

"Hi, Darla. My deputy and I are here to see your boss. Is he in?"

"Yes, he is." She set down a bottle of diluted bleach and a cleaning cloth. "Mr. Crawford has been gone most of the day, but he came back an hour or so ago. He's in his office." She indicated the direction of the big glass windows that had enclosed the owner's office since Mitch's father opened up for business. A slogan painted on the window still endured: WE'LL STAND ON OUR HEADS TO MAKE YOU A GREAT DEAL.

Mitch was on the phone; his back was turned to face the car lot when Emily and Jason approached. When their reflections appeared on the glass, his body tightened and he turned around.

"Gotta go. Have some visitors here." He hung up and stood, his manner stiff and unwelcoming. "What do you want? Are you here to mess with my head some more?"

Emily inched closer. Jason lingered just a few paces behind her.

"No," she said. "We're here with what may be upsetting
news."

"What could be more disturbing than having my wife and
baby killed by some creep and having half of the town I love
think that I'm the one who did it?"

"I'm sure it has been very hard for you, too," Emily said,
her voice cool. "But you've put yourself in this position,
Mitch."

"Are you here to tell me how to act?"

The conversation was escalating to a place that would
have no victors. "No. I'm not. As I said, I'm here with some
very disturbing news."

Mitch folded his arms across his chest. "Yeah? What?"

"DNA results indicate that the baby your wife was carrying was not yours."

Silence. His dark brown eyes looked around the room and
his mouth tightened.

"Mitch, did you hear me?"

He turned and looked across the dealership. It was the
end of the day and the balloons had fallen to the ground. A
pair of salesmen, young and in need of commissions, stood
at the ready in case someone came on to the lot in search of
a deal.

"I heard you. And you ask me if I knew? Let me tell you
this. What you're saying is a goddamn lie. My wife would
never cheat on me. She would *never* do that to me. She knew
I could *never* forgive that. Now, get out. I don't ever want to
see you here on my lot again. Get your next car somewhere
else. I don't care. Leave me the hell alone."

Before he turned his back on them, Emily and Jason
thought they'd seen a tear in his eye.

Chapter Thirty-five

The next morning, Camille Hazelton gave the word and Mitch Crawford was arrested for the murder of his wife and daughter. There was no fanfare. No TV-style chase toward a chain-link fence. It was mundane, as criminal cases often are. Emily and Jason picked him up as he was going into the dealership.

"This is the biggest mistake you ever made," he said, setting his briefcase down. "And you've made a lot of them."

He looked right at Emily and she just dug her eyes deeper into his gaze.

"That's fine," Jason shot back. "We learn from all of our mistakes. Guess you don't."

Jason kicked the black briefcase to the side.

"Hey that's pig leather! Be careful or I'll sue!"

"You have the right to remain silent," Emily began. The words came from her lips, and with each one she thought of Mandy and her baby. This monster standing cuffed in front of her would never hurt anyone again.

The Cherrystone jail staffers—and two guys in custody for driving under the influence—could barely contain their glee over the arrest of Mitch Crawford. He came into the jail kicking like the brat that most of his advance publicity pegged him to be.

"These coveralls smell bad," he said. "I can't wear this filthy thing."

"You'll wear it or you'll walk around naked," a jailer said. "You pick."

The car dealer with the dead wife and baby had a complaint for everything. The food was bad, the place was filthy, and the staff was unprofessional.

"He thinks he's on a damn vacation," one of the DUIs said to the other with whom he was sharing a cell.

"Yeah. Cry me a river. This is no all-inclusive resort, that's for sure."

When it came time to shower, Mitch Crawford begged for unused flip-flops so his feet "didn't have to feel the slime of the vermin who've been here before me."

That didn't win him any friends, in a place where he probably could use one. It wasn't that anyone was going to "shank" him for a pack of smokes. It was more like someone might rough him up a little just because they could. It was also because in jail, outside of watching TV for an hour and hoping for a litter detail, there wasn't much to do.

Mitch Crawford was fresh blood and a welcome break from the jailhouse ennui that ensured long days.

"Shut up, you big baby," the older of the DUIs called over when the murder defendant complained about the filthy conditions of his holding cell. "Your dad sold me a lemon and I might just take it out on you."

As Emily continued to work on what she knew was a thin case, she skipped out on the arraignment and the bail hearing the next day. While it was true she was busy, she also saw no need to see Cary McConnell argue on behalf of his client. *It would be,* she thought, *like a barracuda cuddling up with a great white shark.*

Camille Hazelton called her from the courthouse. Emily could hear the sound of the prosecutor's heels as they smacked the marble floor.

"Interesting morning in court," she said.

"I'm guessing that he's already out."

"You'd be guessing wrong then."

"How much?" Emily expected the bail figure to be around $1 million. There weren't many murder cases in the history of Cherrystone, but the few such cases in recent memory usually ended up with the suspect behind bars pending the outcome of their trials. Few had the means of a successful businessman like Mitch Crawford.

Camille presented her words like she was pulling a table-cloth from under a china tea set.

"I asked for—and got—five million."

"You're kidding. How did you manage that?"

"I really don't know. I mean, I know I'm persuasive, but even I didn't expect that. I threw the number out, stating all that was true—flight risk, private plane, more money than God. Cary objected, of course, but he didn't challenge me on the flight-risk aspect, which was key. He told the judge that his client's wealth shouldn't hold him to a higher standard, but it was halfhearted."

"I love it when Cary has an off day."

"Yeah, there aren't too many of them."

"How long do you think it will take for Crawford to raise the money?"

"It'll take some doing. We've seen his finances. Very few of his assets are liquid. I'm not sure he'll put up the dealer-ship—and I'm not sure if he can. Seems that his stepmother still owns a chunk of the place. And they haven't spoken in ten years."

Chapter Thirty-six

Garden Grove

The first time that Olivia Barton saw the news clipping in her husband's wallet, she was doing laundry in the basement of their tidy house in Garden Grove, California. Olivia was an exceedingly organized woman who somehow managed to get all the laundry done, folded, and put away before her Saturday was shot. She hung sheets and towels outside because she and Michael liked the crispness that came with a line-dry. Darks were tumbled because no one liked a pair of jeans that stood on their own.

That morning Danny and Carla were watching the Cartoon Network with cups of Cheerios and apple juice drink boxes. From the downstairs, she could hear the TV and the relentless laugh track. It was the comforting soundtrack of her weekends.

Michael had left his wallet inside his jeans pocket and when she pulled it out, a small laminated newspaper clipping protruded. She'd never have opened his wallet to see what was inside. She'd learned from her own mother's mistakes—"Never look into something that doesn't concern you ... you just might find something that does."

It was silly advice, convoluted, like most of her mother's, but she got the essence of it.

Don't look for things that will break your heart.

That day she did just that, and her heart indeed shattered. It wasn't because of a motel receipt or a canceled check for an expensive gift that he never gave to her. That she could deal with. That she could scream about.

Not this. She looked at the clipping and started to cry. The picture of a little boy and a toddler girl wearing Mickey Mouse ears and sitting in a police station shook her. The boy looked like her son, though she knew it wasn't.

It was her husband.

Boy, Girl Abandoned at Disneyland

By Gwen Trexler,
SEA BREEZE GAZETTE Reporter

Disneyland is supposed to be "The Happiest Place on Earth" but not for two children who were abandoned there Wednesday when a woman—presumed to be their mother—asked an amusement park attendee to watch her son and daughter while she searched for a phone.

"She said she had an emergency call to make," Martina Montoya of Tustin said Thursday morning when contacted by the SEA BREEZE GAZETTE. "I waited for an hour. She never came back. I hope she's okay."

The park closed an hour later and Disney security searched for the missing woman. Her children, ages believed to be 10 and 2, are now in police custody.

Olivia wanted to cry, but with her own children around, she held it together. She couldn't fathom why Michael's mother had left her children. *How could anyone do that to a child?* Michael had told her only snippets about his past, including the fact that he'd had a sister that had been adopted by another family.

Later that afternoon, Michael, all sweaty from planting two small date palms and an enormous fan-shaped bird of paradise plant along the crisp white stucco wall that ran along the backside of the property, came inside.

Olivia's expression told him something was wrong, though she hadn't tried to show it.

"You OK?" he asked, pulling a gritty T-shirt over his head and tossing it into the now-empty laundry basket.

"I'm fine," she said.

There were things they never talked about. Things about his past that just seemed to be silent between them. Olivia's parents had known great hardship when they sneaked across the border at Nogales and made their way up to Washington State's Yakima Valley, where they picked apples and sent as much of the money home to Mexico as they could. That meant no new clothes, no books, no "extras" of any kind. There were days when they had nothing to eat but blocks of government surplus cheese and pinto beans.

Olivia made light of those days.

"Try living in a two-room shack with five brothers who have eaten nothing but beans, and you'll know what a nightmare really is," she'd say in her canned answer to those who asked about her past. It was always said with a laugh. Yet there was hurt there, too.

She'd been the reason her family came across the border that night. Her mother had her a week later in a motel outside of El Paso. When she was well enough to travel, they swaddled her and took a bus up north. In the years since, her three oldest brothers became naturalized citizens and successful businessmen. The two youngest never bothered.

All of that was an open book. It had to be. She needed her own children to understand where she had come from in order to be more than she'd ever dared to dream.

But not her husband. Michael was closed off from his past and even the slightest nudge toward some information about it brought rebuke. Sometimes even anger.

"I saw the clipping in your wallet," she said, her voice tentative. Her big eyes stayed fixed on him.

"That was a long time ago," he said.

"I know. But you've never told me about it. About your *mom*. What happened?"

"I'm not going to start now, Olivia."

He pulled off his jeans and took off his underwear, toe-kicking it into the basket. He was a pretty good shot and if she hadn't been trying to uncover more of his life she might have said so just then. She might even have said something about his physique. The workout in the yard left his muscles bulging and he'd looked more like an underwear model, sans underwear, than he did a computer systems geek. He turned on the shower and stepped inside, keeping his distance from the icy spray while waiting for it to warm.

Olivia stood by the glass door.

"Michael, I just want to know you better," she said.

He ducked his head under the water and she wondered if he'd heard her at all.

"I love you, Olivia, but I can't talk about that, babe. Don't ever ask again."

Olivia stood in the bathroom, the steam swirling from the shower and the image of her husband standing before her growing more and more distant. It was more than a metaphor for who he was, but who he'd always be.

Inside the shower, Michael Barton's tears mixed with the water.

* * *

The thought that just scuttled through his mind almost made him laugh, had it not been so painful. Robert and Helen Hansen had the first foster home that he and his sister had been assigned to after their mother failed to show up after leaving them at Disneyland. The Hansens were what he would later call "K4Ms" or Kids for Money—the kind of family who pretends to want to help children, but really only wants the $300 per head they get from the State of California each month.

Although state law prohibited keeping more than two children in a bedroom—and they had to be two children of the same gender—Michael and Sarah slept in a back bedroom of the Hansens' house in Tustin with four other children. The Hansens outfitted the room with three bunk beds that Robert Hansen had built himself out of pressure-treated timber he stole from a landscaper three blocks away. The chemicals in the wood made the kids sick, which made Helen Hansen madder than usual.

The first time that Robert Hansen abused Michael was a couple of weeks after he and his little sister arrived for foster care. Michael and the oldest boy in the house, a lanky kid with red hair and a swarm of freckles, were watching TV when Mr. Hansen came into the den. Mrs. Hansen, a morose brunette with spider veins that practically crocheted the skin around her ankles, had gone to the grocery store. The other kids were napping in the little warren of beds that met the minimum requirements for youth housing.

"Tim, you watch the kids," he told the redhead.

"OK, Papa," the boy said, barely looking up from the TV.

"Son, I want to show you something," he said, taking Michael by the hand and leading him to the garage. A cat meandered past them, and for a second, Michael thought that he was there to play with the cat. But the cat kept going, and Mr. Hansen said nothing to stop it. It was a two-car garage, but inside there was a single car and a workbench, a bed for the dog, and an old sofa.

Mr. Hansen was working on a Corvette that he'd been restoring for months, if not years. Its red fiberglass body was spotted with Bondo.

"Hop in," he said, holding open the passenger door.

Michael climbed inside. The car fascinated him at first. He'd had a Hot Wheels car similar to it back in Portland, though that, and everything else he owned, had been left behind.

"Beauty, huh?"

Michael watched as the man slid into the driver's seat. He reached over and clicked the automatic garage door opener and the gears overhead started to grind as the hinged panel rolled down, shuttering the sun from the garage. It went from a blast of light to a slit, to near darkness. Michael felt Mr. Hansen take his hand and press it into his crotch.

"That's a good boy," he said.

Michael wasn't sure what was happening, but he knew it was wrong. He tried to pull his hand away, but Mr. Hansen wouldn't let him.

"Hold on, cowboy," he said, leaning closer, his hot breath now against Michael's cheek. "You're gonna make Papa feel good."

The rest of what happened was lost in his memory. It wasn't because it wasn't traumatic, because to Michael Barton, it absolutely was. It was lost because, over time, Michael just turned it off.

"Suck on me until I tell you to stop," Mr. Hansen said.

Michael looked up and started to cry. "I want my mom."

"Stop crying and suck. Your mom dumped you because you were a bad boy."

Michael protested some more, but Mr. Hansen palmed

the back of his head like a volleyball and pressed it to his groin.

"Yeah, that's a good boy. That's my good boy."

It seemed to last a long time. *Horrifically long.* Inside his head, Michael sang the Itsy Bitsy Spider song over and over. It was a mantra that helped him through the hours he'd ended up spending in the Corvette, the laundry room at the end of the hall, the bathroom when Mrs. Hansen had gone to bed. As time went on and the incident was repeated, Michael knew it would end. He could read Mr. Hansen's body for the telltale signs that it was almost over. Mr. Hansen would stiffen his legs, moan about how good it felt, and then relax.

Mr. Hansen was a cigar smoker who liked to light up afterward and wave the cigar around, taunting the boy.

"Bet you'd like this in your mouth, too?"

While Michael was able to push most of the repulsion and shame that he felt out of his mind, whenever he smelled the pungent smoke of a While Owl cigar, his stomach would roil into knots.

Years later, he pushed the memory aside. Only temporarily, of course. He pulled a paper towel from the bathroom rod and patted his face. The mask was on. He looked good. He looked in control.

Chapter Thirty-seven

Dixon

It was strange how quickly they started coming and leaving things on the steps leading up to the big Tudor that was Beta Zeta House at Dixon University. A bouquet of carnations with the cellophane from the Dixon Kroger on West Cannonball Street was the first item. It had probably been dropped off there within two hours of the discovery of Sheraton's bloody body. From the settee in the front window, Jenna Kenyon and Midori Cassidy watched the other students come from across campus. They were carrying flowers, cards, candles—and even a beer bong.

"Sheraton would have liked that," Midori said.

Jenna looked at the girl, unsure how to respond.

"I mean, she would have thought that was funny," Midori quickly added. "You know?"

"I get it."

A plainclothes detective entered the living room and smiled at the young women. Her name was Kellie Jasper. She wore round-framed glasses that were far too large for her face. Her hair was curly and clipped short—a symptom of a woman too busy to care, or one who'd just given up.

"I know this has been a horrendous morning," she said from across the room.

The words brought Midori to tears again and Jenna patted her on the shoulder.

"Midori and Sheraton were very close."

"I know. I'm so sorry, darlin'," the detective said, taking a seat next to them so she'd no longer tower over the grieving girls. She turned to face Midori—a crumple of a human being, her long black hair limp and askew.

"We all have to work together, now. Sheraton is gone, but we will make sure that whoever did this to her is caught."

Midori looked like she was going to cry again and Jenna squeezed her hand.

"I'm going to take you in my car to the justice center, and another officer will bring you back."

"That's fine. I understand procedure," Jenna said, realizing that she sounded like some lame junior detective or a TV watcher who stayed glued to police procedurals.

"I understand that your mama's in law enforcement."

Jenna nodded. "She's a sheriff back in Washington."

Detective Jasper led them out the front door and down the steps.

"Yes, I remember reading about her, and, of course, reading about you."

Midori, who'd stopped crying, looked over at Jenna. She was clearly puzzled.

"Long story," she said, not wanting to go into it, but seeing that Midori could use a diversion. "OK. Basically, my mom and I were captured by a serial killer. He's dead now."

Inside her cruiser, the detective turned the ignition. "Not just any serial killer. Dylan Walker."

"Yeah, him," Jenna said, fastening her belt and wishing that she'd sat in the backseat instead of Midori.

"I've read about him," Midori said.

The statement surprised Jenna. She hadn't thought Midori *read* anything.

"I'll tell you about it sometime," Jenna said, knowing that she never would. She didn't like to revisit those days any more than her mother did. They never talked about it. They were glad that the media ignored the five-year anniversary of the handsome serial killer's death in that bunker on the Washington coast. They celebrated the fact that true-crime TV movies and books had fallen on hard times, and that none had been written or produced about the man and his crimes—and their role in his death.

"Yes, that was quite a story," the detective said, clearly angling for more information.

But Jenna wasn't going to bite. She'd said all she had to say. She turned away from Midori and faced the passenger window as the BZ house and the makeshift memorial faded from view. She played some images of those days of terror from five years ago in her mind, but she didn't let any of those images seize her. *How could she?* It seemed like so much nothing compared with the murder of her sorority sister, Sheraton Wilkes.

The offices of the Dixon Police Department were about on par with Cherrystone's, where Jenna had spent most of her teenage years popping in to drop something off, get some money, or just say hello. She recognized the conference room where the officers gathered at the beginning of their shift to catch up on what was happening. The weekend cops—some reserves, she guessed—had left a greasy box of apple fritters.

Those wouldn't have lasted back home, she thought.

She saw the bulletin board that was affixed with at least two hundred police and sheriffs' patches from across the south. Back home, Sheriff Kiplinger had started one of those, too. She remembered how happy he was when she brought in a patch from an Oregon county that he hadn't ever seen.

She'd won it on eBay for three dollars plus shipping, and she'd never seen a happier man.

Detective Jasper sat Jenna and Midori on folding metal chairs in a room that overlooked the parking lot of a Cracker Barrel Old Country Store and Restaurant. She set out a pad and a pen. She offered them coffee or sodas, but neither Jenna nor Midori felt like drinking anything.

Midori just wanted to cry.

"All right," the detective said, "I want to talk to you two, for a couple of reasons." She fixed her gaze on Midori and pushed a box of tissues toward her. "Midori, you are her best friend. We need to know everything you can tell us about Sheraton. Who were her friends? She have any enemies? Any run-ins with anyone? That kind of thing. OK?"

Midori dried her eyes. "OK."

"And you," she said, now looking at Jenna, "you were with Midori and Sheraton last night at dinner."

"Right. But I barely knew the girl. I'll be as helpful as I can be, though."

"Understood. Midori, tell me about Sheraton."

"What do you want to know?"

"Boyfriend troubles?"

"She was dating Matt Harper, but it was going all right."

"We know about Matt, and another detective is talking to him now. Any others? She was pretty. She probably broke a few hearts on campus."

Midori pulled the zipper on her hot pink Juicy tracksuit top. "She was a big flirt, but it was all in fun. Everyone liked her. If anyone's told you otherwise, they're lying."

"Everyone liked her but the killer."

Of course, the detective was right about that.

They discussed dinner the night before, how Sheraton had wanted to go out and party at one of the fraternity houses when they got back. Jenna stayed behind in the BZ house and Midori said she was out only until about twelve-thirty.

"I just wasn't into it. Sheraton was. She told me to go home and she'd be right behind me."

"What was she doing?"

"We were at the Tri Gamma house. She was on a couch talking to some guys and some other girls. There was nothing special about it. She was just talking, having a good time."

They talked for a little while longer. The detective took copious notes, though Jenna couldn't see what she was writing down.

There really wasn't that much to say. No one saw anything. This had to be some kind of random happening. There was no stalker. There was no person bent on revenge for some silly transgression. Whoever had slashed the life out of Sheraton Wilkes had done so out of a sickness for which she had only one word: *Evil.*

"So, Jenna," the detective asked, as the two young women stood to leave, "is there any reason anyone would want to kill you? You were supposed to be sleeping in that room, correct?"

Jenna slung her purse over her shoulder and gathered her coat.

"No," she said.

Midori's eyes widened and she stared at Jenna, then the detective.

Detective Jasper followed the pair as they started to leave. "No one harassing you? Bothering you? Threatening you?"

"No. No one at all. And thanks, Detective, I really needed you to say that. Nice."

Chapter Thirty-eight

Tustin, California

The dog's name was Maggie. Michael Barton called her Maggot.

She was a ten-year-old liver-and-white Springer spaniel mix that, by most observers' accounts, had to be the love of Mrs. Hansen's life. There was even proof of it. The wall next to the TV had been outfitted with shelves that gave clear and incontrovertible testament to the dog's place in the family— there were a dozen pictures of Maggie in silver and gold frames. There were none of any of the children who lived there with "Mama and Papa," as they were instructed to call the Hansens. Not a single one, not even a Polaroid. But there was Maggie on the beach in the surf, barking lazily at the sky. A shot of Maggie sprawled out on the sofa. Maggie with a Frisbee in her mouth, looking brightly at the camera.

How Michael grew to hate that canine. Certainly jealousy was a factor, and later in life, he'd figure that out. The dog was more important than any of the kids in the house.

One time when he didn't eat the rancid lentil soup that Mrs. Hansen had made and left on the stove for four days, she ladled some of it over the dog's kibble and made him eat

it there, on all fours like he was nothing more than an animal. When he cried and screamed and finally succumbed to
her demands, she laughed and turned to her dog.

"Don't worry, baby, I'll wash the bowl after he's finished
so you won't have to get any of his germs."

The dog seemed to smile.

But there was another reason to hate Maggie. The dog
was a cheerful witness to Michael's repeated humiliations at
the hands of Mr. Hansen.

Sometimes when Mr. Hansen had his pants unzipped and
his pelvis pressed into Michael's face, Maggie would sit in
the corner, panting like she was enjoying what the smelly
man was doing.

*Maybe the dog was happy that she didn't have to lick her
master there?*

Michael tried to talk to Maggie by sending messages
from his brain, to hers.

*Bite him! Make him stop! Bark! Do something! Stupid
dog!*

But Maggie sat there, almost smiling at what was happening.

Please help me, he thought.

Instead, she wagged her stub of a tail.

Michael was sure the dog understood just what he was
saying, just what Mr. Hansen was doing to him. The dog, he
reasoned, was evil.

The first time that Michael hurt Maggie was entirely by
accident. He was coming down from his bunk bed and didn't
see the dog curled up on a sleeping bag that held the newest
arrival, Kenny.

Maggie yelped when Michael planted his foot on her
hindquarter. Instead of dropping down to see if the dog was
all right, Michael felt an odd surge of something that he
couldn't quite peg at first. Something about hurting that animal, though accidental, felt good.

He did it again. This time, he put some effort into it.

Maggie growled and the noise only served to excite Michael. He wanted to jump up and down on the dog, busting its ribs into shards, cutting through the dog's organs, the lungs, the heart . . . and stopping her from that stupid dog smile.

"Hey, you're hurting her!" Kenny said, sitting up, wide-eyed with fear.

Michael pulled himself together, the vision of Maggie flattened into a bloody mess passed. "She's in the way!"

The new boy cradled Maggie. "Leave her alone."

Michael grinned. He didn't know it then, of course, but he'd just found something that gave him both pleasure and control. The smile that he gave Kenny had nothing to do with genuine joy. It was an involuntary, natural response to another person's fear.

In time, Michael started kicking the dog when no one was around. A while later, he graduated to other animals in the neighborhood. The first one that he killed was a neighbor's tortoise that had free rein of their backyard, eating bugs, vegetation, and enjoying the California sun that filtered through the eucalyptus and sycamore trees. Michael stole a screwdriver from Mr. Hansen's workbench and drove it through the reptile's shell. He sat there and watched the life drain away.

Two days later, he cut off the head of a cat that he'd beaten with a plastic baseball bat. It was easy to do, and it felt good, too. The tabby hadn't even put up a fight. It just looked up from the garbage can and he landed a blow, stunning it. He'd stolen a box cutter that he'd intended to use on Mr. Hansen's penis one time, but never found the nerve for it. But the cat was different. The cat couldn't get him in trouble.

Michael was surprised how easy it was to cut through the tabby's matted fur. It was nothing to slice through the skin, the tendons, and the vertebrae. Then, like a plucked orange from the mini citrus grove two doors down, the head fell off. So easy and so very final. He crouched behind the house next to the corral Mr. Hansen had built for the garbage receptacles and watched, coolly absorbed in the sight of a pool of maroon fluid as it slowly filled the spaces between the crushed white rocks that Mexican workers had hauled in the week before.

"That's so pretty," Mrs. Hansen had said. "Like a fairytale beach."

Not anymore, he thought. He felt nothing for the cat he'd decapitated. It had been a nuisance, anyway. It shouldn't have been in the trash in the first place.

When Mrs. Hansen saw the blood on his shirt later that afternoon, she said nothing. She didn't bend down to see if he was hurt. There was no running to the bathroom for a bandage and antiseptic as his mother might have done. No offers to kiss him and make him better.

She didn't chide him for making a mess of himself. She didn't do a damn thing.

He was sure he knew why.

She thinks Mr. Hansen hurt me. She's a stupid fat cow.

Chapter Thirty-nine

Cherrystone

Donna Rayburn, the lawyer who'd filled in for Cary Mc-Connell at the Crawford lineup, stood at the gas pump in $300 jeans, stiletto-heeled boots, and a creamy white leather coat that looked so soft it had to have been spread on her. Cherrystone, Washington, didn't see people like her too often.

Emily Kenyon doubted her Ethan Allen leather sofa cost as much as Donna's coat.

"Nice coat," the sheriff called to Donna from her gas pump, a row away—too close to pretend she didn't see her. She wanted to say something about how the coat's coloring was a near ringer for Donna's BMW, but thought better of it. "You look like you're headed off somewhere."

Donna nodded in Emily's direction. "Cary and I are going to his cabin. You know how he loves the great outdoors."

It was the first acknowledgment between the two women that they'd both dated Cary. Emily was relieved that her liaison with Cherrystone's most narcissistic lawyer was long since past. At the same time, she almost felt sorry for Donna. She was sleeping with the devil and didn't even know it.

"Oh yes, the cabin," Emily said. "I'm sure you'll have a wonderful time."

Donna turned off the pump and waited for her receipt.

"Only going for one night," she said. "Cary is such a workaholic." Donna slid into her car, waved at Emily, and drove off.

Emily finished filling the Crown Vic, wondering how on earth the department could justify the gas-hog that barely got fifteen miles to the gallon. She also wondered who approved such a hideous kelly green livery for the small fleet of department cars. Mostly she pondered how long it would take Donna to wise up about Cary.

She'd been up to the cabin a couple of times in the beginning of her relationship with Cary. It was a few miles from the Schweitzer Mountain Resort, in northern Idaho. The whole place was a shrine to Cary and his quest to be the most formidable at all the things he did. Everything was the best. His snowmobiles, fishing gear, and ski equipment. Weekends at the cabin were exhausting, and not for the reasons most being romanced would hope.

Poor stupid, BMW-owning Donna. She'll just have to figure out things on her own.

Chapter Forty

Stanton, California

Michael Barton was never quite sure how it came to be that he and Sarah were taken from the Hansens' foster home to the Ogilvy Home for Children in Stanton, California. Was it something he did? The dead animals? The little fire he set? Maybe it was that he was no longer wanted once a younger boy named Jeremy came to stay.

Maybe he was really worth nothing after all?

Years later, he'd tell Olivia about it, in terms that suggested a kind of rescue, but he really felt more regret than anything.

"The Hansens were despicable," he said one time when he let her inside a sliver of his dark past, "but it felt like home. Sick. But home. Ogilvy always felt like a concentration camp for the lost."

"It couldn't have been that bad," Olivia said. "It was state approved, wasn't it?"

Michael allowed a wide smile across his face. Inside, he wanted to scream at the woman to whom he sought to make himself whole, normal.

"Of course. But Ms. McCutcheon did things her way."

* * *

Marilyn McCutcheon was the floor director of the "intensive" unit of the Ogilvy Home. The building that housed the home for the wayward and the disposable had once been part of Stanton High School. It had a cafeteria, gymnasium, and forty-four classrooms which were converted in 1961 into dormitory rooms and offices for a staff of eighty, full- and part-time. Most who worked there, caring for the 220 children on the way station to either reform school or a foster home, were there because they couldn't get a better-paying job elsewhere. If they were half decent in their appearance, skill, and work ethic, they'd be there no longer than six months.

But not Marilyn McCutcheon. The fiftyish, prematurely gray-haired, giantess of a woman with big hands and a lumbering gait was there because she loved it. She loved it because for eight hours every day at Ogilvy, she was in charge of her floor. She ran it the way she wanted. No one told her what to do or when to do it.

It wasn't that way at home. When McCutcheon got home, her mother and father, both in their late seventies, yelled and screamed at her for being the lousy person they said she'd always been.

"I should have had my tubes tied before you were born," her mother said at least once a month.

"No wonder you couldn't find a man," her father would say. "You are bigger than a football player. No man would want a woman like you."

Marilyn wanted to kill them. She certainly thought of ways to do it. One time she even left the house after turning off the oven pilot light. She imagined that she might even hear the explosion all the way over at Ogilvy. But it never came. When she got home, she found that the oven had automatically shut off.

Her parents yelled at for her being late and all she could

think of was how happy she was shopping after work, thinking they'd be dead.

Marilyn lived for the job. It was her sanctuary. Being there was her release. The children were her therapy. They were her punching bags.

The social worker told Michael and Sarah they would be at Ogilvy "temporarily" until another home opened up.

Michael was glad to leave the Hansen place. He never told anyone what Mr. Hansen had made him do, though he almost confided what had been going on to a teacher one time. It was so close; the words begged to come from his mouth as the teacher's sympathetic eyes drew him in. *She'll help me. She'll protect me. She'll save me.*

"Are you all right, Michael?" the teacher, a woman, asked. "I know it's hard with your mom gone, but you can tell me. I care."

"It's very bad," he said.

"Tell me what you did," she asked.

What he had done?

If he'd spoken up, he might have changed the trajectory of his life. Her words stopped him cold. For a flicker, he thought that maybe he had deserved what Papa had done to him. After all, as far as he could tell, he'd been the only one in the Hansen household to have to do those terrible things. Maybe he had been bad? Maybe what he was doing was his fault?

No, he thought. *She's wrong. She doesn't know what she's talking about.*

What stopped him was the dark threat that Papa lobbed at him when his face was buried in the man's smelly crotch.

"You tell on me and I will kill your sister. Papa doesn't like little girls anyway, cowboy."

The teacher looked at the wall clock. She had something to do.

"We can talk about it later. And, I promise," she said, gathering her purse, "that I will help you."

"OK," Michael said, knowing full well that he'd never tell her. He'd never tell anyone. The danger to Sarah was too great. The door had slammed shut.

"I can tell that you're nothing but trouble," Marilyn Mc-Cutcheon said when she came upon Michael and Sarah ten minutes after intake. "And I won't have it."

"You," she said, pointing to Sarah, "are a dirty little bird."

"She's *not*," Michael shot back, while his sister sat on one of the stained green couches that lined the family visiting area that had once been a high school library. Shelves, though empty of books, were a visual cue that would not have been lost even on an eleven-year-old.

Marilyn grabbed Michael by the wrist and wrenched him from his seat. He started to cry out and she shoved her big hand tight over his face.

"Don't. Don't *ever*. Don't ever defy me," she said. Her words were a wretched vomit, spewing out of her mouth and all over the little boy. He was nothing. He was garbage. "This is my floor. You got it?"

He started to squirm.

She twisted him tighter and pushed so hard against his mouth and nose that he couldn't breathe.

"I said, do you understand?"

His eyes were flooded with terror. Sarah sat still, almost catatonic, watching the big woman wrestle her brother.

He nodded.

"Good. You don't ever want to mess with me."

His head bobbed again.

Later that evening, with his sister in classroom 14 down the hall, Michael Barton wet the bed for the first time. It was the beginning of a cycle that he feared would never end, even in manhood.

Every morning, Marilyn McCutchcon would haul Michael's two-inch-thick mattress out in the hall and hand him a brush and a steel pail of soapy water.

"You'll clean this up or I'll beat you," she said, her cold blue eyes burrowing deeply into his. "You got that?"

Of course, he did. Other kids laughed at him. The staff called him "Michael the Flood."

Olivia Barton knew better than to have any books on child abuse in the house. She knew how angry Michael became when she appeared to be studying the subject. That meant no novels, no nonfiction on the subject. Anywhere in the house. She'd been a frequent visitor to the Garden Grove West Library on the corner of Bailey and Chapman where she practically owned the 150s of the Dewey Decimal system—all forms of psychology contained in four rows of books at the branch. For a time, she'd been sucked in by every *Oprah* or *Dr. Phil* TV show that even hinted at child abuse as a subject. Bonus points came when the program touched on the subject and how it might impact the lives of an adult survivor.

Olivia liked the word *survivor* when it was applied to her husband. She was sure that his experiences in foster care, in the state institution, maybe even in the years *before* his mother abandoned him, had likely been bad—but not *Oprah* or *Dr. Phil* bad.

How could it be, she asked herself over and over, *when Michael is so normal now?*

Chapter Forty-one

It was a shock wave of fear. If it was meant to stop everyone in the middle of what they were doing, it did so. The unintelligible scream coming from the kitchen was undeniably blood-curdling. All throughout the home, the children and their keepers turned toward the sound. Even the kid who sat in front of the TV day after day with a frosted strawberry Pop-Tart on his lap and the empty look of a lost soul glued to a video of SpongeBob SquarePants moved toward the horrific scream that ricocheted throughout the facility.

Something very bad just happened. Something worse than someone wetting the bed, trading their meds, or stealing extra food.

The next scream came with words. "Oh, my God! What could have happened here! Please help me!"

The voice belonged to Consuelo Ramirez, the cook.

"She must have cut herself again!" another voice called out, as the sound of a score of feet went clacking down the linoleum corridor to the kitchen. Something very, very bad had happened. One quick-thinking employee swung open the wall-mounted first aid kit and grabbed tape, gauze, and a fistful of bandages.

Indeed, when staff and a few children arrived at the

kitchen, there was blood and the stink of death. At first, no one saw Consuelo. A rapid scan of the room found her sitting on the floor, crouched in a near-fetal position.

"Sweet Jesus, who would do this to our Boots?" Consuelo looked up at those who had arrived to her aid. She held the black-and-white body of Boots, the cat that Marilyn McCutcheon had found in the parking lot seven or eight years before. It was a black-and-white cat, named very unoriginally for its white paws. To be fair, the name could have been Mittens just as easily, but Marilyn had loved Nancy Sinatra so much that she named the cat Boots and frequently found time to whisper-sing "These Boots Are Made for Walking."

"What happened?" Marilyn said, rushing to the lifeless body of her beloved cat.

"I don't know." Consuelo was in tears then.

"Where did you find her?" Marilyn held gently took the cat from the head cook's arms. A bloody Rorschach blot was smeared on her light blue blouse. The form looked a bit like a snow angel; the bloody fur had smeared in such a way that it looked like the cat had left the imprint of wings.

One of the kids started to cry, and soon others joined in.

"She was in the mixer. It must have turned on somehow. She liked to curl up and sleep in tight spaces, you know." Marilyn didn't cry, but the look on her face indicated a meltdown was coming. Children and staff who knew her only hoped that she'd take out her anger on someone other than them. "There's no way Boots turned it on," she said, looking around at the horrified faces.

She was right, of course, but there was no way anyone was going to say so.

On the other side of the facility, Michael Barton stepped from the shower and got dressed. He'd put his bloody pajamas into a plastic bag he'd stolen from the supply room and wrapped that in a cocoon of paper towels in case someone looked through the trash. He also stole clean pajamas from the laundry room and hid them under his clothes.

He'd prepared.

The cat hadn't really put up much of a fight. He didn't get a single scratch. It had taken a quick turn of the animal's head, a snap, and then he could do anything he wanted to with it. It was a furry bag of dead.

A broken neck was quick and decisive. It got the job done. But ultimately, it was no fun.

How to make it fun?

A knife was the answer. It beckoned from the counter next to the sink. In a second, in a flash that was too fast for him to really grasp, he made it fun. Michael gingerly gutted Boots with a small paring knife, splashing the smelly fluids—mostly blood—over the front of his pajamas. His heart rate remained normal. It was odd, and he'd ruminate over that later in life. Though he was excited by what he was doing, he wasn't scared.

He set the cat's corpse with his entrails oozing into the in-stitutional-sized mixing bowl and turned it on the setting called Pulse.

Funny, she doesn't have a pulse, he thought in apprecia-tion of the irony of what he'd just done.

He knew how much Marilyn McCutcheon loved that cat. It might have been the only thing she ever loved. He'd see her from across the TV lounge, holding the cat in her lap talking to it in a kind of sickening baby talk.

"Who's the prettiest kitty in the whole wide world?" Mar-ilyn asked, scratching the cat under the dollop of white fur under its chin. "You are, that's who."

The cat didn't know Marilyn was a terror to everyone else. Marilyn had scooped her up from the cold outside and given her a cozy existence. If it hadn't been for the annoying children at the group home, it might have been perfect.

"How's my precious little fluff ball?" she'd ask.

How was it that a cat was worthy of love when a little girl or young boy was only the focus of derision and scorn?

Later that day, when the excitement of the horror of what happened to the cat had died down, Michael and Sarah played together in the corner of the TV lounge that had been set aside for reading. It wasn't really a library, of course. Just as the place wasn't *really* a home, though it had branded itself as one.

Marilyn came through on her rounds and looked over at the pair.

Michael looked up. No expression. Nothing at all. Then he returned his gaze back to the book he was reading to Sarah.

The Cat in the Hat.

Chapter Forty-two

Garden Grove

Michael Barton cried when the ultrasound technician turned to him as she moved the jellied wand over his wife's abdomen, looked at the monitor, and said, "You're going to have a son."

Olivia tilted her head up from the table to get a better look herself. The image was a little grainy, but to a mother-to-be it was a portrait done by American impressionist Mary Cassatt.

A tear ran down Michael's handsome face and stopped on his nose. He almost breathed in his tear before reaching for a medical wipe from a large cardboard box on the tray table. He stayed silent for a second, and tried to smile. He had hoped so much that the baby Olivia was carrying would be a girl. He'd read the statistics, of course, and he knew that those who are abused are likely to become abusers themselves.

"Honey, I feel the same way," Olivia said, looking at her husband's silent tear. "I'm so excited and scared at the same time."

Scared? He thought. *Olivia doesn't know fear.*

He did.

Michael was a facile liar by then, and he knew it. He thanked God for the practiced skill. Being able to skirt past the truth without batting a lash was an ability that had served him well. It allowed for survival.

"Having a son has been a dream of mine," he said, his voice very soft. "I want to give him the boyhood that I never had."

"I know. Me, too," she said, lifting her head, this time toward her husband, so that he would kiss her. He bent down, and pressed his lips against hers.

As the technician started to mop the gooey globe that was on Olivia's swelling abdomen, she grinned and shook her head slightly. There was so much joy in seeing people's dreams come true. The tech pumped the foot pedal and dropped the used wipes into the stainless drum garbage can.

"You're going to make a beautiful family," she said exiting the examining room.

Olivia got dressed, euphoric with the news. She wanted nothing more than to get on the phone and call her mother.

"A boy!" It would be the first boy in her family in years. She gave Michael another kiss and dialed her mom with the news.

"I'm going to go to the bathroom," he said, leaving Olivia to her call.

The bathroom was one of those family-oriented configurations, with a changing table and a toilet. Best of all, it had a lock on the door. He clicked the lock, turned on the water, and splashed it all over his face. He looked into the mirror.

What am I? A man or a monster?

Michael wasn't sure. All he knew was that all the things that happened to him, that made him who he was—whatever it was—were seeded long ago.

* * *

It started with the idea that if he stopped drinking a glass of water before bedtime, he wouldn't wet the bed. Soon it was if he'd stopped drinking anything after lunchtime that surely would stem the nighttime occurrence that brought him such overpowering shame. Sometimes, he woke up in the middle of the night and put his hand to his crotch hoping against hope that the wetness that he'd felt had only been the result of seminal discharge and not the flood of urine that taunted him over and over. It was like a pelvic waterboarding, hitting him over and over, telling him that he was useless, a loser, a freak. Every now and then he woke up in time to strip the bed silently and bundle the sheets into a pillowcase so he could hide them from the staff. Those were the best mornings.

Those were the mornings without the taunts from the others.

Michael the Flood! Michael the Flood! Michael forgot to row the boat ashore!

When he was fourteen, he created a contraption from a plastic Coke bottle and a pair of Ace bandages. He fashioned the bottle into a kind of homemade bedpan, which he held in place with the bandages strapped around his waist and thighs. He became adept at his stealthy subterfuge. He still didn't drink past noon. He still hated the smell of his body, only more so because of the urine.

If he'd have believed in God or anything good, holy or kind, he would have held hope that whatever was wrong with him would pass.

That he'd never want to hurt anyone again.

But now and then, throughout his teenage years, he couldn't stop himself from looking for ways to kill someone and not get caught. It was merely a thought, and never put into practice.

Maybe he'd found a way to cure himself?

* * *

Michael had only one piece of paper that seemed to give concrete proof that he'd ever had a life outside of foster care or a state institution. It was the small news clipping about when he and Sarah were found at Disneyland. He'd used it to call the police department to see if there was a case file, but the cop who'd been mentioned had transferred to another jurisdiction.

The idea that his mother could dump her children like garbage made the bile rise in his throat like a choking acid.

The Ogilvy Home for Children had a two-bit computer lab of obsolete PCs and printers that didn't work. It had no Internet access, or he'd have tried to find her. He smuggled a disc from the rickety lab and occasionally kept notes, stories, and thoughts.

He wrote of a staff member who had looked at him with the "evil eye" when he was walking to the cafeteria after morning classes.

He's a fat pig. He even has a pig nose. I'd like to take a knife, slit him up the middle and spill his smelly guts all over the chemistry lab. I'd do it slowly. I'd do it in front of everyone so that when he cried out, I'd tell everyone to shut up or I'd do it to them.

Another time, after she was gone, he wrote tenderly of his sister.

Sarah deserves better and I know she's found it. She's in a sunny place. She's eating fruit that isn't soft and mushy from a can. She doesn't have that weird metal taste in her mouth and she shouldn't. She didn't deserve any of this shit that mom dumped on her.

He never included himself in those rants. He never fixated on why he wasn't worthy of a decent home, the love of the family. He was smart enough to know why. He'd wetted the bed. He was filled with hate for just about everyone. He figured that the rest of the world didn't care about someone like him.

Not until he did something to hurt them. Then, they'd get it. Too late. But they'd get it nevertheless.

Almost everything with a heartbeat seemed to provoke him. He tried to interest the other boys in the institution in doing what he called "frog stomping." Whenever the sprinklers ran long into the night during the summer, the cement courtyard would be dotted with the small jumping creatures. He saw no difference in turning them into splat than adults who'd crushed a bug.

"You're a sicko," said one of the other kids, a Mexican who considered himself a badass, but who didn't like the frog-stomping game.

"You're a faggot," Michael shot back, using the word that he loathed more than anything. It was the word Mr. Hansen had called him a time or two.

"You're a good boy," he'd said as he pleasured himself against Michael's pale young skin. "Maybe too good a boy. Maybe you're a faggot and you really like this."

Michael killed cats and dogs and found that he enjoyed it. Other kinds of animal murder merely brought him a smile. One time, he poisoned the fish in the dentist's office. When the receptionist turned her back, he emptied a Baggie filled with ammonia. By the time he'd left the dentist chair, he was beaming.

No cavities and an aquarium full of floaters. Who could ask for more?

Chapter Forty-three

The morning light filtered through the café curtains that Olivia Barton had made as her first sewing project with the machine Michael and the kids had given her that Christmas. She hadn't liked the frilly selection at the Linen N Things that commanded most of the real estate in their neighborhood strip mall. She wanted simple and chic, not country saloon. She smiled at her handiwork and waited for Michael to notice them. She vowed she'd wait a week if she had to. Maybe *two*.

The smell of orange juice and frying bacon filled the air of the amber-painted walls of the kitchen. The children were still asleep, which was slightly unusual. Olivia didn't mind. Michael had come in late on Friday, and the kids waited up to see their father. Their slumber meant that she'd have time alone with the man she loved.

But something seemed wrong.

Olivia looked at Michael with her dark brown eyes full of genuine concern as he stared at the screen of the small TV mounted under the white cabinets.

"Are you all right?" she asked.

He didn't respond. He kept his eyes fixed on the screen.

A brunette helmet-headed reporter with a shrill delivery

reported on the horrific murder of the girl at Beta Zeta House at the university in Dixon, Tennessee. Michael looked a little flushed. It was more than being tired from the long trip. He just didn't look right. Out of sorts? Sick?

". . . The crime scene was so grisly that FBI profilers tell me that the killer was driven by rage against the victim. This killing, they say, was personal."

"Fine," Michael said. He reached for his *World's Best Daddy* coffee cup. "I'm fine."

Olivia looked at the photo on the screen. It was a pretty girl, young, full of life. Under her photograph, the chyron lettering identified the victim: *Sheraton Wilkes, dead at 20.*

"Sad story. Such a waste," Olivia said as she poured some creamer into the cup.

Michael looked down at his twin piles of hotel and restaurant receipts and took a swig of his black coffee. "Agreed." He fidgeted with the receipts, as though he couldn't find something important. He was really looking for a way out of the conversation. A graceful way out. One that wouldn't cause worry.

"I'm not feeling so well, I guess," he said. "Probably food poisoning from that seafood restaurant."

Olivia felt his forehead. "You know you should never eat seafood if you can't see the ocean from the dining room."

He managed a brief smile. It was as fake as could be, but he hoped she didn't see that. He loved her more than anything. A tear in his facade, and just maybe she'd see him for what he was.

"I know. I know," he said, excusing himself for the downstairs powder room.

"Oh, baby," she said, "I'm sorry you don't feel well."

"It'll pass."

With the door shut and locked, he turned on the fan and ran the sink tap at full force. He flushed the toilet. He did whatever he could to give him a second in which he could let out his anger and disappointment. He paced, but there was barely any room in there to move. He felt the walls move in and out, taunting him.

From the kitchen, Olivia heard the muffled noise and went in search of antacid.

He must be really, really sick, she thought, rifling through the shelf next to the sink that held ten kinds of children's vitamins, cough medicine, and a few things for the adults of the house.

Michael braced his body by grabbing on to the opposite sides of the pedestal sink. He faced the mirror straight on. His eyes were dilated in the dim lighting of the windowless powder room. His mouth was tight, a knothole of anger. He wanted nothing more than to yell out to the world that he was the stupidest man on the planet. A fool. An idiot. All that everyone had told him about himself was true. He had fooled Olivia, but for how long? When would she know what he was? What fueled him? What he'd done to survive?

What twisted lengths he'd gone to to calm himself?

He grabbed a hand towel and shoved it into his mouth, nearly gagging. Sweat poured from his temples. He reached over and flushed the toilet again; the noise of the rushing water filled the small space. At least he hoped so. He wanted to scream, but he let out a muffled yelp.

Sheraton Wilkes.

Jesus, he was the fool they'd all said he was. The bed wetter. The kid no one wanted. The kid who was dumped off at Disneyland by a mother who surely cared more about herself than her children.

Sheraton Wilkes.

He'd killed the *wrong* girl. He'd never even heard of her. What was she doing there, at that time? Sheraton Wilkes wasn't on his list.

Jenna Kenyon was.

He splashed water on his face and then let out a couple of phony coughs.

Olivia stood outside the door. The knob turned a little, but he'd locked it. "Honey, you OK?"

"Be out in a minute." He flushed the toilet for the third time and stared at his face in the mirror. He looked older than his years. He was tired. Angry at the world. "I'm not going to screw up again. I can do this," he said in a soft, but angry whisper. "I can do this."

"Honey?"

"Just a minute, Olivia!" He snapped at her, and wished he hadn't. She wasn't the problem. She was never the problem.

He swung open the door, ready to face the world and plan what he had to do.

"Here you go," Olivia said, handing him a fizzing glass of water. She looked worried, not scared. For that, he was grateful.

He looked at the glass questioningly.

"Alka-Seltzer," she said.

"I hate that stuff. You know that."

"It's not like it'll kill you."

Michael smiled at his wife. If killing were only so easy. Killing, he knew, was sometimes very difficult and, frequently, very disappointing work.

"Let's go wake up the kids," he said. "I need some hugs."

Chapter Forty-four

The offices of Human Solutions, Inc., were on the fifth floor of a mirrored glass building in Santa Ana, California, two blocks west of the courthouse. It was a nondescript location with a trio of dying date palms and clumps of tiger lilies that the garden service should have divided or yanked two seasons ago. A vendor selling sliced melons and churros worked the outer edges of the parking lot. Other than shabby gardening practices, it was as nondescript as any shiny building off any interstate.

Inside, the HSI offices were mauve-and-taupe cubicles with laminate counters and gooseneck lamps. It had a distinct nineties milieu, but that had more to do with the company's frugal nature than the fact that the offices had once been used as the headquarters for a diet center company that went belly-up.

Michael Barton's office was hard-walled with a door. On one wall, he had a framed poster given to him by his coworkers. It depicted four men silhouetted against a fading sunset with the words: *Teamwork: Together We Achieve More.* He found the rah-rah sentiment exceedingly hokey. He didn't think he needed anyone to do anything. Despite all odds, he'd achieved quite a lot, thank you. Despite his compulsions, he had made a life. A picture of Olivia taken on their honeymoon in Hawaii and another of his children sat on his desk. The surface of his desk was in order. All papers were placed perfectly squared up with the edge of the desk. His office phone gleamed from having a daily dusting. His laptop's docking station was as pristine as it was the day it was installed.

Everything about the space suggested a man in control.

The company CEO, a pudgy man with black hair that he VO-5'd to such a degree it dripped, knew that Michael Barton was among his most brilliant consultants. He'd come up through the ranks, first as a programmer, then an engineer. HSI tapped the kid on the shoulder and made him into what he was by paying for his education at Cal Polytechnic. There were things about him that the office staff both admired and found amusing. On the days that he came into the office, he walked in at 8:30 on the dot. It was uncanny. Never a minute earlier, or a second later.

One of the temps from Kelly Services found out why. One day, she saw Michael in the parking lot looking at his wristwatch like a swimming coach with a stopwatch. He didn't move until the second hand told him just when. Once he got the go-ahead, he marched right for the front door, black briefcase at his side, can of Diet Coke or cup of coffee ("caffeine du jour" he liked to call it) in his hand.

No stopping to say hi. No tip of the hat or acknowledgment to a friendly face. Just a beeline through the door and up the staircase. Never, ever, did he take the elevator.

Michael was rigid in other ways, too. He seldom took a lunch break, but instead took a two-mile run down the boulevard and then back to the basement of the building for a shower. He'd return to his office right at 1 P.M., again on the dot, smelling of Irish Spring soap.

Only one time did he deviate from that routine. He came back a half hour late with a big scratch across his cheek.

"I fell down," he said, scooting into his office and shutting the door. He stayed put that day until after everyone else had gone.

The next day, when he returned to work, the sharp-eyed Kelly temp thought she noticed something strange on his face.

"I think Mr. Barton is wearing makeup," she said to an office friend when they were getting Doritos and Diet Cokes. "It looks like he tried to cover up that scratch from yesterday."

The other woman nodded. It did, indeed, appear that way.

"At least it isn't eyeliner. That would make me worry."

They laughed, fished for their change from the slot of the pop machine, and went back to their desks.

Business partners—"never call a customer a customer"— liked Michael Barton for all the reasons that made him dependable. The IT industry had been populated with kids, goofballs and flakes, and a young man who knew what it meant to be where he was supposed to be and do what he said he'd do was refreshing.

In time, Michael Barton became Human Solutions' most sought-after consultant. His business card read: SENIOR CONSULTANT. The demand led to freedoms and perks that eluded other troubleshooters in the office. He was able to work at home one or two days a week. He was able to pick and choose which business partners he wanted to call on.

When he told his boss that he was heading to Nashville to assist a restaurant chain that was having problems with their database, no one stopped him. No one knew that the client hadn't called for support—that it was Michael who called *them*.

"I'm going to be in town anyway, and I thought I'd stop by," he said. "Just a friendly see how y'all are doing, OK?"

The business partner saw no harm.

His boss saw no need to query him. The South was booming, after all.

"Have a great trip," he said. "We're making a killing over there and we have you and your good work to thank for that. Keep it up."

Michael grinned. It was just too funny a comment not to flip it back at his oily-headed boss.

"Oh, I intend to. I really do."

Olivia was in the Barton's home office printing copies of the flyer she was going to post in the neighborhood when she heard her husband activate the automatic garage door opener and pull his car inside. Michael had been gone overnight to a trade show in Portland. With him home, things could get back to normal. She smiled when she heard the car door close and the garage door rumble back shut.

The drama of their missing cat had come to a head.

"Daddy's home!" she called out to Danny and Carla, who were sitting in front of the TV, enthralled by a reality show that they probably were too young to watch. But Olivia hadn't wanted to fight that battle with her husband away on business.

The laser printer lurched into action and after a quick glance, Olivia determined that the toner cartridge would probably hold up for the ten copies she needed.

LOST CAT
His name is Simon and he's very friendly . . .
and very missed by two small children.
__Please__ call if you see him.

She met Michael by the door that led from the kitchen to the interior of the garage.

"Hi, baby," she said, setting the sample flyer on the kitchen table.

"Hi yourself, beautiful," he said, embracing her and they kissed. "Missed you tons."

"Me, too. Good trip?"

"Not too bad. Fixed the problems, and upsold some, but, you know, I always wish I could do better." His eyes lit on the flyer.

"I'll get the kids a dog," he said.

"We're not giving up on Simon. You know, I'm no quitter."

"Yeah, I know. But I think a coyote got Simon. Saw one by the garbage can the other day. A dog would have a better shot at survival around here."

A second later, Danny and Carla came running into the kitchen.

"Daddy's home!"

Michael scooped up his children one at a time and kissed each on the tops of their heads.

"Hey, I think I have a little something for you two in the car."

"What is it?" Danny asked. Having his father come home from a business trip all but guaranteed a surprise of some kind. Sometimes it was just a little token, picked up at the airport gift shop, other times it was the item that Santa had forgot to bring.

"It wouldn't be a surprise," he said, "if I told you."

While the children squirmed in anticipation and Olivia smiled at their excitment, Michael disappeared into garage.

"*Shit*," he thought, looking over at the workbench vise where he'd crushed Simon's head with a final twist. Killing the cat, torturing the cat, had brought a kind of relief. It was like he was a kid who'd gotten the right dosage of Ritalin and was able to focus clearly. It brought a rush, too. But not now.

Not when he saw the faces of his wife and children. They missed the cat. They wanted the cat to come back home. They didn't know, and he knew they couldn't understand anyone's compulsion to crush the family pet's skull.

Maybe no one could.

Maybe there was no one else in the world who could understand him.

The only one who might really understand what had made him who he was had been taken away. She was so young, but she was there. She'd seen it happen. She alone understood what had transpired. But she'd been taken away. The day after his thirteenth birthday, Michael was alone for good. Sarah, almost five, was selected by a foster couple as a "transitional foster daughter" and was moved to Riverside, east of Los Angeles. She was in the queue for full-time adoption by another couple.

They told me they wouldn't split us up, he thought, remembering. She's my blood.

Only one time in their married lives had Olivia seen her husband fall apart in a manner that suggested he might have residual problems from a very difficult childhood. It happened when Danny was just three. Olivia and Michael were in bed, having drifted off to a sound sleep after passionate lovemaking that had Olivia forgetting that she was anything other than a lover to a wonderful man. No wife. No mother. No chief cook and bottle washer. As she lay next to her husband, she counted her blessings. Moonlight scattered across the walls in crisp slits from the miniblinds that she'd twisted only partially shut. The blissful moment was shattered by the sound of her son's voice.

"Mamma?" It was Danny's little voice, as he entered his parents' bedroom.

Olivia awoke and reached for her robe. "What is it?"

"I made an accident." Danny started to cry, waking Michael.

"What is it?"

"He wet the bed. I'll take care of it."

Michael sat up like a shot. "What happened?"

"He wet the bed. Sleep."

"What about his Pull-Ups?"

"I thought we'd try big-boy underwear tonight."

"He's not ready! And now he's wet the goddamn bed. Jesus! Olivia! How stupid could you be?"

"Honey—"

Michael, still nude, bolted out of bed and chased after his son. His lean body was a contorted mass of muscles and anger. Sweat ran from his temples.

Danny's cries turned into screams.

"What are you doing?"

"I will not," he said. "I will not have a boy that wets the bed. You understand? I don't care if he wears diapers until he's ten."

His face was red and his eyes were bulging. Olivia was stunned. His rage was way off the charts. Every little boy makes a mistake or two.

"Calm down," she said, "You're scaring our son!"

Michael gulped for air. "He doesn't know what fear is."

Olivia scooped up Danny and took the crying three-year-old into the master bedroom. "Find another place to sleep tonight." She shut the door.

"I will not have it," Michael said. "I will *not*."

The next morning, Olivia could barely look at her husband. He apologized for what he'd said and done, but no matter what the underlying reason, there was no excuse.

He'd only wet the bed. He's just a little boy.

* * *

Most men hate the idea of changing a diaper. Some consider it "woman's work" or just flat-out avoid it because they're lazy and don't like the idea of foul-smelling, soiled diapers or even the perfumed baby wipes that are supposed to make the task more tolerable. But for Michael Barton, avoiding changing Danny's diaper was about self-preservation. He had no idea what, if anything, he'd do when faced with a tiny penis and a helpless child. He worried that whatever had been done to him, even before Mr. Hansen, had happened when he was so small.

So helpless.

So without the ability to comprehend.

"I just can't do it," he told Olivia when they first brought Danny home. "I can feed him. I can burp him. Just can't see myself changing him. Don't have the stomach for it, babe. Sorry."

Olivia seemed to understand.

He was hopeful that even if he was soulless and without any hope of redemption, he would never pass on the evil that had cursed his own life.

Evil, he knew, was both born and learned.

Chapter Forty-five

The last time that Michael Barton had been to Disneyland was memorable for all of the wrong reasons. It was the place his mom handed his sister and him off to a stranger in front of the Swiss Family Robinson Tree House. It was the last time he'd ever see her, and with her vanishing, the last glimpse of his own childhood.

Before it was stolen by those who did not love him or his sister.

Michael thought of a million reasons why he didn't want to go there, suggesting that Knott's Berry Farm was a superior attraction for young families.

"Knott's is more fun," he said, urging Olivia to reconsider her push for the Magic Kingdom. "I also feel like one of their chicken dinners. You like those, too, Olivia. Remember?"

Olivia did, but she also wanted to see Disneyland with Carla and Danny.

"I know you have some hang-ups about Disney, but, Jesus, Michael, get over it. The kids want to see Mickey Mouse," Olivia said. She held her breath, almost wishing that she could reel in her hurtful words. And yet part of her wanted to shake him from whatever it was that haunted him so that her own children could experience all the joys of childhood. All that he had missed.

"I know they do," Michael said, slipping back to his own memories. He was older than Carla and Danny when he set foot there the terrible week before Christmas when Adriana threw him away. The park was done up in all sorts of Christmas finery. But to an abused boy from Portland, Oregon, the extra lights and plastic snowflakes were merely dollops of unneeded frosting on the most amazing cake in the world.

He fell deeper into the memory. First it was foggy, then clear.

His mom had been agitated the day before she announced they'd be going to Disneyland. No need to pack, she told him. They'd be there only a day or so and could buy new things if they needed them.

"I'll get you a Mickey Mouse shirt and hat," she said.

What she didn't say was that they'd be driving, a grueling eighteen-hour drive from their small house in Portland. Mrs. Barton packed up Michael and Sarah early—before daylight. It was cold before the sun came up and Michael complained about it to his mother, but she ignored him. He tugged on Sarah's blanket and swiped it from her somewhere in the mountains between Oregon and California. Later, he would feel bad about many things in his life, things that deserved major regret, but nothing compared with stealing the blanket.

Nothing seemed as rotten as taking that little piece of comfort from his baby sister.

Adriana Barton took the kids to the Denny's across the street for breakfast because the park wasn't yet open at that early an hour. Outside of ordering pancakes and bacon, she said nothing. Michael had seen his mom sad like that before. He knew that it had something to do with the fact that she and Sarah's father weren't getting along. Hadn't gotten along for a long time.

"Mommy, don't be sad," he said. The words were practiced. He'd said them over and over whenever his mother cried.

"It's OK, baby, you're my big little man," she said. "Always look out for your sister." Her response was equally canned. No feeling. No warmth. Just a rote *don't worry.*

But as much as she appeared to be an automaton as she slid deeper into the booth, blank-eyed, cold, Michael would later remember those simple words as the last words of substance that his mother would ever utter to him.

They parked the family's dark blue Subaru in the Tigger parking lot. Michael could remember how cold he felt that day as they waited for the tram to take them to the gates, past the floral portrait of Mickey Mouse. He could feel the push and pull of the moment. His mom was sad, almost broken. His heart told him something was wrong with her, but all he really wanted to do was to get down to the Pirates of the Caribbean ride.

He gripped the hem of Adriana's coat as she pushed Sarah in a stroller and they snaked through the long line, first under the bridge, then inside the funny smelling mix of children and chlorine that filled the entrance to the ride. And then down, down, down into the magical world of rubber pirates, barking dogs, and gold-painted treasure.

"Are you OK, ma'am?" a girl asked, snapping Michael's mother out of a stupor as she sat in the boat at the ride's conclusion.

"Fine," she said.

As Michael Barton entered the archway that proclaimed Adventureland it was all coming back to him. He felt his heart work overtime, his breathing accelerated.

He gripped his own son's hand and looked over at Olivia and the baby, pushed in a rented stroller. He wondered if it had been the same stroller that had once held his sister, so long ago.

Across from the kiosks that sold pineapple spears and coconut milk in coconut shells loomed the Swiss Family Robinson Tree House.

It looked more real—at least in its design—than he imagined, but more fake, at the same time. It also had a new name. It was now named Tarzan's Tree House, for the animated movie. The Robinsons, it seemed had long since been evicted. Gone. *Over.*

He wished it had been the same for his memories. He thought they'd been vanquished. He remembered how he stood with his sister by that steel and concrete tree while his mother nervously tapped on the shoulder of a woman waiting for her brood to come down the bamboo staircase of the attraction.

"I have an important call," she said. "Will you watch my children? Here." She didn't even wait a beat. There was no time for the woman to say yes or no. The crowd was thick, almost impenetrable. But Michael and Sarah's mother found a little fissure among the throng and in a second, she was gone.

Gone forever.

Before he and Sarah ended up at the Anaheim police station, he remembered hearing someone talking in a low voice over by the pineapple kiosk.

"The woman's been behaving strangely since she got here. She looked crazy, depressed."

A young man in a safari costume joined a group of colorfully attired Disney workers huddled by the river ride.

"God, do we have to drag the damn lagoon? Can't we just drain it? Why do the suicides always come here? Why can't they jump off the log ride at Knott's, or something?"

He didn't know what "drag the lagoon" meant, but there wasn't anyone to ask. His mom was gone.

* * *

How to do it? Why do it at all? The triggers that brought him to the place in which he'd find himself fantasizing about doing evil, doing harm, came at unexpected times. During mundane moments. Always uninvited. When working the ketchup dispenser cleanup detail at McDonald's as a teenager, he found himself caught up in a memory of the first cat he'd ever killed. He hit the pump multiple times to empty it, in nearly a manic performance that brought glances from those closest to him in the fast food restaurant.

The red of the condiment was blood.

"Hey, easy on that, Mike," a pimply-faced crew chief called from the other side of the counter while another worker, a girl, looked on with utter distain. "The dispenser is stainless steel, not titanium."

"Oh, right," he said. Inside his uniform, his heart was a drumroll. He hoped no one could see the excitement that he'd experienced looking at the ketchup. He was thinking of the blood, killing the Hansens' cat.

He felt an erection grow and hurriedly excused himself. He flipped the RESTROOM BEING CLEANED sign into view and did what he needed to do to relieve the excitement.

The excitement that he hated more than anything. Why, he often wondered, had his brain hardwired unspeakable violence to an animal to his sexual organs?

It wasn't all the time. After all, he did have the occasional girlfriend. He wasn't a weirdo in bed. He didn't strangle a girl as he made love to her. He wasn't a killer.

And yet, the compulsion came to him. One time, when he was mowing lawns to make some extra money for college expenses, he flashed on catching a particularly annoying dog. It obviously hated him, sneering and barking whenever he arrived at the house to cut the lawn and weed the garden. He thought of burying it in the center of the lawn, up to its furry little neck, and running over it with a weedwhacker. The idea shifted to something even bloodier. The riding mower. It would be decisive, sending a red, bloody spray from the point of impact over the patio, onto the lawn furniture, arcing on the glass doors to the living room. The thought excited him, as always, but he suppressed it. He wished it away. He even prayed it away.

Then dormant, he'd go.

But the cycle was relentless. For a time, he thought marriage or fatherhood could abate it completely. And it did. He never acted on the compulsion to harm another human being or an animal. That wasn't to say the thoughts didn't come to him.

He thought of killing the loan officer at the bank when he and Olivia were applying for the financing and things were looking a little dicey. Credit scores out of college were always in the five hundreds. They jumped through some extra hoops and prayed that late payments on a big screen TV were not as big a deal as the jerk had insisted. *Killing him would be good.* But, he reasoned, what guy didn't fantasize about killing someone who stood in the way of his future happiness?

The loan came through, and the man's life was spared.

Another time the neighbor's dog barked until all hours. It was the kind of barking that came only when he was desperate for sleep. If he hadn't been so mad, he'd have laughed at the irony that the dog that barked incessantly didn't seem to keep his owners awake. He could have pumped a couple of slugs in the mongrel's head and they'd probably not even stir. But he didn't do that. He simply opened the gate on the chain-link kennel and the dog ran out, chasing whatever it was that he had to chase.

Problem solved, compulsion to kill and torture gone.

He'd done some reading about his own psychological

makeup, but he never really saw himself in the label of anti-social personality disorder. He wasn't so messed up that he was a narcissistic person. In fact, he was too good for that.

Michael Barton never wanted to eat anyone, so he wasn't Jeffrey Dahmer. He didn't capture and torture girls like Joel Rifkin. He didn't stalk young women, à la Ted Bundy.

Yes, he wet the bed into his teenage years. Yes, he tortured a few animals, but they were only animals, and he knew it was wrong. Yes, there was a slight sexual charge that came with the rush of what he was doing, but he could function normally, too.

Michael had his problems. He knew every one of them and how they matched up to evil, but he wasn't like any of those guys.

What he didn't know was that he'd never been pushed. And that was about to change.

Chapter Forty-six

Before Olivia, every move Michael Barton made was meant to hurt someone. She changed all of that. She was forgiving and beautiful. And, most important of all, she soothed him. She might have thought that she understood him. But of course, she could not. He'd let her inside his messed-up world more than anyone he'd ever known. But he could never tell her specifically what he'd done when he was younger.

"My background's not so good," he had told her. "State institutions, a few run-ins with the cops. Let's just leave it at that, OK?"

"But I want to know you, babe. Let me in."

"You're in. You're in as far as I can allow you. Maybe later, maybe down the road, I can tell you more."

His words were a lie. He knew that if she'd known all the things he'd done, she'd leave him, too.

She was his hope. She was his chance not to be a monster anymore.

How could he tell her that when he was serving food in the cafeteria at the Ogilvy Home, he spat on the food, poured salt in the milk, and emptied Visine into the counselors' iced tea because it made them sick and that made him feel good. When the boys found a cache of balloons that had been brought into the institution for a water balloon fight, he filled them with urine. He also filled the balloons with water and froze them so that when he hurled them, the strike would almost break a bone.

Only then did he feel a kind of joy. Holding those frozen balloons—red, yellow, blue—and throwing them at the kids he hated most. The weaker ones. He broke one fat boy's nose with a well-aimed shot, and though he felt a flutter of satisfaction, he also felt a bit of remorse. He wished he'd broken something more vital. Like the fat boy's neck.

There was always cover there for that kind of an act. No boy, no matter how tough he thought he was, would ever tell on Michael Barton for what he did to them. When he offered up a new kid to service one of the security guards, he didn't choose the weakest. He chose a kid from a well-off family in Los Angeles.

"You'll suck his dick and you'll shut up about it," he said.

"I will not," said the L.A. kid, a redhead with freckles and blue eyes that were unable to hide the fear that swelled through his bloodstream.

"You will. Or I'll cut off your head." Michael stepped closer to the boy as they stood in the hallway outside the institution's library. The librarian smiled uneasily through the glass and Michael just smiled a phony smile. *A practiced one.* He put his arm around the boy and leaned forward. "I've done it before." His voice was a whisper, cold and flat. "And I really want to do it again. Welcome to Ogilvy."

The security guard thanked him the next day. And gave him a five-dollar bill.

Michael could care less about the money. He was glad there was someone else to take his spot on his knees in front of a man with a lowered zipper.

Nothing, he knew, would ever get back the years he'd lost in the system. Nothing could erase what his mother had done to him. He was just a little speck of human life, floating around a world in which there seemed to be no place to land. There was nothing to love. And without love, there could be no other emotion but hate.

Michael knew that there were things about him that were so dark, so out of the boundaries of acceptable behavior, that what he'd done was deviant. *Aberrant*. He looked for understanding in the stacks of the Madison library. The psychology books talked about how sociopaths had no ability to empathize with others. How they had no connection to another human being. Isolation from emotion was a term one of the books used. Sociopaths were like pod people who just existed in a world designed for their own empty pleasure. One writer said they could only mimic the feelings of others, unsure how to act or react. They were completely detached.

But that wasn't him. He knew that he did have an attachment. His sister Sarah was out there. He loved her. He wanted her to be free, to be happy. Sometimes he wept for her, thinking that his loss was so great. And at the same time he hoped that she felt at least a little like he did.

He wrote several letters that he never sent because he didn't know where she was.

Dear Sarah,

> *I think it's your birthday this week. I'm not sure of the exact day? Maybe the fifth? I wish I knew. I wish I'd paid more attention to things like that. I'm imagining you in a pretty white house with one of those big chocolate cakes with curls of chocolate stuck to the sides. I'd bet you'd like pink candles, too. I remember how much you liked pink, when you were a baby.*

He stopped and thought how silly that note sounded. Sarah wore pink when she was a baby because their mother bought her pink clothes and blankets. She might have loved lavender or yellow. He crumpled the paper into a tight ball.

He missed her. One day, he told himself, they'd be together again.

While Danny and Carla played amid the array of toys scattered like a cyclone had hit the basement, Olivia continued to rack her brain about their missing cat, Simon. Simon had been a housecat who never ventured outside because he hated the feeling of morning dew on his paws.

"He ran out when I opened the door," Michael had said. "I think the coyote got him."

Olivia asked the neighbors about the coyote that her husband had insisted had been the likely culprit.

"Good news on that one," said Angela Martinez, the retired schoolteacher next door, when Olivia ran into her one afternoon shopping at Vons. "Animal control trapped the miserable animal three weeks ago. Your cat surely wasn't a coyote snack."

The information surprised her. "My husband said he saw the coyote last week."

Mrs. Martinez dropped a couple packages of white and pink Hostess Snowballs into her shopping cart. "Grandkids are coming Friday. Lucky me," she said, with a kind of tone to indicate she was annoyed with the prospect of a visit by her daughter's band of grade-school hellions. "Anyway, I'm sure of it. Talked to the officer myself. Coyote problem solved. Now if I could just find a way to make it through the weekend."

Olivia smiled. "Call me if you need reinforcements."

As she pushed her cart toward the checkout aisle, Michael's words echoed in her thoughts.

"I saw the coyote by the garbage can. I never should have let Simon out."

Chapter Forty-seven

Cherrystone

Camille Hazelton seldom stopped by the sheriff's office. She left that, rightly so, to her assistants who wanted to burn off carbs or see how the *order* tent pole of law and order lived. But today, she'd called ahead and Emily was waiting for her in her office. Camille snapped the door shut. The warmth on her face was absent. She was granite.

"Em, this isn't a social call."

"I figured."

"We've got a problem with Tricia Wilson."

"Is she all right?"

"Far from it. One of our DAs noticed a couple of inconsistencies in her depos and did a little more digging. Sent the kid down to Portland. Good thing I did."

Emily could feel the blood drain from her face. "I'm not going to like this one bit, am I?"

Camille shook her head. "About as much as a kick to the stomach. That's how I felt."

"Go ahead, Camille. Start kicking."

Camille allowed a wary smile across her face. She wasn't

there to beat up Emily. Emily had done her job—and the DA's office had done its job. The two worked together with the single purpose of making a case that would convince a jury.

"She and Mitch divorced, all right. But not because he beat her up. At least, not that we can tell. Patty or Tricia or whatever she called herself back then had more than likely bilked the Portland dealership out of two hundred thousand dollars. She was the pretty wife and the sticky-fingered head of accounting."

"Charged?"

"Nope. It never got that far. Mitch's father must have wanted to kill the girl, but instead they kept it out of the papers and kicked her to the curb, oh-so-quietly."

"What about the abuse? The photos? The threats?"

"Made it up as far as I can tell. One of her old coworkers—you know the type, the woman who worked alongside the nitwit boss's wife and wanted him for herself—she said the photos were fabricated. She used Max Factor and a Polaroid. I guess when it became clear that she was caught, she wanted a little insurance that she didn't go down in flames."

"Hence the photos."

"Right. My guess is she never got over the fact that she'd been caught and didn't get to extort the Crawfords for all they were worth."

Emily sighed. "So coming forward must have been about payback."

"That's my take. She had those photos. Saw the Mandy story on TV and went for it."

"Wonder why the defense didn't bring this up? Why wouldn't Mitch go to the media and blast one of his chief accusers? "

"Good question. I would have. But my guess is that Cary was looking for his Perry Mason moment. All lawyers do."

"So what do you want me to do?"

"My assistant had no luck with her, but for some reason, she said she'd talk to you. She's working for a telemarketing company east of Seattle. Here's the address." She handed Emily a slip of paper.

Chapter Forty-eight

It was 9 P.M. when Chris Collier showed up on Emily's doorstep. She'd called him earlier in the day to share her worry that despite Mitch Crawford's arrest, something didn't feel right.

"How on earth did you get here so fast?" she asked, letting him in and embracing him in the foyer. "I'm going over to Seattle tomorrow."

"Timing is everything," he said, a broad smile on his face. "Caught a flight from Spokane and, voilà, here I am." He set the rental car keys on the console by the door, next to her purse.

Chris followed Emily into the dining room where she had placed a box of case file folders. He took a chair and noticed the wine on the table. "Are you buying that by the case to boost the local economy?"

Emily smiled at his mention of the local vintner. "Maybe. I don't know. I like it. Help yourself."

Chris poured a glass and topped off Emily's.

"I thought wine made you sleepy," she said.

"Are you kidding? I drank about a gallon of coffee between the plane and drive up here. I'll be wired until tomorrow."

She smiled. "Good, because we have a lot to do."

"All right. Let's go over what you've got."

"We have a pregnant woman murdered and dumped outside of town.'

"Cause of death?"

"Strangled."

"Hands? Ligature?"

"We think hands. The body was in pretty good shape, but enough decomp around the fleshy parts of the neck to make it impossible to tell for sure. There were some marks, but Dr. Wilhelm thinks they were fingerprints."

He sipped his wine. "OK. That's the signature of a killer who likely knew his victim. It's very, very hard to strangle someone. It takes some real effort and unless you're coming from behind with a cord or something, you're facing the victim until their lights go out."

"Exactly. Must be a cold son-of-a-bitch to do that."

Chris nodded. "That's right. Especially to a pregnant woman. So taking that into consideration, we're in agreement that the victim was likely known by her killer."

"Yes. And the perp is probably a male or, if not, the strongest woman in Cherrystone."

"That would be *you*." Chris smiled at Emily and asked for a sheet of paper and wrote down what they'd agreed upon.

"I have all that in the Crawford Murder Book," she said. "Let me get it."

He watched as she opened the big black binder. "No offense to you and Camille Hazelton, but your Murder Book is part of the problem. We're not looking at the evidence, but at what we think about it. You know? We have to look at each piece of evidence anew. OK?"

Emily didn't like the idea and her face showed it. There were reams of documents to go through and the hour was getting late.

"OK," she said, "no shortcuts. But I want to remind you

that we have to give the defense notice about Tricia Wilson's perjured deposition by five p.m. tomorrow. Camille is doing us, I mean *me*, a favor."

"Then we better get going. What's next, the DNA?"

Emily pulled up the lab work sent over by Dr. Wilhelm on the DNA swabbed from Mitch Crawford, and the victims, Mandy and Chrissy. The ME had attached a note written in his own handwriting, oddly legible for a doctor.

"There is absolutely no chance that this full-term female fetus was fathered by Mitch Crawford. Not a snowball's chance in hell."

"I love his medical terminology," Chris said.

Emily set down the file. "He's a legend for about a million reasons."

Chris wrote down on the paper: *The baby's father is the key*.

"Look at it this way: Either Mitch killed Mandy because he caught her cheating, which I'd say is the best bet. Or the baby's father killed her, for what reason, I don't know."

Emily could see the plausibility in either scenario. "We figured that. The big problem for us is that we've never been able to find out who fathered the baby."

"Who was she seeing?"

"No one knows."

"Friends? What about her girlfriends?"

"I've mined that field, Chris. No one seems to know anything. No one noticed anything strange."

"What about coworkers? Sometimes a woman will share with those outside of her inner circle?"

Emily set down her wineglass and stared at Chris. "Wait a second. Her friend Samantha Phillips had a strange encounter with Mandy not long before her disappearance."

"OK, Em, what did she say?"

"She told me two things that were interesting. One, that

Mandy had told her the sex of the baby, but not her husband."

"What do you mean?"

"It was something about how Mitch had wanted a son so much, but that it was a girl she was carrying."

Chris wrote down: *Baby not a boy? Did Mitch kill her because Mandy was having a girl?*

"That's a bit farfetched," she said. "Even for around here."

"Happens in China every day and probably a thousand times on Sunday."

Emily looked upward and shook her head. "OK, fine. But I highly doubt it."

"You never know. Anything more?"

"Let me see," she said, looking through her notes from the first interview with Samantha Phillips. She used a pen to guide her tired eyes across the paper. "Here it is. She had an encounter with Mandy around Halloween. Nothing much here. Says that Mandy was acting evasive about something and gave her the bum's rush at the door."

Emily set down her notes.

"What is it?"

"I don't know, I got the distinct impression that Samantha was holding out on me. Like she'd suspected something was going on with Mandy when she went to her house."

"Like what?"

"They were best friends. Samantha stopped by to check on Mandy and she didn't invite her inside."

"Are you thinking what I'm thinking?"

"She wasn't alone, was she?"

Chris wrote down: *Talk to Samantha Phillips. What does she know?*

Next up was the Darla Montague file. It was a thin folder, with only two sheets of paper inside.

"This is the girl who had an affair with Crawford," Emily said.

"Jesus, Emily, what kind of a town is Cherrystone, anyway?"

Emily knew what Chris was getting at, but she brushed it off. "Like every other town, I guess."

They talked about Darla and how she'd had "one or two, well, *two*" sexual encounters with Mitch Crawford at the office.

"She's a nice girl," Emily said. "Mixed-up and stupid, but nice. She's not a part of this. Just a bystander in the way of a man who takes what he wants no matter who gets hurt."

"OK. I'll accept your assessment on that. Let's leave her alone tomorrow."

It left one key witness, Tricia Wilson.

"I've got Tricia handled. I called in a favor to a buddy at one of the financial institutions. If I gave you the initials, you'd have to kill me, Emily." He smiled and she returned the gesture. "I guess it's good to have friends who can help out now and then."

"Like you're helping me." She looked into his eyes. "Thank you, Chris. I really want to nail this bastard."

"We'll get him tomorrow. But we can't do it unless we get some shut-eye."

Emily looked at the clock. It was almost 1:00 A.M.

"Shit, I'll look like hell tomorrow," she said.

Chris completely disagreed. "You'll always look beautiful," he said.

With that, they turned out the dining room chandelier and padded down the hallway to bed. Too tired to make love, they snuggled together under the covers. As they drifted off to sleep, Emily found herself enjoying the closeness of the man she loved in a tender and gentle way. She breathed him in. The next morning, he returned to Seattle on the plane and she drove across the mountain pass.

She needed time to think. About Tricia. About Mandy. About Jenna. And even a little bit about herself.

Ten employees of Evergreen Marketing were huddled under a blue tarp on the west end of the company's parking lot. Recent state law had shoved smokers far from the doorways and picnic tables by the Dumpsters where they'd once congregated. The tarp kept them dry as they smoked and chatted about how much they hated their jobs, their kids, their spouses. None ever seemed to say a word about their smoking shanty and the constant push to make their lives more miserable. Emily parked her car and glanced over. But no one in the smoking mass was Tricia Wilson.

Evergreen Marketing commanded a single floor of a five-story building in Renton, a city known for a Boeing plant and pretty views of Lake Washington. She presented her card to the receptionist. She smiled, and buzzed for Tricia to come to the front desk.

"You have a visitor. Please come at once."

Patty emerged from a cipher-locked door. When her eyes met Emily's it was with more a look of resignation than of concern. Her blond hair had been highlighted since Emily had last seen her. She also wore an exceptionally nice pair of camel slacks and a wheat-colored twinset, likely cashmere.

"Hello Sheriff Kenyon. After that DA creep tried to trash me, I sort of expected you'd come to see me."

"I'm here, Tricia. Is there someplace we can talk?"

"Sure." She turned to the receptionist. "Fatima, we're going to use the Rainier conference room."

"Very good," Fatima said, logging a note into her PC.

"She's here for training," Tricia said softly as they walked toward the conference room. "She's a VP with a company we're working with. My guess is that we have about six months. Then, poof, our jobs are gone."

"I'm sorry," Emily said as Tricia flipped on the lights. "I'm grateful that no one has found a way to outsource the legal system."

Patty smiled. "Just wait. I'm sure someone will find a way."

They sat down in the windowless conference room with a massive mosaic of Mount Rainier, Washington's tallest peak, covering an entire wall.

"I'm in trouble, aren't I?"

"I'm not sure. That depends."

"On the truth, right?"

"Yes, the truth."

Tricia swiveled in her chair and put her hands on the table. "OK. Well, what I told you wasn't completely a lie. Mitch was an asshole. He treated me like dirt, and he did push me around a few times."

Emily locked her eyes on Tricia's. "Did he beat you?"

She looked down at the table. "Yes, he did abuse me. But not really, not physically."

Emily pushed a little harder. She knew a crack in a story when she saw one. She needed to force the issue. "Does the name Maggie Emery ring a bell?" she asked, again her eyes fixed on Tricia's.

Tricia's face tightened at the mention of the name of her coworker from the dealership. Her blue eyes flashed.

"You talked to that bitch?"

"I didn't. But one of Prosecutor Hazelton's assistants did."

"I can imagine what she told you. She hated me. She wanted Mitch for herself. I should have let her have him. That would have been sweeter revenge."

"Has this been about revenge, Tricia?"

"Revenge would be too simple."

"What about the photographs? Were those doctored?"

Tricia Wilson was trapped and she knew it. "OK. I did doctor my makeup and hair for those pictures. But I want you to know that he really did abuse me."

Emily wanted to abuse the woman herself just then. She could barely keep her cool. "How, Tricia, how did he abuse you?"

Tricia swiveled in her chair again. "He was cheap. He never let me have a dime. He was, I swear to God, the biggest control freak this world has ever known. Everything had to be done his way. I just wanted to buy myself some new furniture. We had the money. But he said, no, no, no."

"So you started to bleed the dealership."

"I saw a lawyer so I know that the statute of limitations has run out on that, so yes. Yes, I did. I'm not sorry about it, either."

Emily pushed herself back from the conference table and stood.

"Don't you know what you've done?" Her voice was loud and she didn't care. "Mandy Crawford was murdered. Mitch Crawford was arrested, in part, because of your fabricated statements. You've not only embarrassed me, but you've shamed yourself in the name of women who have been abused."

"He was a jerk."

"So get a divorce. A husband who doesn't let you have new furniture is a lout, not an abuser!"

"You try living with a control freak."

Emily let the words "been there, done that" play only in her mind. Her ex-husband had been a jerk, but she'd never give Tricia Wilson the satisfaction of knowing that they shared something in common.

"I'm done with you. Go back to your phones and think of Mandy Crawford and her baby and how you've single-handedly screwed up a double murder investigation."

With that, Emily departed for the lobby, and made her way past the smokers' tarp for her car.

Fatima pressed the mute button on the Rainier conference room to the OFF position. She looked down at the Cherrystone sheriff's business card and scooted it under her telephone console.

Chapter Forty-nine

No matter what the other parts of the country were going through in terms of economic growth and recession, the Puget Sound region seemed bulletproof. Expensive developments with chichi names popped up in places that ten years before had been the modest homes of factory workers. Underperforming strip malls were dozed in favor of restaurants, movie theaters, and big-box electronic stores. Emily, still fuming over the stupidity of a woman like Tricia Wilson, drove north on 405 toward Interstate 90, then across the floating bridge to Mercer Island. As she drove, she fumbled in her purse for the MapQuest directions she'd printed out before she left Cherrystone.

It was for 4545 Lake View Terrace, which was David's address. She felt silly for doing a drive-by to her ex-husband's new digs, but curiosity had gotten the best of her. Jenna told her mother that the house on the water "wasn't all that great." But something in her daughter's voice indicated a white lie.

It wasn't that Emily was jealous of David's success or his new life with Dani and their child. It just seemed that after he'd left her, he simply went on to a new life. She didn't. She stayed where she was, mentally, emotionally, and romantically.

She'd dated a few times. She hated revisiting that time of her life. She'd found love with Christopher Collier, or at least she allowed herself to entertain the thought. But not a new life. Jenna had graduated from college and was working toward her own future.

But not Emily. For some reason, Emily didn't seem to know how to move herself forward.

She made a sharp left, then a right, and followed the road that looped around the island.

At least his view isn't of Seattle, but of Bellevue, she thought, as she tried to rack up whatever consolation she could.

Lake View Terrace met the main road and dropped down an incline to the water.

"Dad says to add a million to each house the closer you get to the shore," Jenna had said when she was first describing the new house. "I'd rather have a house with horses and a view of the mountain than that silly lake. Too cold to swim in, anyway."

Emily drove down toward the water. The last house, 4545, was gated. She pulled up to the gate. The house was a monster. It had to be five thousand square feet. It was all arches and porticos, as though every Italian architectural gewgaw had been thrown into a blender and poured onto the foundation.

A deep purple 700-series BMW was parked out front on the smallish circular drive. Smallish, Emily figured, because the house had taken up most of the lot. She squinted her eyes to make out the license plate.

The plate read: HOTDOC33

Oh, David, she thought. *What has Dani done to you?*

"I thought I saw you on the video cam." It was David, emerging from the front door. Emily wanted to die just then. "So now you're a stalker, huh, Em?"

She'd been caught. There was no way out of it. No way

out of her stupidity for driving by. She wondered if she'd been like one of those criminals who wanted to get caught, for some repressed reason.

"I just wanted to see where our daughter's education fund ended up," she said, feeling bitterness take over embarrassment.

"I see." David's eyes were cold, unfeeling. He stood on the other side of the wrought iron gate with his arms folded. "Maybe you'd like to come inside and see what you're missing?"

The things she hated about him started flooding back. "I'm not missing anything."

"Really? Then why'd you come?"

"Curiosity. I wanted to see what misplaced values and too much money gets these days."

"Maybe you should just move on, Emily."

"Oh, I have, David. I *have*."

She got into her car, pressed the accelerator and drove off to see Chris at his condo in Seattle. She'd called him earlier in the day to say she might come by, but she didn't know when. After playing stalker on her ex—and having her case crumble—she could use the love of the man she adored.

Chris swung open the door to his twentieth-floor unit and without missing a beat, put his arms around Emily. The look on his face was surprise.

"Why didn't you buzz me?" he asked.

Emily managed a smile, though not a convincing one. "A woman downstairs let me in. I must look like I live here."

Chris hugged her again. "You look upset. What is it?"

"What isn't it? My case is imploding. My life is a mess."

He led her to the living room where the windows framed a magnificent view of a ferry pulling in to the pier.

"Maybe I can help with both."

"Maybe," she said, stopping herself as her gaze landed on the coffee table. Fanned out on the table were five business cards from various real estate agents.

He followed her eyes to the business cards.

"Yup, I've listed the place."

"I see that."

"I had some brokers come over, you know, give me the song and dance about how much dough they can bring in versus the other guy. I just did the listing agreement about an hour ago."

"I don't know what to say or what it means for us, Chris."

"There's time to figure that out. The market's slow." He laughed and stretched out his long legs. He wore dark-washed blue jeans and a light gray sweater.

Emily put her hand on his knee and looked into his blue eyes.

"All right."

They curled up on the couch for an hour, discussing the case. How Tricia Wilson had lied about her abuse, and about the ramifications the disclosure might have on the case.

"You still have the computer evidence? You still have his aberrant behavior, right? His affair with his office girl?"

Emily nodded. "Right. We still have all that. But I'm not sure it's enough. There's not a single bit of physical evidence to tie him to the crime."

"I get that," he said. "Let's dig a little deeper over dinner."

"Can't do it," she said. "And you know I want to. I have to get back to Cherrystone."

"Please call me," was the message that Fatima Hussein left on Emily's voice mail. The woman's tone was polite, but with an unmistakable sense of urgency. Emily pulled over to the side of the road. Listening to voice mail while driving was one thing, but making a call and focusing on a conversation involved too much distraction on a snowy highway. The call must have come when she was going over the mountain pass—a location where she never seemed to get cellular reception.

Emily searched her memory. She didn't know anyone by that name.

"Is this Fatima Hussein? This is Sheriff Kenyon returning your call."

"Yes. Thank you very kindly for answering my call I made to you. Please hold for one moment while I forward my other calls."

By the time Fatima came back on the phone, Emily had made the connection. "You're with Evergreen Marketing, aren't you?"

"Yes, we met in the lobby. I was doing phone training, practicing my American accent with people as they call in."

"I remember you," Emily said as cars whizzed by one after another, kicking slushy snow in her direction. "How can I help you?"

"I am U.S. citizen. I wanted you to know that."

"OK, that's wonderful," Emily said, unsure how to respond.

"That's why I am phone calling you. It is about our civic duty."

"What do you have to tell me, Fatima? Is it about Tricia Wilson?"

"Yes. You are correct. I want you to know that something has been going on with her. We all have noticed it here."

"I don't see how I can help you with a work performance issue."

"No that. It is about her new car and her clothes."

"What do you mean, Fatima?"

"She bought a new Lexus and she's wearing new garments every day. She is not even close to a top performer. We don't understand how she could afford all of that."

Emily remembered how impeccably coiffed and attired Tricia had been when she came to Cherrystone, and again, at the offices of Evergreen Marketing. She was the very picture of success, one of those women in magazine ads or on TV.

"I thought she was an executive there," Emily said. "She just seemed so in charge, so professional."

"Oh, not at all. She's one of our phoners."

"Phoners?" The term puzzled her.

"She does outreach calls. Surveys, things of that kind of nature."

"I see."

"I thought that you should know. I do not want to be involved. But it was my duty to tell you."

Emily thanked the woman. Civic duty was one thing, of course. But the call smacked a little of getting even. Or maybe even housecleaning.

Tricia Wilson, you've just been outsourced, Emily thought, pulling back on to the highway.

PART THREE
Jenna

Chapter Fifty

Cherrystone

Camille Hazelton didn't like what she was hearing one bit. She leaned close to Emily Kenyon and jabbed a finger at her. *Tricia Wilson was a liar.* Close, but it didn't touch. They met in Hazelton's office and associates and clerks who probably already knew the score scuttled by, hoping for a glimpse of some fireworks between Cherrystone's most powerful women.

"This is a huge mess, damn it, Emily."

"You don't have to tell me. And you don't have to poke me to get me to listen. I get it."

"I'm sorry. But these walls are cheaper than justice these days and I don't want to raise my voice. But this probably means we have to drop the charges. You know that, don't you?"

"Can't you give me a little time?"

"For what? To dredge up another winner like Tricia Wilson? We should have vetted her from the onset." Camille caught herself, she'd used the word *we.* She knew that the error in judgment was shared. "Cary McConnell is going to have a field day with this."

"She was sworn in. She's perjured herself in that depo. I'm going to make sure she goes to jail for that. It's the least I can do. Honestly, paybacks are hell and I intend to make sure Miss Patty or Tricia or whatever her name is understands that."

"Look, Camille, I think I can do something here. Something's not right and I'd like a chance to repair it."

"Oh my God, Emily, are you looking for redemption? Hasn't the meter on that one run out by now?"

It was a cheap shot at things long since past. It was meant to sting and Camille Hazelton hated herself for saying it. She liked Emily very much, but she'd been pressed to her wit's end. She could read the headlines the next day. The thought of them made her blood boil.

Car Dealer Released From
Trumped-Up Charges

Camille sat down at her desk and Emily slumped in the chair across from her.

"I'm sorry," she said, doing her best to cool off. "I didn't mean that."

"I know," Emily said, wondering if the thought of the little girl who had died because of a mistake she had made so many years ago as a Seattle cop was always on the back of everyone's minds. The wound that would never heal. Did they see her at the mall and think to themselves, "Oh yeah, that's the woman who let Kristi Cooper die in that underground dungeon." Did the woman who always chatted so amiably when she had her hair cut say to the other women when she left the room, "Oh that's her. That's the one I've been telling you about. The one who let that kid starve to death."

"Really I am. It's just this case. I know you do good work.

We're going to be crucified by McConnell and Crawford. You know how much I'd hate to be tarred and feathered."

"From a woman with some experience there, let me tell you it's no picnic."

Emily managed a smile, a gesture that meant a call for a truce. "We're on the same side, Camille. Give me twenty-four hours before we go to McConnell and the judge."

Camille looked at her watch, an expensive Cartier that she surely didn't buy at Rondo's Fine Jewelry in town. "I'll time you."

"Thanks. I think."

"I was kidding. Let's see what you can come up with by the end of the day. Go bust some heads, shake some trees, do whatever it is that you gun-toting sheriffs do."

"Are you asking me to shoot Cary McConnell?"

A look of horror came over Camille Hazelton. "God no, Emily! No such thing!"

"Just kidding," she said. It was a gotcha that felt only a little bit good. She still had no plan. No hope for one. She thought of the one person she could call.

Chris Collier was eating a can of tortilla soup that he'd microwaved in a measuring cup because all the other vessels that could hold soup were dirty. He wasn't a slob, he was just the kind of guy that liked to run a full load of dishes. And that meant about once a week. Cooking for Emily was one thing. Cooking for himself? A chore. When the phone rang, he set down his spoon and answered.

"Hi, baby," he said, seeing it was from her. His mood lightened. "Miss me already?"

"You know I do. But it's more than missing you right now. I need you, Chris. The Crawford case is crumbling. Can you come over to Cherrystone?"

He didn't ask why. There was no need to. "Of course. I'll leave in fifteen minutes. I have to put some food out for the cat."

"You have a cat?"

"Sure." A kind of mischievous look came to his face. "And you thought you knew everything there was about me."

"I guess I did."

"Actually, I'm feeding the neighbor's."

That was more like it. She hung up feeling a sense of relief. Not because the man liked cats—always a good sign in her book—but because whenever she needed him, Chris Collier had always been there for her.

He never, ever wavered.

Emily pulled all the Crawford files and carried them to her car.

"Need some help, Sheriff?" It was Jason.

"No, I can manage."

"I heard about Ms. Wilson," he said.

If Jason had heard, it wasn't from her. The word was getting around fast. Too fast. The minute Cary McConnell got wind of it, he'd be in front of the judge in the same breath.

"Let's keep a lid on it, please, Jason." Her tone was more scolding than she meant it to be.

Jason looked hurt. "I'm not stupid, Sheriff," he said turning on his heels and leaving her to deal with the big box of files.

Emily called out after him, but he either pretended not to hear or the sound of traffic drowned out her call. She felt about two inches tall, and ashamed that she'd treated him with such a dressing-down. It was uncalled for. With all that was happening—in her life, in Jenna's life—upsetting Jason Howard was the last thing she needed.

As Jenna would say whenever something had gone awry with the sorority job, "My life sucks royally right now."

Like daughter, like mother.

She put the car in gear and went home, thinking that nothing else could happen to make the day any worse.

Chapter Fifty-one

Emily Kenyon couldn't sleep. *Something is so wrong about this Crawford case.* It was more than Tricia Wilson, too. She was dog tired, but rest eluded her. She'd tried, of course, but her thoughts kept returning to the blue sleeping bag—Mandy's down-filled body bag. She got dressed, clipped her hair back, and took a Diet Coke from the refrigerator. She cleared a space and sat down at the kitchen island and reread Jason's reports. *Nothing remarkable.*

She pored over the photos taken by the forensic team when it had been examined at the lab in Spokane. She reread Jason's reports. Her eyes landed once more on the five-inch square hole in the fabric. She wished right then that her eyesight was better, that the hour wasn't so late, or that she had a photographer's loupe. Something was percolating in her mind, but she couldn't quite grasp it.

She looked at the kitchen clock and sighed. It was after 4:00 A.M.—that time of day when it was too late to go to bed and too early to go to work. Emily decided to go take another look at the sleeping bag. Photographs and a report—no matter how finely detailed—weren't working.

*   *   *

The evidence vault for all of the sheriff's cases was the size of a walk-in closet—and quite frankly, didn't need to be much larger. Cherrystone, thankfully, was that kind of place. Emily pulled the clipboard from behind the counter and signed her name and Crawford's case number. She searched her key ring. She seldom needed the vault's key, because there was always someone on duty—even with a tightening budget. Evidence was serious business, of course. She flipped on the light. Inside, six black metal Gorilla racks purchased at the Spokane Costco held the bits and pieces of criminal cases still in work. When cases were adjudicated, key materials were dispatched to a secure storage vault in an undisclosed location managed by the state of Washington.

The sleeping bag was cataloged with a code, but there was no reason for Emily to locate it by an accession number. Among the file boxes, it stood out because it was kept in a clear plastic bag. It looked like a puffy blue pillow.

Emily put on a fresh pair of latex gloves and initialed the tag on the plastic bag. When she opened it, it released a musty odor that reminded her of a wet dog, or maybe a men's locker room. Not overwhelming, but a heavy presence, nonetheless. That was at the first whiff, but by the second or third she'd wished she'd dipped her nose into Vicks, as the smell of Mandy's corpse filled the room. Emily brushed it off and unfurled the bag on a table in the center of the small room. Next, she pulled on the reflective metal shade of a gooseneck lamp clipped to the edge of the table.

The deep blue sleeping bag lay there, doused in the light, like a moonlit ocean.

"Now," she said to herself, "let's see what that hole is really telling us."

She pointed the light onto a spot near the top of the bag. The five-inch square void winked at her. She bent down closer. The edge of the fabric was fringed from the stress of being in the water, being moved and jostled as Mandy's body began to bloat when the icy depths of the pond began to warm. She noticed that the fringe of the unraveling nylon fabric was slightly uneven in several places.

She looked up as if to speak to someone, though no one was there.

The fabric hadn't been torn. It had been cut. Most likely with scissors, maybe the blade of a razor.

Emily looked at the top edge of the bag and followed the lines of the machine stitching. It was clear that there was a start and stop to the seam. It wasn't one continuous line of thread.

She dialed Chris's number and he answered.

"Early for you, isn't it?" after hearing her voice.

"Chris, I know it's early," she said, knowing he wouldn't mind as he went running along the Seattle waterfront at 6 A.M. every morning anyway. "I've been down here looking at the Crawford evidence."

"Either you've got insomnia or you're overly dedicated."

"Somewhere between the two, if you must label me. Anyway, I'm not sure what it means, but I was looking at the sleeping bag. Remember the tear on the bag?"

"Sure. I guess so."

"It isn't a tear. It's a cut. Someone cut out a window of fabric."

"I guess I'm not following, Em."

"When you rip nylon, it is a clean tear between the threads. There's some jaggedness here. It's subtle, but unmistakable."

"OK. So what you're saying is someone cut that hole in the sleeping bag and they did it on purpose."

"Right," she said, "I'll bet the killer cut the hole to remove something that pointed to him as the owner of the bag."

"OK. So the person had their name written on the bag."

"I doubt that," she said. "This fabric's too dark for someone to ink a name and address. Even the fattest Sharpie would get lost on it. And really, why would you put your name there anyway? When the bag is rolled up you couldn't see the name and address."

"Again, I'm not following you. Sorry, babe."

Emily exhaled. "No worries. You haven't seen what I've just seen and you've never sewed a stitch in your life. I have. I made most of Jenna's Halloween costumes." The mention of it brought a warm smile to her face. "Anyway," she said, returning her thoughts back to Mandy and the sleeping bag, "it looks to me like the top edge was re-sewn."

"What does that mean?"

"Not sure," she said. "You driving or flying over?"

"I'll be there for dinner. I'm driving."

They exchanged their "I love yous" and Emily snapped her phone shut and signed out of the evidence room. Despite the lack of sleep, she felt energized. *Why re-sew the top end of the bag?*

Gloria Bergstrom was fixing coffee in the break room when Emily emerged from the basement. "The best little dispatcher in Cherrystone" as she called herself, was wearing a pretty black-and-white wool dress with a toffee-colored cardigan.

"You look lovely. Something special about today?" Emily said.

Gloria filled the coffee carafe with water and poured it into the coffeemaker.

"Not at all. Every now and then I dress up just to prove that I still can." She smiled and Emily returned the favor. "Hey, you're in mighty early today. What's up with that?"

"Couldn't sleep."

"Personal or professional?"

Gloria had a knack of cutting to the chase. She knew that Emily and Chris had gone through their ups and downs. Although Emily tried to keep a reasonably tight lid on her personal life, privacy was hard to come by in a small place like Cherrystone. Besides, during those ups and downs, Emily's mood sometimes betrayed her need to stay professionally detached from those who worked for her. Working day in and day out, Gloria, however, had become family.

"Professional, thankfully," Emily said.

"Crawford, of course. I've lost sleep over that one, too."

Emily rinsed out a mug and watched the brown stream of fresh coffee fill the carafe. She explained how'd she'd gone into the evidence vault and how she'd seen the irregularities of the tearing on the nylon sleeping bag.

"Interesting," Gloria said, trying to mull it over, but coming up empty. "But what does it mean?"

Emily poured her coffee and looked for a package of Equal. "The only explanation I can find is that the square of fabric that's missing once held a monogram."

Gloria, once more, looked mystified. "A monogram? Who monograms their sleeping bags?"

Emily gave up on the Equal and poured some sugar into her black coffee.

"Someone with a big ego and too much money, that's who."

Recognition clicked behind Gloria's eyes. "Mitch Crawford?"

"Seems like the type to me. I'll dig into that some more. See what Jason can turn up with embroidery shops around here."

Gloria smiled and let out a laugh. "Oh boy, he'll love that one."

Emily laughed, too. Jason had expected a lot more out of

police work than running around sporting-goods stores and embroidery businesses.

"This is the kind of excitement that never makes TV," she said, disappearing down the hallway.

Chapter Fifty-two

Garden Grove

The invitation to be heard was almost too much. Michael Barton looked at the comment feature on Jenna Kenyon's blog. He read what some of the other readers had to say.

> Jenna! You rock! You are the most awesome consultant in the whole world. I don't know what we would do without you and your advice!
> —Cherie, BZ, Biloxi

> Hey! If you ever come back to Huntsville, we have to hook up! You are smart, funny, and a blast to hang out with. Don't forget your BZ sis Megan!
> —Megan, BZ, Huntsville

> I have some more ideas to brainstorm with you. I'll send you a PowerPoint with the particulars! You know me, I love bullet points!
> —Donatella, BZ, Bowling Green

Michael clicked the pencil icon that indicated he could leave a comment. A window popped open. The blank space stared at him. Yeah, he wanted to leave a comment. But what he had to say wasn't going to be so upbeat. What he wanted to say could be traced back through his Internet provider or IP address.

He started to type.

Hi bitch! You think that you're something pretty special, don't you? You think that you're so smart, talented, pretty. You're a piece of garbage, that's what you are. I'd like to use a dull knife and take my time hacking off your head from your bony ass body. I'd like to take dynamite and stuff it in every orifice and light the goddamn fuse. You're nothing. You and your sisters think that you rule the world. But you don't. I won't let you. You're indifferent to anyone who doesn't fit into your predetermined plan. Bitch! Do you even remember Sarah? Do you ever think about her? Pretty soon you will. Believe me, it will be the last thing you ever think about!

He heard his wife stirring. Olivia was coming down the stairs. He minimized the window and opened another file. He looked up and smiled.

"Hi, baby," she said, "it's late. I want you to come to bed." Her beautiful dark skin glistened from a bath. She smelled of the faintest hint of lavender. As she put her hand on his shoulder and tugged, her nipple protruded from the slit of her robe.

Michael looked in her eyes. "Hold that thought," he said. "I'll be right up."

"You better. I'm a lonely girl."

"I'll power down now."

Olivia disappeared up the stairs and he went back to Jenna Kenyon's blog. He waved the curser over the box that said "post." It was so tempting. He wanted so much for that girl to know that her fate was something to fear. Her future belonged to him.

He closed out the blog without saving it.

No need to warn her, of course. No need to get caught.

Chapter Fifty-three

Something was wrong and Olivia Barton could feel it in her bones. The first indicators were trivial, silly almost. She smelled cigarette smoke on Michael's clothes and asked him about it. He said someone at work smoked in the conference room. She knew that was a lie. Human Solutions, like all California employers, offered a totally smoke-free environment. She figured he'd been stressed out and started smoking again. It pained her. He'd quit before Danny was born.

"I want to live a long life to take care of my boy," he said. *Why are you smoking now? What's going on with you?*

As the uncharacteristic behaviors escalated, she began to worry. Worry turned into action. She knew that some wives pick their husband's pockets hoping to find something that will indicate a love affair. Olivia knew something was awry with Michael, but an intimate physical betrayal was simply not at the top of her list. She sought more clues as to the changes in his behavior that she worried indicated a possible breakdown. *Something was wrong.* She wondered if there had been some trigger that had brought back problems long since buried.

She'd seen an episode on *Dr. Phil* about repressed memory syndrome and how childhood trauma is frequently revisited in adulthood. Sometimes a woman or man relives the incidents of the past that they've never quite resolved. They become stuck in dramas that quietly play in their heads. No one knows it. No one but the victim. Shame is a silencer.

The things that told Olivia that a problem was percolating were small but powerful. She remembered how she'd noticed on at least two occasions that Michael had stripped the bed of its sheets and laundered them. One time, he said he'd spilled coffee. Another time, when she detected the smell of urine, he said that Simon, the cat, had peed on the bed. It was possible, of course. But Simon never did it again. He went missing shortly after that.

All of that would have been believable if not for the obvious lie. She looked at the online report from the state of California that indicated how much money was drawn from their bank account for the Fast Pass, an electronic transponder that allowed access to carpool lanes and expressways for a fee.

"What's with all the trips on the Fast Pass down to San Diego? You don't have that region," she said referring to his service territory for Human Solutions.

He looked at her, then down at the printout. "Nope. Must be an error. I've heard about a bunch of transponders that have sent screwed-up signals to the reader. Remember that article in the *Times*?"

She looked at him with blank eyes.

"We talked about it, Olivia."

She searched her memory, but she knew that there had been no discussion. His insistence alarmed her.

"I guess so," she said, finally. "I'll call them tomorrow and straighten it out."

"Don't bother. I'll do it. I hate paying for something we didn't use and I'll let them know that we won't stand for it.

Stupid government computing systems. Jeesh, I'd like to consult for them and see if we couldn't save the taxpayers some dough."

His little rant satisfied Olivia until she caught him in what had to be a lie. It was a crumpled cash receipt for coffee from a San Diego Hardee's restaurant. The date was the same day as the date on the Fast Pass report.

He had, in fact, been there. He had to have been. *But why? Why did he lie?*

There was something else that ate at her. When he arrived home from Dixon, he came with only one bag.

He'd left for Tennessee with *two*. The larger of the two was a garment bag that held three pressed long-sleeved shirts and a pair of suits—though, depending on the client, he usually only wore a suit the first day. The second was a smaller bag with wheels that held his socks, underwear, and shaving supplies.

"What happened with your bag?" she had asked, eager to get him unpacked and the suitcases put away so they didn't hog the space of their small master bedroom.

"I must have left the other in the car."

She knew that was wrong. "No, I just looked in the car. Empty."

"Damn that airline." Michael's face started its slow turn to red. "They probably lost the other piece."

Olivia wanted to ask how it was that he didn't notice that he'd come home with only half of what he brought. But she held her tongue.

Something wasn't right. *Why invent a story?* When concern morphs into fear, a woman revisits the things that bothered her only a little.

When he was sleeping she snuggled up next to him, spooning his back. She flicked the hair at the nape of his neck and looked closely at the row of small circular scars. There were five. They were in perfectly spaced sequence.

Dear God, what did they do to you?

Michael felt his wife's touch and the warmth of her body and breath on his back. He rolled over and kissed her.

"I love you," he said.

She whispered back the same words.

He rolled over and pressed his body against her, nuzzling her. He smelled, as always, of mint toothpaste and Irish Spring. He explored her body with his hands, whispering all the while how much he adored her. But as he did so, Olivia's own interior monologue was at odds with the moment.

What happened to you, baby? What did they do to you? Why are you slipping away? Where are you going?

In the dim light of their bedroom she could see his handsome face as he made love to her, his eyes intense, his body taut and hard where hers was soft and smooth.

"I love you, Olivia," he said, "I love you more than you know."

"I love you, too."

Again, the monologue that she had running in her head:

Tell me, tell me. Something's wrong. What, baby, what do I need to know to make it better?

Later, when Michael fell asleep, Olivia went downstairs to the office and logged on to his laptop. She knew the password because he'd called her from the road one time when his laptop had failed and he needed to retrieve some client data from his backup computer, a Sony desktop.

"Sorry, honey," he said, "But I'm in a bind. Do you mind?'

"Of course not." They chitchatted for a moment about his trip as the computer warmed up and she asked for his password when the log-on prompt came up on the screen.

"OLIVIAMYLOVE," he said.

She typed it in, smiling as she went.

"Nice password. I thought you might have used the cat's name like everyone else."

"I've used this password or a variation thereof from nearly the day that I met you."

It was a sweet memory. But as she sat waiting for the screen to light up, she wasn't sure how far she was willing to go to find out what it was that was troubling the man that she loved so much. *Maybe some secrets*, she thought, *are best hidden?*

Her heart rate accelerated a little when she heard the creak of the stairs, but it was a false alarm. No one was coming. With the light of the computer screen as the room's only source of illumination, it took three times to get the password correct. She'd almost given up, thinking that he might have changed it.

The desktop picture was a familiar image, taken by a Japanese tourist at the Santa Monica pier as the sun started its dip toward the Pacific. The family stood in front of the carousel, their features washed with the golden light of the hour. It was captioned: *The Bartons Get the Runaround.* The image brought a quick smile, but it was rueful rather than joyful. Their perfect family was at stake.

Olivia dug in to his e-mail first, but found nothing of interest—though some sexually related e-mails from spammers gave her brief pause. She pulled down his list of favorite websites. Amid the stock report sites, the news sites, a half-dozen tech sites, and even a gardening web page, one caught her eye.

It was a blog written by a young woman from Washington State. It was out of the ordinary, for sure. Olivia couldn't readily see why her husband would "favorite" something so far removed from any interest. For a second, she wondered if it was a porn site.

. . . the national office sent out an advisory, that I'm sure you have already read. I'm going to put it up on my blog anyway. It really bears special attention. OK? Click here and read the message.

Olivia moved her cursor and clicked. A pop-up window opened up with the following message.

The brutal murder of our Beta Zeta sister Sheraton Wilkes has devastated our chapter at Dixon University, Dixon, Tenn. Along with the heartache of a life taken from us too soon, we must also implore each of you to maintain a watchful eye over each other. We have four tips [4 Safety!] that we urge you to take to heart. Your continued safety will be a tribute to Sheraton Wilkes.

Always travel in pairs.

Always make sure that several people know where you are going and when you will return.

Always heed the midnight curfew.

Never be afraid to call campus security or 911 when you feel threatened in any way.

There was an explanation for her husband being on Jenna's website, of course. Olivia remembered how the murder of the sorority girl had been on the news when he returned from Tennessee. She and Michael had discussed it. He seemed somewhat interested because he'd been there. It was the same connection she felt when she learned that a jetliner had crashed in the mountains of the Cascades—not far from where she'd grown up.

Sometimes you want to know everything when evil or tragedy comes so close.

Olivia looked at the time. Once again, the Internet had sucked away another hour. It was almost 2:00 A.M. She powered down and went back upstairs.

Whatever she was looking to find wasn't there.

* * *

He could feel the covers move and the mattress give way as Olivia crawled back into bed. He looked at the clock. She'd been downstairs for more than an hour. He pretended to sleep as she settled herself back down.

What had she been doing?

Chapter Fifty-four

It felt like a small betrayal, but Olivia Barton had good reason for it. As the highway to Acton unrolled in front of her in a seemingly endless belt of blacktop and skid marks, she told herself that Michael would see that she loved him— *if* he ever found out what she had done. She planned to be careful, of course, so that they'd never have that conversation.

She couldn't come up with any other way to ferret out her troubled husband's past. State records for juveniles were sealed. She'd tried the "I'm a family member desperate to find my brother" ploy on a records clerk who snapped gum and told her that "they're sealed for a reason and the reason is they don't want anyone in those records." She tried talking to Michael about his past, but he was evasive. Sometimes even dismissive, as if there was nothing there to really tell. He'd told her time and again that he'd moved on. She knew that to find out about his past, the time to do so was when they were first together.

Only in the beginning of a relationship, she thought, *can a woman make a stand and rummage around, gently of course, in the past of the man she loves.*

When you marry him, you unwittingly shut the book and

you accept him for all that he is. All that comes with him. His past. His family.

Two days before the drive from Garden Grove, she found Gwen Trexler's phone number on an online phone directory. She took a deep breath and made the call.

"Ms. Trexler?"

"Yes. Who's calling?"

"Did you used to be a reporter for the *Sea Breeze*?"

There was a short silence. Olivia could hear Etta James wailing "At Last" in the background.

"Yes, I was."

"I'm calling about my husband, Michael Barton."

"Come again? Barton? The name doesn't ring a bell. I haven't been down in Orange County for years. Finally wised up and got into PR."

"He was the little boy you wrote about. They found him at Disneyland with his sister."

Another short silence came from Gwen Trexler's side of the line, but this one had more to do with instant recognition of the sad story of the two little kids, dumped by their mother.

"I've thought of those children forever. I wish I could have done more for them. Especially the boy, he was so messed up. I wish I could have helped more."

Olivia wondered what the former reporter meant by that, but she let it slide. Over the phone wasn't the venue for what she was after.

"I don't suppose you'd be willing to talk to me?" Olivia asked. "You might be able to help now. I think he's having problems. It might be related to what happened to him back then."

"All right. I'm up in Acton. Got a pencil? I'll give you an address."

Olivia looked at the computer screen. "You still on Antelope Way?"

"Yes, I am. Nice work. You should be a reporter. That is if you want to give up your life for meetings, breathe in everyone's smoke, have no money, get no respect . . . don't I sound bitter?"

Olivia laughed. It was a break in the tension of making the call that she needed.

"Just realistic, I guess. Thanks, Ms. Trexler. See you tomorrow afternoon."

The conversation played in her head after she dropped off the kids with her mother and headed north. Olivia told her mom she was going to have lunch with friends and spend the day on Melrose, then the Beverly Center. She couldn't explain why her husband wouldn't talk about his past. She loved him so much, but there was a stinging hurt over being with a man who had no connection to anyone from a past longer than a couple of years.

If there had been an easier way, one that hadn't required deception, she would have gladly gone that route. But the *Sea Breeze* had been purchased by a major newspaper chain in the late 1980s. The archives were summarily dumped by the new owners. So much for history. The only saving grace was that Gwen Trexler was still alive and very much willing to help.

Now almost seventy, Gwen Trexler was living in a duplex in Acton, her PR firm having given up the ghost. It was a spotless place, with a manicured flowerbed that in a month or so would be the envy of any garden magazine. The duplex was painted a bronze tone with orange trim that while strange, somehow worked. It was clear coming up to the front door that Mrs. Trexler likely lived alone—everything was in perfect order. Next door was another matter. A swing set and a debris field of toys indicated that a family with kids had taken up residence on the other side. It was order vs. chaos. Family vs. alone.

Gwen Trexler was a tall woman, at almost six feet, with a slim and muscular build. Her features were angular, almost Cubist. She wore a cotton blouse and a denim skirt that almost touched the floor. Her eyes matched the jade on the pendant that swung around her neck.

She opened the screen door and ushered Olivia inside.

"I made some mango smoothies," she said. "No sugar. I use honey and whey powder to give me a little pick-me-up in the afternoons."

Olivia thought it sounded awful, but her mother taught her to take a sip and "pretend to enjoy because that makes the host happy."

It was a rule she lived by.

"Sounds delicious," she said, taking a glass.

The living room was surprisingly large, facing out to a valley view that held several hundred head of cattle. There were so many that it was hard to see where one animal ended and another began.

"Seems like a stockyard, I know," Gwen said, regarding the sea of black and brown undulating less than a mile away. "The wind's in my favor today. Thank God." She set down a pale yellow smoothie, complete with a straw.

"Delicious," Olivia said, only half-lying. She'd tasted worse.

"I know you want to know more about your husband, so why don't you just ask him?"

Olivia sipped on the drink, buying time and trying not to feel embarrassed because she'd been shut out of Michael's life.

"He won't talk to me. It really is that simple, Ms. Trexler. He has nothing to say."

She brushed away several strands of white hair from her eyes. "Have you ever heard of letting sleeping dogs lie?"

Olivia had. Her own mother was a major purveyor of

homespun advice like that. "Believe me, I've thought of that. Maybe there's something so deep, so dark, that he just can't go there and get it. I understand that. But . . ."

"But there's something that's propelled you here today." Gwen Trexler glanced out the window, noticing Olivia's car. "I see from the fingerprints on your windows that you have kids. Is that it?"

"A boy and a girl. And, no, that's not it. He's just been so distant lately and he's lied a couple of times about small things."

"Like what?"

"Where he was, nothing big."

"This isn't about an affair?"

Olivia shook her head emphatically. The idea of an affair was ludicrous. "No. Not at all. Just lately, he's been crying in his sleep."

Gwen narrowed her gaze at the pretty young woman. An affair had been a stupid suggestion. "I see," she said.

"I just have a feeling that he's trying to deal with all that happened to him, and if I knew, I'd be able to help."

Gwen looked over at the file. She tapped her opalescent nails on a yellowed folder she retrieved from a side table. "What little I have is right here."

"Do you keep copies of all the stories you write?" Olivia asked.

"Heavens, no." Gwen swished the spoon in her drink to loosen the frozen concoction. "Only what interests me."

There was something foreboding in the former reporter's tone and Olivia let it pass.

Gwen opened the file and spread out the clippings on the coffee table. The one on top was the one that Michael had kept.

"I wasn't sure there would be more than the one I'd already seen," Olivia said. "May I?"

Gwen watched as Olivia reached over to pick up the brittle stack of clippings, preserved like pressed flowers from a young girl's high school prom.

"Help yourself. I won an award for it. Best spot news reporting for a paper in the lowest circulation category for a daily newspaper." She laughed. "Back then, I was young enough to think that you could actually get somewhere in the newspaper business by being good. What a joke."

There were three stories, including the original with the photo. The headline on the second clipping almost made her gasp.

Disney Kids Mother Found?

The article detailed how the body of a woman had been found in a bed at the Igloo Motel on Katella Avenue, across from Disneyland three days after Michael and Sarah Barton had been found.

"I don't understand," Olivia said, looking up. "What happened to her?"

A gray tabby cat jumped up into Gwen's lap and she inattentively started to rub its ears.

"Good question. We really don't know. There were no signs of a struggle. There were no obvious injuries. Mrs. Barton checked into the motel the same day that her children spent in the park. She paid for three days in advance. It was all she had."

She added: "I thought the headline was irresponsible. We didn't have any connection to those kids."

"What do you mean?"

"All we had was a dead woman. No drugs. No signs of violence. Nothing."

"Who was she?"

"Who knows? Coroner said she'd given birth to at least one child, maybe more. We never made an ID. No one could. She paid cash. No purse. Nothing. They even showed a ghoulishly retouched photo of her to the boy, but he couldn't ID her. "

Olivia looked back down at the clipping. "Then how did she die?"

"The coroner thought she died, possibly, of asphyxiation. But I think that a mom who would dump her kids like that maybe died of a broken heart."

Olivia could scarcely think of *any* reason a mother would leave her children. She would die before she allowed anything to happen to her own. She knew most mothers were that way. But not, it seemed, Michael's mother.

"What has your husband told you about his family?" Gwen asked.

Olivia felt a flush of defensiveness take over and it bothered her. It was as if the reporter was challenging her on the closeness of her marriage to Michael. She wanted to tell her that she knew everything, but it would be an obvious lie. The reason she'd come up to Acton was for a little piece of the puzzle, a piece that would bring her closer to the man that she loved.

"I don't mean to be too nosy," Gwen asked. "Would you mind answering some questions?"

"That seems a little formal. You're not writing about it, are you?"

"Of course not. Like I said, I've often wondered about your husband and his sister."

"Well, all right. What?"

"The articles don't mention it, but your husband had been severely abused by someone."

"What do you mean, *abused*?"

"Physically abused." Gwen searched the younger woman's eyes. "Does he still have the scars on his neck? The little round scars?"

Olivia remembered seeing them for the first time. She was helping him put on a tie for one of those awful company events he had to attend. It was an almost perfect row of small circular scars faded by time, hidden by the hair that brushed against his collar.

"What's this?" She asked, looking at his face in the bathroom mirror.

"What?"

"These little scars, Michael. What are they?"

His eyes narrowed and he shrugged off her inquiry. "Oh, *those*. Bad acne. I scarred up pretty bad on my shoulders and neck."

"Scars from acne, he told me," Olivia said.

Gwen set her cat on the floor. She touched her fingertips to her lips and shook her head.

"That wasn't from acne. When we found Michael and Sarah, the back of his neck was still scabbed over from the burns. On his hand, too. Some, it seemed, had been quite recent."

Olivia felt her stomach turn. *Burns?* What she was hearing was beyond anything she could have imagined. *Who burns the neck of a child?* "You mean, burned flesh?"

The horror of the scenario welled up in the younger woman's pretty dark eyes.

"Yes," Gwen said, softly, taking her questioning tone down a notch. "It appeared to us at the time that he'd been tortured with a cigarette."

Olivia couldn't help herself. She started to cry. She had come there for answers, not tears.

"Look, I know this is hard." Gwen got up and looked for a tissue, finally producing one from a crocheted dispenser on the top of her upright piano. "I'd never seen a kid more abused than Michael. He could barely speak to us. He was a wreck. His sister, being younger, I always felt had a fighting chance. But Michael. . . ." her voice trailed off as she handed the tissue box to Olivia. "Well, you brought me a bit of a miracle today."

Olivia dabbed at her eyes and looked up. "What? How?"

"He has *you*. He has two children. That poor little boy has survived and made a life out of what was handed to him. I thought for sure he'd end up in the system somewhere, giving back to the world what his mother and father had given to him."

As she got up to leave, she offered to take the empty glass into the kitchen, but Gwen waved her away.

"Ms. Trexler," Olivia said her voice slightly tentative, "one thing I don't understand."

The older woman put her hand on Olivia's shoulder, a gesture meant to comfort. It did.

"What is it?" she asked.

"How come you thought the woman was Michael and Sarah's mother? Did she look like them?"

Gwen looked out the window. "It wasn't that. I mean, there was a resemblance, of course. It was something else."

"What?"

She returned her gaze to Olivia. Her face was full of regret and worry. "She'd been burned on the nape of her neck, too. She had a row of scars that matched what he had."

Olivia felt sick. It was more than the smoothie and she knew it. "Sarah?" she asked.

"None there. Her neck was flawless."

"Was the body ever claimed?"

"No. Buried in the Potters Field behind the old Westward Ho Motel and Casino."

"Thank you," she said, tears running down her face. Olivia turned on her heels and headed for the door.

"I wish I could have been more helpful. I'm glad to know your husband's a survivor. The girl, too?"

"We don't know," Olivia said, without looking back. "They've lost touch."

As Olivia drove, the Etta James song that had been playing in the background when she called Gwen Trexler kicked back into her consciousness.

Yes, *at last.*

When Olivia and the children arrived home around 7 P.M., the house was still. She found Michael in the bedroom dressing to go running. He sat on the edge of the bed.

"How was your mom?" he asked, lacing his shoes and not looking up.

"Oh you know my mama—a little good, a little bad."

"I guess so. You can always count on that with her. Thought you'd be home earlier," he said.

"Traffic was worse than usual. I don't even know if there is a usual anymore."

"You three had a good time?"

"Yeah, nothing exciting. I managed to break away for about an hour. I got you a shirt from the Gap. On sale." She smiled.

He looked up and returned the smile. "Great. I'll try it on when I get back from my run."

"All right, baby. See you in a bit."

Michael took off and Olivia went into the kitchen. The message machine had already been played. But there was a new message on it, so she hit the button.

Her mother's voice came on the line: *"Hi Michael. The kids want me to take them for ice cream to their favorite place. For the life of me, I can't remember what that place is called. Neither can they! Oh dear. I know you're working at home today, but Olivia's cell must be off and she's not expected back for the rest of the day."*

Olivia felt a chill run down her spine. She had no real way of knowing what her husband had thought of the message and her obvious lie. He might have thought the very worst; that she'd been cheating on him or something crazy. All she had been doing was seeking the truth. She felt the truth would set him free from his torment.

That was about to change.

Olivia, stop. Olivia, please.

Michael Barton, running around the Rancho Alamitos High School track, used the speed and repetition of doing laps to focus his thoughts. Why was it that she seemed to think that *her* digging into his life was something that would benefit *him*? He'd loved her so much. He thought that she and the children had been the cure for the disease that ravaged him since he was a little boy. Her big brown eyes looked at him with nothing but love when they were first together. Now, all he saw was the reflection of her suspicion.

Olivia, stop. Don't make me stop you.

He saw a young woman doing stretches by the long-jump pit and he looked around. The parking lot was empty, save for his car and a blue Mazda, which he assumed was the woman's. She wore green sweats with a big gold and green V on the back of her jacket, a nod to the Vaquero, the school mascot. *A student.* He ran past her, his heart pumping blood and adrenaline like a fire hose.

Olivia, I want to love you. I want to know what it is to be normal. Stop. Stop. Don't make me do this.

He moved closer to the girl as he turned toward the stretch in front of the bleachers.

She reminded him of his wife a little, small-framed, with dark hair that she held out of the way in a loose clip. Her brown eyes held his for a second. She turned away as he ran past. His running shoes pounded the spongy black track, and he fought the urge.

She's not on the list. Got to stop. Can't keep doing this. No. Olivia, please don't make me angry.

Chapter Fifty-five

Lily Ann Denton. There was a kind of familiarity with the name. Olivia hadn't given it a lot of thought, but as she sat in the kitchen with the TV going and the coffeepot brewing, the name came up on the morning news. It triggered something. She wasn't sure what. The news report indicated that Lily Ann had been found murdered—butchered—off a highway near San Diego. According to the reporter standing in front of the coroner's office in a crisp blue shirt and wine-red tie, the girl was twenty-two.

The case was now considered cold and the family had put up a $50,000 reward for any information leading to the arrest and conviction of their daughter's killer.

"Lily Ann was many things to her family and friends, a creative interior designer, a loyal sorority sister, and a loving daughter. But right now, the family wants to put all of that aside," the earnest reporter said.

The next cut showed a man and woman, well-heeled, sitting on a leather couch with an ocean view behind them. It was likely their home. Despite the somewhat dated furnishings. But they were clearly loaded. The woman had ice-cube size diamonds on each stretched earlobe.

"Our daughter was our life. She was our only child. We

want to find out who did this to her. . . ." Mrs. Denton's voice trailed off and her husband reached for the mic to take over.

"We want to catch the SOB who killed Lily Ann. Please help us."

Olivia poured some coffee, but it smelled burned and made her sick. Her stomach was in knots. Something about the name seemed to call to her, but she wasn't sure. She didn't know Lily Ann Denton. She didn't really have that many friends down in San Diego.

It niggled at her brain throughout the day.

He thought of Lily Ann and how he killed her. He'd done some reading on serial killers and knew enough that he wanted to mix up his technique to throw off the investigators who would want to stop him before his work was done. Animals had taken care of his first victim, Tiffany. The investigators knew she'd been murdered, but they didn't know that he'd wrapped an electrical cord around her neck. He'd taken a washcloth soaked in chloroform and covered her lip-glossed mouth until she fell limp. He'd shoved her in the back of his trunk and gone for a snack.

She was alive when he took her to the rest stop and opened the trunk.

"Please don't do this," she said, crying so hard that she could barely spit out her words.

"You shouldn't have done what you did."

"I don't know what you're talking—"

He pulled her out of the trunk in the middle of her sentence.

"Shut up. Shut up or I'll kill you."

He loved the lie. The promise of false hope that his words gave.

It was dark and the sound of the freeway rolled like an

ocean. Save for a lone trucker sleeping with his refrigerated truck idling, the place was empty.

"Are you going to rape me?" she said.

The thought of raping her made him recoil. He'd never rape anyone. He'd known firsthand what that was like.

"I won't tell anyone," she said, pleading with terror-filled eyes.

Everyone's last words.

He pulled out battery-powered hair clippers. The buzz almost roared in her ears as he held her still. He tightened his grip. All she did was cry as her beauty fell to the dirt.

He was mute as he reached for the knife in his jacket and drove it through her chest. Lily Ann Denton barely gasped as the life drained from her blue eyes. She slumped to the ground and he sliced her flesh like the belly of a fish. Her organs, shiny in the glow from the parking lot lights, spilled onto the dirt.

This is messier than last time.

It bothered him that she'd thought he was going to rape her. He would never do that.

The last thing he did was snap the golden chain from her neck, careful not to let the two special letters fall into the clump of ice plant pooled with her already coagulating blood.

Now he had two such souvenirs. *A very good start. Almost done.*

Chapter Fifty-six

Dixon

Sometimes when investigators review the evidence in criminal matters they miss the most obvious clues and connections. Sometimes it takes a sharp young woman with a love of Google to find the answer that eludes the most seasoned investigators—even her own mother.

Jenna Kenyon had mourned the deaths of her sorority sisters Tiffany Jacobs and Sheraton Wilkes. She only knew Sheraton for a few hours, but she'd worked with Tiffany during recruitment for a new batch of pledges the season before.

Although Beta Zeta House had been cleared for the girls to return after 7 P.M., none did. Sororities across the Dixon campus opened their doors to the BZ sisters. Ten of the young women were too traumatized even for that kind of accommodation—they went home to their parents. The national office authorized a hotel room for Jenna and she checked herself into a Ramada Inn in downtown Dixon.

She got out her laptop and looked at the BZ message boards. Several sisters had offered "virtual" flowers in Sheraton's memory. Bonita Rayburn of Tucson, Arizona, posted a message that chilled Jenna to the depths of her bones.

These are hard times for our BZ sisters. So much tragedy. First Lily Ann Denton, Tiffany Jacobs, and now Sheraton Wilkes. My heart goes out to their families.

Jenna stared at the laptop monitor. *Lily Ann Denton?* She knew Lily Ann. She and Tiffany Jacobs had worked with her for BZ recruitment at Cascade University.

She put "Lily Ann Denton" into the search field and clicked. One article came up.

SD Woman's Body Identified

The body of a young woman found behind a rest stop near the San Diego County line was identified as Lily Ann Denton, 22, San Diego, the medical examiner announced today.

"I'm classifying this as a homicide," Dr. Ken Jensen said. "But there are some irregularities that we'll need to review."

Dr. Jensen refused to deny or confirm police reports that Denton was murdered as a part of a black market human organs scheme out of Tijuana.

"I'm not going to go there," he said.

Jenna looked at her phone for the time, and figured her mom would be home and probably getting ready for bed. She pushed speed dial number 1.

It rang and rang. *Pick up. Pick up.*

Finally, it clicked, and Emily answered. "Hi, honey. You caught me just as I was sliding under the covers. A nice way to end the day," she said.

"Mom, I'm so glad you're there. Something weird I wanted to tell you about."

Emily could detect the concern in her daughter's voice. Her words were tight, constricted. She'd had that kind of affect since she was a little girl. Jenna was tough, but when she was scared, her feelings could not be masked.

"Are you all right, Jenna? You've been on my mind all day." Emily turned to look at Chris, who'd rolled over on to his side and snuggled next to her. He could feel her shift from romance to worry.

Jenna felt her heart start to race, as the fear welled up inside. She'd been unnerved a moment before, but the sound of her mother's voice let her fear build. She let herself go, only in the way that a child can do for a mother she knows will always be there for her.

She fought tears. *Something's wrong. Something's wrong. Only my mom will understand.* She didn't want to cry.

"I'm fine. But, Mom, I was online looking at the message boards and someone mentioned that another girl, Lily Ann Denton, had died. Murdered, mom. Tiffany was murdered. Sheraton was murdered!" Her words came machine-gun rapid, firing across the country, cell-tower to tower.

"Slow down," Emily said, now sitting up in her bed. "Lily Ann Denton?"

"Yes. I'm reading about her online. Mom, that's too much of a coincidence, don't you think?"

A couple of BZ sisters walked past and Jenna turned. She didn't want them to see her cry.

Emily was on her feet then, reaching for her robe. She wanted Jenna to get out of Dixon as soon as possible. "I'll call the Dixon Police and tell them what you've told me. Get the first flight out in the morning."

Emily could feel her hands tremble as she held the cell phone to her ear. "Nationals doesn't open offices until ten and I can't get a reservation."

"You still have your dad's Visa card? You know the one for 'emergencies only'?"

Jenna looked over at her purse. "Yes, I think so," she said.

"Fine. This is an emergency."

Emily set down her phone and looked over at Chris, under the covers in bed but no longer in either a sleepy or romantic mood.

"What was that all about?" he asked, sitting up.

"I told you about the Jacobs girl. The bones the Idaho police found?"

"Jenna knew her, yes. You told me."

"There's another girl, another BZ sister who's been killed."

Chris wasn't really getting it and the puzzled look on his face made it clear he needed more information to connect the dots that Emily was firing at him. "You mean Sheraton Wilkes, right?"

Emily shook her head. "No, Jenna just found out that there's been another of her sisters killed. This time a girl in San Diego." She told herself to be calm. Jenna's fears had become her own.

"Well, it's got to be nothing more than a tragic coincidence," Chris said.

Emily shivered. "I hope so. But, Chris, I have a bad feeling about this. You see, Jenna knew two of the three girls.

"Tiffany and Sheraton, right."

Emily's eyes suddenly widened in fear. "Sheraton was the only dead girl she didn't know well. She knew the San Diego girl."

That night, Jenna Kenyon packed her bags. She wanted to get out of Dixon as soon as first light. She was going to a place she felt safe—home.

The Sorority Killer, as the perpetrator was first dubbed by a *Dixon Chronicle* desk editor, was immediate fodder for discussion by talk radio hosts and psychologists with a lust for the red light of a TV camera. All agreed that the killer had sought a *type* of girl—young, pretty, privileged.

"Look," one of the experts told Nancy Grace on her true-crime talk show, "I have no doubt a serial killer is at work, stalking young women all over the country. If I were a father or mother of a young pretty girl, I'd arm them with pepper spray and tell them to keep an eye out."

The host batted her eyes and shook her head, asking the guest, a criminal profiler with a dubious curriculum vitae, what exactly they should be looking for.

"White male, very strong, probably in his twenties. I'm sure of it."

That very thin description, of course, was the problem. The police knew just about as much. That description could fit half the men on college campuses across the country.

Dixon Police Detective Kellie Jasper had the case with the greatest hope for resolution. The Jacobs girl was nothing but bones and the Denton girl found near San Diego had likely been killed somewhere other than the rest stop. But the crime scene at the BZ house was Tupperware fresh. The detective was hopeful there would be some DNA or fibers found at the house.

The big problem was there was so much of it. The FBI combed through the scene of Sheraton's murder and carted out a mountain of evidence. With more than fifty girls—not to mention all of their friends, family members, and support staff—it was apparent that it would take months to go though the evidence to decide who left what. It was easy to exclude the girls living there, but not every person that came and went and left prints, hair, and fibers.

It's almost one of those cases that once we know the killer, we can dig into this stuff and build a case against him, she thought.

That, of course, only worked if the perp was known. But as far as anyone could tell, the only connection the women had with each other was the sorority. Lily Ann and Tiffany knew each other from Cascade University. That was well documented. But while Sheraton Wilkes was a BZ girl, she didn't know either one. At first, it was thought they'd been to the same Pan-Hellenic conference in Washington, D.C., but it turned out that Lily Ann had boyfriend problems and had stayed home.

Was it a coincidence that Jenna Kenyon knew well two of the three dead girls and just happened to be at the scene of the third girl's murder?

Kellie Jasper didn't think so. She got Jenna, now home, on the phone in Cherrystone.

"There has to be something here with you and Sheraton. Think. *Think.*"

"I've told you, we just met."

Kellie pushed harder. She had to, there was nothing else. "But she's in your sorority. You must have met her. You must have been connected."

"There are three thousand girls nationwide who have pledged BZ."

"Think. Please. We need to catch this guy before he kills again."

Jenna could feel her blood pressure rise. "You think I haven't thought of this, Detective Jasper? This is all I think about."

"Fair enough. I'm sorry. But I'm counting on you."

After the call ended, Jenna found her mother in the kitchen. She was making a chicken dish with olives and diced dried tropical fruits.

"It smells really good in here, Mom." There was a flatness to Jenna's voice.

Emily picked up on it and her smile faded when she looked up to see her daughter's worried expression.

"What is it?"

Jenna let out a long sigh, one she meant to help her relax and lessen the stress of the call.

"The detective from Dixon called again," she said. "She thinks that I must know something about Lily Ann, Tiffany, and Sheraton. There really isn't anything to know, Mom. I don't know what connects the three of them, beyond their pledge to Beta Zeta."

Emily set down her spoon and put the lid over the chicken sautéing on the gas range. She lowered the heat, bending down to check the level of the blue flame.

"There's a link," she said. "Let's talk some more at dinner."

Chapter Fifty-seven

Cherrystone

Chris Collier had always been partial to the task of following the money in a criminal case. It was the surest way to catch a killer when insurance, payoffs, and, of course, murder for hire were the suspected motives, even though this time, neither he nor Emily suspected any of those scenarios. He'd done it more than a time or two as detective for the Seattle PD.

His most famous "follow the money" collar was made when he proved that the wife of a Seattle city councilman had hired a hit man to kill her husband. The scheme was as simple as it was dumb. She asked her brother to do the job ("nothing like keeping stupid in the family," Chris told Emily over coffee the morning the case broke), promising a small down payment and a fat insurance check later. Chris worked the finance angle sorting out the multiple accounts and discovered ten checks of $500 all made out to her brother. She was convicted and given a life sentence for murder and conspiracy to commit murder. Now she was an inmate at Washington Corrections Center for Women in Purdy, where she taught accounting classes to other inmates.

Tricia Wilson's recent influx of cash as related by Fatima was likely related to the lie she told about her ex-husband.

The question was just how? And, more important, who had given her the dough?

Chris drove his rental PT Cruiser on the highway to Spokane. As he looked out across the orchards and ranchland and drank his coffee from Java the Hut, he grinned. It wasn't the wet side of the state; it was green only where irrigation ditches and enormous sprinklers deigned it to be.

He was ready for a change. He hoped Emily was, too.

When he arrived in the parking lot at the bank in Spokane, Chris knew that without a warrant, getting any information at all would rest on who he selected to ask. He was tired from the night of wine and files, so charm would have to be forced. Not always a good mode in which to win over a potential witness.

As he entered the bank, he noticed a circular counter with a young woman named Britannia Scott smiling from the center of her Lucite and brushed-steel domain. She was the bank's personal greeter. Her wide eyes and warm smile as much as her name-tagged role made her the best shot for the first approach.

The first approach without a badge to back him up.

"Good morning! Welcome to your personal banking center!"

Chris immediately returned her smile. *This girl is overdrive-friendly. Good. That's what I need.*

"Hi, Britannia," he said. "I see you have coffee there. Could sure use a cup. What have you got today?"

"Viennese roast. Let me pour it for you," she said, walking to the other side of her circle and pumping the cinnamon-scented coffee from a black carafe.

"A real cup," he said, as she handed over a blue ceramic mug with the bank's name in silver. "This is better than Starbucks."

"We try a ton harder than anyone. What can we do for you today? We have new rates on equity loans and free checking specials."

"I'm actually here for some other kind of help."

"What's that?" Her tone was suddenly wary.

Chris slid a photo of Mitch Crawford toward Britannia. She looked at it, and it was clear she recognized the man.

"Are you a police officer? My manager can help you. I'm not authorized to do anything like that."

"Well, I am a cop. But I'm not here as a cop. I'm here helping another jurisdiction with an investigation."

"I can't help you," she said.

"All I need to know is whether or not this man is a customer of your bank."

Britannia pushed a button on the console under the counter. For a second, it flashed in Chris Collier's mind that she was activating a silent alarm and in three minutes he'd be on his stomach with a Spokane police officer's gun bearing down on him.

Instead, a small woman with dark birdlike eyes, a sharp, pointy nose, and close-cropped hair that made her look like a boy—*a bird boy*—clacked over from her desk across the room. She looked completely irritated.

"What is it now, Britannia?" The woman was impatient before she even knew the problem. "I told you the helium tank is empty, a replacement is on its way from the Valley branch, and you'll have to make do."

Britannia shrank with embarrassment and Collier felt sorry for her. "It isn't that, Ms. Davis. This man is seeking some information. He's working on that case from Cherrystone."

Chris hadn't said where he was from and he knew that meant Britannia had ID'd the photo.

"Where's your subpoena?" she asked, virtually spitting out her words.

"I don't have one. Look, I just want to know if this fellow is a customer of the bank. What would that really hurt?"

"Either open an account or leave," Ms. Davis said. "We might be the friendliest bank in town, but we follow every rule. And really, would you want to bank with an institution that didn't?"

She calls this friendly? I'd like to see her when she's not so congenial.

Ms. Davis spun around, and called over her bony shoulder, "Britannia, review the employee handbook. See the section on information requests. It starts on page thirty-two."

Chris Collier returned to his car. He'd come so close. He knew that the young woman in the circle knew something. She'd mentioned Cherrystone. She had the unmistakable look of recognition on her face when she saw the photo. It was something. Not as much as he hoped. But better than a complete zero. As he started to back out, Britannia Scott's lacquered nails rapped on the passenger's window. He struggled to find the window release.

Damn rental car!

"I'm quitting this job Friday, so I don't care if Ms. Davis fires me today. I've been here six months and that's half a year too long."

"No kidding. About the photo? You recognized the man, didn't you?"

"Yes. I think so. I've followed the case from the beginning. I've seen Mitch Crawford on TV. That's him in the photo, right?"

Chris pointed at the photo. "Is he a customer here?"

Britannia looked back at the bank's front doors. "Like I said, I don't really care if I get fired. But, no, he's not a customer here. I see everyone who comes in. I'm in the 'Customer Circle.' I'd know."

"Maybe under another name? Banking under a company name?"

She let out a sigh and shook her head in an exaggerated manner that was meant to drive the point of her exasperation to the moon. "That's all I can tell you. I have fifty balloons to blow up. God, I hate this job."

He thanked the young woman and she disappeared inside the bank. He could see Ms. Davis descending on the younger woman and giving her the "what for" for going outside to speak to him. Britannia's eyes met Chris's as she stood in the circle, being read the riot act by her boss. For a second, Chris caught a slight smile on her face.

Chapter Fifty-eight

Garden Grove

The desire to kill can gestate like an evil spawn. Michael Barton could feel his rage and hate grow, darker and deeper, the summer before the sorority girl killings started.

The summer he found his sister. The summer he lost her.

For those who kill for sport, it was easy to see why prostitutes are such an easy target. They're always lurking in the shadows, as if just waiting to be killed. "Like shooting fish in a barrel," a 1960s serial killer once famously said of strangling hookers. Michael Barton could see it. Hookers put themselves at risk every time they hopped into a guy's car and slid over to complete the transaction that brought the customer relief and the hustler the dough. Unless they have a pimp that keeps them on an electronic monitor—as some of the more tech-savvy had started to do in South Florida— they do what they want, when they want, *who* they want. There's no one to worry about them, no one to mourn them when they vanish.

Just an angry pimp with a slot to fill.

Michael thought of killing prostitutes when rage fueled the desire to kill, when he'd outgrown mowing a kitten or stabbing a tortoise with a screwdriver. One time when he was cut off by a snot-nosed debutante in a midnight blue BMW on Sunset in L.A., he saw a young girl in a too-short skirt, her white thighs sticking together in the heat of a summer's day.

She's Midwestern. Corn-fed. A cow. I could kill her and grill her bones on a hibachi, he thought. *If I was that type. If I was like the others with the compulsion. But I'm not. I'm not. I am, most emphatically, not.*

He was proud of his ability to contain the compulsion. He knew that by containing it, part of who he was inside was dying, but that was fine. He was a father, a husband, but he could tell no one what else he was.

What else he'd been.

By holding back, by not killing a hooker who caught his eye or a waiter who gave him lousy service, Michael felt he was doing his family a favor. Nothing, he knew, was more important than his family. That meant Olivia and the kids. And his sister.

He had to find Sarah.

Despite the fact that he knew his way around complex computer systems, how to find back doors that programmers sometimes left just for the sheer fun of it and how to dig so deeply in a system yet remain undetected, he failed at every turn. The state's records were in deep encryption because a teenage boy had hacked into the California Department of Social and Health Services to find his birth mother. He did. The story might have ended up happy enough, the boy meeting his long-lost mother. But not this one. Trevor Wilson was pissed off. He found his mom all right. He also set fire to the house she shared with her husband and three children in Tarzana. Two of the children died; the husband was burned on more than 60 percent of his body.

It was not a happy reunion.

Michael figured he'd have nothing to lose by going the

conventional route. He placed an ad on the FindaRelative. com site:

MISSING A SIB

Brother looking for Sister. My name is Michael. Your name is Sarah. We were abandoned by our mom at Disneyland when you were little. We were in foster care before you were adopted out. I love you. Write to me in care of this site.

A few private investigators contacted him within days of the posting—reminding him of the days after he and Olivia went to a Wedding Expo in Anaheim and stupidly entered a drawing for a discount honeymoon.

"Never," he said to Olivia, "give your address or e-mail or phone number to anyone whose sole purpose is to reach into your wallet."

Olivia urged her husband to continue his search. She prayed on it whenever they went to church. She knew that Michael had been hurt deeply by what his mother had done. She wasn't sure that he'd been abused, but she knew some terrible things had happened to him when he was so very young.

"A piece of his heart is missing," she told herself. "Maybe Sarah can help put him back together."

It was after eight, and Olivia had just put Carla to bed for the third time when the landline phone in their spotless kitchen chimed its too-loud ring. She and Michael always let the phone go to voice mail, because the only people who seemed to use the old house number—and not their respective cell phones—were charities and election organizers.

As the announcement played, she ran the tap into the teakettle. It was Michael's voice.

"We're not in right now. If you're selling something we're not interested. If you're telling us who to vote for, we've al-

ready made up our minds and we don't need any sugges-
tions. If you must leave a message, please do so. At the
tone."

"Michael," the voice said, a woman's voice, tentative, and
soft, "I hope I have the right number. I'm Sarah, your sister."

Olivia bolted for the phone and sprung it from its cradle
as fast as she could.

"Sarah? This is Michael's wife, Olivia. Is this his sister?
Is it really you?"

The young woman on the other end of the line gulped.
"Yeah," she said, "it's me."

"Oh, how I've prayed for this—how we've prayed for
this!"

"Me, too." Sarah's voice was soft, tentative.

Olivia felt a surge of adrenaline. "He's not here. He's
away on business. He'll be back tomorrow night. Do you
want his cell number? Or, wait, let me get your number and
I'll have him call you."

"I'll call back. My folks don't know that I'm trying to
find my brother."

"I see. OK. No problem." Olivia's heart was aflutter. Her
husband, whom she loved more than anything had found his
missing piece. He'd be able to be whole.

*Sarah had called. Thank God! Whatever connection he
needed from his past was there.*

"You have no idea how much this will mean to him,"
Olivia said, a tear rolling down her cheek as the kettle, now
hot, finally whistled.

"Tell him I love him. Tell him that I'm doing OK."

Olivia looked down at the caller ID panel on the phone. It
said: PRIVATE CALLER.

"Where are you living?" Olivia asked.

"I'm in Seattle. Things are great. Gotta go. Tell him we'll
talk tomorrow."

They both said good-bye, and Olivia leaned into the counter, facing the window. Moths had gathered around the patio lights, creating a beautiful halo of movement and light. She felt like breaking down and letting her emotions pour from her. In all her life, she'd never been so happy. *Michael had found his sister.*

She was so sure that Michael would now find himself.

She reached for her cell and dialed her husband. It was late in Chicago where he was away on business, but not so late that he wouldn't want to hear from her. Not when the news was as welcome as this would be. She retraced each word of the conversation in her head. Sarah hadn't asked her not to tell him that she had called. There was no "dibs" on who was going to break the news to Michael. She didn't allow herself to think for one second that the call was a hoax. No one would do that to a man so lost as a brother in search of a sister.

She got his voice mail.

Michael, where are you?

Chapter Fifty-nine

Olivia Barton considered that previous summer the happiest of her life with Michael. He was a new man. A happy man. The sometimes sullen expression that came over him for no apparent reason had been eclipsed by the joy of finding the one positive connection to his life before Olivia.

His sister, Sarah. The exchanges between the two were tentative and emotional phone calls, then e-mails took over.

Hi Mikey,

It was fun talking to you last night. I was scared that maybe you wouldn't want anything to do with me. You know, old, bad memories. You have a lot of those, don't you? I really don't have any memories of Portland, so I'll have to trust yours. I guess I really don't want to know, so if I ask, promise me you won't tell me. OK? It is so strange to be talking to you again. Should I call you Mikey? We're all grown up, but I still think of you as my big brother, but not that big. Not even a teenager.

Love always,
Sarah

Dear Sarah,

You can call me Mikey. No one else can. You are my only sister, so I guess you can get away with anything. I think it is a good idea not to talk about Portland too much. It was bad for both of us. I want you to know that when they took you away they told me that it was the best thing for me not to contact you. I fought them on it. I didn't want you to think that I abandoned you like mom abandoned us at Disney.

Mikey,

The weird thing is, I never thought that. I just sort of imagined that you and I were on different airplanes or something, going to different airports. One day, we'd meet up at the same place. Do you know what I mean? Like we were supposed to be apart because it was part of the plan. Tell me about your wife and kids and I'll tell you about my college plans.

Love, S

Dear Sarah,

Olivia and the kids really are my greatest blessing. I know that I don't appreciate them as much as I should, given the kind of upbringing I've had it is really hard to stay positive about anything or anyone. I wonder if you've ever felt that way? You know, like people were disposable? Anyway, I don't feel that way about Olivia or the kids. They are the only things that have kept me sane. Tell me more about your family.

Love, your big bro

Mikey,

My adoptive family is great. I've been so lucky.
Dad is an aerospace engineer, subcontracted to
Boeing. He's not the most exciting person. He
sometimes talks in a strange emotionless code.
Whatever you've heard about engineers is true.
Mom is an art teacher for the junior high school a
mile from our house. She's fun, pretty, and helps
make dad a whole person instead of a walking en-
cyclopedia. They couldn't have kids of their own,
and, lucky me . . . they picked me.

Michael remembered the day he'd heard that Sarah had
been selected. He'd moved on for a short stint at the Madison
Home for Boys in Chino, when the state of California sent
him a letter saying that his sister had been adopted and that
she'd be moving away to another state. He brought the letter
to his counselor, a man with gray eyes, gray hair, and a protruding belly who thought he was the hippest man in the facility.

"Kid, you just gotta let go of this," he told Michael. "Let
her be free. Let her start over somewhere, while she can."

"But she's my blood," Michael said.

"Blood doesn't matter anymore," the counselor said.
"Didn't your mom prove that?'

Michael glared at him. The remark was beyond cruel. He
wanted to grab the pair of scissors off the man's desk, open
them, and stab out both of his eyes—which, it flashed
through his mind, was exactly what he'd once done to a Jack
Russell terrier.

"You think you know about all of us here," he said. "But
you don't know shit about anything. All you can do is *talk*
about stuff. You've never *lived* any of this."

"I don't have to *live* it to help you," the counselor said, his
tone clearly defensive. He looked at his wristwatch. It was a

dismissive gesture if Michael Barton had ever seen one, and as much as he hated to admit it, it hurt. "Look," the man said, "we're about out of time for today. We never got to the occupational education brochure."

He handed Michael a brochure that detailed the kinds of jobs that the counselor felt most suitable for him. Restaurant work (dishwasher), newspaper industry (pressman), retail (clerking), and so on. Most of the training would have him working on the lowest rung, the ricketiest rung, of any corporate ladder.

"I'm interested in computer science," he said.

"You mean, data entry?"

"No, I mean programming or network engineering." Michael had turned his anger into defiance just then, and for a second he felt his rage melt away. He was smart enough to do something more than the Madison counselor could ever envision.

"I'm afraid that's not in our program here," the man said stiffly. "You might be better served by taking the TV repair training."

Michael imagined himself coming into the counselor's living room in his crummy Chino apartment. The man bending over to point to the TV connection or something that wasn't working properly. Michael pulling out a screwdriver from his tool kit and slamming it right into the man's neck. Sweet Jesus! Blood spurting like one of those chocolate fountains at a chichi wedding in Beverly Hills. Twisting the handle of the screwdriver, feeling the man's vertebrae snap as he slumped to the beige-carpeted floor.

"You listening to me?" the counselor said.

Michael snapped back. The fantasy of violence had been rudely interrupted.

"Yeah. And I'm leaving now."

He walked out of the counselor's office and searched for a bathroom, on the hunt for a place of relief.

* * *

If her husband had always seemed a little melancholy, even in the midst of the happiest days of life, Olivia Barton always put it off to his dark history. She knew that he was the sum of everything that happened to him. She also knew that where her life with her impoverished family was bathed in love and light, his own was fraught with abandonment and terror. After he made contact with Sarah, some of that cloud seemed to lift. He seemed to enjoy his children more, her more. He even seemed to think that her cooking was border-line gourmet even though he had once sheepishly urged her to take one of those cooking classes at a kitchenware store in the mall.

"When are we going to meet her?" Olivia asked while Michael gathered his things for work.

"Soon, I hope."

"What's the delay? I thought one of you would be on the first plane you could book."

"Me, too," he said, still very upbeat. "She's got some is-sues with her folks. I understand. They adopted her. They've tried to protect her from her past."

"But not from you?"

"Oh, no. Not from me. She's just going through some things. That's all. I've waited for a long, long time. I can wait until she's ready. She'll still be my sister."

It was after dinner, that quiet time when the children were settling down and the sun was low in the sky. Peaceful. *Hopeful*. Olivia looked over her husband's shoulder when he opened the MSN chat window to see if Sarah was online. She was. Since the first contact from the adopted siblings' website, there had been numerous e-mails and online chats. Phone calls had been more infrequent because of Sarah's family situation.

MichaelTech: Hi sis. Olivia and I here.

Sarah: Hi Mikey. Hi Olivia!

MichaelTech: You know you're the only one that calls me that. Olivia says hi back.

Sarah: I'm special, huh.

MichaelTech: Yup. You are. What's going on this week?

Sarah: Nothing.

MichaelTech: Nothing?

Sarah: OK. Something pretty big!

MichaelTech: Out with it.

Sarah: I got the scholarship! Four years!

MichaelTech: Are you serious? Wow!

Sarah: My parents are so proud of me. We're going to Cascade to tour the campus next week.

MichaelTech: Awesome. I knew you could do it.

Sarah: Thanks. That's my news. What's yours? Olivia OK? The kids?

MichaelTech: Everything's good. Everyone wants you to come down here. Or we can come up.

Sarah: Still haven't told my folks yet. But I will.

MichaelTech: Understood.

Michael seemed elated by the exchange, but Olivia felt less so. She wondered why it was taking so long for Sarah to tell her folks that her long-lost brother had been found.

"I wish she would tell them," she said.

Michael closed the chat window. "She will. This is a hard one for her. She doesn't want to hurt them."

They had had the discussion once before, so there was no need to state the obvious. *It isn't like you are her birth father or something. You're her brother!*

Chapter Sixty

Cherrystone

Jason Howard entered Emily's office with a file folder and that kind of cat-that-killed-the-canary look that Emily knew all too well. She knew immediately he had something to go on.

"Didn't Samantha Phillips say that she and Amanda stopped talking?"

Emily nodded. "Yes, not by her choice, I gathered."

"She lied, Sheriff." He pulled out the phone records addressed to Mitchell Crawford, 21 Larkspur, Cherrystone.

"What have you got?"

"Ten calls."

"Ten?"

"Yeah, between Halloween and the date of her disappearance."

"Good work, Jason. Anything else?"

"A bunch of calls to and from different dealerships, his lawyer's office, and calls to Mandy's folks in Spokane. Not much else."

Emily looked the list over. Jason had highlighted the calls to Samantha.

"When someone lies," she said, "we just need to find out why, now don't we?"

"That we do."

A call to the Phillips' grand residence was answered by a housekeeper named Anna, who sweetly informed Emily that Samantha, "the lady of the house," was volunteering at her children's school for the day.

Lady of the house? Emily thought, *Why can't I be the lady of the house? Why can't I have a housekeeper? Oh, yeah. I'm a top elected official and I make $53,000 a year, that's why.*

Emily grabbed her coat and keys for the drive to Crestview Elementary School. She knew the school well, of course. Jenna had attended there, just as she had. She parked by a maple tree that she could remember being a sapling when it was planted to commemorate an Earth Day celebration. In winter, it was an enormous skeleton, with four bird's nests still clinging in the frozen air.

She parked and made her way into the office.

"Hi, Sheriff Kenyon," said the woman behind the counter. Her glossy dark hair was held tight to her head, and her eyes were magnified behind the thick lenses of her glasses. Her name tag read Ms. JONAS, but Emily didn't know her.

"Good morning," she said.

"Everything all right? Mr. Gray is out at a conference in Boise. I'm Heather Jonas, his assistant principal."

"Nice to meet you," Emily said, extending her hand. "No problems here. I just need to speak to one of your parent volunteers. Can you tell me how to find Samantha Phillips?"

Heather set down her clipboard. "I'll ring her right now. She's in computer lab helping Ms. Brennan's class." She retreated to the telephone/intercom console one desk over and made the call.

"She's on her way. Would you like to talk somewhere privately? You could use Mr. Gray's office. He has a nice visitor's table. Maybe I can find some refreshments in the staff room. I have a key to the fridge."

"That would be wonderful," Emily said, thinking that the very idea of "refreshments" seemed out of place when she wanted to dig in and see what Mandy Crawford's best friend was holding back.

Five minutes later, Samantha's mask of charm failed her as she took a seat in the principal's office at Crestview Elementary to face Emily Kenyon. She looked irritated and in a hurry. She carried her purse and coat as if she planned on leaving the building after she was done talking with Emily. The housekeeper had told her that Samantha volunteered for the "entire day" at the school.

"I've told you everything I know already," she said.

Emily ignored the chilly reception. "Good morning, Samantha."

Samantha caught herself, and tried to find her good manners. "I'm sorry. Good morning, Sheriff Kenyon."

"I am sorry to bother you, but you might be our only hope in Mandy's case."

Samantha fidgeted with the big Chanel clasp of her purse.

Emily smiled inwardly. *Figures. It's real. She has a housekeeper, too.*

"What help do you need? You've got her husband locked up already."

"Yes, I know. He still has to be tried and convicted."

"Look, I've told you all that I can. All that I know."

Emily fastened her eyes on Samantha's. "Are you sure?"

"Yes, I'm sure. Do I need a lawyer or something?"

The answer was a bizarre non sequitur and it jarred Emily. "Why on earth would you need a lawyer?"

Samantha continued to open and close the clasp. Over and over. "I feel like everyone's pushing me, pressuring me."

"Everyone? What do you mean?"

"I just want to be left out of it. OK?'

"You know something, don't you?"

Samantha shook her head. "No. I don't."

"Samantha, why is it that I don't believe you? Is it about Mandy's affair?"

"You are harassing me. I don't know *why*. Leave this alone. I don't know what you're talking about."

"You do. You saw something when you visited her that day, didn't you?"

"You don't understand, Sheriff. I *can't* tell you anything more."

"Why can't you? She was your friend. Don't you want to make sure that her husband gets what's coming to him?"

Samantha looked away. A row of bright yellow school buses had converged out front. The morning kindergartners were going to line up soon to be taken home.

"I loved Mandy. But this isn't about her anymore. OK? Please just leave me alone. Please, I'm begging you, Sheriff Kenyon."

"What do you mean, isn't about Mandy? Are you all right?"

Heather Jonas opened the door with two cans of Diet Coke, but before she could say a word, Samantha stood up and started for the door. "I've said more than I should say. Please. Let it go."

"Is everything all right?" Ms. Jonas asked, stepping out of Samantha Phillips's way.

Neither Emily nor Samantha responded as they trailed out the door. No response was needed. Things were clearly far from all right.

Emily stopped Samantha as she opened the driver's door of her Volvo wagon.

Samantha looked up. Tears were streaming down her face.

"Look," she said, "I got a call right after Mandy disappeared. The person told me if I didn't keep my mouth shut about what I knew, my kids would die."

"Oh, Samantha, who was it? And what is it that you know?"

Samantha got into the driver side and reached in her purse for a tissue. She was sobbing and her tears made it hard for her to see anything in the car's dark leather interior.

"I really don't know who it was. I don't know anything. Mandy was having an affair, but I don't know who it was. She wouldn't tell me."

"Was it Mitch who threatened you?"

"No. No. It wasn't him at all."

"Are you sure?"

She dabbed at her ruined eye makeup. "I'm sure, Sheriff. The caller was a woman." She turned the ignition. "Please," she said, "I'm begging you. Keep me out of this. If I knew something I'd tell you. I promise. I'd like to kill the bastard and the bitch who've made me feel like Cherrystone is no better than L.A. or Chicago."

Emily drove back to the office, nearly out of breath from the shock of Samantha's disclosure. Who was it? Was it Tricia Wilson? Who and *why* would anyone threaten Samantha with the death of her two little children?

Were all roads leading to Tricia Wilson?

Her cell rang.

"Hi, babe." It was Chris on the phone, calling from the drive back to the airport for a flight to Seattle after checking things out at the bank in Spokane. "Tried you earlier. How's your day going so far?"

"Hang on." Emily searched for a spot to pull over. Frozen snow crunched under her tires as she pulled into a parking place in the Mayfair Market lot. "You tell me how the bank went first," she said.

"Is this like 'Show me yours, I'll show you mine'? We've already done that."

Emily ordinarily would have laughed and teased him back, but she was still reeling. "I'm processing my talk with Samantha."

Chris didn't catch the anxiety in her voice. Emily could hold it inside and she chose to do so just then.

"OK," he said. "Bottom line here is that Mitch Crawford has never been a customer of the branch that sent the cash to Tricia Wilson. Absolutely not. I got it from the woman who works the circle."

"The circle?"

"Yeah, the customer circle. It's a bank thing. Don't ask."

"So, if the money came from there, someone else paid off Tricia, right?"

"Yeah. We just don't know *who*. What about Samantha?"

"All right. I don't think she's a liar. She says she was threatened. She's a mother. Once she told me of the threat, she's not going to protect some creep."

Chris understood, at least he said so. "All right. I'll talk to you tonight when I'm back in Seattle."

"I love you," she said.

"Back at you."

Before pulling away, Emily hit the speed dial for Camille's private line.

"Camille, it's me."

"Yes? Do you have something so soon?"

Emily could feel the lift in Camille's voice. "No. Hold on. I have until five. Here's what I know. Bank employees confirm that whoever made the transaction—and remember this is without a warrant, thank you—it was *not* Mitch Crawford."

"We need a warrant, of course. Cary McConnell will be all over this. He smells blood like a shark."

"Don't I know that," Emily said. "Based on what we know, Mitch didn't pay off Tricia."

"Who else would do that? Who else would tamper with a witness?"

Emily was surprised at the prosecutor's question, but she answered it anyway.

"The only person I can think of is someone with a whole lot to lose. Someone with more to lose than Mitch."

The line was silent for a second. "Who?"

"I don't know. I wish I did. I also talked to Samantha Phillips. This thing is bigger than just Tricia Wilson's bank account."

Camille paused. "How do you mean? You think Samantha's involved?"

"No. No. She's frightened. Someone threatened her after Mandy's disappearance."

"Threatened her? *Why?* How?"

"Her kids. Killing her kids if she talked."

In her mind's eye, Emily could see Camille's face just then. Anger turned her face a shade of pink. A vein on her temple had likely risen to the surface of her otherwise flawless skin.

"That goddamn Mitch Crawford's a complete snake!"

"Cammie, it wasn't Mitch. Sam said it was a woman."

"What kind of woman would threaten another's children for that monster? Darla?"

Emily liked Darla and saw her as a young woman who'd already figured out that she'd made too many mistakes. "I don't think so. She's not the type."

"Tricia?"

"Could be. Or someone else."

Chapter Sixty-one

Garden Grove

Michael Barton's meeting with his long-lost Sarah never took place. It had been planned. It had been dreamed about, at least by him, since the day they'd been separated. But two days before Michael and Olivia were going to catch a flight to Seattle, a call came from a woman whose voice Michael did not know.

"Mr. Barton?"

"Yes?"

"This is a hard call to make. One that I don't want to make." The woman was on the verge of tears. Her words were held tightly in her throat before each emerged, one at time in a staccato sequence. "You were my daughter Sarah's biological brother."

The word "were" caught him off guard. He knew something was wrong. He spun around his office, and stared at the window.

"Is Sarah all right?"

"She's dead."

It was such a cold and thoroughly devastating way of relaying such horrific news. No preamble. No "I regret to in-form you" or something along those lines. Just a quick cold *She's dead.*

Michael could feel the air escape his lungs. "What are you talking about?"

A beat of silence. An audible gulp of air. Then the words: "Sarah took her own life."

Michael stood and steadied himself, his free hand against the glass of the kitchen window. He looked out. Danny and Carla were playing on the swing set. An orange tree's waxy green leaves fluttered in the wind. "What do you mean? What happened?"

The woman on the other end of the line was doing her utmost best to convey the most difficult news. Her voice splintered as she spoke. "She hanged herself in her bedroom closet here at home. I thought you would want know."

Want to know? She's my little sister!

If the woman were telling him in person, he'd lunge at her just then. He'd grab her by the bony neck and snap it like a peppermint stick.

"But why?" he asked. "Why did she do this?"

"We aren't sure. The police found some things on her computer. She was distraught. She'd been rejected by some sorority at Cascade last year."

"Why would she care about that?"

"You probably don't know this. But Sarah had a way of hurting herself. When she was eleven she set fire to her playhouse and was seriously burned on her face. She had many surgeries, but the doctors could never make her exactly as she was. She had severe scar tissue on the right side of her face."

Michael, of course, had no idea. She'd sent photos, but they'd all been flawless.

"She never told me," he said, his own words choked with emotion.

"She wanted you to be proud of her. She was so pleased, I

want you to know, so very pleased that you'd come back into her life. She was going to change her major to information technology at Cascade because of you."

He noticed his grip on the phone was so tight, he needed to tell his brain to lessen his grip. "She told me. She seemed so happy."

"She was. Until those girls at Beta Zeta got through with her."

"What happened? She was my only sister."

She was also his only link to his past.

The woman stopped, catching her breath. Maybe drying her tears.

"The police found some e-mails from the rush committee at the sorority. They made some cruel remarks about our daughter. They said she wasn't pretty enough. She wasn't BZM."

The code puzzled him. "I don't understand. Come again."

"Beta Zeta material."

Michael was reeling just then. He wondered if he was screaming at the woman, or if their voices were low and quiet, appropriate for the office.

"This is so stupid. So senseless."

"I know. But, Mr. Barton, these are the times we're living in. There are no happy endings any more. Not even for a little girl left with her brother at Disneyland."

From his reflection in the window, Michael Barton observed something he'd seldom seen on his own face. A slight shimmering stream ran from each eye.

What was that?

Michael's affect was oddly flat when he told Olivia that Sarah had committed suicide. He sat at the breakfast table, swirling the orange pulp in the bottom of his glass. He was casual. Unconcerned.

"You and the kids are the only family I need," he said.

She put her arms around his shoulders. He was stiff.

"I'm so sorry, baby," Olivia said. "I know how much you wanted to have her in your life."

"That's OK," he said. "I'm pretty busy, you know. Don't really have time to get everything done that I need to do anyway. I'm making a list."

Olivia kissed him on the forehead. She didn't know that the list he was making had the names of three young women. Three young women that he was going to make sure paid the price for the wheels they set in motion.

For taking his sister away forever.

Chapter Sixty-two

Everyone has a quirk. For some, the habits are hidden, undetected for a lifetime. The fat woman who eats like a bird throughout the day, but at night sneaks into the freezer for a carton of ice cream. Or the dentist who waits for his patients and staff to go home so he can take a hit off the nitrous tank. Or the mom who sips a passable California chablis in the afternoons as her toddler sucks on the plastic straw of a juice box. Some are less apparent. Almost all have a root cause— pain they seek to diminish, or memories they seek to cloud.

The pantry in the Barton house always smelled like the laundry detergent aisle in the supermarket. No matter how much Irish Spring soap Olivia carted home, Michael always seemed to ask for more. It was, she thought, the only obsessive behavior that he engaged in and she figured it was harmless enough. After all, it was soap.

When they first got together, like all young couples, they couldn't get enough of each other. Showering together in the morning after sex or just plain having sex any time of day fueled their desire for each other. It was during that first shower together in his apartment before they married that she noticed that the scent of her lover was the green-and-white striated bars of soap. She made a joke of it, by aping the Irish lilt of the old slogan from the TV commercials of her youth.

"Ah. Irish Spring! Ladies like it, too!"

"I guess, I really, *really* like it," Michael said as he lathered her up, the water splashing through the shower curtain as the two of them huddled near the hot water to keep warm.

What he didn't tell her, what he *couldn't* tell her, was why he liked it so much. The green soap was his salvation. He sometimes used a bar of Irish Spring every two days. He'd let it soften in a deep soap dish that he'd rendered useless by most accounts—he'd plugged the drainage holes with plumber's putty so it would *hold* water. By doing so, it became almost a jelly on the underside of the bar. That allowed him to rub the soapy paste over his body, particularly on his chest, armpits, and genitals. He knew he was compulsive about it, and that nothing else seemed to meet his needs. *Just that soap.*

Irish Spring had been the only soap that masked the smell of his own male body. Michael had been teased in junior high and high school about not participating in a team sport. He couldn't. The sweaty smell of a locker room, the musky smell of another male body made him nearly convulse in spasms of nausea. He took up running, then swimming . . . then he gave up on all sports. He refused to disrobe and shower with the other teens in gym class. It wasn't that he didn't want to play sports, be with the guys, it was just that whiff of maleness that made him ill.

Irish Spring was the only thing that erased it.

His mind had been imprinted with the smell of Mr. Hansen's body as he unzipped his fly and slid his pants to his ankles in the Corvette.

"Get down on me. Be a good boy," he'd said. "I want you to drink it all gone this time."

It was a musky scent of cotton boxers, sweaty body parts, and, after his work was done, semen. He could barely breathe as he did what the man told him in a voice that seemed to know absolutely no gentleness whatsoever. *Just do it. Satisfy me, cowboy. Get it done. I've got things to do now.*

When the phrase "comfortable in his own skin" became common in the late 1990s, Michael Barton almost wanted to laugh at the very concept of it. He couldn't stand the smell of his own skin. Before he was able to rein in some of his compulsion, he used to scrub his skin so hard that he left track marks on his thighs and stomach. A couple of times he even bled.

This is stupid, he thought. *What happened to me in that garage with that freak doesn't define me.*

He learned to bathe with a gentler hand. He learned ways in which he could get even.

It doesn't own me.

Deep down, he knew it did.

The morning Michael's impulses could no longer be subdued by logic flashed through his mind. The morning had been cloaked in a veneer of ordinariness that easily masked his rage. *His intentions.* And yet, he knew it was the point of no return. He was getting ready for the flight out of town. Olivia poked her head into the shower and was nearly overcome by the scent of Irish Spring. She caught a soapy glimpse of her husband's muscled torso, creamy clouds of soap rolling down in the hot spray.

"God, honey," she said, "you think you could switch to Dial or something sometime?"

It was a joke, of course.

Olivia knew that her husband had his hygiene quirks. She knew that he'd have that scent on him when he was lowered into the ground.

We all have our quirks, she thought. *At least, my man is a clean one, a decent one. Who could ask for anything more?*

"I wish you didn't have to go," she said, handing him a towel.

"That makes two of us." He wrapped the towel around his waist and faced the mirror to shave. "I'll only be gone a couple of days. Just long enough to get in and get out."

"I know, but you just got home." Olivia stood behind Michael and looped her arms around him.

He bent down and kissed her quickly. "Gotta make a living." He ran the shaving gel over his face. "I'll be gone only as long as it takes to get the job done."

He meant that. Every word of it.

He'd booked a flight to Seattle, then on to Spokane, Washington, where he'd rent a car for the drive to Cascade University. The girls, the stupid, evil, girls had made it easy, blogging about their lives, hopes, and dreams. He'd kill them one by one. First on his list was Tiffany Jacobs. Next, he'd go after Lily Ann Denton, down in San Diego. The last would be the chapter president. Her name was Jenna Kenyon.

He'd kill her last.

Chapter Sixty-three

Seattle

Irvin Watkins, a retired Seattle cop, was watching the TV—actually *reveling* in the majesty of his TV, was more like it. Just sixty-three, with a thatch of snow-white hair and lively blue eyes, Irv sat in the dark and drank some beer and took it all in. *Life was so good.*

He'd just upgraded to high-definition TV and felt like everything he'd been seeing on the screen now dazzled. Sporting events were now so crystal clear that he could almost smell the sloshed beer on the bleachers. The local newscasters looked like they'd aged twenty years as every wrinkle and pore seemed to be diamond-cut.

As he was watching the Seattle news, a blond newscaster who'd been on the air for decades updated viewers on the Mandy Crawford case across the state in Cherrystone. It caught his interest for two reasons. One, he knew of Emily Kenyon mostly by reputation from her days in Seattle. But he also knew that she'd been dating his old partner, Chris Collier.

"The husband of the missing woman—Mitchell Crawford—has been unable to make bail and awaits trial in a cell at the Cherrystone jail."

"Wait a second," he said aloud, though no one was there to hear him. He lived alone. *Had been alone since his wife died in August.* Irvin set down his tumbler of pinot noir. He didn't need his glasses as he studied the man's face on the TV. The HD made sure of it. The guy on the screen was eerily familiar.

He reached for his old worn-out phone book, old school all the way, and dialed. The call didn't go through and the operator's recorded voice indicated that he should check the listing and dial again.

He did, to the same results. It seemed. Chris's number was dead.

"He must have gone to a cell phone," he said, again, to himself. *The whole world had.* He dialed a buddy at the downtown precinct where he'd worked before retiring. Within two minutes he had Chris Collier's cell number. He dialed again, this time getting voice mail.

"Hey Chris, Irv Watkins here. I think I've got something you might find of interest. Call me. Or better yet, come by and see me."

It was stone cold that night and despite the man lying next to her, Donna Rayburn couldn't get warm. She cuddled up next to her lover, but his cool body offered no comfort at all. She got up, grabbed a robe, and went in search of an extra blanket. She used a flashlight to guide her way down an unfamiliar hallway to a linen closet. The contents of the closet were as ordered as the linen section of Saks. Nothing was out of place. All colors were coordinated. On the edge of each towel on the shelf just below her eye level she noticed they were monogrammed with the initials of her host. She waved her light up another row, looking for a blanket.

Those, too, were monogrammed. Donna gave her head a shake and pulled one from the top, exposing a blanket with another set of initials—ML. *Who was ML? A wife, she'd never heard of?* She thought it was creepy that he didn't get rid of those towels. The guy wasn't cheap. He had to have kept them because he wanted, rather than *needed* them. She took a blanket and went back to bed. She made herself a mental note to ask about the unfamiliar monogram in the morning.

Donna didn't know that her question would be the last she'd ever ask.

Chapter Sixty-four

Cherrystone

The Cherrystone jail was in the basement of the county-city building next to the sheriff's office. Jeffery Kirkpatrick had been the jailer for at least twenty years, though he professed not to have "a real fix" on the exact number of years. He figured whenever anyone wanted to know how long he was there it was either to push him to retirement or celebrate an employee anniversary. He didn't want either. He was reading a *Newsweek* article on eco-vacations and thinking that a sunny day in Costa Rica might be in order.

Whenever it is that I damn well decide to retire, that is.

Jason Howard signed in the visitors' log requesting to see inmate 43992, Mitch Crawford. He noticed on the sign-in sheet that visitation outside of his lawyer had been sparse.

"Didn't know you were a friend of Crawford's. You're about the first one. His dad never knew a stranger, but this little jerk doesn't seem to have much in the way of any loyalty reserves. That's what I think, anyway," Jeffery the Jailer disappeared down the corridor, leaving Jason in the processing area with its library table, Formica, and, oddly, a collection of framed Winslow Homer prints.

Jason knew what he was doing was at best, out of the ordinary. At worst, grounds for some kind of disciplinary action. He didn't care. He'd grown weary of having Emily treat him as if he was the coffee-fetcher. She seemed to go to Chris Collier for everything.

Discussions they'd had should have been between the sheriff and me.

He could do more than look over phone records. He didn't want Emily's job, just the kind of respect from her that indicated she knew he wasn't a pimply-faced kid anymore.

Jeffery the Jailer came lumbering into view. "Says he'll see you. Trial coming up. Maybe you're here to wish him luck?"

If Jeffery was fishing for information, Jason didn't offer any.

"Something like that," he said.

Even if he hadn't been a deputy, there was no search required. The Cherrystone jail was old-school, with visitation carrels separated by one-inch-thick safety glass. Chris took a seat in an orange molded-plastic chair and looked toward the door.

At the end of the row of carrels, a woman was talking animatedly through the glass. He could only see the back of her head and it was moving back and forth like a slingshot.

"Damn you, Luis, I'm not doing this again," she said. "I'm done with you!"

Luis Guzman was the only other man in the jail.

That must be Mrs. Guzman, he thought, recalling a name he had seen above his on the sign-up sheet. *Give 'em hell, honey.*

Mitch Crawford approached from the other side of the room. He no longer looked like the self-absorbed prig that most said he was. His clothes were far from designer; he wore light blue pants with a drawstring waist and a T-shirt that hung loosely over his frame. His skin looked somewhat ashen and sweat beaded along his upper, unshaven lip. He slid into the chair and picked up the phone.

"What do you want?"

"I just want to talk to you."

"Are you stupid or something? Without my lawyer, I'm not saying a word. You people have had it in for me from the minute Mandy went missing."

Jason did feel stupid just then. The visit could get real ugly, when he'd only come to try to get a better handle on the Tricia Wilson deposition.

"I'm here about your wife," he said, pausing, "your ex-wife, Patty."

"You mean Tricia? That lying bitch!" Mitch's eyes flashed hate.

"So you say. But can you prove it?" Jason held his tongue. He wanted to end the sentence with a snarky *dude*. He could see in two minutes why everyone hated Mitch Crawford. "Can you?"

"No. My word against hers. The jury will probably believe her. They always take the word of a woman. They can turn it on, you know."

"Seems she might have come in to some money," Jason said. "You wouldn't happen to know how she could have got her hands on fifty grand?"

"That lowlife bitch? She'd have to blow a lot of guys to make that kind of money, so, no, I don't know where she could have come up with it. You tell me."

"Hey, I'm fact-finding here. Let's go over a few more things. Your computer. Anyone have access to it? House-keeper? Other family members?"

Mitch shook his head. "No. We run a tight ship at home. I tried to keep Mandy from pissing away our money. You know, tried to keep her on a short leash."

I'll bet you did.

"OK, I know that you've said you don't think Mandy was having an affair with anyone, but, of course, we know otherwise. So who do you think it was? Who was she cheating with?"

Mitch Crawford's face went scarlet, his lips white.

"You don't think I've tried to figure that out? I've thought of everyone that bitch came in contact with. Maybe she was boning the mailman? Her doctor? Someone at work? I have no goddamn idea! If I did, I'll tell you one thing, I wouldn't be here under false murder charges. They'd have me here for the real thing. I'd kill the guy who screwed my wife and screwed my life."

"This isn't about pride. This is about finding out what happened the day Mandy disappeared. You know, the day your wife and unborn baby were murdered. Don't you want to know, even if just to save yourself?"

A smile came over the inmate's face. "Of course. I want to clear my name. I don't want people thinking that I was some pussy who got cheated on by his no-good wife."

"All right. Question."

"What?"

"Who had access to your home computer? Think."

Mitch stared through the glass panel. "I told you no one. We lived alone. We didn't have cleaning staff. I did keep extra house keys at the dealership, if that makes a difference. I liked to take new cars home, so it was always easier to have some spares around."

Jason brightened a little. "Now we're getting somewhere. Who had access to your house keys?"

"No one except Darla, of course."

"The girl you were banging?" Jason hated the term, but as Mitch Crawford thought of himself as some tough ladies' man, he just went for it.

"Yeah, *her*. I'm not proud of it."

"Did she have anything against Mandy?"

Mitch shrugged. "Just mad that she got everything she wanted. She had me, you know."

An hour later, Emily found Jason in the front office talking with Gloria. He barely glanced at her. She could feel a chill in the air and knew it had nothing to do with the weather outside.

"I need to talk with you," she said. "In my office, if that's OK?"

Emily looked at Gloria, then back at Jason.

"All right. This sounds serious."

They faced each other across her desk.

"Jason, I understand you went to the jail to see Mitch Crawford. What in the world were you thinking?"

"Were you spying on me or something?"

"God, no. Cary McConnell called. He says that his client called. This isn't how we run a case. You know that."

Jason's eyes were downcast.

"You've been treating me like some kind of lackey around here, Sheriff."

"I don't know what you are talking about."

"You do. You go to Chris for everything. He doesn't work here. I do."

Emily knew Jason was right and she felt so foolish for not considering his feelings, and even more so for not recognizing that his ability was far beyond coordinating witness statements and helping Gloria with the monthly case reports.

"Jason, we're a team. You and I."

"Treat me like a member of your team."

"Fair enough. Did you find out anything when you saw Mitch?"

Jason told her about the house keys being under Darla's control and Emily wondered if perhaps she'd been wrong about Darla. Maybe she had been the one threatening Samantha Phillips.

"Want me to go over there and check it out?" Jason asked.

"Yes, please." She waited a beat. "Jason, *you* are my deputy. Chris offered to assist."

"Yeah, but I heard you deputized him."

"Only so he could help. He's not here to replace you. OK?"

Jason looked down at the floor. "I'm glad to hear that, Sheriff, because I thought you and I worked well together. I'm not so green anymore, you know. I have more to contribute."

"I know," she said, now feeling a twinge of shame for keeping him outside an investigation that he had every right to be part of. "That's why you need to see Darla. Find out about the security of the keys, all right?"

"Yes. Will do."

Chapter Sixty-five

Steffi Johansson turned off the TV. Her heart had almost stopped beating. *Spokane Afternoons* had just aired a segment on the Mandy Crawford murder case. She had watched with keen interest, having been down at the Cherrystone jail looking at the lineup of potential suspects. She had wanted so much to help. There was something very unnerving about the handsome stranger who'd come into the coffee shop after supposedly traipsing around the woods in search of a Christmas tree.

The local TV show had done a nice job, showing Mandy's mother and pictures of a little girl who would grow up only to be lost before she reached her fullest potential.

"All my daughter ever really wanted was to be a mom," Hillary Layton had told the host. "She said she wished that someday she'd be as good of a mother as . . . I was to her."

She felt her knees go weak as she went toward her purse and the telephone.

Oh, my God, she thought, *I really did see that woman's killer that night. I can identify him.*

She looked for Emily Kenyon's business card in her wallet. *Where was it?* Credit cards, receipts, and a punch card from a sandwich shop that she forgot she had. When she found it, Steffi started to dial.

* * *

The Crawford car dealership had undergone the kind of change in vibe that was usually reserved for a new model introduction that actually brought in prospects and rang up sales. The smell of hot dogs rotating on a little wheel in the front window still excited or turned the stomach, depending, of course, on how one viewed hot dogs. The abundance of helium balloons and strands of crepe paper still signaled that the dealership was a cool and fun place for the entire family. Jason Howard noticed that everyone working there seemed to be in good spirits.

Maybe having a boss arrested for murder is a real boost to morale? Jason asked himself as he came upon Darla, who was shuttling coffee and files from Stan Sawyer's office. Sawyer was the acting manager, filling in until Mitch came back.

Jesus, she's even whistling.

"Hi, Darla," Jason said.

"Hi, Deputy," she answered, a warm smile on her face. "You want some Starbucks? That's what Stan's offering to customers these days. Says he wants our customers to 'wake up and smell the coffee.' Isn't that cute?"

"Pretty cute," he said. "But I'm not here for coffee. I'm here for information. The sheriff sent me."

The smile fell from Darla's face. "I'm not going to have to testify now, am I? Not about you know what?"

"Oh, gosh, I don't think so. Anyway, that's not why I'm here. I'm here about some, you know, odds and ends."

"What kind of odds and ends?"

"We're just crossing the t's and dotting the i's before trial."

"OK. How can I help?"

"Well, what we need to know about is the key situation with Mr. Crawford. He says that he had several sets of house keys at the office."

"That's right. He took a different car home two or three times a week. You know how when you buy a new car and there's like sixteen miles on it? That's from a dealer like Mitch driving it. Important to have product familiarity, you know."

"Cool. I didn't think of that."

"Not many people know what happens behind the scenes in a car dealership. It's kind of like what happens behind the scenes at McDonald's." Darla paused. "You just don't want to know."

Jason had worked at McDonald's in high school. He knew what she meant and he smiled. "Yeah. So about his keys. Could anyone get them or were they kept in a secure place?"

"I kept them with all the dealership's master keys. In the vault. So, yes, they were always secure. I log all vault entries."

"I was hoping you did. Can you do a favor for me and look up who came and got keys on November twenty-fourth or twenty-fifth?"

"You mean, when Mandy disappeared?"

Darla was young, a little reckless considering her affair with her boss, but she was sharp. Her immediate recollection of the date surprised him.

"Yeah. Can you?"

"Sure."

She walked across the showroom and retrieved a logbook in a metal case next to the vault.

"Only one thing jumps out at me."

Jason drew closer. "What's that?"

"Cary McConnell. I remember how he came over to get some keys to help out when all this started with Mandy."

"OK. Anyone else?"

"Just me. And trust me, I really did learn from my mistakes."

As Jason went for the door, he got a whiff of bleach coming from Crawford's office. The smell triggered a memory. Bleach had been smelled at the Crawfords' place when he'd first been questioned. At the time, it had been an odoriferous alarm that Mitch might have done something to his wife and used bleach to obliterate the evidence of his crime.

"What's with the bleach?" he asked.

"It's Friday."

Jason looked puzzled.

"Every Friday we do a wipe-down of all surfaces in Mitch's office. Even when he isn't here."

"Why bleach? Why not Fantastik or something else? This stuff smells."

Darla looked around to make sure no one was in earshot. "OCD," she said, lowering her voice. "Doesn't want anyone to know. But Mitch is a little crazy when it comes to germs. I used to have to do his house, too. Finally, someone convinced him that it wasn't my job to clean his house."

Jason could relate. Emily sometimes had him photocopy things that Gloria could have done just as well. He carried a badge, after all, not a degree from a clerical college.

Having her call go to Sheriff Kenyon's voice mail was exceedingly frustrating, given what Steffi Johansson had to say. She tried three times to dial the number, but in her haste and fear, her fingers felt fat and kept hitting the wrong keys on her touch pad. Finally, after getting the voice mail a second time, she hung up. She dialed the alternate number which went to Gloria, at the dispatcher's desk.

"I need to talk to Sheriff Kenyon right away."

"She's not in right now. Is this an emergency?"

"Yes. I guess it is."

"What is it?"

"Look, she told me to call her if I had something to say. This is Steffi Johansson. I was at that Crawford lineup a while back."

"Yes, Steffi. Can I help you?"

"No. I really need to talk to Sheriff Kenyon."

"She's out. How about Deputy Howard? I can patch you through."

"I guess so."

The line went quiet and then beeped. Steffi knew that the spaced intervals of beeping were an indicator that her voice was being recorded; she'd worked as a telemarketer for a camping company before coming to the café.

"Deputy Howard speaking."

"Hi, Deputy. I'm Steffi Johansson."

"How can I help you?"

There was silence for a second as she found her courage. "I know who killed Mandy Crawford," she said.

When he asked her *who* and she answered, he felt a rush go through his body like the shock wave he once felt while fixing his uncle's electric cattle fence wearing soaked leather shoes. If he was standing when she said the name of the man, he surely would have stumbled to the floor. It was that jarring.

"Are you sure you saw *him*?"

"Yeah," she said, her voice catching with a little emotion. "One hundred percent."

Jason Howard tried Emily's cell phone three times. It went to voice mail. Finally, on the second try, he decided to leave a message.

"Emily, Steffi Johansson's coming down here. She can ID the man she saw that night at her coffee place. Get over here, OK?"

Chapter Sixty-six

Seattle

His condo now in escrow, Chris knew that Emily would have to marry him or he'd have to find a new place to live. He knew she'd never leave Cherrystone. He'd tell her that they'd reached their moment of truth.

Either you love me or you don't. I know that you do. Let's spend our lives together.

He swung by Irv Watkins's house in Normandy Park, a fir-canopied enclave south of Seattle. The house was a two-story contemporary with sweeping views of Puget Sound and Vashon Island to the west. Chris pulled alongside a cobalt blue Miata next to the garage with a FOR SALE sign taped inside the passenger window and parked.

Irv Watkins poked his head out the front door and shook off the chill of the northwest winter gloom. He wore a purple and gold University of Washington sweatshirt and faded brown corduroy trousers.

"You're a hell of a guy to reach," he called out. "I had to call downtown to get your cell number." He waved for Chris to get up the steps.

"I guess I like it like that. But it's always good to hear your voice. Irv, how's it going?"

"No complaints, considering."

Chris winced at the thoughtlessness of his own words. Randi, Irv's wife of forty years, had been gone such a short time. The Miata had been hers. He stepped inside the Danish modern–furnished home and Irv shut the front door. A cat scampered past. Irv motioned for Chris to follow him to the living room. The place was familiar. Chris had been there years ago for a party. The exact occasion escaped him just then.

"I'm sure it's been hard."

"I'm doing better. Miss her every day, you know."

"I'm sorry. I'm glad you're hanging in there."

"Coffee? Beer? Soda?"

Chris passed with a smile and Irv went on, clearly glad to have company.

"Hey, you still seeing Emily Kenyon?" he asked.

"Every chance I get."

He took a drink. "That's what I heard. Any-who I saw a clip of the case she's working on over there. On TV. Last night."

"Mandy Crawford?"

"That's the one."

"It reminded me of the Harriman case."

Irv had Chris's interest. "Belinda Harriman?"

"Yeah, you remember that one?"

Chris pondered the name. Of course he did. *Everyone did.*

Belinda Harriman was a law student at the time of her disappearance. Anyone who lived in the Seattle area at the time could easily remember the photographs and handbills that were plastered all over the region. The mantra from her friends and family members was loud and decisive in their aim to bring her home: *Leave no telephone pole without a handbill! All the way from Tacoma to Everett!*

As the memories came back, Chris took a seat in the brown leather recliner that matched the one Irv commanded.

Belinda, a tall, slender, redhead with ice blue eyes and a freckle-splashed nose, was last seen playing pool at Sun Villa, a bowling alley with ten lanes and six pool tables in suburban Bellevue, east of Seattle. She'd been there with a group of friends from the UW law school. She rode home with her boyfriend, who dropped her off in front of her University of Washington district apartment building around midnight. Belinda told friends at the bowling alley that she had a big test the next week and needed to study. She waved good-bye and disappeared.

The police—both Seattle and Bellevue—investigated. Every inch of her apartment and the bowling alley was examined for evidence. But nothing turned up. Belinda's parents packed up her belongings after Christmas, knowing in the way that parents often do that their child is dead.

In late February the following year, a girl on the hunt for evidence of early spring for a science project, found a patch of long red hair on the frozen edge of Phantom Lake, a small body of water more akin to a large pond than a real lake, a few miles north of the bowling alley. Her eyes followed the red hair to a tangle of dead cattails. Arms akimbo, faceup, was Belinda Harriman, entombed in a sodden sleeping bag.

"But Belinda Harriman's killer was apprehended, convicted, right?" Chris asked, not really seeing the parallels that seemed so apparent to Irv.

"He was. Rick Deacon was his name—the boyfriend, remember?"

Chris scratched his head. "Sorry, Irv, guess I'm getting a little rusty. I don't see the connection with Mandy. Was it the body dump site that caught your attention? The fact that it was a young woman killed in winter?"

Irv retrieved another beer from the mini fridge next to his chair, his TV command central, and Chris motioned "no thanks" with an outstretched palm.

"Gotta drive," he said. "Heading over the pass to see Em."

Irv swallowed a couple of big gulps of his beer. "Sure, a frozen pond and a strangled young girl are ringers, but for crying out loud, that's hardly enough to get you over here."

"Then what is it?" Chris wasn't losing his patience. He liked Irv. He simply remembered that Irv was the kind of guy who could turn a minute into an hour. He could drag a thought out until the damn thing had nothing left anymore.

"Like I said, I saw the TV interview last night regarding the Crawford murder case."

"So you said."

Irv poured some more beer down his throat.

Jesus, is this guy another retired cop with a booze problem? Chris asked himself, though he knew the answer.

"When I was watching the show, it sort of hit me. *Hard.* I recognized someone and it got me to thinking."

"Rick Deacon's still in prison, Irv. He couldn't have done it."

Irv got up from his recliner, set down his empty green bottle, and strode over the coffee table in front of a matching leather sofa. "Oh, it wasn't *him*. I know that." He picked up the remote control and punched the button to play back the DVR. "Isn't this cool how I can do this?"

"What's that, Irv?"

"You know, record without a tape. I record the news—in case I'm, you know, if I'm busy or something. I can keep up."

Irv fast-forwarded past the commercials, the story about a Seattle bus accident, layoffs from a Redmond software company, before stopping on the anchorwoman with a graphic of a yellow chalked outline of dead body with the words CHERRYSTONE MURDER behind her. The story continued with various townspeople talking about Mitch Crawford and what he might have done to his wife.

"That guy!" Irv said, freezing the image. "Right *there*."

Chris was on his feet, staring at the screen. He looked back at Irv, unsure of what or who he was supposed to be seeing.

"I think that's Rick Deacon's best friend. In fact, I'm *positive* it is. I remember my buddy working the case said that Rick's buddy had just as many good reasons to lie about the night that Belinda disappeared as Rick did. In fact, he once told me that if James had come to the police first, they might have been able to pin the murder on his pal."

Irv pulled out a videotape and stuck it into a player with cords that snaked from the new flat screen.

"Randi was a big fan of *Evening Magazine*. She made me tape it for the 'Washington Getaways' segments that featured places to go. But on this one, there's an update on the Harriman case . . . and our guy's in the shot, putting up a poster."

Chris extended his finger and aimed it the image on screen.

"Be careful! Don't touch the TV. Ruins it!"

Chris pulled back his hand, but stepped closer. He could feel the blood drain from his face as the pixels grew larger and brighter. He wanted Irv to be wrong.

"What do you think?" Irv asked. "You think it's him?"

Chris looked at Irv. "The quality's not so good. There's a resemblance, of course."

"Not the TV's fault, you know. Picture's good."

"I didn't say it was, Irv. I know you love your TV. But it's a lot of years ago, man."

Irv took the final foamy gulp of his beer. "I think there's something there. Could be a coincidence, but I kind of got that little chill on the back of my neck when I saw him."

Chris didn't say so, but he felt that little chill, too. It was like an icy finger tapping lightly at the tiny hairs on the nape of his neck .... *pay attention . . . pay attention.*

"I need to leave now," he said. "Long drive."

"Can't you stay for a beer? I feel like cracking open another."

Chris dismissed the offer out of hand, but gave the impression to his old colleague that he mulled it over. "Later. OK? Thanks, Irv."

"Don't you want this?" Irv held out a couple of white pages. "I still have a friend or two downtown, you know."

Chris looked down at the first paper. It was a state driver's license photo of the man on the TV taken at the time of the event, obviously from the case file, and on the second sheet was his image as it appeared on his current license.

Jesus Christ, Chris thought, *that really could be him.*

Chris wondered if he'd taken his blood pressure medicine that morning. He needed this to be one of the days he didn't skip because he had something else on his mind. He dialed Emily's number, but no answer. He got Gloria on the phone and she said Emily had been out on the case and she was up to her neck "in alligators."

"Four bookings in the last hour—three drunks and a peeper. Don't know when the sheriff will be back in, Chris. Keep trying her cell. Stop by when you can. Things are just strange around here lately."

She has no idea, Chris thought as he hung up the phone and left for the airport. There was no time to drive to Cherrystone. Good thing a plane left for Spokane every hour.

The text message on Emily's phone came earlier that afternoon from Donna Rayburn, the associate from Cary McConnell's law office.

If u get this, meet me where u found M. I'm out of
range. So can't call. I'll be there at 4. Come alone.
Do not tell Cary. DR

For the first time, Emily noticed that Donna had made
several attempts earlier in the day to reach her, but no calls
lasted long enough to leave a message. Cell reception was
spotty at best in some parts around Cherrystone. No carrier
could really claim total coverage.

For a moment, Emily considered calling Camille to get
her take on talking with a lawyer from the other side of the
Crawford case, but she thought better of it. Her need to meet
likely had nothing to do with the case. If Donna had something to say to her, she might as well hear it. Maybe she had
wised up about Cary and wanted an experienced and sympathetic shoulder to cry on?

Chris Collier stood in the security line at SeaTac while a
young, blond-haired and dreadlocked TSA agent with a neck
tattoo covered by a Band-Aid waved an electronic wand between his legs and down his back.

"Just checking, sir."

"No problem." Chris wanted to laugh a little because as
he heard the young man's words, he impulsively edited them
to: *"Just checking, dude."*

He could hear his cell phone ringing from the plastic
caddy that held his shoes, belt, coat, and wallet.

It was probably Emily calling him back. Damn!

He put on his shoes, grabbed the paperwork he'd passed
through the X-ray machine, and found his way to the departure gate. A baby's piercing cry filled the gate area, but Chris
merely offered a smile in the direction of the young mother.

His own kids were grown, but he never forgot what it was like to have little ones on an airplane.

It's only an hour flight, he thought.

He dialed Emily back, but no answer. This time when it went to voice mail, he left a message.

"Em, I'm on my way to see you. Something could be breaking on the Crawford case. I'll explain when I get there."

He hung up. He chose to be somewhat cryptic. Saying more would be too explosive.

The young man's voice was matter of fact, though given in a slight whisper.

"Hey, sir, this is me, Devon Little of the DMV. We got a request yesterday on your license photo and information. Seattle PD. The requestor came from Seattle PD. Wanted your photo from today and your pic from back when you were my age. Pretty funny haircut. Don't forget to send me the money right away. I'm going on vacation next week."

The man shut his phone. A bead of sweat trickled down his temple. He knew the day was coming. He just didn't think it would be so soon. He looked across the room at the woman fussing with the makings of a salad.

It looked good. Too bad she wouldn't be having any of it.

Chapter Sixty-seven

Cherrystone

It was her late work day, so Gloria Bergstrom was at the desk answering the one or two calls that would come in until 9:30, when Renata Klug would come in to relieve her. She looked up when Emily came in.

"I just tried you," she said. "Jason called. Steffi's coming in to the office. She needs to amend her statement. Jason says she can ID the man who was at her shop that night."

Gloria looked at the door, then back to Emily. "He should be here in five minutes. Went to get her. Says this is big."

Emily checked her office phone and locked up a second time for the night. Just as she returned, Jason and Steffi came inside the office.

Jason looked like he was going to burst. Steffi looked as if she was about to cry.

"You have to hear this, Sherrif," he said.

"Hi Steffi. Are you all right?"

"I'm scared," she said.

"Don't worry. I'll help you. Let's go to the conference room."

Gloria sighed. It was clear she hated being left out.

When the three of them sat down, Steffi started to shake. She put her palms flat on the tabletop to steady herself.

"I was watching TV, you know, about Mandy."

"On the Spokane show," Jason added, as though the detail was helpful.

"Did it trigger a memory or something?"

"More than that." Tears started to fall.

"Tell me. Take your time."

"The man who came into our café. The one I told you about?"

"Yes? The one who was injured?"

"Yeah." Steffi fidgeted with her hands. "Well, that man was on the TV."

"We've already done the lineup," Emily said. "We can't go there again, just because you can ID Mitch Crawford now."

Steffi looked over at Jason, then back at Emily. She'd stopped shaking and seemed to find firmer footing.

"It wasn't Mr. Crawford I saw."

"Then who was it?" Jason asked.

The young woman looked at Jason, then Emily. "It was his lawyer. Cary McConnell was the man I saw that night."

Emily's pulse spiked, but she hid the surge in adrenaline that came with it the best that she could. "You think the man you saw that night was Cary McConnell?"

Steffi shook her head and the gesture brought Emily a second of relief.

"No, I don't *think* it, Sheriff Kenyon. I'm absolutely certain."

Jason leaned toward Emily. "Look, it makes sense," he said, in a low voice. "McConnell wasn't there at the lineup, right? He had an associate there. Remember?"

Emily recalled how disappointed she and Camille had

been when Steffi came up empty-handed. She remembered
how Cary had been too busy to come in. He was a man who
liked to do battle head-on. But not that day.

"He had access to the Crawford house. He could have
faked that note."

Emily could feel herself nearly lose balance. She was
grateful that she was sitting in a chair. Cary McConnell was
a sleazebag lawyer. And the world's worst boyfriend. But
they were suggesting that he was a killer.

"That's a pretty big leap," she said. The defensive tone of
her remark shocked her own sensibilities.

Why in the world would she defend him?

Jason knew and he answered right back. "I know you
have some history with McConnell."

Jason was right, of course. He could read her well. He
could see the shame she felt in her own judgment. He saw
how compromised she'd been over this whole thing.

She looked at him. She didn't say the words, but she
hoped her look was clear enough. *Let's talk about this later.*

Jason got the point. He looked back at Steffi.

"Are you going to be all right?"

"Yeah. I guess so. I feel bad about Mr. Crawford."

Emily nodded. "If he's innocent, he'll be let out soon
enough."

She told Steffi that Gloria would take her statement, but
that she and her deputy had to leave.

"Donna's waiting for me at Miller's Marsh Pond. I'm
going there. She texted me an hour ago."

Jason stood and put on his coat. "Not without me, you're
not."

Emily smiled, a forgiving smile. She wished that she'd
been a better mentor. Jason Howard was a great deputy and
had always deserved her respect. "Of course not. But you'll
take your own car and keep a distance away."

"Emily, I don't know about this," he said.

"I do. I think she's about to tell me what's really going on and I want to hear it."

"You're making it sound personal."

"It is. But not about me. This is for Mandy and her baby."

"You think she's behind the threat to Samantha Phillips? The payoffs to Tricia?"

Emily smiled. "You're good. Those things crossed my mind about ten minutes go."

"Right behind you," he said.

Chapter Sixty-eight

Miller's Marsh Pond, outside of Cherrystone

It was early March and the snow had finally gone. Spring had begun to emerge. Cattails were sending up new green spikes and the willows along the edges of Miller's Marsh Pond where Dan Fletcher and his kids had discovered Mandy Crawford's body just after Christmas were popping with green buds. Emily had felt a shudder of horror at the sight of a half-frozen corpse wrapped in a sleeping bag, but the chill had faded now with the realization that she'd been wrong the entire time.

Mitch Crawford probably wasn't the killer. She edited her thoughts. *Mitch Crawford was innocent.*

Emily parked the Crown Vic next to Donna Rayburn's BMW.

She recalled how Steffi had said the man had a pickup the night he came in for coffee.

Out of the corner of her eye, she saw Jason's cruiser as he parked fifty yards away.

As she walked down the path, the light dipping low behind a grove of alders draped with new catkins, Emily wondered how she could have been so stupid. How she had

wanted to believe something about Mitch Crawford so oner-
ous, so unforgiving, that she'd trapped herself. Camille had
pushed hard, of course, but the blame wasn't hers alone.
Emily was the investigator. She had been in pursuit of a
killer to avenge a woman's and a baby's deaths.

*This case went too far too fast. It was like we just wanted
it to be Mitch. So neat. So much easier.*

It wasn't Donna she saw at the water's edge. When she
saw him, everything crystallized. Emily remembered the
monograms on the guest towels in his mountain cabin in
Idaho, at his big house in Cherrystone. She remembered
how she shopped for a tie tack with the letter M because
Cary hadn't wanted any jewelry unless it was personalized
in some way.

"Why wear anything if it doesn't say something about
you?" he asked her back then when they were dating.

All of it was from a time she wished she could sift from
her memory.

Cary McConnell was facing the water. He turned around
when he heard Emily approach, as her steps echoed softly on
a boardwalk weekend fisherman had laid over the sodden
path. She kept one hand close to her gun, its cold barrel reminding her of the danger of the moment.

"There's nowhere for me to go, Emily," he said. His eyes
were red. He might even have been crying before she got
there.

"You can come clean, Cary."

He turned away from her and looked at the water, dotted
with ripples of gold. "No. No, I can't."

"You *can*. Tell me. What happened with you and Mandy?"

He answered, with his back still toward her. "It isn't so
hard to figure out. You are pretty smart. Not smart enough to
avoid getting involved with me, though."

She chose her words carefully. "That was awhile ago."

But I was smart, she thought, *I dumped you.*

"What happened with Mandy?"

"It was stupid. She was the wife of my biggest client. She was lonely. I was lonely. It was wrong, I know that."

"This is more than an ethical violation, Cary. Mandy's dead. What happened?"

Cary looked over the water, now cast in the yellow light of a very late afternoon. "She wanted to tell her husband. She wanted to be with me. Jesus, I didn't want that. I told her to stick with Mitch. Let him think the baby was his. She kept telling me that she didn't love him, that she could make a life with me. Right? Like I could give up my biggest client for her and that baby."

It was the first time he mentioned the baby.

Emily inched a little closer. She wasn't afraid. "What did you do, Cary? Tell me what happened."

"It was stupid. She made me mad. I don't like to be pushed. She kept pushing. She even started to call Mitch and tell him. I couldn't have that. I put my hand around her neck. She clawed at me. But I had to shut her up."

For the first time, Emily noticed the barrel of the gun that Cary pulled from his coat pocket. She hadn't expected that and she took a slight step backward. She pulled her own gun.

"Drop it," she said. "You don't want to do that."

"You don't know what I wanted. I wanted you, remember that? I loved you, Emily. If you hadn't broken up with me, none of this would have happened."

"I'm sorry. I wish things could have been different."

It was such a hollow lie that she was sure he could see right through it. But it was the first thing that leapt to her mind. *Promise the potential suicide anything. Stall for time. Time might save a life.*

"You're a good man," she said. Again, another lie, one so egregious she nearly choked on her words.

The barrel of the gun moved slightly.

"I'm garbage. Everyone says so. I couldn't even manage to cover up my own mess."

"But you did a good job. You paid off Tricia, didn't you?"

A near smile came over his face. "That was pretty good, wasn't it?"

"Brilliant. Now, please set down the gun."

A flock of ducks flew overhead, and for a second, Emily moved her eyes from Cary. In that very instant, he pulled his arm from his body and in one rapid move pointed the weapon at his face.

"No!" she screamed.

A gunshot sounded, and blood spatter sprayed over a stack of firewood someone had assembled like a giant Jenga game. Cary slumped to the muddy ground.

"You shot me!" he said.

Jason was right behind Emily, a curl of smoke drifted from the nose of his Cherrystone Sheriff Department issue.

Cary writhed in agony. His shoulder had been pierced by Jason's bullet. A cleaner shot had never been fired. Emily picked up Cary's gun, its handle gleaming with engraved lettering: CAM. She put it out of reach.

"Where's Donna?" she asked. She was cool, direct. She meant for the son-of-bitch coward slumped in front of her to give her an answer. "Tell me. Now."

Cary's eyes were ice. "You think I will tell you?"

"Don't mess with me, Cary! Where is Donna?"

Cary put his left hand on his right shoulder as blood oozed through his wound. He struggled to pull himself together as if he'd just been stung by a bee.

"You'll find her when the time is right. Like the others," he said.

Cary's words took Emily's breath away.

Like the others? Mandy? Donna? Who else?

"Ambulance will be here in five minutes," Jason said.

Emily looked at Cary, then at Jason. "Tell them no need to rush. Maybe he'll bleed out."

Cary McConnell just smiled.

Two hours later after gunfire sounded across the waters of Miller's Marsh Pond, Chris Collier showed up at the sheriff's office in his rental car. He was agitated, sweaty. Cursing the airline for its delays, the rental car company for putting him in a car that smelled like an ashtray. That was small stuff, of course. The real reason his blood pressure soared was because he hadn't been where he'd wanted to be. *With Emily.* To make sure she was safe.

He'd picked up most of the information on the shooting from talking to Gloria on the drive from the Spokane Airport.

"Jason picked Cary off in the shoulder just as he was about to blow his own brains out. Jason's too good of a shot if you ask me," Gloria said. "Idaho police are up at the cabin, but no sign of Donna."

"Emily's OK, isn't she?"

"She's been through worse. You know that better than anyone. She's tough. She made me call Jenna and fill her in on everything, of course. She didn't want her to worry in case the news started churning out stories about the shooting up at the pond."

Gloria said that Emily was holed up with Camille Hazelton and the investigators from the state were on their way to make sure that Jason Howard's shooting of the suspect was clean.

When Chris arrived at the sheriff's office, Gloria was on the phone. She waved him past her, mouthed "media," and rolled her eyes. He poked his head in Jason's office to thank him, but he was gone. When he turned around, Emily was right behind him. Without a word, she melted into Chris's arms. Emily didn't cry, but she could feel his strength and it soothed her, making her feel that as horrific as the day had been, it would not always be that way.

"He said there were others, Chris. I think he killed someone besides Mandy and Donna."

"I know," he said, letting her go so he could look into her eyes.

"You know?"

"Oh, Emily, I tried to get ahold of you all afternoon."

"I saw your calls."

He told her about Irv Watkins's beloved DVR and how he'd recorded a TV magazine show's segment on Belinda Harriman's murder.

Emily's eyes flooded just then. "I remember that case. She was found at Phantom Lake, wasn't she?"

"Yeah, in a sleeping bag," Chris said, pausing to let the words sink in. "Em, in the background of the video you can clearly see Cary, putting up posters. He was a law student back then. The police questioned him. They just liked the boyfriend better for the crime."

"They convicted the boyfriend, didn't they?"

"Yes, he's still in prison."

Within hours, the media swooped in on Cherrystone to cover the story of the crooked lawyer and the client he'd almost defended right into a date with the gallows. Mitch Crawford had retained a new lawyer by then, threatening all the players in the saga with a lawsuit "the likes of which Cherrystone had never seen."

Emily tried to stay out of the fray as much as possible. Certainly a killer was captured, but there was nothing to be gleeful about. It wasn't justice at all. Just a twisted end to a very sad saga. She felt sickness in the pit of her stomach when the Idaho police investigator said they'd found Cary's pickup a half a mile from the cabin. She wondered if hidden in the grooves and spaces around the rivets were pieces of Mandy. *Her DNA. Her hair. Her blood. Or Donna Rayburn? What about her?* She knew that no matter how many times he might have detailed that truck, something would be there that would scream to the world that Mandy had been back there. Heaped like garbage, wrapped in a cocoon.

To be hidden away in a frozen pond.

I like hauling stuff around on the weekend, he'd told her.

She thought of how Cary had touched her. How they'd made love. How he told her that she was beautiful, sexy, smart. *How he wanted to possess her.* A shiver went down her spine.

Instincts, Emily, she thought. *Trust your instincts.*

She took a deep breath. She'd be OK. She was strong.

Emily didn't know that someone had come to Cherrystone with a dark payback plan that could cost her everything.

Chapter Sixty-nine

Garden Grove

Olivia Barton had never been a stupid woman. No one could say so. But as the hours melted she thought back to the moment of truth, the time when her life's lessons–forged brilliance should not have been dimmed by her love for Michael Barton.

What happened the morning her husband left for the Pacific Northwest weighed on her. It was an anvil on a chain around her neck, choking her, reminding her that what she had with Michael Barton might have been nothing more than an illusion. It was like a slice of the skin, an opening so wide and bloody that it would never heal. She played it over and over.

Late again! The truck from St. Vincent's would be at the Bartons' later that morning, after Michael left for the airport. On the corner of the bed sat Michael's suitcase, opened, packed with everything but toiletries. While he showered, Olivia carried a stack of old kids' clothes to some boxes he had set aside for the charity collection in the garage. She'd meant to be more organized and was grateful to get the things out of the house and into the hands of someone who could use them.

Olivia had always taken great care with Danny and Carla's hand-me-downs. She'd been through hard times with her own family growing up, and knew how much a little boy or girl would appreciate that what they'd been given was truly a gift and not someone else's garbage. Her mother told her that a decent person knew the difference between giving something to someone who needed it, and boxing up junk no longer wanted.

Four cardboard boxes were lined up next to the flawlessly organized workbench. Olivia bent down with the stack of baby blankets that she'd ironed into perfect squares and placed into separate gallon-sized plastic Ziploc bags. They were, she knew, as good as new. She imagined Danny and Carla as babies. A bittersweet smile came to her lips. She felt the surge of love that comes with the reminders of how tiny, how precious her children were.

Good memories in these blankets.

She looked around to see if there was anything else she'd be able to offer up before the St. Vinnie's truck lumbered down the street. *And there it was.* A perfect candidate up on a shelf along with some paint cans, gardening supplies, and a minigraveyard of kitchen countertop appliances.

"Someone out there could use a pizza cooker more than we did," she thought as she pulled the box from the shelf. It had been a wedding gift. Never used. Never really needed by anyone, but it was brand new and might make someone happy. She blew off a very thin layer of dust and the particles illuminated in the morning sunlight from the garage's east-facing window fell like tiny stars to the cement floor. She looked back up at the space where the pizza cooker had been. Another, smaller box had been behind it. A picture on the side indicated that the box held a Waterford vase.

"I don't remember getting that," she said, aloud.

It was heavy, but not Waterford heavy. She pulled off the top and peered inside.

"What?"

Coiled like snakes were a half dozen dog collars and chains.

Olivia pushed her fingertips through the cardboard carton, moving the collars and chains to get a better view. She tilted the box toward the window to catch more light. A silver B and Z glinted from a slender cable chain. She recognized the Greek letters.

Michael stood in the doorway, proffering two steaming mugs. "Honey, coffee's ready!"

Her back to him, Olivia slammed the lid shut and set it behind the stack of baby blankets. She wasn't quite sure what she'd seen. She knew, however, that it was not meant to be seen. Her pulse accelerated. She spun around and put on an exaggerated grimace.

It was false affectation and she worried that he'd think so. He could read her so easily.

"So much to get rid of," she said, taking a cup from Michael's outstretched hand and willing her heart to stop pounding.

She didn't know it, but her husband had been thinking the very same thing.

"Isn't that the truth," he said, his eyes moving across the garage from the box of hand-me-downs to the shelf where the pizza cooker and Waterford box had been.

The flight from LAX had been uneventful. Michael Barton changed planes in Seattle and took a midday flight that landed him in Spokane at a little after three. During his downtime at the airport, he had a cup of coffee and answered some e-mails from work and an "I miss you already" note to Olivia. They'd talk after he got settled in Spokane. He checked into the Davenport, one of Spokane's grand old hotels, built originally in 1914 as the first hotel with air-conditioning—a monumental feat of its day. It had fallen on hard times, but had been restored in recent years to its former luster. Uniformed bell captains and front-desk clerks were back in force.

The Kmart on Spokane's South Hill had one of those parking lots that covered about ten acres, though one or two would have sufficed even on the busiest shopping days of the year. On a rainy day, all slick and wet, it was a black sea anchored by a pier of blocky buildings outfitted with a giant red K.

Michael Barton parked his rental car farther from the front door than necessary and walked inside. Despite the season, he wore dark glasses. He wore a hooded sweatshirt that made him look like a Unabomber wannabe. He wore the getup so that he wouldn't be noticed, couldn't be identified. Past the Martha Stewart collection, past Jaclyn Smith, and on to the store's well-stocked hunting section. There, he picked out a Camillus Buckmaster's blade with a gut hook.

The nearly eight-inch blade looked serviceable enough.

"Need a whetstone?" the clerk asked, a roly-poly man with a walrus mustache and failed hair plugs.

"Is it sharp now?" He twisted the high-carbon stainless-steel blade in the flat light of the store. A nice glint deflected light into the clerk's eyes. He looked back down at a little card extolling the virtues of the blade: *Precision skinning is guaranteed. Hairsplitting sharp! No meat-souring "accidents" with this superstar blade at a chorus line price.*

"You could gut a live deer in ten secs," the clerk said, pausing for a gruesome punch line, "and she wouldn't even feel it. It works almost like a zipper pull."

Michael nodded approvingly. "Nice, but no whetstone."

What he didn't say was that he didn't need a whetstone because he had no need to use the knife a second time.

"OK, $24.97, with tax. Guns and knives are paid for here, not up front."

He put down a twenty and a five.

When the clerk attempted to hand over the three pennies, he shook his head and pointed to the share-a-penny dish on the counter.

"Put 'em in there."

He looked at his watch. Everything was right on time. Jenna Kenyon's online schedule had her back in Cherrystone already.

He was going to finish a job that he'd failed once before.

The trauma of the McConnell shooting had taken its toll on Jason Howard. He'd never fired his weapon at a person before. He'd been interviewed for hours by men and women from the state who'd never faced danger head-on. Hitting a suspect with a bullet to save his life did not guarantee absolution. One investigator suggested that if Emily's deputy had killed the serial killing lawyer, there'd be less of an investigation. *Less concern.*

"No one would be screaming about his rights, if he was dead," Chris told Emily as he went out the door for a couple of coffees. He'd stayed over a couple of days just to "make sure" she'd be all right.

"Back in fifteen minutes," he said.

Emily never wanted him to leave. She knew just how much she loved him. If he asked her again, she told herself that she'd say *yes.*

* * *

Shali Patterson's car was in the shop, so she walked from her house over to the Kenyons'. She'd had that old VW forever, and knew that it was about time that she'd have to quit fixing it, and buck up and buy a new one. For their shopping trip that day, Jenna would have to drive her reliable but boring Honda Civic.

A man approached Shali in front of the Kenyons' big white Victorian.

"Hi," he said.

"Hi yourself," Shali replied, never one to rein in her considerable flirting skills. He was a good-looking man, in jeans and a hoodie. Older than most of the guys she dated, but undeniably handsome with lively brown eyes and wavy black hair.

"My car broke down," he said, looking over his shoulder. "My cell's dead and I have to use the bathroom. TMI, right?"

Shali smiled. "That sucks. You can use my phone. My friend lives here and I'm sure you can use her bathroom. This isn't the kind of neighborhood where we want guys peeing on the bushes."

"I didn't think so," he said, a bright, white smile across his face. "Thanks."

Shali knocked on the door and Jenna answered, looking quizzically at the man a step behind her best friend.

"This is?" Shali said, looking back at the man in the hoodie.

"Michael," he said.

Shali turned her gaze back at Jenna. "Michael's car broke down. He needs to call Triple-A or something. More than that he needs to use a bathroom."

Michael shifted his weight from one foot to another once, then again. It wasn't exactly the "gotta go" dance, but a subtle hint that there was a little urgency. He needed the bathroom *now*.

"Stupid rental car," he said. "I'm here checking out the real estate. Thinking about moving here. Your hospitality is amazing. This just might be the perfect town to bring my wife and kids."

"I'm Jenna Kenyon. You've met Shali."

He smiled, his white teeth perfect on the top, crooked like a busted fence on the bottom. "Nice to meet you. Thanks for helping out a stranger."

As he stepped into the foyer, Jenna noticed a bloom of water on the fibers of Michael's sweatshirt pocket.

"Looks like you're springing a leak," she said.

He looked down sheepishly at his crotch.

"Oh, not that!" Jenna said as embarrassment took over. Her face went red. "Your sweatshirt pocket."

He felt the damp bulge. "Water bottle," he said, though he didn't pull it out to tighten the cap.

"I hate when that happens," Shali said.

He grinned.

"Powder room's down the hall," Jenna said.

Chapter Seventy

Her phone was a sleeping cobra. She didn't want to pick it up. Olivia Barton knew that it was the hardest call she'd ever make. She knew that by dialing the number of the Cherrystone Sheriff's Department, she'd be ending the life that she had dreamed of as a child. She was going to snuff out all of it—the loving husband, the stable environment in which to raise their children, the pretty house with an orange tree in the backyard. There was no one to talk to about what she was thinking. She was alone, looking at that dangerous phone and the damage it would do. She had written down the phone number she found on the Internet. She picked it up and dialed.

It rang and Gloria Bergstrom answered.

"Cherrystone Sheriff's office. Is this an emergency?"

"Um. I want to speak with Emily Kenyon," she said, her words constricted in her throat. "The sheriff, please."

"Is this about a criminal matter?"

Olivia knew that it was, but what she said next wasn't entirely a lie.

"No, it's personal."

"I'll patch you through. Hang on."

"Sheriff Kenyon."

"Sheriff, my name is Olivia Barton." Her voice faded like an echo.

"Yes. Do I know you?"

Olivia tried a second time. She knew every word she had to say, and she understood the urgency that came with it. "Sheriff, I think my husband might not be well. He might be a dangerous man."

She couldn't bring herself to say serial killer, but it ran through her mind.

"Are you safe right now?" Emily asked.

Only because he's not here. I think so. But your daughter isn't.

"Yes. I'm OK. I guess."

"Can I come to you? Where are you located?"

"No, I'm calling from Garden Grove, California."

"All right. I must be missing something. Is there a connection to Cherrystone? Is your husband from here?"

"No, he's not. But I think he's up there. I think he plans on killing again."

Emily opened a notepad, and took down Olivia Barton's name, her husband's, and other personal information. Although she could easily detect the genuine angst in the woman's voice, she had serious doubts that anything she was saying was true. For all Emily knew, Olivia was a woman seeking revenge against a philandering husband. *Or maybe just a crackpot with no real ax to grind?* Calls like hers, less some of the drama, came in every single week.

"All right," she said, "tell me what you're worried about."

"I'm worried that he's come up to Cherrystone to kill someone."

"What makes you think that?"

"Sheriff, I think he's killed before. Maybe many times. I think that he . . . well, he might have killed a girl back east."

Emily hadn't a clue where this was going. The woman on the line, this supposed killer's wife, wasn't being direct.

"How do you know this?" she asked, firmly. "Did he tell you?"

Olivia hesitated. "Oh, no. He doesn't even know that I know. He's been acting strangely and I've been trying to find out why." She started to cry. *Hard.*

"I'm sorry, Mrs. Barton. Please try to tell me what I need to know."

"He killed that sorority girl back east."

Even though the information was conveyed in the vaguest of terms, Emily knew who she was talking about. And it sent a shiver down her spine.

"Sheraton Wilkes?"

The line was silent.

"Mrs. Barton, are you saying Sheraton Wilkes?

A loud cry came, and a single word: "Yes."

Emily could feel her muscles tighten a little and her brow moistened. She brushed at the hair that grazed over her forehead. She wished she hadn't blurted out the name. Perhaps she'd given the cue that the woman on the other end of the line needed to continue a false statement.

"And you know this how?"

Emily could feel Olivia Barton try to pull herself together.

"I read some things on his computer," she said, "but mostly I've put two and two together."

Oh, no. One of those women who watch Law & Order *reruns by day and fight crime by night.*

Emily thought of the days of the Green River Killer investigation in Seattle. She hadn't worked it, but as an investigator on the periphery of the case that chased the killer of dozens of Seattle-area prostitutes she knew of dozens of instances when a woman tried to pin the blame on a boyfriend or a husband.

"I see. You said there was more than one victim. So you're saying your husband is a serial killer?"

Again, more tears. "Yes, I guess. I mean, he could be. I don't know."

Emily didn't want to make the same mistake twice. "Do you know who the other victim was?"

"There were two others. Tiffany Jacobs and Lily Ann Denton. They were sorority sisters. Michael's sister killed herself last summer. She'd been trashed by the Beta Zeta girls and, I guess, from what he told me and from what I've read on his computer . . ."

When Olivia stopped, Emily pushed her to carry on.

"Go on, please. What about Beta Zeta?"

My daughter's a BZ. She knew Tiffany, Lily Ann, and Sheraton.

"I think he wanted to pay those three girls back. I know it sounds crazy, but my husband's had a really bad past. His sister was everything. He feels those three girls caused his sister to kill herself."

She felt her office inhale and consume her. The room became small and dark. She knew those girls. She knew the connection they shared with her daughter.

"Sheriff Kenyon, I'm calling you because my husband made a big mistake."

Emily drew a breath. "What kind of a mistake?"

"He didn't mean to kill Sheraton Wilkes."

No. No. No.

Emily set down her pen and looked at the caller ID on her phone, hoping the call was coming from somewhere in Cherrystone and not California. The area code was 714. She wasn't sure exactly where it was, but it was a call originating in California.

"Sheriff, are you there?"

"I'm here."

"Jenna. *Your daughter*. That's who he meant to kill. I'm so sorry. Please."

As the room constricted once more, Olivia Barton explained how her husband had been troubled by his sister's death. Blame had somehow spun into rage. Rage became a vendetta of a kind of unimaginable evil.

"My husband is ill," she said. "He was a good man and a good father. I've found out things about him that I never knew. Things that explain maybe why he's as sick as he is. I'm sorry. I just hope I'm not too late."

Emily felt a deep shudder of fear. Jenna and Shali were going to a movie later. Or were they going shopping? She really hadn't paid any attention. On her trips back to Cherrystone, Jenna had tried to get in as much as she could in the way of visiting old friends.

"Mrs. Barton," Emily said, "I'm going to call Garden Grove PD and have them send someone to see you. This will be for your protection."

"Don't worry about me. I'm so worried about your daughter. Michael has been stalking her online. He's been reading her blog. He knows everywhere she goes. He's supposed to be on a business trip, but his client told his boss he never showed."

"All right. I'm going to hang up now. Stay where you are. The local police will be there as soon as they can. This might scare your children, so if you have a place to take them, please do."

"I took them to my mother's this morning. I've driven up and down the freeway trying to figure out what to do."

"You did the right thing," Emily said. With that, she ended the call. She gave Gloria all of Olivia Barton's information and told her to see if Garden Grove PD would send a car to the Barton residence immediately. She paced, wondering where Chris was with those stupid coffees. Her heart began to race.

"I'm going after Jenna," she told Gloria. "Tell Chris to meet me at the house."

Chapter Seventy-one

Cherrystone

Emily drove her not-so-agile Crown Vic as fast as she could. It was a kelly green blur. There were no sirens or flashing lights to alert Cherrystone pedestrians and drivers to get out of the way. It flashed through her mind that someone would see her run a red light and report her to the sheriff's office. The local paper would have a field day with that one: SHERIFF KENYON "BRAKES" THE LAW was the inevitable play-on-words headline for an editor who could not resist a pun. But she didn't care. She had a daughter in potential danger.

She had tried Jenna's cell phone and the landline at the house. *No answer.* That could mean one of two things. Either Jenna wasn't at home, or she was in trouble and she couldn't get to the phone. There was no way she wouldn't have answered multiple attempts by her mother to reach her. The days of marathons of *America's Next Top Model* or *The Real World* putting her into a TV-watching-zombie state were long since over.

Please let her be safe.

She dialed Chris's cell number.

"Hi, babe," he said. "The coffee place across the street is closed. Pipes busted. I went—"

She cut him off. "Chris, this isn't about the coffee." Her voice cracked with concern. "This is very bad. The Sorority Killer is after Jenna."

There was a crack in the reception and Emily worried that the service failed again. But Chris's voice came back on.

"What are you talking about?"

"His wife called. His name is Michael Barton and he's on some kind of revenge trip against the girls of Beta Zeta, Jenna's sorority. She told me that her husband's sister killed herself after she was dumped by the sorority. He blamed Tiffany, Lily Ann, and Jenna."

"What about Sheraton Wilkes?"

Emily could feel her chest tighten as made a hard right turn on Orchard Ave. "An error. He thought that Sheraton was Jenna."

"Hang on. I'm coming."

"Chris," Emily said, "Olivia Barton says her husband is already here. I'm on my way home now."

She passed a car that was unfamiliar to her. She knew every car on Orchard Avenue. Even as she sped by, she could see the car had come from a rental car agency, its familiar yellow decal displayed on a side window.

Michael Barton faced the mirror as he had a thousand times before. His task was now far more complicated with Jenna and her friend being there together. He'd never had to kill more than one person at a time. Part of him, a very small part, liked the challenge of the scenario. The rush he had gotten from his compulsion was better than sex. If so, killing two at once would be a veritable orgy.

He'd done everything right. He looked down at his fingertips. They felt hard and crunchy. He'd coated each one with superglue back in the motel. He'd leave no fingerprints in the bathroom of the house that was about to become the bloodiest of murder scenes—a nightmare of his own creation. Controlling two young women would be very difficult. He'd have to make a fast move for one, plunge the knife into her heart or slash her neck. It would have to be done with horrific and unexpected speed.

Otherwise, the one left standing could run.

He unzipped his fly and urinated into the bowl. He was careful to hit the center of the reservoir of water to make as much noise as possible. He wanted the girls to hear that he was actually doing what he'd said he needed to do.

Instead, he was standing there, sucking up the courage to do what he *had* to do.

For Sarah. For himself.

He flushed the toilet and felt for his hunting knife. *Razor sharp*. He'd used it only once—to cut the landline that came inside the Kenyon's home—before Shali showed up.

In a minute, everything would be over. He'd find relief. He'd go back to California. He'd never do this again. He knew he'd promised himself that before. But this time was different. It was the way it had to be.

He opened the door to the hallway.

Emily pulled into the driveway. Shali's car wasn't there. She hoped that meant that they'd gone off shopping in Spokane as they'd planned. *Please be safe. Please be all right,* she thought as she turned off the ignition and grabbed her gun.

A thousand miles away, Olivia Barton opened the front door of her dream house in Garden Grove to find two police officers. Seeing them was concrete proof that the action that she'd taken to save a young woman in Washington State had truly closed the curtain on everything she held so dear. She knew the wheels were in motion.

She let the officers inside.

"No matter what he's done," she said, "there are parts of Michael that are so very good. I want you to know that. I love him. Our children love their father. He's only partly a monster."

Chapter Seventy-two

Michael Barton emerged from the powder room and found the young women waiting in the foyer. Jenna was by the door, which was still slightly cracked open. Cool spring air poured inside.

"Thanks for the use of your bathroom," he said.

"No worries." Jenna smiled. "That's the kind of place Cherrystone is."

Shali held out her cell phone. "Use mine to make your call. I have unlimited minutes."

He reached over to take the phone with his left hand. The flash of a piece of metal—a knife—caught Jenna's eye.

She screamed. "What are you doing?"

As if in slow motion, Shali turned her head and looked at Jenna, then back at Michael as he plunged the knife into her stomach. A pool of blood the size and color of one of Emily's dark red dahlias formed. Shali gasped and slumped to the floor.

"What did you do?" Jenna dropped to her knees. Shali grabbed at her own stomach and started to gag, then coughed up blood.

"Jenna, help me," Shali said, gasping.

"Drop your phone," he said. "Drop it or I'll cut off Shali's head right now."

It was so fast. So frightening. The blood just kept coming. Shali went completely white. Her body slumped backward against the door, slamming it shut.

Jenna dropped her phone. It started to ring. She could see it was her mother calling.

"Mom, help me. Something's happening. Mom," she said in a loud voice inside her head, a voice that no one could hear.

"I'm not going to hurt you," Michael said, surprised that lying was so easy, even in the midst of utter chaos and crisis. He hoped it would somehow disarm her. It was a fantasy, a dream. *Just do as I say and none of this will hurt so bad,* he thought.

"What do you want?" Jenna asked. "My friend needs a doctor! We have to call an ambulance."

"I came for you, Jenna. I'm sorry about her."

Jenna was terror-stricken and confused. "Came for me?"

His eyes were like a reptile's, devoid of compassion for what he'd done as Shali's blood oozed around them.

"Yeah *you.* You were the third of the bitches that trashed my sister."

Jenna tried to take a step backward, but there was nowhere to go. Her eyes moved rapidly from Shali to the man with the dripping knife.

"What are you talking about?" she asked. "I don't know you! I don't know your sister."

"Sarah Barton."

Jenna's face stayed blank, pinched in horror. Tears ran down her cheeks. "I don't know her."

"Sarah Cleary was her name. Sarah Barton Cleary." Michael taunted Jenna with the blade. "You said she wasn't good enough to be in your stupid club. You, Lily Ann, Tif-

fany . . . the three of you. You told her that she wasn't smart
or pretty enough. Do you even have a clue how much you
hurt the girls who want into your little club?"

Jenna racked her brain, but things were happening so fast
she couldn't grab on to any memory of any Sarah Barton. "I
don't remember Sarah, I'm sorry. I'm sure she was a nice
girl."

"You set her up. You told her she was 'in' and then you
took it away from her. You crushed her. You have no damn
idea what her life was about, how much she struggled."

Jenna continued scanning the room for a way out, a
weapon. *Anything.* "I really am sorry. Please. We need to get
Shali a doctor."

"She's collateral damage. I came for you. I missed you
once at Dixon University and I'm sorry about Sheraton
Wilkes. But you two look alike and she was wearing your
damn coat and she was in your room."

Jenna remembered how Sheraton had borrowed her coat
that night at the restaurant, how she'd vacated the chapter's
guest room for the sleeping porch the night Sheraton was
murdered.

"You deserve this," he said.

Emily Kenyon turned the unlocked knob on the front
door and pushed, but something was in the way. She pushed
a second time, a little harder.

Shali Patterson's unconscious body was blocking the
door. Each time she pushed, a smear of blood grew larger
across the hardwood floor, but she couldn't see it.

Dear God, what's going on here? She pushed harder, this
time using her shoulder like a battering ram.

Chris Collier's rental car pulled up and he ran across the
driveway to Emily, who was hunched low by the front door.

"Something terrible is going on here," she said, her words

hushed, and her face awash in worry. "You cover the backyard. Shali's hurt."

"Where's Jenna?" he asked.

"I don't know. Call for help. We need an ambulance and
backup."

"Already called. I'll check out the back of the house."

"Be careful," she said.

Chris Collier rounded the backyard with such haste that
he nearly fell over a planter on the patio. He steadied himself, bent down low, and peered into the living room window.
What the? He could see Jenna walking backward toward the
kitchen, a man with what looked like a knife moving toward
her. He could see a slice of light come through the front door
as Emily pushed and pushed from the outside of the front
door.

Emily stuck her head inside and screamed. "Jenna!"

The man with the knife started to lunge for Jenna and
Chris did what he knew he had to do. *This has to be the
cleanest shot I've ever fired*, he thought. He aimed his gun
and fired at the man in the hoodie. The window shattered and
glittery pieces of glass rained down all over. For a second he
couldn't see what, if anything, he'd done.

"Jenna! Emily!" he called out.

"I'm all right," Jenna said.

Chris rolled his body through the broken window and ran
to Jenna just as Emily came inside. Shards of glass clung to
his chest and pant legs.

"Mom," Jenna said, pulling her mother toward her in a
desperate embrace. "We have to help Shali. That freak stabbed
her."

Emily hugged her daughter as tightly as she could. "The
EMTs are coming, honey. They'll take care of her."

Tears rolled down Jenna's face. "Mom, I'm sorry. I shouldn't have let him in."

She squeezed her daughter with the kind of hug that promised to never let go. "Don't blame yourself."

Chris bent over Shali and told her in a gentle voice that she'd be all right.

"You're a fighter, Shali Patterson," he said. "Fight this one. Hang on."

Sirens screamed down the street, growing louder as they came toward the Kenyon house.

Jenna was crying and shaking. She was nearly inconsolable, the kind of breakdown that happens when one feels safe enough to just let go.

"He said he killed Lily Ann, Tiffany, and Sheraton," she said.

Emily held her with the might of a mother's love. "I know. I know. Baby, it's all over." She looked over at the dead man on her living room floor. A puddle of bloody water formed around him. Michael Barton had been shot in the chest. The knife was still clutched in his hand. For a second, Emily felt the look on his face wasn't anguish or menace.

It was a dead man. *A sick man.* A monster at peace.

Epilogue

Noplace was more lovely than Cherrystone in the full of a spring day. The cherry blossoms planted along the main arterials by the Boy Scouts in the 1960s were in their pompom prime. Whenever the breeze came down from the north, a little flurry of white petals filled the air, drifting around tires and along the curb. The winter had been beyond turbulent—but the spring promised, as it always did—a rebirth.

Jenna had been accepted into law school and would be attending Stanford in the fall. She was more than ready to pursue a career in criminal law. No young woman had seen so much, yet stayed steady and optimistic. She quit the BZs with an e-mail the same day that her mom agreed to marry the man she loved.

"We need to get on with our lives," Emily had told her daughter. "We can't always count on a second chance coming around again."

Jenna and Shali decorated the gazebo in the Kenyons' backyard with massive bouquets of cherry blossoms.

"I had no idea that you had so many cherry trees at your house, Shali."

Shali rolled her eyes. "I know why you're saying that."

"You do?"

"Yeah, I know that you know we don't have any at my house. But hey, it's your mother's wedding and I *like* her. So I did a little snipping here and there last night two blocks down."

Jenna measured another length of ribbon. "I hope my mom doesn't get arrested for having stolen property at her wedding."

Shali grinned. "I hope she does. We'll get on the news for sure."

Both girls laughed. They hadn't laughed like that in a while, not since that terrible afternoon when Shali had been stabbed by Michael Barton. Her injuries had healed, and she was conscientiously attending her prescribed physical therapy sessions. Jenna marveled at her friend's indomitable spirit. She'd be all right. They all would.

They stepped back from the gazebo. Indigo blue ribbons and white cherry blossoms were carefully braided around each post. It was, both girls knew, as beautiful as a dream.

"So your mom's not going to run for a second term, huh?"

Jenna surveyed the yard. Things looked perfect. "Nope. Jason is, though. Mom and Chris are going to open their own investigative agency."

"Like private eyes?" Shali's eyes grew wide with intrigue.

Jenna picked up the roll of indigo ribbon. "Kind of like that. But Mom says, not half as exciting. Mostly hunting down deadbeat dads and working on insurance scams."

Shali let out a laugh, touching her abdomen, still a little tender. "I'll give her my dad's last address."

Jenna returned her best friend's smile.

"Let's go inside," she said. "The wedding starts at two."

ACKNOWLEDGMENTS

I'd like to acknowledge Michaela Hamilton, Susan Raihofer, Jessica Rose Wolfe, Jean Olson, Tina Marie Brewer, Bunny Kuhlman, Jim Thomsen, Charles Turner, and Kathrine Beck for their much-needed advice, guidance, and general good sense on this project. Also, to Claudia for being the best reader a writer ever had. I love you.